AND JUSTICE FOR ALL

And Justice for All

ERIC WILEY

Copyright © Eric Wiley 2023

All rights reserved.

The characters and events portrayed in this book are fictitious. Any similarity to real persons, living or dead, is coincidental and not intended by the author.

No part of this book may be reproduced, or stored in a retrieval system, or transmitted in any form or by any means, electronic, mechanical, photocopying, recording, or otherwise, without express written permission of the publisher.

ISBN: 979-8-888962-985

Library of Congress Control Number: TXu 2-348-386

Printed in the United States of America

This book is dedicated to my wife, Emily.
I did it. It took me forever, but I did it. However, I couldn't have done it without you. Your support as well as your critiques meant the world to me. I hope you enjoy...again.

| 1 |

For reasons unknown to himself, Tommy could now smell the sharp twinge of last summer's fresh coat of paint. He was standing in the doorway of his bedroom. The bedroom that he didn't want to leave behind. He liked his room. And for as far back as he could remember, it was the only one he had ever had.

He begged his father last year during summer vacation to paint it blue instead of the dingy, bland, tan color it had always been. And after about a week of begging, and what he was sure was a bit of influence on his mother's part, his father left for the store one afternoon and when he returned, he was carrying a gallon of paint. There was a little blue spot dried on the top about the size of a dime. Tommy stared at that blue spot on the lid of the can with a smile on his face that he could remember even now. It hadn't been quite the blue Tommy had imagined when he had pled his case. But at eight years old, blue was blue. He was just happy his father had finally gotten the paint.

He spent most of the next day painting with his mother and father. Though his part of the painting mostly consisted of him letting loose in the middle of the wall with a roller and a modest amount of paint while his parents took on the more careful task of cutting in around the baseboards, floors, and ceiling. It was a good day. It was one of his favorites.

Tommy thought this summer was going to be just like every other summer he could remember. Trips to the beach with his mother's best friend, Tracy Neil, and her son Todd. Their mothers would often get their names confused when calling for their respective child to not go too far into the water without them or to just stay close in general. When their mothers did join them in the water, Tommy would just float in the shallows. His feet flapping out in front of him, arms extended and a peaceful smile on his face. Not a care in the world. Any time out of the water was spent with Todd trying to build anything that resembled a sandcastle, or lying at the water's edge and letting the dying waves roll over them. They liked to pretend they were being toppled by monster, boat-crushing waves. The water would roll up the short length of their bodies and over their faces giving them the slightest feeling of being adrift in a swelling, unforgiving ocean. It was where Tommy felt his happiest. His peace.

The last couple months before school let out for the summer, Tommy spent gearing himself up for another "fun in the sun" summer. He could practically taste the salt water. But that was also when he started to notice that things between his parents seemed as though they were starting to unravel. His mother seemed to be deeply upset with his father about something. Not for just a little while like she had before. Or even a whole day. It didn't seem like it was going away. And his father just seemed to get upset about everything.

"Tommy!" his mother called up the stairs, pulling him back into reality.

He was still standing in the doorway staring at his empty bedroom. The barren blue walls, the empty wood floor. He tried to soak in every memory he could think of.

His mind raced, looking for any excuse it could come up with to stay. It even crossed his mind to try and muster up the nerve to run down to the moving truck and demand that they stay. He did not want to move. He didn't know how far it would get him. He didn't kid himself into thinking it would work. But he was desperate. He didn't want to trade everything he had ever known for the promise to see snow for the first time. Or for the new friends his mother said she was sure he was going to make to make. He didn't care about the darn snow. And Todd was his best friend. He didn't understand it. He just knew he didn't want to leave.

"Tommy!" his father called, in a shorter, more demanding tone. "Come on, we gotta hit the road."

"I'm coming," he replied, just loud enough for his father to hear.

He was already defeated. And he hadn't even gotten to shoot his shot.

He turned away from his room immediately wishing he had ignored the calls of his parents for even a few seconds longer. But he knew it was no use. He walked sluggishly down the stairs and could see both of his parents standing at the bottom waiting. His father turned and walked back out towards the moving truck once Tommy came into view. His mother just stood there waiting at the bottom of the stairs, looking at him through more sympathetic eyes.

She knew he didn't want to leave. They both did. His mother just seemed to care about it a little more. The truth was, she didn't want to leave either. At least that's what Tommy suspected. He remembered the night they had told him that they were going to be moving. The look on his father's face seemed neutral enough, but his mother's face told a different story. It told him that it wasn't really their decision at all. They were making it, but he could tell there was more that they *weren't* going to tell him. In fact, none of what they were going to tell him was true. Even at eight years old, he had been sure of that.

"Do we *have* to move?" he asked his mother in a last-ditch effort to change their minds.

"Yes honey, we do," she said softly. She took his face in both her hands and smiled at him. "You're going to love it in New York," she added. "You'll get to see the seasons change; you'll make all sorts of new friends."

She had said all of this to him before. Although this time he thought maybe she was repeating it for herself as well.

"This is new and exciting for all of us."

He knew she was trying to cheer him up. Though part of him didn't want her to. He didn't want to be happy in New York. Or anywhere else for that matter. He wanted to be happy here. He wanted to be happy at home. Back in his room that he never thought about leaving. That he never thought about missing. He just couldn't see how he would ever not miss this place, let alone forget about it completely.

They walked out the door toward his mother's SUV. The thud and final click of the front door closing for the last time seemed louder than it ever had before. The sound echoed in his head as he turned and looked at the house one last time. He tried to take in whatever he could and then climbed in the back seat. He made up his mind right then that he was going to stay awake as long as he possibly could on the drive. At least until they were out of Florida. He wanted to see everything he could one last time.

Tommy had never been outside of Florida. Not that he could remember anyway. He didn't even know what the rest of the country looked like. Except what he had seen on tv. And based on what he had seen about New York, it didn't seem all that appealing.

The dark, wet streets, glistening with the reflection of every color light you could imagine. The steam pouring from the manhole covers adding a creepy texture to the already unsettling backdrop of the city at night. The blacked-out alley ways lit only by the faint, flickering glow of a burn barrel revealing the silhouettes of the multitude of homeless people who resided there. He just couldn't understand why his parents thought this would be a fair trade for sunny weather and beaches.

They hit the interstate, and the vehicle speed increased effectively erasing the faint possibility that this was all some elaborate hoax, and they were going to turn around any minute and head back home. Tommy didn't know why he had even let that possibility grow in his mind. But he was desperate.

The miles continued to fly by, and he thought of the hardwood in his now *old* bedroom. They always creaked just loud enough to give him away when he would try to sneak out of bed. He was never able to make it all the way to the door before hearing a voice from downstairs instructing him to go back to bed. He never thought that would be a memory he would want to hold onto so badly and felt saddened at the thought of ever getting frustrated that the hardwood gave away his attempts at evading bedtime.

"Welcome to Georgia. We're glad Georgia's on your mind," the blue and white sign read.

Ugh, Tommy thought, detesting the pleasantness of the welcome sign.

Panic hit him as he suddenly realized that if they were in Georgia, that meant they weren't in Florida anymore. He unbuckled his seatbelt and frantically turned around in the back seat. He was resting on his knees and staring out the back window. His sudden change in positioning startled his mother. He was almost in tears. He watched the palm trees that landscaped the border between Florida and Georgia fade into the distance. Smaller and smaller they became until they were nothing more than a memory.

"What are you doing, Tommy?" his mother asked, peaking at him through the rearview. Her eyes still wide and panicked.

But Tommy didn't answer. He just stared out the window and watched until he was sure there was no more Florida to be seen. Once he knew it was gone, he turned back around and slumped back into his seat. He buckled himself back in and returned to mindlessly staring out the window at the vast, endless greenery Georgia had to offer.

"You ok, honey?" his mother asked, understanding now what Tommy had been doing. What all the commotion had been about.

Silence filled the vehicle as the miles continued to fly by. Tommy sat in the back seat with a sad, pained look on his face that he didn't feel he would have been able to change even if he wanted to. He periodically glanced at the rearview mirror. His mother had adjusted it so that she could see his face. He tried to avoid it, but his eyes seemed to flick on their own in that direction. He stared out the window unsure of what lay ahead. Both on the road and in his future. He felt lost. For the first time in his eight years, he didn't know what anything in his life was going to look like. He was scared. Scared that all the good things he had been told were just lies. A false sense of security to get him to go along peacefully. Not that he would have been able to put up a huge fight anyway. He was scared of the unknown he had been forced into. Scared that he would forever feel the way he did right now. Lost.

The loud squeal of the brakes on the moving truck coming to a halt next to his mother's SUV woke him up. He didn't realize he had even fallen asleep. Which meant that being back at the beach with Todd had only been a dream and he wasn't about to be carried in their house by his mother. He was somewhere he had never been before. *It felt so real*, he thought trying to remember the fading dream. For a brief moment, he swore could even taste the saltwater again. He sat there grasping at the scattering details of his dream, trying to catalog each one he could, when his mother opened the car door and broke his concentration.

"Hey! You need to go to the bathroom?" she asked smiling at him.

"Where are we?" Tommy asked unbuckling and climbing out of the car.

He had unintentionally ignored her question about the bathroom. He was more concerned with it being the first time his feet were going to touch the ground somewhere outside the state of Florida.

"Tenn-e-ssee," she said with a grin and the strong hope that even a little of her positivity would rub off on him. "It took forever to get through Georgia, but we made it."

She watched him looking around for a few seconds.

"We are going to stop for the night once we're in Kentucky," she said and closed the car door as he stretched in the gas station parking lot.

Tommy didn't know anything about Tennessee. And the only thing he had ever heard about Kentucky was that they raced horses. And maybe something about blue grass. *Do they really have* blue *grass?* he wondered. He remembered that most of the horses had long, weird names that didn't make any sense. At least not to him. He remembered that his parents would have people over and there would always be a cookout. During which they would all gather in the living room and watch the Kentucky Derby. He liked seeing the horses jump out of the gates then run around the track as fast as they could. Not to mention all the funny hats that the women on TV wore. He always found himself wondering why the race was so short. Why they only ran one lap? And why they only raced once a year? He would always stop whatever he was doing for a couple of minutes and watch the race, trying to imagine what it must feel like on the back of a horse that was running that fast. Besides, the guys on the horses didn't look much bigger than he…

"How much longer?" he asked looking up at his mother and interrupting his own thought.

"Well," his mother said. She paused doing her best to maintain her enthusiasm. "We should be stopping for the night in the next two or three hours." She paused and stared at him. "Maybe they'll have a pool," she added, smiling. "That'll be fun, huh?"

"Yeah, I guess," he replied.

He continued to sulk even though he loved his mother for the effort.

"Listen buddy," she said kneeling in front of him. She gently grabbed both his arms. "I know you didn't want to move. It's going to be a big change for all of us. But we'll make this change together. And that's what counts."

He loved the sound of his mother's voice. It always seemed that no matter what problem he was having, the soft, breeze-like tone of his mother's voice made him feel at peace.

"Is what dad said true?" he asked her. A question that had been circling in his head for days now. He wasn't sure if he meant for the question to pop out. Not right now, anyway. But the words had flown from his mouth no sooner than the thought had reappeared in his mind.

"What do you mean, honey?" his mother asked.

It was too late to back out now. He had asked the question, and he did really want to know the answer.

"He said that we had to move because they needed police officers like him in New York. Is that true?"

She paused for a second and stared at him. He couldn't help but notice the slight smile forming on her face. But it wasn't her usual smile.

"Yes honey," his mother said and brushed his brown hair off his forehead. "Your dad has been offered a great job in New York and he took it because he thought it would be good for all of us."

As hard as his mother tried, her face told a different story. And for him, someone who had unknowingly studied every expression his mother had made since the moment he was born, it was as obvious as the sun in the sky. It told him that there was more to it than just a good job offer.

After a brief bathroom break, they loaded back up and hit the road again. By this time, after sleeping through almost two states, he had accepted that this was his new reality. He didn't know anything about what was going to happen, only that he was going to have to find some way to be okay with it.

They arrived at a hotel in Frankfort, Kentucky around 9:00 pm. He climbed out of the back seat and stretched again. This time his stretch seemed to go on forever. As they walked through the automatic door of the hotel into the lobby, he picked up on the faint smell of waffles and eggs from that morning's continental breakfast. Admittedly, it made him a little excited for breakfast the next morning. He was a big fan of waffles. His father stood talking to the man at the front desk and worked on getting them a room for the night and he and his mother stood waiting.

He took the opportunity to scan the rest of the lobby. The tile floor was an almost yellow tan. And although there had been a clear attempt to keep it looking shiny and new, Tommy couldn't decide if the yellowing was part of the original color or just a sign of aging. A clear path had formed, leading from the front doors, from years of guests walking in and out of the lobby. It ran past the desk and faded out in different directions. The hotel had placed a long runner mat over top of the developing path to slow the wearing process and hide what progress had been made. But the attempt had not been completely successful.

The walls were covered with a bland, oat colored wallpaper, spruced up with navy blue pinstripes. Several pictures took up random spots on the wall, each and every one of them of a horse. Some more than one horse, others were close ups of single horses with what looked like roses hanging around their necks. Those pictures had little metal plates at the bottom of the frame with what Tommy guessed was the horses name. But he didn't make it close enough to read any of them.

Seems about right, Tommy thought to himself as he continued to look around the room.

His investigation of the hotel lobby was interrupted by the sound of his mother's voice asking the man at the desk if they had a pool.

"We sure do, ma'am," the man said, handing the room key to his father. "Closes at 11:00," The man glanced over at Tommy and smiled. "Anyone under the age of 12 has to be accompanied by an adult," he added.

His mother turned to him and smiled. She was still desperately trying to break through. He smiled back for the first time that day. Half-hearted as it was, but he did it for her.

Tommy and his parents took the elevator to the second floor. Directly off the elevator were vending machines and an ice machine. The smell in the empty hallway reminded him of the musty odor that would fill their old house (God, how he still missed that house) sometimes when his mother would vacuum. She would complain about the smell for a bit, usually for a month or two, maybe even longer, before she finally decided to replace the vacuum all together. The smell would always disappear for a while with the old vacuum gone, and the house would smell like their house again. But it would eventually return. As they entered their room the stiffening cold from the air conditioner caused the three of them to shiver almost simultaneously.

"Ooh, James! We're going to have to turn that off," his mother said looking over at his father.

"Don't turn it all the way off," his father said to her. "Just turn it down. It'll get too hot in here."

It was cold enough in the room that Tommy almost thought twice about going swimming. But a quick review of the day left him with no other choice. He decided that swimming was going to be the only good thing about today. Now he *had* to go. He and his mother changed into their bathing suites and left the room. The hallway was warmer. The elevator ride back down to the first floor was quiet. His mother stood there waiting for him to speak and even though he had a ton of questions, he remained silent. He didn't want to give the impression that he was coming around to the idea of living somewhere new too quickly. He knew he would have too eventually. He just wasn't ready to let go. Not just yet.

They arrived in the pool area just as a family of four was finishing up their swim. The sounds of the other children's voices echoed throughout the closed-in pool area. Tommy watched listened and studied the parents and the children for a bit as they were collecting their belongings. He watched the parents wrap their children in towels and then dry themselves off. His father, however, had elected to stay in the room to watch the Yankees game. That was his idea of relaxing. And that was fine. Tommy didn't mind either way. Although, the overly cheery family of four did spark the realization that most of the good times he could remember in his life only involved him and his mother. He secretly envied the brother and sister. Not only for having a someone to play with and annoy built right into the family, but for also having a father that seemed to actually want to do things with them.

Tommy heard his mother sigh and looked to see a smile stretching across her face when she noticed that the pool area was also equipped with a working hot tub. He approached the edge of the pool deck and stood there staring at the water while his mother settled slowly into the hot tub. Immediately, he began thinking about the ocean. He wondered when or if he would ever see it again. He looked over at his mother. She had her head back against the side of the hot tub and her eyes closed. The smile still emanating from her face showed that she was slowly morphing into a state of complete relaxation. All the questions he had about the move seemed to resurface in his mind. But he didn't want to interrupt. He dipped his toe into the lukewarm water which was still just cold enough to send a chill scurrying through his entire body. He remembered again that this was the only thing he had had to looked forward to all day and he didn't intend to waste it.

He took a deep breath and quickly exhaled letting all the heavy emotions he had felt throughout the day out with the breath and leapt off the edge of the pool into the water. He hit the water trying to make the biggest splash he could, as all young boys do. He intentionally sank down toward the bottom as far as he could. The chilled blanket of silence surrounded him as his body shook off the minor shock of the water's temperature. Sinking felt eerily comforting. Coupled with the silence, it allowed his imagination to spring to life.

He imagined that he had been sitting on the side of a large boat drifting in the middle of the ocean. The vessel rocked back and forth by the unforgiving waves. With no land in sight, he had dove into the silent depths of the world below. It was now all his to explore. He straightened out his body and began kicking his legs and waving his arms to propel himself further down. He swam down as far as he could and reached the bottom. He tried his best to stay there. But as the seconds ticked by, he knew he would have to resurface soon. He pushed off the bottom as hard as he could launching himself toward the opposite side of the pool. His body began to drift upward and forward as he moved. He was determined to reach the far side before having to come up for air. He could feel his young lungs begging for air. His heart pounded in his chest. But he wasn't giving up yet. He held out his arms. His fingertips inching closer toward the side of the pool. And then they found it. The instant his fingers touched the rough interior of the pool wall, he popped up out of the water and grabbed on to the edge.

Don't gasp for air, he thought, *that's not heroic.*

He scanned the empty pool area, ignoring the decorative trees and towel racks and beach chairs, attempting to maintain the visual of his mind's eye that he was still adrift in the middle of the ocean.

"How's the water, hun?" his mother's voice faded in from the hot tub, dissolving the imaginary seascape he had created and bringing back into view the lazily decorated pool area.

"It's fine," he replied, wiping the water from his face. "Not cold, not hot."

He flopped onto his back and pushed off from the side of the pool. He floated and stared at the ceiling thinking again about the fleeting details of the pseudo-reality he had just created for himself. When the last detail had faded away and was out of reach, he thought only about the beach. He thought about the saltwater and the noise. The crowds of the afternoons and the emptiness of the evenings. He remembered times when he had been there with just his mother. Lying on the sand in the surf letting the incoming, dwindling waves roll over his legs and onto his stomach. He wanted to go back so bad. But he knew that that was no longer an option. As terrible as it sounded, he knew he was going to have to accept whatever lie ahead in this move.

The thought crossed his mind to intentionally make tomorrow a better day, but that was quickly overshadowed by a still festering desire to continue showing his parents how upset he was. He hated everything about this move. Every attempt his parents, mostly his mother, had made to make this move sound great, he had purposely ignored. He didn't want to be happy about it. He didn't want to get used to it. He wanted to go home. But he knew that home was going to look different now. The only references he had to envision it were the dark, scary streets of New York City he had seen on TV, and that certainly didn't give him any reason to think that he was going to enjoy it.

He and his mother spent the next hour in the pool area, each relaxing in their own way. His mother got out of the hot tub and slowly walked down the steps into the shallow end of the pool and continued walking toward the deep end until the water reached her chest. Then she went completely under, popping back up with a chilled look on her face. After the chill wore off, she wrung the water out of her hair then made her way out of the pool and returned to the hot tub.

Tommy just continued to float on, drifting aimlessly in the middle of the pool. He would try to swim the length of the pool underwater. Going the distance most times, only coming up short in a couple attempts.

He popped up out of the water after one of his underwater swims and saw his mother standing on the pool deck staring down at him. She just smiled and said that it was time to go because the pool was closing. He climbed up the side of the pool and sat on the edge with his feet still in the water. His mother grabbed one of the fluffy white hotel towels from the rack and wrapped it around him. He immediately smiled and thought about the parents he had seen wrapping their kids in towels as they were packing up to leave when he and his mother arrived at the pool.

"Feeling any better?" she asked as she sat down beside him on the pool deck.

He briefly re-lived everything he had been thinking about while swimming and decided that he was going to give his mom what she had been working towards all day.

"Yeah, I think so," he said, looking over at her and smiling.

A smile stretched across her face from ear to ear. The biggest one he had seen in a while. It was worth it.

| 2 |

The next day Tommy and his parents made their way downstairs for breakfast after re-packing the few things they had taken into the hotel room the night before. When they got off the elevator in the lobby, Tommy immediately recognized the smell of waffles from the night before. Only this time it was much stronger, and scent felt warm. He could eat waffles any time of day. It didn't matter. They sat down and ate as a family in the dining area of the hotel lobby. His father would look at his watch periodically, itching to get back on the road and get the miles behind them. Tommy agreed with his father in this aspect. Although he was not excited about spending another whole day in the car, he desperately wanted the driving part to be over with.

After breakfast they retrieved their bags from their room, checked out at the front desk, and walked back out into the parking lot. Tommy reluctantly, and with the facial expression to match, climbed back into the back seat of his mother's SUV. His father climbed back in the moving truck. Each one of them as prepared as they could be for another very long day on the road.

He got a little excited when he remembered that he had put his Game Boy in the bag he kept with him in his mom's car. His "carry-on," she had called it. At least that would give him something to do instead of staring out the window the entire time. After all, from what he had seen, except for the palm trees, the scenery hadn't changed much since they left Florida.

"You ready to see our new house today?" his mother asked, peaking at him through the rearview.

He sat for a brief second thinking about his mother's question, sifting through all his thoughts and emotions from the day before. He could see in her eyes looking back at him in the mirror that she was smiling and hopeful.

"Yeah, I think I am," he replied. And he was surprised to find that he actually meant it.

The miles came and went quicker than he anticipated. He would play his Game Boy for an hour or two, or until he got frustrated with the game, then he would stare out the window. He found himself longing to see something other than just greenery and billboards. The interstate in West Virginia seemed to be more of a slow rollercoaster ride through the wooded mountains than anything else. He held on as long as he could, but after stopping for dinner he was done for. Somewhere around Pennsylvania he slipped off to sleep hoping that when he woke up the car ride would be over. He got his wish.

It wasn't until his mom opened the door and woke him up that he realized it was finally over. Tommy felt a slight fear grip him before he opened his eyes.

What if I really do hate this place? he thought.

He moved around just enough so his mother would know that he was awake. He was hesitant to open his eyes but felt a bit of relief as soon as he did. It was dark. It both comforted and scared him. He wouldn't be able to see much of the outside of the house or the neighborhood. But the inside of the house was a different story. He sat up and slid out of the back seat. As his feet hit the ground, he dropped his bag and stretched as far as his body would let him. So far in fact, that he almost fell over. Once he regained his footing he tried to look around and see what he could of their new neighborhood. But the streetlights didn't offer much insight into the darkness. He picked up his bag while his mother grabbed a few things out of the back of her vehicle.

"I'm just going to lock this thing up really good for the night and we can unload it tomorrow," his father said, walking towards his mother and shooting a thumb over his shoulder toward the moving truck.

"That's fine," she replied, waiving a hand toward the large truck. "I don't feel like messing with it either."

They walked towards the house with air mattresses, blankets, and not much else. The knot in his stomach tightened just a bit as his father turned the key to unlock the door. As his father stepped inside the house, he ran his hand along the wall just inside the door to find the light switch.

"Ah! There it is," his father said.

On came the light, illuminating the single room just inside the door and giving Tommy a limited first glimpse of his new life. He stepped through the door onto the hardwood floor. He thought again about the floors in his old room and the noises they made. He stood there in the doorway scanning the room and trying to see anything that the light would allow. The slightly off-white walls stretching the length of the empty living room leading into the kitchen, reminded him of the color his old bedroom walls had been before last summer's paint job. He wondered if his new room was going to be the same color.

His mother looked around at the inside of the house, smiling and glancing at him every few seconds trying to gauge his reaction. But Tommy felt unable to embrace their new house at the moment.

"Well, no weird smell, so that's good," his father said, breaking the silence.

His mother laughed as if she had been holding it in for a while. Tommy thought she was just glad that someone had said something. She looked at Tommy again, still a little unsure of his opinion of their new home.

He walked further into the living room still examining whatever he could find. There was a smell, but not a bad one. *Definitely cleaning products,* he thought. He walked past his father and into the kitchen and flipped on the light. The kitchen was noticeably bigger than the kitchen at their house in Florida. *So far, so good,* He thought.

"Where's my room?" Tommy asked, turning to his mother.

"Oh, right this way, sweetie," she said. He could tell that she was happy that he had finally said something.

She led him down the hallway to the last door on the left. They both stood in front of the door like they were about to embark on some treacherous journey and through this door is where it would all begin. For him, that's what this move had been. A treacherous journey. And not one he had taken lightly. But he hadn't been given a choice. However, this door represented both the beginning and the end. The end of the journey and the beginning of everything new in his life

"Well?" his mother said looking at him with encouraging eyes, urging him to open the door.

Tommy grabbed the knob and turned and pushed the door open. His mother reached in and flipped the light switch giving life to the room and for the first time, Tommy was now standing in the only piece of this move that was his alone. An unintentional smile forced its way onto Tommy's face as he scanned the empty room. He couldn't help picturing where his belongings would go. His bed would go here, his dresser there. He concluded, and rather quickly, that his new room looked to be bigger than his old room.

He passed his mother and stepped through the doorway. He started to verbally map out where all his things would go. He looked back at her and genuinely smiled a large, toothy grin. And he could tell that it did her heart good to see that he was happy in that moment.

None of this had been easy on him. Knowing that they had to move, all the packing, the two-day drive. At least for now, it seemed that the weight and stress of the move would soon be a forgotten memory.

"Mom, this is great!" Tommy said, with more enthusiasm than she had seen since they told him about the move.

"I'm glad you like it, honey," she said, letting out a quiet sigh of relief.

"I can't wait to get all my stuff in here," he continued.

"I know," she said. "You know, I bet if you ask your dad, we could probably get some blue paint for these walls."

A brief silence took over the room and instantly his mother thought that maybe she had pushed a little too far, too soon. She wished she had just stood there and enjoyed the moment.

"Nah," he said, enthusiastically, erasing her fear. "Maybe something different."

His mother breathed a second, not so quiet this time, sigh of relief that she hadn't completely ruined the one thing that had seemed to turn this move around for him. She slipped out of the room and let him continue planning the layout of his new room and returned a couple moments later with an air mattress and some blankets.

"Hey," she said, interrupting his process. "It's late, honey. And we all need some rest. You can plan all you want tomorrow, but we still have a long day of unpacking ahead of us."

He considered playing the "sad card" to get a little extra planning time but going back to sleep did seem like a good alternative. Plus, if there was anything that he had learned from past Christmas Eve's, the faster you go to sleep, the sooner you get to wake up.

He helped his mother put the blankets on his air mattress. Then he climbed under them, and she tucked him in.

"I'm *so* glad that you're happy with your room," she said, kneeling on the floor beside the air mattress.

He stared at her momentarily. The soft orange hue from the streetlights pouring through the window illuminated her brown hair and gave her face a sort of heavenly glow. The way he imagined an angel would look if it were kneeling where his mother was now. Of course, to him, she was an angel. She was *the* angel. And he had made her happy. Even if he had started out faking it, this place was already starting to grow on him. And he hadn't even seen it all yet.

"I love it," he said, continuing to stare at her in the orange glow.

She leaned down and kissed him on the forehead, unintentionally tickling his nose with her hair.

"Goodnight, little man," she said.

"Goodnight, mommy," he said, watching her walk toward the door.

"Hey momma," he called out, stopping her at the door. She turned and looked at him. "I'm sorry for being so upset the whole time. I think I was just scared." He paused and considered his words. "A little angry, but mostly scared."

His mother smiled and walked back toward the bed. She sat down on the floor next to him and began brushing his hair across his forehead with her fingers.

"It's ok, sweetie," she said. "You know, we moved around a lot when I was a kid. Starting at about the time I was your age. Your grandfather was in the Army and every few years we would have to pack up and move some place new."

"Really?" Tommy asked. "Where you scared too?"

His mother leaned in and kissed him on the forehead once more.

"Every time," she said. "It never got easier. In fact, the older I got, the harder it was to move across the country. I made and lost some really great friends because, after a while, we would have to move again. I hated it."

"Can we stay here?" he asked. "I don't want to move around anymore?"

"That's the plan, baby," his mother replied. "Now get some rest. You've got to set this room up tomorrow. I'm very interested to see what you come up with."

Tommy just smiled and watched his mother walk to the door. Just before she closed his door for the night, she turned back and looked at him with that smile that he loved so much.

"I love you, little man," she said, smiling her beautiful smile

"I love you too, mommy," he said

Tommy rolled on to his side, still facing the window, looking at the orange glow that was now falling across the floor of his new room. He stared through the glass and wondered what all was on the other side that he hadn't seen yet. All he could see right now was a streetlight and part of the roof of one of the neighboring houses. He closed his eyes and thought about the last couple of days. His last moments standing in his room at his old house, the awful drive that took two whole days, and on top of that, all the frustration he had felt. He certainly didn't think that on his first night in his new room that he would be excited about anything. Especially arranging his new room. Tommy drifted off to sleep to the sound of his parents' muffled voices down the hall. He had a smile on his face and couldn't wait to get started in the morning.

He woke the following morning with a yawn and a stretch. The brisk air filling his room made it that much harder to climb out from under the warmth of his blankets. He looked around at his empty room and immediately began visualizing again. Down to how he was going to arrange his shoes in his closet. He knew everything wouldn't stay exactly the way he was imagining. Besides possibly the furniture. But still, it was an important part of the process. He could hear doors opening and closing and the sound of his father walking up and down the ramp on the back of the moving truck. A sound he had detested hearing in Florida. Every time he heard his father's feet going up and down the ramp then, he knew they were just that much closer to leaving that life behind forever.

Eager to get his room together, he slid out from under the covers and walked across the cool hardwood floor toward his bedroom door. Just as he reached for the doorknob, one of the boards beneath his feet creaked, thrusting him backwards in his mind to his last moments in his old room. Guilt flooded him, and he missed his old room all over again. He felt a twinge of anger at himself for being taken with his new room so quickly. Florida hadn't even crossed his mind since he'd woken up. Never mind that it had only been a few minutes.

He stood there rocking his foot back and forth re-creating the creak and lost in the memory of their old home. He turned and looked once again at the bare walls and empty floor of his new room and began sifting through all the different emotions he was feeling. He struggled for a moment, debating on which feelings he was going to allow to set the tone for the rest of his day. Then he realized something. It was okay to feel both. Just because he missed his old room and was still sad about leaving Florida, didn't mean that he wasn't allowed to enjoy his new life here in New York. Wasn't that what he was so worried about when they left Florida? Wasn't he worried that it was going to be terrible here and he that he was going to be miserable? *But it's not,* he thought. *I found something I like about it. and quicker than I ever thought I would.* A smile crept back across his face, and he opened the door and walked out of his room feeling a bit wiser than before.

Heading down the hallway he noticed the morning light pouring through the windows of their new home gave life and color to what had only been a blank canvas of silhouettes the night before. He looked around taking everything in for the first time and exploring as much as he could with his eyes before reaching the kitchen.

"Hey sweetie, good morning!" his mother said in a chipper voice.

He could tell that she was excited about the getting the new house in order.

"Did you sleep good last night?" she asked.

"It was ok," he said. "I hate that air mattress."

"I know honey, we just had to get through the first night," she said, her smile growing at the thought of furnishing their new house with all their belongings. "But hey, I'm sure we can get your bed set up today. Are you hungry?" she asked.

"I'm starving," he replied as his father walked through the door and sat at the table next to him.

"You gonna put those muscles to work today, boy?" his father asked, looking over at his mother. "I could use some help getting that truck unloaded?"

Tommy smiled back because it was the polite thing to do.

He loved his father, but their relationship was lightyears away from the relationship he had with his mother. He was from the "Seen and not heard generation." His mother was too, but that part didn't seem to stick with her. She was nurturing and made him feel safe and loved. She listened to him. His father on the other hand, worked a lot.

And that part was fine. Tommy had come to understand that sometimes that was just part of it. But most of the time he wasn't working he seemed to be on edge. And Tommy never knew why. Whenever his father would spend time with him it always seemed half-hearted, like his father was not fully present in whatever it was they were doing. He knew his father loved him. Their relationship just seemed to be disconnected. With his father, it seemed to only exist when there was time for it to. It had been this way since he could remember. He even had weird dreams about his father sometimes. Dreams that would leave him feeling even more disconnected from his father. And sometimes, they even frightened him.

"Sure," Tommy replied with a smile. Mostly because he could not wait to get his stuff out of the truck and begin setting up his room.

"Here ya go, boys," his mother said interrupting his thoughts. She sat their plates down in front of them, then sat in front of her own.

"Our first meal in our new house," she added, smiling at both him and his father.

They ate as a family, which was not an everyday occurrence, but today seemed different. His mother asked his father about what he had seen of the neighborhood in his few trips from the house to the moving truck and back. He didn't give much detail. He told her that it seemed like a pretty typical neighborhood from what he had seen.

Once they were finished with breakfast his mother opened one of the boxes sitting in the living room and pulled out some of his clothes.

"Here ya go, hun," she said. "Go get changed, so we can help your dad."

He grabbed the clothes and ran to his room to get changed and then ran outside.

As he walked out the door, he could feel the warm summer sun across his face. Something he didn't expect from Northeastern weather. He just assumed that it was always wet, cold, or both. At least, according to his father. He remembered hearing his father talk about how bad the snowfall had been in the Northeast this past winter, and how he wanted no part of it. In fact, that had been one of the first things Tommy had thought of when they told him they were moving to New York.

As he reached the back of the moving truck the house across the street caught his eye. He stared at the house, wondering who might live there. He wondered if there would be anyone around his age that lived close. He stared a little harder and noticed someone that someone peering through the window, watching them from the house across the street.

"Here ya go, Tommy, this one's yours," his mother said, grabbing his attention.

He took the box and started back toward the house, looking back over his shoulder across the street once more before rounding the front of the truck and heading inside. Whoever was watching them was gone. The closer he got to his bedroom door the more excited he got. *The first box,* he thought to himself. Nothing else mattered today except getting all his belongings into his new room and placed where he wanted them.

He rushed into his room and sat the box down. He stared at the tape holding the box closed and debated on opening it to see which box it was. But he didn't want to get distracted by what he might find if he opened the box and began digging through. He wanted to get all of his things in his room before unpacking anything. He walked back outside and over toward the back of the truck. Only this time he didn't hear the sound of his parents shuffling boxes around in back. He heard voices. Voices he didn't recognize.

"Tommy!" his mother called out.

He walked around the side of the truck and saw a man standing there talking to his father, and likewise, a woman talking to his mother. The woman could've easily been mistaken for his own mother. Long brown hair, styled just about the same. She had a similar nurturing voice and from what he could hear that same contagious laughter. Her smile matched his mother's as well. Next to her stood a boy who appeared to be about his same age. The boy stood there leaned up against his mother and looked a little annoyed about the whole situation. Tommy's mother turned to yell for him again but noticed that he was just a few feet behind her. She smiled and waved him over to where she was standing. He walked up next to her mirroring how the other boy was standing.

"This is our son, Tommy," his mother said. "Tommy, this is Mrs. Christopher, they live in the house across the street.

They were just looking at us, Tommy thought, but didn't say.

"Hi, Tommy," Mrs. Christopher said, smiling down at him. "I'm Stephanie, and this," she said placing a hand on the boy's shoulder crowding her leg. "Is Owen."

| 3 |

Tommy made a couple quick glances at Owen while pretending to listen to his mother's conversation with Mrs. Christopher. The boy seemed a little standoffish. Inconvenienced by the whole encounter. Which is exactly how Tommy felt at that moment as well. He was supposed to be standing at the back of the moving truck waiting for a box with his name on it. Just one more piece of the puzzle he needed to get his new room just the way he wanted it. Just right. But here he stood, the same as Owen. Both equally trapped in this meet and greet while their parents carried on conversations about careers, long drives, and the overall climate of the neighborhood. After a while though, Owen and his parents returned to their house. But not before Owen's mother made the offer to show Tommy's mother around the area whenever she was up for it.

Tommy's father hopped back in the moving truck once the Christopher's were back across the street and continued unloading what was left of their belongings. With each of his boxes his father uncovered, Tommy's trips in and out of the house became quicker and quicker. Until finally, he had the last box, and he could start unpacking. He opened all of the boxes at once and scanned the top layer of what was inside trying to decide where he wanted to start. In the end, it only took him about three hours to get everything exactly where he wanted it. Less the thirty-minute break for lunch and the time it took his father to put his bed together. His bed was the very last thing to go in his room which officially completed the job.

He stood there looking around his room. He was proud of how well it looked. Proud of what he had accomplished, and the day wasn't even over yet. He promised himself that he was going to try really hard keep it that way. But deep down he knew that it would only last for a little while.

He stared at his bed and thought about the air mattress he had slept on the night before and how it always seemed to partially deflate somehow in the middle of the night, and the air inside would get really cold, and he'd wake up freezing. He really hated that thing.

It was about five-o-clock in the evening when his father brought the last box into the house. Just in time too, it seemed, because his mother had just finished dinner. He heard the door shut and then the all too familiar pop and hiss of a beer can being opened. There were a few seconds of silence, then the crinkling sound of the can being crushed and thrown away. This was quickly followed by a repeat of the pop and hiss of his father immediately opening a second beer as he walked into the kitchen and sat down at the table. Tommy walked into the kitchen just as his father began telling his mother about the different struggles he had run into while getting everything unloaded. Items that had shifted around during the drive, hindsight on how things could have been more efficiently packed into the truck versus how they were. All of which Tommy suspected was normal end of day conversation after any move.

"Boy, if you were a little bit bigger you would've been right out there with me," his father said smiling at him and moving the beer can towards his lips.

He took a healthy gulp and sat the can down on the table. Tommy could tell by the sound of the can hitting the table that his second one was almost empty as well.

His father was a difficult man to please. Tommy mostly felt that no matter how hard he tried he always seemed to be doing something wrong in his father's eyes. Other times it seemed as if his father didn't even know that he existed. Tommy always tried not to focus on feeling that way. Mostly, he just tried to stay out of his father's way. That at least made it harder to be blamed for anything. Harder, but not impossible.

He sat there eating quietly listening to his father continue about his unloading issues. His mother would try to sneak in a decorating or renovation idea that she had for the future of their new house whenever she could. Then they discussed the new neighbors. His father thought it was nice gesture for the Christopher's to come over and welcome them to the neighborhood. But wasn't thrilled about the fact that their little visit had set him back about nearly a full hour.

Tommy listened and only stopped eating to talk when he had been asked a question. His only focus was finishing his dinner and getting back to his room. Right now, that was the only place in the new house he wanted to be. Plus, he wanted to take the time to properly marvel at his accomplishment before his mother called for lights out.

The rest of the house was still littered with open boxes, but not his bedroom. His bedroom was complete. Tommy finished his dinner and asked to be excused, then hurried back to his room. He noticed once he closed the door that his mother had managed to sneak in at some point throughout the day and put his curtains up. He didn't remember seeing her do it, but he was happy that she had. Now the streetlight wouldn't be glaring through his window tonight. Although, the soft orange glow had been comforting for the first night in and empty room of a new house. *Everything looks great,* he thought standing just inside the closed door of his room.

He walked over to the window and pushed the side of his face against the glass to see what else he could of the neighborhood before it got too dark outside. He hadn't really taken an opportunity to look around too much during the day. He had been way too focused on his room. There wasn't much to see from what he could tell. Just the Christopher's house and the ones following the sequential line on down the street, a few passing cars, and the unlit streetlights spaced out along both sides of their street.

He thought long and hard about Florida. He thought about his old room and the beach. He thought about how much he really did still miss those things. He was pretty sure he would never see his old room again. Except in the memories. But there was nothing saying that he would never see Florida again. Or the beach for that matter. This realization comforted Tommy. It even made him laugh a little, that he hadn't thought of it that way sooner. Despite the weight of the stress leading up to the move and following the heartbreak of actually having to leave Florida, Tommy decided in that moment that he was probably going to like New York. He had dreaded coming here. All of the unknowns. There were still plenty, and he knew that. But something as simple as getting his room completely unpacked had started to change his mind. Dare he say he felt at home surrounded by all his things. He felt a touch of guilt at that last though but shook it off quickly. He had decided that he wanted to be happy here. As happy as he had been in Florida. And that was okay.

The next morning Tommy was awakened by the sound of his mother's voice calling his name. First in the hallway and again as she opened his bedroom door.

"Hey Tommy, it's time to get up, sweetie," his mother said. "We're going out for a little bit with Mrs. Christopher and Owen. They're going to show us around town."

He lay there looking up at his mother from his bed with one eye still closed against the daylight seeping through a gap in his curtains. His blankets were pulled up, covering half of his face in a blue, diagonal slash from his ear to his chin. He wanted nothing more than to stay in the bed. But apparently, thanks to two thirds of the Christopher family, this was not on option.

Mrs. Christopher had made a second visit this morning and told his mother that she had some errands to run and invited her and Tommy to tag along.

"Tommy!" she said again in a snappier tone. She stepped further into his room and turned the light on.

"I'm *uuup*," he slurred up at her from his bed, both his eyes closed again to block out the overhead light on his ceiling.

His mother gave a small chuckle watching him slither out of his bed and onto the floor. He sat there slumped in a pile like discarded laundry with a disgruntled face. His mother walked over to his closet and grabbed some clothes and sat them on his bed.

"Here sweetie, put these on," she said. "I'm going to finish getting ready," she said walking toward his door and out of his room. "We're leaving in just a few, so get up and get ready," she yelled as she started back up the stairs.

Tommy sat there for another minute or so before he accepted that going back to sleep was not an option. He got dressed and walked to the kitchen hoping to get a quick bite to eat before they left. He stood there looking in the pantry for something quick but was interrupted by his mother.

"We're gonna get something while we're out, hun," she said.

Tommy, still in no mood to talk, closed the pantry door and sat down at the kitchen table waiting for his mother to give the word that she was ready to go. They walked out the door and he noticed again that the summer weather felt nice. He immediately felt thankful that they had been greeted to the Northeast by the summer heat and not blistering cold of a northeastern winter. He didn't feel like he would have turned a corner so quickly on this place if had been the ladder.

He and his mother reached the end of their driveway and began crossing the street. He noticed that Owen was sitting in his front yard. He appeared to be playing or messing with something. Tommy still wasn't sure what to make of Owen. He had only met him the one time and he had been pretty sure that they both had the same opinion of that forced encounter. But now, they were officially going to be spending the day together. Forced encounter again, yes, but surely, they would come up with something to talk about. Tommy hoped anyway. He loved his mom but being stuck in a vehicle all day with nothing but the sound of her chattering on with another mom was not his idea of a good time.

"Oh look," his mother said. "Why don't you go play with Owen and I'll get Mrs. Christopher?"

"Hey, Owen," Tommy's mother said to him and waved. "Is your mom inside?"

"Yes Ma'am," Owen replied, looking up at her, then back down at the ground.

Tommy's mother nudged him. He looked up to see her smiling, nodding her head in the direction of where Owen was sitting. Tommy looked back at Owen and started over to where he was without a word. He sat down on the ground across from Owen and realized wasn't playing, he was digging in his yard with a small stick creating a small, seemingly pointless hole. Tommy silently watched for a minute. He remembered his friend Todd back in Florida. He and Todd had been friends as far back as he could remember. He had just always known Todd. There was never any awkward moment where they had to become friends or be introduced or have an awkward, silent second encounter. Much like the one he and Owen were sitting in now. Todd could be found somewhere in nearly every good memory that Tommy could think of. He had never been forced into something like this. But still, here he was.

Owen hadn't said anything yet either. He hadn't even looked up since Tommy's mother asked him if his mother was inside. It made Tommy wonder if they had that in common. Not being too keen on new introductions. Although, it didn't look as if mattered to Owen whether he had sat down with him in the yard or chose to go inside with his mother.

"I'm Tommy," he said, after staring at Owen for what felt like forever.

Owen remained silent for another few seconds, and the finally spoke.

"Yesterday was weird, huh?" he asked.

"What do you mean?" Tommy asked feeling unsure about the path their conversation had started down.

"I mean the whole 'us coming over' thing, bothering you guys while you were trying to get all your stuff inside."

Tommy nodded silently in agreement. It had been a little weird. But Owen saying so had relieved a bit of the tension right off the bat, because now, he and Owen had something that they agreed on.

"Yeah, I guess so," Tommy said nudging the conversation along. "But I think it's just one of those things people do when someone new moves in close to them.

"I'm Owen," he said looking up at Tommy for the first time.

He dropped his stick and extended his hand toward Tommy. Tommy couldn't remember ever actually shaking anyone's hand before. Certainly not someone his own age. He suddenly realized that he was a little unsure of the proper protocol. Still, he reached out and grabbed Owen's hand and engaged in what he believed to be his first real handshake.

"So," Tommy picked back up. "What's there to do around here?"

"Me and my dad go fishing sometimes," Owen replied. "And we have a pool. I think you do too, but I've never looked. The last guy who lived there was old, and kinda mean."

"Yeah, we do," Tommy said. "But it's empty. My dad says we're gonna get it if filled sometime after he starts work."

"What's he do?" Owen asked.

"He's a cop," Tommy said. "He was transferred here... or something. He was a cop in Florida too.

"That's pretty cool," Owen said with a hint of excitement.

"What's Florida like?" he asked. "I've never been, but I heard it's really warm. Like all the time"

For a brief moment Tommy was walking down the stairs of his old house again. All of the emotions and feelings as fresh as the day they left Florida. He thought about being in his mom's car, sitting at the stop sign at the end of their old street, taking in the last glimpse of their now old house.

"It is," Tommy said smiling uncontrollably. "It stays pretty warm all year. I heard it gets really cold up here. I've never seen snow before"

"What?" Owen exclaimed, stiffening his back. His jaw dropped wide open. "It doesn't snow in Florida?"

"Nope, not at all," Tommy said, laughing at his new friend's reaction.

"Just wait till wintertime," Owen said. "You'll see more snow than you know what to do with."

Tommy and Owen continued laughing until their conversation was cut short by the sound of Owen's mother.

"Let's go boys," she said as she and Tommy's mother came walking out of the house.

Tommy had reasoned at the beginning of their conversation that Owen was probably just as unsure about him, as he was about Owen. Although now, they seemed to have hit it off pretty well despite what they both felt was an unnecessary, awkward introduction the night before.

They climbed in the back seat of Owen's mother's car and Tommy immediately started telling Owen more about life in Florida. He talked about the beaches, the little lizards that ran around their yard, anything he could think of that he thought Owen might think was interesting. He admitted to Owen that he was a little nervous about his first New York winter. And Owen couldn't get over the fact that Tommy had never seen snow before. Owen even paused their conversation to relay that information to his mother. Having never lived anywhere except New York, Owen was very accustomed to the changing of the seasons.

He told Tommy more about things that his father would take him to do, fishing, trips to the park, or going into the city to catch a Yankee's game. He even elaborated just a little on the old man who used to live in Tommy's house.

"He had a really cool, old car and he *hated* people walking on his grass," Owen said. "Even if it was an accident."

Tommy found himself a little jealous that he didn't have much to add about things he had done with his father, so he just sat and listened to Owen. He tried his best to seem as interested as he could, though he wasn't sure how well it was coming across. During a story Owen was telling about a Red Sox fan dumping popcorn on his dad at a Yankees game, Tommy started remembering bits and pieces of a dream he had had about his father a couple weeks before the move.

The memory was mostly fuzzy, and he couldn't remember any specific details now. Just that the thought of it was enough to make him feel sick to his stomach.

They stopped for breakfast, then back on the road. Their mothers sat in the front seats going on about husbands and jobs and everything else moms talk about when they get together. They seemed to be instant friends. Laughing and sometimes speaking to each other in hushed tones so Tommy and Owen couldn't hear.

Owen's mother spent a great deal of time talking about their neighborhood and pointing out places to Tommy's mother as they would pass them on the road. Tommy heard her say that the worst thing she had ever heard of happening in their neighborhood was their dog, Friday had been hit by a car. Owen stopped talking when he heard his mother mentioned their dog being hit. His eyes fixed on her, and his brow furrowed. But Tommy didn't think he was actually looking at her. It was more like his eyes had just landed there and something in his mind, a memory perhaps, was the cause of his anger. He snapped out of it after a few seconds and turned back to Tommy. "He's okay," Owen said, referencing their dog.

There was a lot to see on the drive. Every so often Owen, who seemed to take the cue from his mother, would point out something or someplace he had been with his parents. Laser tag, bowling alleys, parks. It didn't really seem that much different from Florida. Still no palm trees though. *Day two and I've already made a friend,* Tommy thought.

As the day went on, Tommy found himself feeling even better about New York and could feel the gigantic change that had just taken place in his life start to grow smaller and smaller. They spent the entire day together and got to see a large part of the town. It was no surprise to Tommy that by the time they pulled back into Owens driveway, that he and Owen were making plans for the next day.

Once they were out of the car, Tommy and his mother said goodbye to Owen and his mother and walked back across the street to their house. They walked in the house and Tommy's father was sitting on the couch watching TV. The stale smell of beer hung in the air. That was where he could be found most nights. After saying good night to his parents, Tommy walked down the hallway to his room. He sat on his bed and thought about what a fun day it had been. How it started with him being nervous about even going across the street and ended with plans for the next day. All it had taken was one long ride in a car. Today had been a good day. He felt like he really had made a friend.

4

Tommy and Owen spent almost every day left of that summer vacation together. They would ride their bikes around the neighborhood and swim in each other's pools (Tommy's once it was filled) or just find something to get into. Owen showed Tommy all the places he was allowed to go without one of his parents tagging along and Tommy's mother had graciously agreed that those boundaries were good enough for him as well. They became inseparable. They stayed gone most of the day unless one of them had to go somewhere else with their parents. But when they would return, they were back at it again. The Christopher's and the Collins' became friends as well. There was an open line of communication about where the boys were or who had seen them last that hadn't given them much of a choice. At least for their mothers.

The parental relationship happened organically as well. Their mothers, Lori, and Stephanie could be found having coffee or talking on the phone nearly every day. Grocery trips, salon appointments, all the sorts of things moms do together. Their fathers would spend their free time chatting about sports or cars or work. It was less frequent than their mother's, but they still seemed to get along okay. Owen's father, Robert even told Tommy's father to bring his uniforms to the dry cleaning and tailoring shop that he owned, Christopher's Cleaners, and he would keep them pressed free of charge. He even said he would be happy to bring them back when he came home in the evenings to save Tommy's father the second trip into the city.

A couple weeks before school was to start up again, Tommy began to get nervous. Moving had been hard enough, but starting at a new school was a whole new animal. He ended up having a fairly typical "new kid" experience, during his first school year with Owen. Owen had given him a bit of a rundown before summer break ended. Starting with the names of the two or three kids to stay away from if he hoped to avoid being mercilessly picked on and ridiculed for no good reason at all. Tommy did get a lot of the "who's that" looks from kids who had spent their first few years of school surrounded by the same cluster of faces looking just a little bit older each time they would return to school after summer break. They asked more than their fair share of questions, especially when they would find out that he had moved from Florida. "Can you surf?" seemed to be a popular question. A lot of the kids, surprisingly, had never been to Florida. That particular question always brought back brief flashes of the emotional aches and pains Tommy had felt when he learned that he and his family were leaving Florida. Learning to surf was something that Tommy had wanted to do since the first time he caught a glimpse of someone riding a wave during one of his trips to the beach with his mother.

 The aches and pains never stuck around for long though. Tommy refused to let them. It only took a few weeks for the new to wear off and Tommy found that he had become just another face in the crowd. And that was alright with him. He wasn't much in favor of all the attention anyway.

 The first school year came and went, as did the next one. Eventually they just seemed to fly by just as the years tend to do. Tommy and Owen would put all their effort into the school week and spend their weekends ripping and running. But when summer would arrive, they were back to their sunup to sundown schedule.

 As they got older their parents loosened the reigns a bit and allowed them to venture off further and further from home by themselves. Tommy and Owen eventually worked their way far enough away from their houses and managed to talk old Mr. Thurman, who lived in the very back corner of the neighborhood, into letting them swim in his pond. Owen's father had talked about Mr. Thurman before and how when he bought his property, he managed to swindle some extra land right out from under the developers during the negotiations. He said Mr. Thurman was just as surprised as everyone else was that it actually worked. Mr. Thurman spoke with Tommy and Owen's parents about the boys being in his pond and told them that he didn't mind one bit. It quickly claimed the top spot as their favorite place to go during the summer. And it was all theirs.

The summer that Tommy and Owen turned twelve was no exception. It started out just the same as the others had. Sunup, to sundown. Rotating between each other's pools, and the pond. Rushing to get home before the streetlights came on with the all-consuming fear that if they didn't make it in time the next day would be a bust. Summer was going great, just as they had planned. Until the third week.

Owen waited outside one morning, but Tommy never showed. He stood fast for about forty-five minutes, riding in circles and figure eights in the middle of the street between his and Tommy's houses. Then finally, he decided to go knock on Tommy's door. He thought maybe Tommy had slept in or something. Both cars were in the driveway, and Mr. Collins' police cruiser was even parked on the street outside their house. But there was no answer. Owen began to feel flustered. It wasn't like Tommy to not show up. They had been at this same routine for years now. Owen rode his bike back across the street into his own yard and dropped his bike in the grass. He walked in the house to see if his mother knew anything about where Tommy was.

"Where's Tommy?" he asked his mother, half expecting that she had already spoken with Mrs. Collins at some point during the morning.

"Well, how should I know, honey?" she replied. She sat the dish down that she had been cleaning and peered out the kitchen window at the Collins' house. "All the cars are there. He's probably just sleeping in. You boys run non-stop. It was only a matter of time before one of you shut down."

"That's what I thought, but no one answered the door," he said.

"I don't know, sweetie," his mother said returning to the dishes.

Owen walked back outside and picked up his bike and continuing to ride in the street for another fifteen minutes or so. Tired of waiting, and having no answers, he set out for Mr. Thurman's pod. That's what they had planned to do that day, so whenever Tommy decided to wake up, he knew Tommy would know where to find him. As he rode his bike down the long gravel driveway that led down to Mr. Thurman's house, he saw him standing out in his back yard looking up at his house.

Mr. Thurman was a very large man. Somewhere in his late fifties or early sixties at the time. He was one of those people you could just look at and tell that they knew the meaning of a hard day's work. He had fought in Vietnam half a lifetime ago and liked to think he was still able to be as physically active as he had been back then. Although nature and time often teamed up to prove otherwise.

Mr. Thurman waved Owen down as he started to pass the house on his way to the pond. Owen came to a complete stop and dropped his bike in the edge of his yard just off the driveway, and walked over to where Mr. Thurman was standing

"Where's Tommy?" Mr. Thurman asked. He grabbed a bandanna out of his back pocket and wiped the sweat from his forehead.

"I'm not sure," Owen said, halfway laughing. "I think he slept in."

I don't think that man's slept a day in his life, Owen thought, staring at Mr. Thurman

"Well, I was hopin' I'd catch you boys coming down through here today," Mr. Thurman continued. "I wanted to see if you boys minded helping me out here just a bit before you head down to the water."

Occasionally, Mr. Thurman would flag the boys down on their way to the pond and have something around the house that he needed help with. It had become part of the deal sometime after he okayed it with their parents for them to swim in his pond. Needless to say, their parents were not opposed to them trading a little manual labor for the privilege to swim in his pond. Although, on occasion, he would slip them a few bucks when they were finished. If he felt the task warranted a little more compensation than just passage to the water.

It was never anything too difficult. Mostly just things Mr. Thurman had become unable to do by himself. A couple times during the summer when Mr. Thurman's family would visit, he would ask Tommy and Owen if they minded letting his granddaughter, Rhiannon tag along with them to the pond. She was a scrawny, little thing. Probably a year or two younger than they were. And therefore, immediately annoying.

She had stringy black hair that came down past her shoulders, and slightly tanned skin, and she liked to talk. *Really* liked to talk. It seemed on some days the boys couldn't get a word in edgewise. Still, they included her in whatever it was they were doing.

One day in particular, they were each taking turns flipping off the dock into the water. It had actually been Rhiannon's idea, because she had seen them do it before, but she had never been able to complete a flip herself. Tommy showed her, then Owen followed, and then she would try. She would always run to the end of the dock, then stop, and lean forward and bend her knees. But when she would jump, she always managed to turn about halfway through her attempted flip and land on her back. So, they continued showing her and she continued flopping onto her back.

During one of Tommy's attempts, Owen and Rhiannon were talking as Tommy sprinted down the length of dock and flipped off into the water. He had asked her how she liked living upstate, and to his surprise, she said she didn't care for it very much.

"It's nice and all," she said. "It's really beautiful. I would just rather be down here. I don't feel like I really fit in up there." It was then that Owen noticed a look in her eyes as she started talking about how she wanted to go everywhere she could when she got older. It was a gleam. A deepness he had never noticed before. He struggled to find the word that fit how he would even begin to describe it. It just seemed... *Wild,* he thought. The word came from nowhere. But it was like her eyes should have belonged to someone much older. It almost made him laugh at first, but it fit. He told Tommy about their conversation but made sure to keep that part about her eyes to himself.

Today's task was cleaning gutters.

"I have trouble on that ladder sometimes," Mr. Thurman said, looking up at his roof.

"Damn hearing and eyesight decided to pop smoke at the same time, now my balance has gone to shit."

"No problem, Mr. Thurman," Owen said, walking over to the ladder.

Tommy and Owen didn't mind helping him out. Especially on the days that they got paid in addition to having access to the pond. In fact, as far as they knew, they were the only ones he had ever given permission to swim in his pond. And that made it even better.

"It'd go by a lot quicker if you had Tommy helpin', ya," Mr. Thurman said with chuckle. "Next time we'll make him do it by himself and we'll split a beer, how's that?"

"Sounds good to me," Owen said laughing along with him.

It took about an hour, but Owen finished the gutters for Mr. Thurman. He half expected to see Tommy rushing down the long gravel driveway to meet him at the pond. But he never came.

Owen went on to the pond after finishing up with Mr. Thurman, but he only stayed for a bit. He got in the water, mostly just to cool off, then back out and just sat on the dock and waited to see if Tommy would show. As he rode back down their street, the closer he got to his house, the more he noticed that nothing had changed at Tommy's. All the cars were still there and in the exact spots they had been parked when he had waited in the street this morning. It didn't even look like there were any lights on inside the house.

He surveyed Tommy's house for a moment and listened for any voices that may be in the Collins' fenced in back yard. But he heard nothing. He parked his bike and walked inside. He half expected, *hoped* was more like it, to hear his mother on the phone with Mrs. Collins. Or to even see Mrs. Collins sitting at the kitchen table with his mother. Then, hopefully, he would have a reason as to why Tommy wasn't out today. But again, there was nothing. In fact, his mother and father hadn't seemed to notice that their almost daily interactions with the Collins' hadn't happened, at least not to the extent that he had.

"Hey, honey," his mother said. "What did you boys get into today?"

"There was no 'we,'" Owen sighed. "Tommy never showed."

"I don't know, honey," his mother replied seeing the questions written on her son's face. "I haven't talked to Stephanie today; I don't know where he could be. Maybe he's sick"

"Maybe," he said, turning and heading toward his bedroom.

Owen closed the door behind him and walked over and sat on his bed. He was still wondering what was going on with Tommy. It probably wouldn't have weighed so heavily on his mind all day if someone had answered the door at Tommy's house. Or if either one of his parents had spoken to either one of Tommy's parents. The likelihood of those two things taking place in the same day seemed damn near impossible. He couldn't remember a day like this one since Tommy moved into the neighborhood. It didn't feel right. It just––didn't feel right.

| 5 |

Three--whole--days. That's how long it was before Owen heard from Tommy again. Three days of riding around in the street between their houses for no less than an hour. Three days of knocking with no answer. And three days of eventually giving up and riding off without him. Even on that third day, Owen still waited for Tommy in the street for a good forty-five minutes before taking off on another solo trip to Mr. Thurman's pond. It seemed that it was becoming the thing to do. Wait, get tired of waiting, head to the pond.

He got about halfway to Mr. Thurman's, when he heard the unmistakable sound of a car behind him, heading up the street in his direction. He looked back to see how close it was to make sure he was out of the way and saw Tommy on his bike peddling toward him. Tommy moved up onto the sidewalk to let the car pass. Owen moved up on the sidewalk as well and hopped off his bike and waited for Tommy to catch up. Tommy sped down the sidewalk toward where Owen was standing. Owen stood there holding his bike up, watching as Tommy drew closer. Tommy hadn't even come to a complete stop before Owen knew that something was wrong. Tommy's bike screeched to a halt no more than a couple of feet from Owen's.

"Hey," Tommy said, as if he hadn't been missing for the last three days, but Owen wasn't buying it.

"Hey, yourself," Owen said. "Where the hell have you been, man? I've been knocking on your door for three days."

Tommy stared at him for a few seconds, and said, "Just at home." Tommy leaned back onto the seat of his bike.

Owen's frustration was beginning to cloud the bit of concern that had surfaced. That answer didn't fit. It didn't answer any of what Owen had remembered about the last three days. Their cars had never moved. No one answered the door. For three straight days.

"How come nobody answered the door?" he asked.

I don't know, man. Maybe there was…maybe they…," Tommy stammered.

"What the hell's going on, Tommy?" Owen asked. He tried to meet Tommy's eyes as they looked anywhere, but at him.

"Nothing, man. I swear," Tommy said, his voice starting to crack.

"Bullshit," Owen said.

"Forget about it, man," Tommy said. "Let's just go to the pond."

Owen stood silent and slightly shocked and agitated as Tommy hopped on his bike and rode past him headed toward the pond. It took him only a few seconds to realize that Tommy wasn't looking back, and he wasn't slowing down either.

Owen hopped back on his bike and followed. He peddled as fast as he could to catch up. Thankfully, Mr. Thurman wasn't outside, so there was no work to be done or no granddaughters to keep up with today. They maintained their speed down the gravel driveway, past Mr. Thurman's house and through the gate that led down to the pond. Owen watched as Tommy rode straight toward the dock and jumped off his bike before it had even come to a complete stop. Owen followed close behind, barely stopping his own bike before jumping off and following him to the dock.

Tommy stood there staring out at the water, his unsettling demeanor causing Owen's imagination to run wild with questions and possibilities. Their cars hadn't moved in three days. Owen knew they were home. But something in his gut told him that whatever Tommy was hiding was bigger than any inconvenience he had experienced over the last three days.

Tommy's silence continued, as did Owen's, until he couldn't stand it any longer. So much so, that he felt his gut was going to explode if it were wrenched any tighter.

"What the hell's going on, Tommy?" Owen asked, fearing what the answer would be.

"Nothing, man!" Tommy yelled. "Just leave it alone." He said, calming his tone a bit.

Owen could hear the breaking in his voice. Tommy stood for another few seconds before crumbling to the surface of the dock as if something had been holding him up with marionette strings the entire time and finally let go.

Owen rushed over and stood beside him.

"It's him." Tommy said, sitting on the dock. "It's my dad!"

"What do you mean, it's your dad?" Owen asked, feeling even more confused than before.

"The son-of-a-bitch won't leave me alone!" Tommy shouted.

Pure adrenalin shoved Owen a couple involuntary steps backward. But he was stopped in his tracks when Tommy shot back to his feet and pointed a stiff finger at him.

"Never repeat what I'm about to tell you, Owen," Tommy said as tears began to well up in his eyes. "You hear me? EVER! I don't know what he'll do if he finds out."

"Okay, okay, not a word, I promise." Owen said, constantly gripping, then having to re-grip his composure. "Just tell me what the hell happened."

"He just won't leave me alone." Tommy repeated in a large gasp and sat back down on the wood surface of the dock.

Owen sat down beside him. He was scared of what Tommy could have meant. He hoped that when Tommy finally explained that it would somehow be even the least bit palatable in comparison to the horrible thoughts and questions that had begun to surface in his mind. But somehow, he knew that wouldn't be the case. Owen didn't dare speculate on what could have possibly happened. He just stared at his friend sitting there on the dock. His head hung and his breathing showing no signs of slowing down.

"He touches me," Tommy said, his face still aimed downward.

"What do you mean--'touches you?'" Owen asked hesitantly. His voice cracked as the words left his lips. The same as Tommy's.

"I mean, he drinks too much, then he comes in my room late at night and touches me when I'm sleeping," Tommy spilled out angrily. "He's been doing it for years."

There was a silence that seemed to last for days before Tommy spoke again.

"And up until three days ago, he had me convinced that I had been dreaming all this time. And that there was something wrong with *me*. He always told me I shouldn't tell anyone about the dreams, because they would take me away from him and my mom. And I believed him. Sick fucking bastard."

Owen sat speechless staring at his best friend. The weight of what Tommy had just confided, pushing down on him as if a dump truck had just turned over on him. And in a roundabout way, he supposed it had. It felt so heavy that it might push him through the dock and into the water. He tried frantically, but quickly realized he was completely incapable of getting his brain formulate anything to say in response to the horror Tommy had just described. Let alone have the courage to let it escape his lips if it did.

"I...I...," Owen stuttered trying to mutter something. If nothing else, just to fill the silence.

"I don't know what to do," Tommy said looking up at Owen. The tears pooled in his eyes and quickly spilled over and streamed down his face.

Owen did the only thing he could think to do. He sat there and listened.

"For some reason the other night, it just popped into my head that I seemed to only be having these *dreams* about my dad when he would drink. And not just the usual three or four he has at the end of the day. Specifically, when he would drink *a lot*." Tommy paused and shook his head, his eyes focused on the boards of the dock beneath them. "The more I thought about it, the more it seemed like more of a fact than a thought, ya know. So, I decided that next time I noticed that he was drinking like that, I was going to find out for sure. And three nights ago, I got my chance. He was drinkin' a lot that night. Like, one right after the other. He even got into whatever it is that he keeps in the cabinet above the fridge. He was pretty wasted by the time I went to bed. And my mom went to bed around the same time. Only I had a plan. I was going to stay awake as long as I could and see what happened."

Tommy paused and looked back down at the dock. Owen couldn't believe it, but Tommy still trying to catch his breath. Or maybe it had slowed, it was just getting faster again.

"S-so what happened?" Owen asked, his eyes glued to Tommy, following his every subtle movement. He barely blinked. His mouth hung open so long it had become dry.

"I got in the bed," Tommy sighed as he continued. "And I laid there waiting in the dark. Trying as hard as I could to hear what he was doing in the living room. All I could hear was the sound of the TV and every once in a while, I would hear him open another beer or he was doing something with a glass in the kitchen. He wasn't exactly quiet about it. I fought to stay awake. And man, it seemed like forever. I didn't think I was going to make it. But just as I was about to give up, I realized that I couldn't hear the TV anymore. I sat up in my bed listening as hard as I could. And I heard him crush a beer can and throw it on the coffee table. Once the rattling stopped, I heard his footsteps. I couldn't tell at first, what direction he was headed in until it was almost too late. He was walking down the hallway. I laid down as quick as I could and pulled my blankets up and pretended to be asleep. Then the footsteps stopped."

The world around them had disappeared. Owen hung on every word of Tommy said. Every breath. His mind tried to wrap around what Tommy was saying. It all just seemed so unreal. Yet, it was.

"I tried to be as still and quiet as I could," Tommy continued. "I was still listening for more footsteps, but by then, he was right outside my door. I heard my doorknob rattle just a bit, so I closed my eyes. He walked into my room and closed the door then walked over and stood by my bed for a minute. I could feel him standing there, Owen. Just staring at me. I wanted to be wrong. I so badly wanted to be wrong. I just wanted him to walk away. But he didn't. My covers started to move, and everything in me screamed for me to hold onto them. *Don't let him pull them down!* But I had to know. I had to know if I was crazy, or if he was actually..."

Tommy stopped talking again. He took a deep breath and continued.

"I could feel his hand on me. On my back at first, then he moved it around to my chest," Tommy looked as though he was about to vomit. "Then he put his hand down my shorts. I didn't know what to do. I laid there for a second, frozen, wondering if I was really awake or if I had fallen asleep and it really was a dream. I was so scared, Owen. Then I started getting mad. I mean fucking pissed. I thought, *If I fight back, I'll find out if I'm awake or not,* so that's what I did. I jumped out of bed and started screaming at him to get the fuck off of me. He seemed shocked at first, b–but then he got pissed and started hitting me. I just fell on the floor, and I was screaming for my mom, but he wouldn't stop. I didn't know if she could hear me from upstairs. I thought I heard her running down the stairs, but I couldn't tell for sure over the sound of him hitting me and yelling at me. She must have heard me––or both of us because she came bustin' through the door and started screaming at him and shoved him off of me.

"Holy shit!" Owen said before he even realized the words were there.

"He tried to tell her that he was just coming in to check on me, because he thought he heard me up doing something when I was supposed to be in bed. It's fucking summer vacation!" he said looking at Owen. "I yelled, 'bullshit!' And then I told her what had really happened. What he did to me. And that it had been happening for years now. She started screaming. I didn't know if she was screaming at him or if she was just screaming because she couldn't handle everything I had said. Either way, she just ran over and grabbed me and ran out of the room."

Tommy continued with the account of what happened. He told Owen that for the next three days their house had felt like a prison. During the day it was so silent that it was almost physically painful. His father refused to let either one of them leave the house, which Owen had already put together. It also explained why none of their vehicles had moved for the last three days and why no one would answer the door.

He told Owen that he spent most of those three days in his room. Sunup, to sundown. Just as it would have been if he had been outside with him. He told him that he had even seen him through the window, waiting in the street for him every day. He was just too scared to try and make any kind of contact. He was afraid of what his father would do if he caught him.

"My mom didn't speak to my father during the day," Tommy continued. "Hell, she barely spoke at all. She even had a hard time looking me in the eyes. I don't think she knows what to make of all of it," Tommy sat silent for a moment. "He forced me to hide it from her too. He really had me so convinced at one point that if I even said anything to her about the *dreams*, that she would send me away. And it wouldn't be to get help. It would be because she would think there was something wrong with me and that she would be disappointed and ashamed of me. How fucked up is that?"

"I can't imagine," Owen said.

"At night, I guess when my mom thought I was asleep, I could hear them arguing," Tommy said. "My mom was just begging him over and over again to leave and to just leave us alone. He just refused and told her to shut the fuck up about it. She would just cry louder and then the shouting match would begin. Eventually, she would just run to her room and that would be the last I would hear from her for the night."

Tommy sighed. For the first time since Owen had seen him today, he didn't seem panicked or scared. He wasn't exactly at peace either. He just seemed… there. Away from the danger for the moment but knowing he would have to return.

"I couldn't make it all out," Tommy continued. "But I did hear my mom yelling something at him about the real reasons why we had to leave Florida. And it wasn't for a change of scenery like he had told your dad or for a better job like they had told me. From what I could make hear, he had gotten mixed up with some bad people in Florida. People he should've arrested. But instead, he ended up doing favors for them. Next thing you know the department was questioning every case he was involved in. It was suggested that he take a leave of absence until it got cleared up if it ever did. We just ended up moving here instead."

The two boys sat on the dock in the silence, listening to fish jump out of the water and the frogs croaking off in the distance. Owen wanted to say something to his friend. He tried to think of anything at all to say. Something to at least break the silence.

"I'm really sorry, Tommy." Owen finally spoke. It was the best he could do.

Tommy just sighed and laid back on the dock and looked up at the sky.

"I know, man," Tommy said.

"So, what changed?" Owen asked. "I mean, why'd he let you leave the house today?"

"He didn't want to," Tommy said. "At least that's my guess. But I think my mom convinced him that if he kept me inside much longer that it was going to start looking suspicious. People would have questions, ya know? He told me I better not be out here runnin' my mouth and I honestly wasn't going to. I didn't know if anyone would even believe me. But it was just too much. I mean, you knew something was wrong, and clearly, I'm not good at hiding it, but you can't say anything, Owen. You can't. I'm scared to death of what he'll do to us if he finds out I told you."

They stayed at the pond for a while, until they absolutely had to head back. They walked home that night, pushing their bikes, taking every extra moment they could. Owen knew Tommy was in no hurry to get home and Owen was certainly in no hurry to get him there.

Their walk home was mostly filled with silence except for Owen's attempt at making plans for the next day. Tommy only said that he hoped he would be allowed out again, but he wasn't sure if his father would allow it.

As their houses came into view, Owen could see the sadness in Tommy's eyes soon clouded by fear. It looked heavy. It looked like more than Tommy could carry. He wanted to tell Tommy to just come home with him and they could talk to his parents. But he knew he was too scared to risk it. He knew that Tommy had no idea what to expect when he walked back into his house. He looked so tired. Not a normal tired, but more like "staying awake, to stay alive tired."

They reached the point in the road where they usually parted ways with the understanding that they would see each other the next day. Only this time there was an uncertainty looming over their departure. It was thick and so clear to each of them that they both knew the other could feel it. Tommy said goodbye and started walking toward his house.

Owen watched for a second and said, "See ya tomorrow," mustering a half smile.

Tommy did his best to smile back. "See ya tomorrow," he said

Owen turned and walked toward his own house. As he walked through the front door, he was met with an earie silence. He couldn't remember it ever being this quiet in his house. He was a little unsure if it was actually that quiet or if all he could hear was Tommy's horrifying story playing on a loop in his head. The back door creaked open, and the sound filled the empty house.

"Owen?" his mother called.

Never in his life had he been so happy to hear the lulling sound of his mother's voice. He instantly felt the comfort of her presence come over him as she walked into the living room. The sight of her made him feel as if the only thing he wanted in the world was to collapse into her arms. He just stared at her. She smiled back at him, and he thought about Tommy. About how it would be quite the opposite for him when he got home. He had nothing like this to look forward to. No comfort. No soft place to land.

"What's wrong, honey?" his mother asked, her smile turning to a look of concern.

"I don't know, my stomach hurts." he lied. "I think I'm just tired." he lied again, thinking of something quick. Something that wouldn't be questioned.

His mother knelt in front of him and gently grabbed his face. She smiled at him radiantly. "See," she said just above a whisper. Her smile gave him goosebumps. "I told you. You boys run non-stop, and it's going to catch up with you."

She smiled again and kissed him on the forehead. Then she wrapped her arms around him, and he could feel his legs wanting to give out. He walked to his room and changed clothes. His mother walked in just as he climbed under his blankets. She sat down on the edge of his bed and brushed his hair back with her hand and smiled. She quietly began humming a tune. It was one that he immediately recognized.

Imagine, by John Lennon, was one of her favorite pieces to play on the piano. Sort of her go-to piece for any impromptu performance. She would always close her eyes and sway ever so slightly, back, and forth when she played. She used to sing it to him quite often when he was younger. Especially if he wasn't feeling well. It had been a few years but for some reason she chose tonight. Owen felt so comforted, so loved. He just lay there staring at his mother, trying to focus on her song. But he was unable to stop the horror Tommy had described from creeping its way in.

His mother finished the song and leaned down and kissed his forehead once more. She told him that she loved him and left the room. Owen lay there in the dark, the residual of his mother's bedside serenade quickly replaced in his mind by thoughts and images of what it might be like at Tommy's house. He imagined Tommy sitting in his room alone and scared.

How could someone take what is supposed to be a comforting moment between a parent and a child and turn it in to such a hellish nightmare? he thought. He didn't expect to sleep at all that night. But somehow, he drifted off.

The next day started just as all summer days had before Tommy's mysterious absence. Tommy and Owen met in the morning and went about their business throughout the day. There was a haze around any of the conversation they tried to have. But they both avoided it like some contagious disease. They filled their day with talking about the fast-approaching school year, other kids they went to school with, and of course, a trip to Mr. Thurman's pond. Owen was able to coax a laugh out of Tommy at one point reminding him about the time Joey McDonald tripped while running down the hallway at school. He had so much momentum that he slid a good fifty feet once he hit the floor. Owen counted the day a success.

They arrived back on their street just as the streetlights came on. Still, they took their time, trying to squeeze every last second, they could outdoors. They arrived at the point where they could see their houses. They stood in the street and continued talking about anything to suppress the thing that Owen was sure was one both their minds. They got ready to part ways, again with the promise that they would see each other the next day and Tommy stopped. He looked as though he had something to say, but that he was struggling to get the words out. Owen let him try, though it seemed clear that it had to do with the one topic they had spent the day avoiding.

"What's on your mind?" Owen asked.

Tommy hesitated for a moment. "I just wanted to say thanks," he said. "Thanks for listening."

"Man," Owen started, quickly realizing that he didn't really know what to what the right thing to say would be. "That's what I'm here for."

They smiled at each other turned and walked to their houses. Ready and hopeful to do it all again tomorrow.

A little over a week had passed and Tommy and Owen had done their best to revert back to something of a normal summer. There were good days. Although, they never could completely escape the topic of Tommy's father. Neither one of Owen's parents seemed to notice that anything had changed. As far as he knew, neither one of Tommy's parents had said so much as a word to his parents in over a week. Owen figured they would have asked at some point, or he would have at least heard them talking about it. But there was nothing. He just figured that in the adult world it's easy to assume that everyone else is just as busy as you are. And that stagnant communication periods of may be a result of that.

Tommy's father returned to work and Tommy's mother started to leave the house again. Tommy hadn't said too much else about his father, except that he had become like a stranger in the house. Tommy still wasn't sleeping really well. He told Owen closing his eyes to go to sleep had become so terrifying. He would just lay there, listening, trying to make sure he didn't hear his father's footsteps coming toward his room. Eventually, he would fall asleep, but he said he usually woke up in a panic, fearing that his father would be standing over him. Aside from leaving the house again, his Mother's Day-to-day behavior hadn't changed since the night everything fell apart. She had been drinking more and Tommy could still see the tears ready to burst from her eyes every time she talked to him. She didn't seem to her bearings anymore. Everything that made her who she was, a fun and loving mother, seemed to trail behind her in a shadow. It was like she had started to deteriorate. On a couple of occasions, Tommy had awakened in the middle of the night, frightened, by noise in his room, only to find his mother sitting on the floor next to his bed sobbing quietly. She would always try to quickly disguise her tears, but Tommy knew. There was no mistaking.

Another summer day had ended, just as they all did, too quickly. Owen made it his mission to keep Tommy out of the house as long as he could, but their time for today was at its end. They parted ways and

Owen walked into house as his parents were finishing the after-dinner clean up.

"Want some dinner, honey?" his mother asked.

"No thanks, I'm not hungry. We had some snacks earlier," he lied. "I think I'm going to go take a shower."

"Okay, sweetie," his mother said.

Owen walked into his room and closed the door behind him. He stood there with his back against the door and was able to feel the heat radiating from his face. Despite all his efforts to reroute Tommy's train of thought throughout the day, it had become increasingly harder and harder to watch Tommy walk to his house every night. Owen always wondered if Tommy was going to be left alone or if his father will have gotten drunk enough to create some fresh hell that Tommy was now going to have to navigate through. Owen told Tommy a few days ago, before they parted ways for the evening, that he would leave his window unlocked and if he ever needed to run, he had a place to go. And he had thought about that every night since, as they would make their way up their street and stand in the road between their houses before heading in for the night. *Would tonight be the night that Tommy would come running, banging on his window in the middle of the night because things had erupted again? This time to a potentially deadly situation.* No one, not Tommy nor his mother knew what Mr. Collins was truly capable of. After everything that Tommy had confided in Owen, the abuse, both sexual and physical, and what could only be described as a three-day hostage situation, there seemed to be no depth he wouldn't go to.

Owen couldn't say anything even though he desperately wanted to. He had made a promise to Tommy. And they both feared what would happen if he broke that promise. Still, Owen wanted so badly to tell his mother. He wanted to tell her so he could break down too. He wanted to break down in hopes that it would somehow extinguish the weight that Tommy, and now he, was carrying. But mostly for Tommy.

Owen walked away from his bedroom door and into his bathroom. He turned on the shower, hoping that he would feel any better after letting the hot water attempt to soothe his nerves. After his shower, he said goodnight to his parents. Being reminded again, that something as simple as a "goodnight," was not something that Tommy had anymore.

He climbed in the bed and lay there staring at the ceiling, completely uninterested in sleeping. Thousands of thoughts ran through his head, none of them pleasant, and most all of them emanating from knowing that Tommy was most likely sitting in his room alone and scared. Just waiting for the next horrible thing to happen. He began to worry that the weight would become too much for Tommy and if his father didn't get to him first, Tommy may do something to himself. It scared Owen to think that Tommy could possibly take his own life. Especially with Owen knowing everything that had happened. Keeping his promise meant possibly losing his best friend. But so did breaking it. Every instinct Owen had was telling him to get out of bed and run into the living room and scream at his parents, everything that had happened to Tommy. Then they could call the police, and *they* could take care of it. *But his dad's a cop,* Owen thought. *Would they even believe that he had done all of those things? Would his dad panic if the cops showed up and hurt Tommy and his mother before they could even get to the door?* The risk of that happening scared Owen back into the solitude of keeping his promise.

He wished he had drug Tommy to *his* house the moment he found out and told his parents everything. Then maybe the whole situation would look very different right now. Especially for Tommy. But it was too late for that now. All he could do now was be there for Tommy during the day as much as he possibly could, and stress about it at night, hoping that the worst would never come to be.

| 6 |

Tommy woke the next morning feeling surprisingly well rested. He couldn't remember any of his dreams, but he knew they were there, lingering just out of reach. Not only had he had them, but he also had the feeling that they had been pleasant. A welcome change from the current climate in their house. He lay in his bed allowing his eyes time to adjust to the morning sun seeping through his window. He listened for any sign that someone else in the house was awake. Everything and everyone in the house was silent. Except for the low, unintelligible voices from the TV in the living room, which he assumed meant that his father was awake.

Tommy opted to stay in his room. At least until he was sure his mother was awake. He had not been alone with his father since everything blew up, nor did he want to be. His mother hadn't been much company since then either. But Tommy didn't blame her. She was sorting all of this out in her own way. *Probably,* hopefully, *working on a way to get us the hell out of here,* Tommy often thought.

He sat up on his bed and grabbed his Game Boy from under his pillow and quickly found himself lost in a game of Tetris. Block after block fell as Tommy rushed to fit them into the open spaces needed to complete his rows. He frantically pressed the "A" and "B" buttons, flipping the pieces ninety degrees at a time and using the directional pad to slide them from one side of the screen to the other.

Outside the clicking of the buttons, beyond his bedroom door, Tommy heard the familiar creak of someone on the stairs. *Mom's awake,* he thought, continuing to build his rows and watch them disappear. He wanted to give his mother a chance to get her morning coffee started, but deep down he also feared being caught in the middle of any conversation that could possibly happen between his parents. They had not spoken to each other in quite a while and if they ever did, it was just her begging him to leave, and him refusing. Same thing every time. Tommy had no desire to be anywhere near his father. Even if his mother was there. Sadly, she seemed to be just as trapped as he was.

All the background noise had faded as the clicking of the buttons filled his head once more. Engulfed in his game and desperately trying to focus on beating his high score, his concentration was broken by the sound of a coffee cup shattering on the kitchen floor. Tommy's head snapped toward the door. The Game Boy nearly fell from his hands. A split second later his mother's gut-wrenching scream filled the quiet house. Tommy froze, the fear weighing him down. He was convinced that the dormant hell they had been only surviving in had finally boiled over.

He stared at his door, still listening. Then he leapt off his bed and rushed out of his room. Down the hallway he ran, the voices on the TV were louder than he had realized before. He could see his father still sleeping on the couch, his head flung back, mouth wide open, and felt confusion starting to set in about what had caused his mother to scream the way she had. Just as he reached the threshold between the hallway and the kitchen he was cut off by his mother. Not missing a step, and her scream still echoing throughout the house, she jerked him up into her arms and ran back down the hallway towards him room.

As she lifted him Tommy saw for himself why his mother had screamed. His father's eyes were opened, just about as wide as his mouth was. The terrified look on his face had been frozen in a single moment of horror. He wasn't asleep. His shirt was saturated, glistening in the sunlight pouring through the living room window and onto the couch, almost as if it were intentionally spotlighted. He wasn't sleeping. He was dead.

Tommy's mother burst through the door of his room, still clutching him in her arms so tight that it had started hurt. She quickly sat him down and slammed the door behind them. She stood with her back against the door for a couple seconds, desperately trying to catch her breath. She looked back at Tommy with her eye so wide that if he believed that if they stretched open any further, they may have popped out of their sockets. She rushed him over to his bed, grabbing him along the way. Sat him on his mattress and knelt down in front of him. She grabbed him by the arms, again squeezing tighter than he was sure she had intended. He could feel her hands shaking. Her voice produced barely audible bits of sound with each exhale. There were tears streaming down her face, although the look on her face wasn't sad. She looked as if she wanted to scream but couldn't quite get the mechanics right. It was fear.

"Suh-sweetie," she said, in two separate, stuttered breaths. "I want you to stay right here until I come back, okay?" She stood up on shaky, barely stable legs. Her eyes darted around his room as if she were frantically looking for something. "Do *not* leave this room. Do you understand me?" she said as sternly as she could.

Tommy just stared at her and nodded his head. His own eyes getting wider as the images of what he had just seen flashed through his mind repeatedly. His mother stood there a second more, her legs shaking, ready to give way at any moment. She was still fighting like hell to gain her composure. She looked frantically around the room and backed slowly towards the door as the tears continued to fall. Only faster now as she looked over at Tommy.

She gripped the doorknob and turned back to him. "Please stay here, baby," she whispered as she turned the knob and stepped out of the room and closed the door behind her.

Tommy could hear her sobbing in the other room. He could hear the quiet beeps of the buttons on their phone amidst her crying. Then there was only the sound of her sobbing quietly until someone picked up on the other end and then she let go of what little grip she had on her composure as she screamed into the phone.

Moments later, as if they appeared from nowhere, the street between Tommy and Owens houses was flooded with police cars, ambulances, fire trucks, and a lone white van labeled "Coroner." Tommy stood at the window in his room and stared at all the vehicles and the people surrounding them. Moving frantically, like ants around discarded food that had fallen to the ground.

The image of his father's lifeless body on the couch replayed in his head on a horrifying loop. He walked away from the window and sat down on his bed. His mind twisting itself inside out. A chill slithered its way up Tommy's spine and burst throughout his entire body. Then it hit him. Like the brilliant shock of jumping into cold water on a hot day. Someone had come into their house while they were sleeping and killed his father. Tommy instantly and unexpectedly found himself longing for his old room at their old house in Florida. The comfort, the safety. He could smell the paint again. He closed his eyes trying to picture it as clear as he could. But the image was washed away by the sound of a knock on his bedroom door.

"Tommy," his mother's voice slipped in as the door eased open. "Tommy, this officer would like to speak with you. He's just going to ask you a few questions, ok?"

Tommy sat rooted on his bed again.

"Hey, Tommy," the officer said. "I'm Detective Joshua Scott with the NYPD. I worked with your dad." He smiled at Tommy, but Tommy sat silently on his bed staring up at him. "I'm here try and figure out what happened to him, and I just want to ask you a couple of questions."

"Okay," Tommy replied. He realized that those had been the first word he had spoken since he'd woke up.

"Now," Detective Scott started, pulling up a chair that Tommy had in his room and sitting down across from Tommy. "Your mom tells me that you and your friend across the street like to ride your bikes around the neighborhood a lot, is that right?"

Tommy's brain was trying to play catch-up. He knew why Detective Scott was asking these questions, but then again, who wakes up in the morning expecting to be questioned about a murder. At twelve-years-old, none the less.

"Ye–yeah, we do," Tommy said.

"I used to do the same thing when I was your age," Detective Scott smiled. "Except we rode all over town." The detective paused and let his smile linger, Tommy knew he was trying to seem nice. But he also knew the detective wanted any answers that he may have. "While you guys are out riding, have you seen anyone around lately? Anyone that you don't normally see or anything strange?" Detective Scott asked.

"No, not that I can think of," Tommy said.

"Okay," Detective Scott said. "Tell me about last night. Did anything wake you up in the middle of the night, any strange noises, anything at all?"

"No. Nothing," Tommy replied. "I don't remember waking up at all until this morning."

"I think that's enough, Josh," Tommy's mother interrupted. "I think he's in shock."

She stepped closer and placed a hand on Tommy's shoulder.

"I just have one more question," he said looking up at Tommy's mother. She stared back at him. Tommy could feel the stare through her hand clinched on his shoulder.

"One more," she said. "And then he needs to be done."

Detective Scott smiled at her, then turned his attention back to Tommy.

"So, nothing strange, huh?" he said, flicking a "that wasn't my one question" glance at Tommy's mother.

"Have you ever seen any vehicles parked outside or near your house that you didn't recognize? Maybe a couple guys you didn't know inside? Anything like that?"

Tommy shook his head and before he could get the word "No" out, his mother had cut in again.

"Okay," she said. "I think he's done."

Detective Scott nodded at Tommy, then his mother, and walked out of the room. Tommy's mother sat down on the bed next to him.

Her hand had moved from his shoulder and taken his hand instead. She still had that terrified look on her face. She stared across Tommy's room as if she were looking through the walls into some alternate existence. She didn't say a word for about five minutes. Tommy could hear the sound of people, other police officers he assumed, conducting their investigations in the rest of the house. She leaned over and grabbed Tommy and kissed him on the forehead. Then she stood up and walked out of the room without saying anything. Tommy stayed in his room. Mostly because he wanted to. And he also figured that his mother's directive to do so was still in effect. He could hear her down the hall talking to Detective Scott, as well as other officers. He couldn't make out anything that was said, only that it was the clearest he had heard his mother speak in a while.

Tommy spent the next few days under the watchful eye of his mother, who, rightfully so, was now in a state of intense paranoia. She wouldn't allow him to leave the house. The first night she wouldn't even allow him to sleep in his own bed. Almost daily, for about a week following the death of his father, Detectives, or other officers would come by to talk to his mother or express their condolences to his family. Tommy was often sent away to his room when there was the potential for details to be shared during these conversations. But from the little pieces he did hear, he knew they had no evidence, no suspects, and nothing to go on.

Tommy spent most of these days staring out the window to see if Owen was out and about. But it didn't appear that he had been up too much either. Finally, on what would have been his eighth full day of house arrest, Tommy stared out his bedroom widow watching his mother talk to a detective in the driveway. Shortly after the detective left and his mother had come back inside the house, Tommy saw Owen leave his house and head across the street. He was headed straight for Tommy's driveway. A spark of hope brought Tommy out of his catatonically bored state and he opened the window and caught Owen's attention just as he started up the driveway.

"Owen!" Tommy shouted as quietly as he could.

Owen Saw him hanging out the window waving one arm and ran over to him

"Man," Owen said. "It's been like, over a week. You doin', okay?"

"Yeah, I guess," Tommy said. "My mom barely lets me out of her sight, but she doesn't talk a whole lot either. It's been really weird."

"I bet," Owen said. "I can't imagine. "Listen, I'm gonna go see if I can get your mom to let you out of the house."

"Ha, good luck." Tommy said, with half a smile.

"I don't know, man. She's gotta let you out some time, right?" Owen said. "I'll see what I can do."

Owen took off to the front door. He gave it a knock and waited for Tommy's mother to answer. Tommy quickly closed his window and ran to his bedroom door. He eased the door open just a crack and tried to listen. He heard his mother answer the door. She said hello to Owen, then both their voices became muffled. He tried like hell, but he couldn't make out what they were saying. And then he heard the door shut and everything went quiet. Tommy tried to listen as hard as he could, but he still couldn't hear anything. He eased his door shut again and stared at it, hoping his mother didn't bother to come and tell him about Owen' visit. Then out of nowhere, his bedroom door swung open and hit him in the head. Tommy took a step back and placed a hand on his head where the door had hit him. He looked up and saw Owen standing in the doorway.

"Come on, shithead, let's go," Owen whispered, a sneaky smile stretched across his face. "I'm bustin' you out."

Tommy didn't know what Owen had said to his mother to get her to let him go, and he didn't care. All that mattered was that he was able to leave the house again. He changed clothes faster than he ever had before and out the door they went with barely a goodbye to Tommy's mother. They grabbed their bikes and sped off down the road to Mr. Thurman's Pond. Thankfully, Mr. Thurman wasn't waiting outside to catch them with some sort of chore that he needed help with. They sped down the gravel driveway and past the house as fast as their bikes would carry them. Once they arrived at the water, they kicked off their shoes, flung their shirts into the grass, and dove in feeling the freedom of summer once again. They swam for a bit then sat on the dock with their feet in the water, enjoying the warmth of the summer sun.

"So, how's it been?" Owen asked.

"Unreal," Tommy replied, "I can't get that sight out of my head. Him sitting there on the couch like that."

"How are you feeling?" Owen asked.

"I don't know." Tommy replied, after a pause. "I've thought about every good thing my dad ever did for me, and how none of it really matters anymore. At least that's how I felt before this happened. But now…I honestly don't know. It's like, I think I'm supposed to be sad that he's dead, but I'm just glad that he's not here anymore, if that makes any sense. Dead or alive, ya know."

"A little," Owen said. "But I think that's understandable, considering everything that happened. How's your mom?" he asked.

"She's a mess, dude," Tommy said. "She did sit me down and talk to me about everything that happened––before all of this, ya know. She told me she was sorry for not seeing it all sooner. And then she cried. She said that if she had known she would've taken me away from him a long time ago. Then she cried some more. I told her it wasn't her fault. I mean––how was she supposed to know about something that he covered up so well? Something *I* wasn't even sure was really happening."

"Yeah, I guess so," Owen said staring at the water.

"I've tried to listen as much as I could when my mom has talked to the cops," Tommy said. "They have no idea who did this. Their best guess is it was someone he arrested."

"Do they think it could be one of the guys in Florida? You know, the ones he was doing favors for?" Owen asked.

"That's the fucked-up part, I don't think they even know about all of that." Tommy said. "I mean, if they did, why would they have hired him in the first place?"

They spent the rest of the day rotating between treading water in the pond and sitting in the sun on the dock. The sun eventually sank low enough and signaled to them that it was time to head home. Sunup, to sundown. Just as they had always played it.

Tommy's mother was sitting at the kitchen table when he walked through the door. She looked up from the book she was reading and forced a smile. Tommy sat down at the table across from her and began fiddling with the saltshaker in the middle of the table.

"I love you, mom," Tommy said, staring down at the table.

She stared at him for a moment over her book before laying it down on the table, the pages flared out to either side. Her eyes had started to regain that familiar loving look that Tommy had seen and loved his whole life. "I love you too, Tommy," she said, her smile becoming even more genuine than before.

"We're gonna be okay," Tommy said.

She folded her hands and laid them on top of her book. "I know we are," she said sighing sharply. "We've just had a lot happen all at once and I'm ashamed to say that I haven't really known how to deal with it all." She paused as her eyes slowly fell to the surface of the table. "I just––I feel like I let you down. I feel unsafe in this house, knowing that someone was in here and we didn't even know. I––I just––It's been a lot. And I know that you know that…"

"Yeah, I do," Tommy interrupted. "But you didn't let me down. *He* did. He let us both down. None of this was your fault."

His mother started to cry again. She covered her face with her hands and sobbed, but suddenly stopped herself. She wiped the tears from her cheek and got out of her chair and walked over to him. She knelt down in front of his chair and wrapped him in the tightest, most meaningful hug he had received from her in a while. He hugged her back as tight as he could and just sat in her arms cherishing the embrace.

The rest of the evening they spent sitting together in the living room floor. Each carefully avoiding the spot where their couch had once been. His mother said that even if the police hadn't removed it from the house, she would have probably dragged the damn thing out in the yard and sat it on fire. They ate pizza and watched TV. It seemed like it had been forever since they had been able to share even the smallest of moments like this with each other. They stayed up until about 11:00 pm, at which point both of them were more than ready for bed. Tommy's mother hugged him again and kissed him goodnight with that genuine smile resting across her face, and they went to bed.

The next day, James Norman Collins' funeral took place at Locust Valley Cemetery on Long Island. It had everything you would expect Hollywood to include in their depictions of a police officer's funeral. The large American Flag, neatly draped over the coffin. The oversized portrait of the officer's departmental photo resting on a stand next to the coffin. And hundreds of his fellow NYPD officers standing by in pressed uniforms. Even the detail of officers waiting to give the twenty-one-gun salute in his honor.

Tommy sat in front row with his mother, followed by a few more rows of chairs mostly filled with NYPD brass, behind which massive crowed mixed with officers and civilians stood watching the ceremony. In that crowd, were Owen and his parents.

Tommy listened as the NYPD Chaplin talked about how God blesses those called to be the peacemakers. Colleagues of his father's would get up and talk about how professional he was. How dedicated he was to the job. And how much of an asset he had proven to be to the NYPD during his years there.

Tommy had started his day simply wanting to get the funeral over with and get back home as soon as possible. But now found himself sitting at the blasphemous ceremony, fighting the urge to stand up and tell everyone the truth about what kind of man his father really had been. He felt even worse for his mother. Listening to what should have been comforting words, knowing that no number of accolades or even the most pristine of service records could overshadow the reality of his father was at home. Tommy felt disgusted. He was sick to his stomach almost to the point that he could vomit. At the end of the service, the chief of police approached Tommy with a neatly folded flag. The very same flag that had been draped across his father's coffin. He knelt down and handed the flag to Tommy. He offered some kind words to Tommy and his mother and stepped away in the proper drill and ceremony manor. Tommy accepted the flag and handed it to his mother, then turned and walked towards the car.

As he neared the middle of the crowd beyond the chairs the first report rang out from the seven rifles for the twenty-one-gun salute. He stopped and looked up and around at the crowd that had parted and made way for him. He lowered his head and continued walking. He could hear the command being given and then the blast of the second report sounded. He reached the back of the crowd with nothing but open cemetery between him and his mother's SUV. And as the third report sounded behind him, he could feel the eyes of the onlookers watching him walk away from his father's gravesite. He knew that everyone would assume that it had all just been too hard for him to handle, and he had to walk away. But he didn't really care what they thought. The truth was, they were right. It was too hard. It was too hard for Tommy to be that close to his father again. Dead or alive.

Tommy and his mother drove home after the funeral and changed clothes. Then they walked across the street to Owen's house. Owen's parents had invited them over for dinner. They thought, in their good nature, that having company may be better than going home after a funeral to an empty house. His mother accepted the invitation to come there rather than host a crowd of people she didn't even want to be around in her own home. She sat in the kitchen drinking coffee with Owen's parents, while Tommy and Owen made their way out to the pool deck, both having had enough adult interaction for the day.

"I'm glad that's over with," Tommy said.

"What, the funeral?" Owen asked hesitantly.

"Yeah. I hated it," Tommy said with a certain degree of disgust. "Sitting there, listening to all the 'wonderful things' he's done. Do you know how many people said, 'you're so brave,' or 'look at you being so strong,' to me today? I didn't even *really* want to go."

"I was kind of wondering how you were doing with all of this. Considering everything," Owen said.

Tommy looked down at the pool deck. "Can I ask you something, Owen?" Tommy said hanging his head.

"Sure," Owen said.

Tommy's eyes moved to the water bouncing around in the pool. "Have you ever been scared by your own thoughts?"

"What do you mean?" Owen replied with a perplexed look on his face.

"I mean--like--have you ever thought something or wanted something that it actually scared you to think about?" Tommy said doing his best to clarify.

"I'm a little lost here, Tommy." Owen said.

"I wanted to see," Tommy blurted out. "I wanted to make sure it was true," He looked at Owen, then dropped his eyes back to the pool water.

"See if what was true?" Owen asked.

"That he was really dead," he said. A look of shame and confusion settled on his face. "I didn't realize that that's what I wanted, but it was. And it kinda scared me."

Owen hesitated a second or two. "Don't let that bother you, Tommy," he said. "It's no wonder you felt that way after everything he put you through. If you want my honest opinion, I think it sounds natural that you wanted some kind of closure, no matter how weird it may have seemed to anyone else."

The shame and confusion seemed to flutter away. Tommy didn't think that Owen was just telling him what he wanted to hear. He had never known him to do that. Except maybe with his parents from time to time, to avoid getting in trouble. But it seemed even more genuine now. In this moment. About his father. Owen was the only other person that knew everything, besides his mother.

"You're my best friend, Owen" Tommy said.

"You're my best friend too," Owen said.

After much contemplation, Tommy's mother decided not to move out of the house. They had started a life there and no matter what that had looked like so far, they were going to make the best of it. She and Tommy sat down one evening and had the hard discussion they had each been silently avoiding, regarding everything that had taken place before his father's murder. They ultimately decided together that mentioning anything to the police about everything that had happened before his father's death was only going to cause more harm than good. His mother didn't want him to have to endure all the lines of questioning that would inevitably follow. No doubt prompting an even deeper investigation into their lives, followed by the feeding frenzy from the media. All wanting the inside scoop on the murdered cop who had molested his own son. Tommy agreed completely. She said she just figured he had suffered enough, they both had. And now that there was no chance of it ever happening again. She didn't see a reason to put Tommy through all of that.

| 7 |

The years of summer freedom, spending their days swimming or bike riding, then starting school again, quickly turned into the high school years. Tommy and Owen spent some, but certainly not all of their summer days working part time jobs at the local grocery store bagging groceries and retrieving carts from the cart corrals in the parking lot. Rain or summer inferno, the customers needed those carts.

Mr. Thurman's Pond remained their favorite place to spend their free time. But having jobs cracked open the door for other exciting summer opportunities. Small pay creates small opportunities, but over the years they did manage to fund a few trips to the city to watch the Yankees play from the cheap seats. As well as the more often, and slightly more affordable, trips to their local movie theater to catch whatever happened to be gracing the silver screen that peaked their interests. Before they knew it, they found themselves preparing to graduate high school and starting to think about college. That was where the real freedom was. *Do what you want, when you want,* was the dream-like thought swimming in and out of focus that fueled their excitement about leaving their respective nests or blowing the proverbial popsicle stand.

Owen went off to study business. No surprise there that he was following in his father's footsteps and preparing to take over his father's business after graduation. Whenever his father decided to retire, of course. But to everyone's surprise, including Owen's, Tommy opted for a degree in Criminal Justice. Everyone surrounding Tommy naturally assumed that this choice stemmed from his father's unsolved murder. And they weren't completely off base. Tommy hadn't mentioned anything to Owen about going in that direction whenever they had discussed possible collegiate areas of study. Partially because everything that had happened with his father had been dead and buried. Literally. And over the years it had become reduced to not much more than a distant memory. A horrible, nightmarish memory, yes. But a distant one, none the less. Tommy himself didn't fully understand the pull in that direction, and he wanted to sort it out for himself. Regardless, Tommy knew he would have Owen's full support.

After graduating high school, they tried to take full advantage of their last summer before becoming college students. Yankee's games, movies, and of course, Mr. Thurman's pond. Soon however, they found themselves all packed up and ready to go. Owen's parents and Tommy's mother all carpooled to drop the two of them off when it was time to move into their dorms at New York University. They were excited and their parents were excited for them. They felt free. As free as one can be holding the key to what amounted to a small, one room apartment. Only half of which you could stake your claim to. Not to mention, the slip of paper bearing the assigned, full course load for the upcoming semester. Either way, they stepped into it with wide eyes and their minds full of possibilities.

They quickly realized within the first couple of weeks, that their college years weren't going to look anything like they had imagined. Their adolescent dreams of tons of free time were quickly shattered, starting with separate housing arrangements, and closely followed by competing class schedules. Weekends, however, were spared. They were just as they had been during high school. When Owen wasn't working with his father at the drycleaners and Tommy wasn't waiting tables at the Hard Rock (secretly being taught how to bartend when the manager wasn't around that is) they would always find something to get into.

They managed this lifestyle through their freshman and sophomore years. Sometimes, their only interaction would be a quick catch up while passing each other on campus during the week. Junior year was not looking much better in terms of social interaction or free time. It seemed to fall as it had a lot during the two previous years. When one was busy, the other was free. It seemed unavoidable.

Their continuously conflicting work and class schedules landed Owen at an off-campus bar one Friday night while Tommy had all but sequestered himself in the campus library cramming for his forensics exam. Owen planted himself at the bar and asked for his usual tall Bud Light draft beer and began to sink into the buzz of voices of the other patrons and the soft hum of an old jukebox playing a mixture of songs he grew up on. As well as some newer songs, some of which Owen could get into, but most of which he didn't care for. He was a couple of beers in when he started getting bored with sitting at the bar and watching ESPN highlights, followed by commercials for shit he either couldn't afford or had no interest in. He Looked through his half empty beer all the way to the bottom of the glass and turned it up to finish it off. With his glass tipped and his eyes closed, he heard a single, soft voice that rose slightly above the low, dull roar of the bar.

"Hey there, stranger" the voice said.

Owen startled a bit as a hand landed on his shoulder and someone jumped onto the barstool next to him. He first met the long dark hair falling well beyond the shoulders. Then the smile and on up to an excited set of staring eyes that there was no mistaking.

"Rhiannon?" Owen said nearly choking on both his words and his beer. "Wow! How the hell are you?!" he asked.

"I'm good. I'm good." she replied, still laughing at his reaction. "How are you?"

"Well shit," he said looking around the bar. "I was actually just about to leave. Just came down to cure some boredom." He grabbed his glass and lifted it slightly and smiled at her. "So, what have you been up to? It's been years."

"Yes, it has," she replied. "We were still kids. And Tommy's father had just––." She paused and her smile stiffened on her face. "Passed away."

He could tell that even after all these years, she remembered very clearly how she felt when she was younger. Knowing that Tommy's father had been murdered. She couldn't even bring herself to say the word.

"And speaking of--death," she continued still trying to shake the feeling. "That's why I'm back in town. My grandfather passed away."

"Holy shit," he said before he knew the words were coming. "I mean, that's terrible. We always liked your grandfather. I'm really sorry to hear that."

"I know you did," Rhiannon said with a smile. "He always liked you guys too. He talked about you two all the time."

Her eyes fell to the floor and Owen could see at once how much she already missed her grandfather.

"So, what about you, where'd you run off to?" he asked trying to change the subject and lighten the mood.

"Oh, I've been all over the place," she replied and the genuine smile she had when she first approached him just moments ago rose again from the corners of her mouth. "I went out West. Spent some time out in California. Hung out on the beaches. And then it was off to Europe. Just traveling and studying abroad."

"Wow! That sounds pretty exciting," he said. "And exactly what I would have expected out of you"

Two drinks turned into four as they sat there catching up for the next few hours. They talked about life and the different places it had taken them. Owen found himself lost in Rhiannon's stories of nights out in small, German towns. The beauty of the Italian countryside or how Ireland was a beautiful shade of green she had never seen before. It all felt very inviting. He thought about the places she described and could imagine her in every detail. Every backdrop seemed to fit her perfectly. Before they had even realized it, they had talked themselves through most of the evening and into the early hours of the morning.

"Oh no, look how late it is," she said as she casually glanced at her watch. "I'd better get going. Busy day tomorrow."

Owen looked at his own and agreed. He had no idea it had gotten so late. Or early depending on how you chose to look at it. "Wow, you're right," Owen said. "Come on, I'll walk you out,"

Owen insisted on paying for her drinks. He settled their bill at the bar, then they both headed towards the door. They stood outside the bar waiting for Rhiannon's cab and continued talking. Though they both found themselves with surprisingly little to say now that the hum of the bar wasn't keeping the conversation moving along.

"So, how long are you in town?" Owen asked.

"Just a couple weeks," she said. "Long enough for the funeral and to help my mom get grandpa's affairs settled. Then it's back to Paris. You're welcome to come," she said, and her cheeks immediately became flush with embarrassment. "To the funeral, I mean," she uttered quickly. "Not to Paris––I mean you *should* go to Paris if you ever get..." She stopped and dropped her eyes to the sidewalk. When she collected herself, she looked back at Owen who was standing there smiling and holding back his laughter.

"Sure, of course," Owen said letting just a bit of the laughter escape. "I'll let Tommy know. He will want to come too."

"Good," she said smiling at him again. "My grandpa would've wanted you two to be there."

The approaching headlights caught her eye and suddenly the night was over.

"Well, I think this is me," she said as the cab stopped at the curb directly in front of them. "I'd better go."

Owen opened the cab door for her and as she sat down in the seat, she looked back at him and smiled. He smiled back and shut the door. He stood there and watched the cab drive away and replayed the whole encounter in his mind. He had been happy to see her again. It was something he could not have foreseen, yet he stood there on the poorly lit sidewalk believing that their chance encounter had been the real reason he had ended up at the bar rather than wasting the night in his dorm room watching reruns or old movies.

The next day he met up with Tommy and told him about running into Rhiannon at the bar. He didn't go into every of detail. He mostly talked about Mr. Thurman and the funeral. He didn't want to give away that he hadn't stopped thinking about her since he closed the door to the cab. He told himself that it was simply because she was someone from his childhood that he hadn't seen since then. But deep down he knew that wasn't really the case. He had thought about her nonstop the same way she had quickly stumbled over her words when she inadvertently invited him to Paris. It was accidental, sure. But the resulting emotional response had been real. He could see it all over her face as she tried to recover.

Tommy however, had not gotten all the studying done he had planned to do. He shared with Owen that he too had a similar experience in the library the night before. While he had locked himself in the library to do some last-minute cramming for his exam, he found his attention stolen by another one of the library patrons. She and another girl were apparently there to do the same. She was a short, blond girl named Alison Taylor. He told Owen he had never met anyone like her. That they had both gone to the library intending on keeping their noses in the books, but found themselves engaged in each other, rather than their studies.

"It literally took one look," he said. "Our eyes just happen to meet one time and then we just kept catching each other looking. So finally, I gave up. After about an hour of the cat and mouse looks, I closed my book and walked over to her and asked if she wanted to go get some coffee."

He said they ended up leaving the library and going to an all-night diner where they just sat and talked. "Just the basic stuff. Where you from? What had led them to NYU."

Owen sat listening to Tommy's story but still only thought about Rhiannon. He remembered the smile she gave him as he closed the door to the cab. And every other smile that had shone on her face throughout the night. He could picture them all. But he let Tommy do most of the talking. Afterall, Tommy had met someone knew. Someone neither of them had ever met before. Owen had run into someone who, in their younger years, used to annoy the shit out of them. And Owen wasn't quite sure what kind of reaction he would get if he told Tommy everything that had been on his mind since he watched Rhiannon drive away in that cab.

| 8 |

The morning of Mr. Thurman's funeral was all too fitting. It was a Sunday. For a funeral that it. The gray sky only allowing only minimal amounts of light to peek through the blanket of grey clouds that separated the brilliant blue from the earth below. The slow and sleepy, inconsistent drizzle of just enough rain to be an inconvenience, concocted the perfect gloomy mixture for the sad day ahead. By the time Tommy and Owen showed up a crowed had already amassed on the funeral home. They stood in line to pay their respects with the other funeral goers, not knowing anyone else, except Owen's parents and Tommy's mother.

As they neared the front, Owen noticed Rhiannon sitting in a chair near the casket, where her mother and father stood shaking the hands of those attending the service. She was staring at the floor and visibly upset by the loss of her grandfather. Owen felt for her. He knew how close she was to her grandfather. He watched her all through the service and noticed that she would periodically raise her head to view her grandfather's lifeless body in the casket for only a few seconds, then it would drop again. On more than one occasion he watched her lean onto her mother or father and begin sobbing. He felt the feeling rising in him to go to the front row and wipe the tears from her face, but he knew he couldn't. He stayed in his seat and watched as the voices of those who took their turns at the podium drifted further and further away in his mind, replaced by the sound of her laughter from the night before.

Once the service ended, Tommy and Owen joined the procession leading to the gravesite. They stood silently in the back, just outside the coverage of the large flock of black umbrellas huddled around the plot. They could hear the muffled sobs of the family rising just above the voice of the funeral's officiant as he recited passages from the Bible that spoke of the paradise where Mr. Thurman's soul had gone to and would remain for eternity. He talked of the place God had prepared for him and how pain and sadness had no place there. He spoke the final prayer, and the family began to approach the casket one last time to say their final goodbye's.

As the officiant concluded the service, the crowd began to slowly slip off in ones and twos back to their vehicles until only the family remained. Once they began to move away from the casket and began to slowly disperse back to their vehicles, the men began lowering the casket into the ground. The casket reached the bottom of the plot as a path cleared to the front. Owen could see Rhiannon still seated in the front row staring at the grave where her grandfather was now laid to rest.

"Come on," Owen said to Tommy, who nodded in agreement.

They walked to the front as the last few stragglers were headed in the opposite direction. They stopped at the foot of the plot and looked down at the casket laying in the ground waiting to be covered by the earth. Owen felt someone walk up beside him and without looking, he knew that it was Rhiannon. She interlocked her arm with his and rested her head on his shoulder. He removed his arm from Rhiannon's grasp and placed it around her shoulders and pulled her in closer. She wrapped her arms around him and sank her face into his jacket and continued crying. They remained at the gravesite for a few moments longer before Rhiannon let go of Owen and wiped her tear-stained face and said goodbye to her grandfather. She tossed a rose on top of the lowered coffin and the three of them turned and walked away.

She grabbed Owen's hand as they walked toward the limousine, she and her family had ridden in from the funeral home. When they reached the car, she let go of his hand and looked at the two of them. She smiled hugged Tommy first and he whispered that he was sorry about her grandfather, but that he was still glad to see her. Then she hugged Owen. She buried her face in his chest and started to sob but reigned in the tears quickly.

"Thank you," she said looking up at him. her face glistened from the mixture of rain and tears.

"It's no problem, really," he said.

She stared up at him for a second and then laid her head back down on his chest.

"I don't really wanna be alone tonight," she said quietly.

Owen barely heard the words over the increasing sound of the rain hitting the nearby trees. But he knew he had heard her clearly.

"Will you come to the pond?" she asked.

He paused for a moment and let the words sink in. "I'll be there," he said.

She squeezed him tighter and then let him go. She walked over to Tommy and hugged him again and smiled.

"Sorry, this is how it is after all these years," she said.

"Don't give it another thought," he said. "We are just glad we could be here for you."

She placed a hand on each of their arms and looked back and forth between the two of them. The tears were still coming, but Owen was sure she had cried herself out by that point and now only a sad smile graced her face as she turned and walked toward the limo.

Later that night Owen left the city and drove back to his old neighborhood. He passed his and Tommy's houses as he drove through the neighborhood and down the long gravel driveway to Mr. Thurman's house. He parked next to the gate that led to the pond and sat there for a moment trying to collect his thoughts. He got himself out of the car and walked through the gate and down toward the pond. The rain had ceased for bit, but the smell was still heavy in the air. As he approached the water, he could see Rhiannon sitting on the dock silhouetted against the light of the falling sun reflecting off the still water. Her arms were wrapped around her knees as she sat there staring up at the fading shades of orange and pink in the night sky as the sun fell toward the horizon. The sight of her sitting on the dock against the backdrop of a day nearly complete created a small knot in his stomach. She turned and looked at him. She smiled, but he could see the tears glimmer on her cheek in the fading light of the day. She waited until he reached the dock before she stood up. He continued toward her and once he reached her, she wrapped her arms around his waist and laid her head on his chest. He held her and let her cry. The crickets serenaded all around them as the smell of the days rain seemed to float away with the breeze.

"I'm glad you're here," she said in barely a whisper.

Owen wrestled with his words, unsure of what he wanted it to say or how he wanted it to sound. Each silent second that ticked past echoed into the night and seemed to get louder and louder.

"I…uh," he stammered.

She pulled her head from his chest and looked up at him. He noted the already short distance between their lips and had the sudden urge to close it urgently and completely.

"I just wanted to make sure you were okay," he said intentionally focusing on her eyes with his own

A smile slowly inched its way across her face. "Owen…" she whispered and paused.

She removed her arms from around his waist and slid them up his chest and around his neck. She pulled his head towards hers and closed her eyes. The soft, earth-shattering impact of their lips colliding sent chills in both directions from head to toe. Owen became very aware that his hands were now clutching Rhiannon's waist. He pulled her in closer, embracing the rest of her. The kiss lasted for only a moment. But for the two of them, it felt as though the seasons had changed.

She grabbed him by the hand as their kiss ended and led him to the end of the dock where she had been sitting. He had never held a hand so soft. As they sat down, Rhiannon laid back on the dock and stared once again into the night sky. All the pastels had faded leaving only a blank canvas of black sprinkled with stars and bathing them in the soft, white light of the moon. Owen stayed sitting up for a moment but then laid back next to her. There had been just enough warmth from day once the rain had stopped to warm the wood of the dock. And now the cool summer breeze wrapped around the two of them like a blanket. Rhiannon rolled to her side and rest her head on Owen's chest. Neither of them said a word. There was nothing that needed to be said.

Owen tried not to think about the fact that she would be leaving again before too long. Back to her life abroad. He feared losing the moment they had found themselves tangled up in. He lay there holding her. His eyes alternating between Rhiannon lying on his chest and the feel of her against him, and the dark stillness of the night sky. He mused at how the beauty of one could be used to perfectly describe the other. *Dark stillness.* After several minutes of uninterrupted silence, only the breeze skating across the surface or the water and the crickets continuing their evening song, Owen realized that she had fallen asleep. Desperately clinging to this moment, he chose not to wake her. He would stay there as long as time and the conditions would allow.

In the early hours of the morning, the moon still hanging full of pride in the sky, a chilly breeze stirred Rhiannon. A sleepy smile stretched across her face when she realized that Owen had stayed with her. Her shiver woke him as well and he smiled back at her. He stared at her there, remembering their kiss. How soft her lips were and the feeling of electricity that accompanied her touch.

"You stayed," she said through her sleepy smile.

"I didn't have it in me to wake you," he replied.

Her smile grew even bigger and was followed by a small laugh. She leaned in and kissed him once more, then placed her forehead against his. He closed his eyes and bottled up everything he could about the moment they had shared. The feeling of her hair being blown against his cheek, the smell of her skin, everything.

"I can't believe we slept out here," she said sitting upright on the dock.

"Who doesn't love camping?" Owen asked jokingly.

Rhiannon tilted her head to the side and laughed.

"I have to help my mom this morning," she said. "She's in no shape to handle all of this on her own."

Rhiannon came up to her knees and placed her hand on his cheek. She rested there for a moment and stared into his eyes before standing. Owen stood with her. They were both unsure of what to say next. A sleepy smile fell across each of their faces. Owen grabbed her by the hand, and they started off towards her grandfather's house. Owen spent his moments during their walk wondering what Rhiannon was thinking and wondering what she was feeling. But any time he would sneak a look in her direction, all that mattered was that she had a smile on her face.

About the time they reached Owen's car, he had mustered up the courage to speak. They stopped at the front of his car, and he reached out and grabbed her other hand.

"So, I guess this is…"

"This is not goodbye," Rhiannon interrupted.

"So that means I'll see you again?" Owen asked.

"I think so," She replied, smiling again.

Owen's smile was permanently plastered across his face. He couldn't have frowned in that moment if he had wanted to. He grabbed her and pulled her in close and wrapped his arms around her. He lifted her off the ground and She quickly wrapped her arms around his neck and pressed her lips against his for a second time that morning. He didn't even have time to take a breath. He lowered her back down and as her feet hit the ground, she smiled up at him again.

Not another word was shared between the two of them. Rhiannon turned and walked toward her grandfather's house, only looking back as she reached the door, then she turned back and walked inside.

Owen watched her close the door and hopped in his car. With the smile still shining on his face, he made the drive back to the city. The thoughts of Rhiannon leaving were long gone from his mind. He wanted to call Tommy and tell him everything and decided to try. *It is a little early,* he thought looking at his clock after reaching Tommy's voicemail. Owen sat in his car outside his dorm re-playing their evening spent together on the dock. Frame by frame, he smiled as they appeared in his mind. He tried to remember every detail that he could, but one thing he was absolutely sure of, he had never felt the way he was feeling right now.

Owen made his way inside and quietly climbed into bed, trying not to disturb his roommate. It took no time to fall asleep, the image of Rhiannon smiling up at him paused in his mind as he drifted off. Later that morning, Owen was awakened by the sound of someone knocking on his door. He stumbled out of bed still dressed in what he had worn to the funeral the day before and shuffled over to the door when he heard Tommy on the other side.

"Owen!" Tommy shouted. "Wake up!"

He got to the door just as Tommy started to knock for a third time. He opened the door and Tommy walked right in and began talking about his date with Alison the night before. It was clear that Tommy had grown very fond of her. He watched as Tommy paced around the room like a mad man. He made a pot of coffee, threw on a different shirt, and listened to Tommy's play by play of his date with Alison.

How she looked, the dinner, the music. The two-hour-walk around campus. All concluding with a forty-five-minute goodnight on the front porch of Alison's sorority house. Owen could see himself in everything that poured out of Tommy. The unbreakable smile, the anxiousness of trying to recall every little detail, the inability to stand still. He had gone through these motions earlier that morning on his drive back to the city. However, there was one difference. The one thing he had forgotten about during that drive. And it filled his stomach with the weight of longing to have what he knew he would soon be without. He knew that in less than two weeks Rhiannon would be gone.

Once Tommy finished his laps around the room he sat down and sighed as if he had told the entire story in one long breath. He looked over at Owen and asked, "How was your night?"

Owen thought about Rhiannon. He thought about her leaving. He wasn't sure if he wanted to share that he was feeling the all the same things Tommy was for fear that the inevitable would then have to be discussed out loud. She *was* leaving. He knew it. He wished he could somehow change it, but deep down he knew he couldn't.

"It was good," Owen replied as casually as he could. "We just stayed out by the pond for a few hours. Fell asleep out there, actually."

Tommy's smile grew larger as he stared at back at him. He could see that Tommy knew that there was more to the story, and he wanted to hear it. It was spelled out all over Tommy's face. Things like this had never been easy for either of them to hide from one another.

"What?" Owen said with a little laugh. "That was pretty much it, man. She was upset. I just went out there to give her some company."

Tommy's stare continued. He was trying to press Owen into giving up details that he simply didn't have. Except for…

"Fine!" Owen shouted playfully. "There was a kiss. There were––a couple of kisses."

"I knew it!" Tommy shouted.

Tommy stared at him as if he were waiting for him to spit out winning lottery numbers.

"So, was that really it?" Tommy asked. "I mean, are you gonna see her again?"

"Well, yeah. I guess," Owen replied contemplating the question himself. "But that's the not-so-good part," he sighed realizing that he was. About to spill everything. "She is still planning to leave in a couple weeks. And I have to tell you, man, I don't know what it is, but ever since I put her in that cab at the bar, I've been thinking about her."

"Why didn't you tell me all of this before?" Tommy asked. "I sat here and went on and on about Alison, and how great she was, what a wonderful time we had. And all you said was you ran into an old friend of ours at a bar. Clearly, you left some shit out."

"Because it was her," Owen said. "Remember how annoying she was when we were kids? I was sure you'd get a good laugh out of it if I told you everything."

"I mean, probably," Tommy said with a chuckle. "But what does that matter? That was years ago. She always did gravitate more toward you than she did me. And remember how smart she was back then? Do you think she could see the future?" Tommy asked with a laugh.

"See! This is what I was talking about," Owen said. There was still a small smile creeping up on his face despite Tommy's jokes at his expense. "Dumbass," he said trying to stifle his own laughter. "Well, now that you've gotten that out of your system, I have to tell you, I don't think I want her to leave."

Tommy swiveled back and forth in the chair at Owen's desk and looked at him. Owen knew what was coming. And he knew Tommy was going to be right. But before the words were even spoken, he had no idea how he was going to go through with it. He had no idea how he was going to ask her to…

"You're gonna have to talk to her, man," Tommy said. He looked at Owen as if he understood every ounce of complication surrounding such a simple answer. It wasn't simple at all. Owen just stared back at him understanding that "just talking to her" could stop everything dead in its tracks. And that meant losing her even sooner.

Owen spent the rest of his Monday staring at his phone and wondering if he should call her. Wondering what she would think if he did. And for that matter, what would she think if he didn't? Later that evening the stress of wondering had reached a boiling point, and he decided he was going to call. He stared at her name on his phone for a long moment before hitting "send," trying to determine how the call was going to go. As the phone began to ring, he immediately felt as though the temperature in the room had skyrocketed. Little beads of sweat began to form on his forehead. The phone rang again, and again, and again. Owen began wondering if the decision to call was the right one. And as the next ring ended, panic started to set in. He was just about to hang up the phone when he heard the familiar click and hum of someone answering, and then her soft voice on the other end.

"Hello," she said.

"Rhiannon, hey–hi–it's–uh…it's Owen," he quickly replied.

"Hey!" she replied. "I was wondering when I'd hear from you again. I figured maybe you were getting some real sleep."

Owen's panic gave way to butterflies. He wanted to celebrate. And he was internally. But he also didn't want to act like a fool while he had her on the phone.

"Good, because that's actually why I called," he said, "I wanted to see what you were up to tomorrow night."

She paused momentarily and he was sure, he swore, he could almost hear her smiling on the other end. "I'm pretty sure I can free up some time," she said.

Yes. She was smiling. And he knew it.

"Okay," he said. "Uh, how about dinner?"

"Sure, that sounds great," she said.

"Great, so––uh, I'll pick you up around 7:00," Owen said still trying to contain his excitement.

"I'll be ready," she said.

| 9 |

Owen hung up the phone and laid back on his bed laughing at the emotional back and forth he had been swimming in all day. Even though, deep down, he still saw it as a necessary part of the process. The next evening came, but not before Owen ran into Tommy again on campus. When Tommy asked Owen what his plans were for the evening, Owen happily relayed that he had dinner plans with Rhiannon.

"Glad you grew some balls and called her," Tommy said.

Tommy took the opportunity to make fun of him once more for going on a date with the annoying little girl that used to tag along with them to her grandfather's pond. Owen just laughed because he had previously thought about how things had been back then. How they hated when she would tag along. But it did pose an interesting question. Had this seed been planted way back then? He shook off the question and looked at his watch and told Tommy that he had to run and get ready.

The night went as well as he could have hoped. A nice dinner at a not too fancy restaurant. Something they both would have likely thought to be too stuffy anyway. Some place where the atmosphere merely suggested that romance was floating somewhere in the air if you wanted to grab it. Drinks afterwards at the same bar where they became reacquainted. And finally, they ended their evening back down at the pond. Owen had to laugh after Tommy's question about their childhood. He now found it funny that being at the pond with her now meant something completely different than it did when they were kids. He remembered how he and Tommy used to get so annoyed about her tagging along. And now, here he sat with her at the same pond. And there was no place that he'd rather be.

"So, how's your mom handling everything?" Owen asked

"She's gotten better since the funeral," Rhiannon said. "We've actually gotten quite a bit done in the last couple days. Getting all of Grandpa's affairs settled."

"That's good," he said. "He had so much stuff in that house when we were kids. I don't imagine it's changed much."

"No, no it hasn't," She laughed. "He loved his stuff."

"I wish I would have thought to come see him one more time before he passed," Owen said.

He mused at how easily someone can fall from your thoughts over time. He realized that until just a few days ago, it had been the same with Rhiannon. She hadn't crossed his mind in years until her hand landed on his shoulder in that bar. Then it was like she had been on his mind the whole time.

They continued talking into the night. Until Owen could tell that Rhiannon was getting tired. He offered to walk her back up to the house, which she gladly accepted. They walked back up the gravel road to the house, hand in hand and taking their time to get there. Owen didn't want to let her hand go. He tried not to let her inevitable departure cloud his mind and therefore the evening, but he knew it was there. He could feel it pressing behind everything he was trying so hard to focus on. He walked her to the door. They shared a kiss, and she went inside.

Week two of her stay was there before either of them knew it and they had seen each other just about every other day since the funeral. Even taking time away from themselves to see Tommy and meet Alison. The four of them went out to dinner a couple times. Double dating was something Tommy and Owen had never done before, but the girls seemed to get along great.

With only a couple of days left, Owen's anxiety surrounding Rhiannon's departure was only growing stronger. Owen had planned what he thought would be a nice evening for the two of them. He picked her up around 7:00 pm and took her for drinks, followed by a walk around town. Owen was waiting for Rhiannon to let on that she was hungry and once she did, they made their way back his car.

"Where are we going?" Rhiannon asked.

"You'll see," Owen said. "It's a surprise."

Rhiannon smiled down at her lap and then over at Owen. As they pulled up to the gate that led to her grandfather's pond, Rhiannon wondered what he had done and how he had done it at her grandfather's pond without her knowing. Awaiting and excited to find out what he had planned for the evening, they exited the car. Owen took her by the hand and led her through the gate. The warm breeze seemed to push them down the path as they walked towards the water. Owen, for the moment, was stress free. Focused solely on maintaining the smile on Rhiannon's face. As they got closer to the dock, Rhiannon's silence broke.

"What have you done?" she asked.

Owen just smiled back at her, keeping his lips sealed. Once the dock was in view, Rhiannon could see that there was something sitting in the middle. The two traded a few more glances before the surprise was finally revealed. Rather than dinner at a crowded restaurant, Owen had arranged a picnic for the two of them by the pond. Complete with a bottle of wine.

"This is beautiful," Rhiannon said, turning towards Owen and kissing him.

"Thank you," Owen said. "I wanted to do something special, something a little different. So, I figured, what better place than here."

"I love it!" she said, looking back down at the display Owen had prepared for the two of them.

They sat down and began enjoying the picnic. With each sip of wine, the laughter at the stories got louder and the looks began to last longer. Before they knew it, the time had gotten further and further away from them. Further than either of them had expected. It was just after midnight. Rhiannon sat smiling at Owen, both feeling the effects of the wine, the meal, and the atmosphere.

"Thank you for this," Rhiannon said.

"It was my pleasure," Owen said.

They sat packing up what was left of their picnic, placing everything in the basket, except the half empty bottle of wine. They stood up and Owen grabbed the basket, and Rhiannon grabbed the wine. She reached over and took him by the hand.

"Walk me home," she said staring deep into his eyes.

They set off back up the road towards the house. As they were walking, Rhiannon locked arms with Owen and laid her head on his shoulder. When they reached the house, without saying a word she opened the door and led him inside the house. Through the darkness of the entry way and into the kitchen they walked. Owen looked around and suddenly realized that the inside of the house, as much as the outside, had not changed since he was a child. He sat the basket full of the picnic remains on the table and followed her into the living room. Still not a word. She turned to face him; her smile replaced by a look Owen had yet to see from her. He took a step towards her leaving barely a breath of space between the two of them.

Their eyes seemed to be tethered together. Neither one could look away from the other. Rhiannon reached out and touched his cheek. She ran her fingers down his neck, twisting them in his shirt, pulling him to her. As their bodies collided and their lips found each other, they shared one hastened breath after another.

Owen's hands began exploring every inch of her body that they could reach. He ran his hand up the back of her neck and under her hair. His hand tightened, firmly but gently gripping her hair, and slowly pulling her head back, giving way to her neck and shoulders. Rhiannon let slip a slight gasp as he plunged into her neck, his lips now doing the searching. He worked his way down to her collar bone. Each touch of his lips on her skin caused her entire body to quiver. Her hand had loosened from the front of his shirt and began uncontrollably squeezing and clawing at the rest of him. Owen continued his descent, kissing along the "V" shaped opening of her dress, then back up towards her lips. With their lips entangled, Rhiannon managed to regain enough composure to grab him by the hand once more and lead him into the bedroom. Crossing the threshold, their hands still clasped to one another, she turned to him again. They each began blindly undressing the other. Discarded clothes fell towards the floor, piling up at their feet, as their bodies revealed themselves to one another. The temperature in the room seemed to rise as the two leafless bodies began trying desperately to inhabit the same space. Finding their way to the bed without so much as a glance in the right direction, Rhiannon laid down and Owen immediately overshadowed her.

His lips crashed into to her neck once more, like they each contained opposite ends of a magnet that had been kept away from one another for far too long, and then suddenly released. He slowly worked his way down the center of her body. Between her breasts. He stopped briefly at her stomach and ran the tip pf his tongue around her naval, then continued further down to her waistline. A spot that Owen recalled glancing at several times since the two had become reacquainted. He spent more than a couple minutes slowly, but intentionally, exploring her waistline and all it revealed. He moved further down gripping her thighs in each of his hands and pushing them in opposite directions. He tasted her. He savored every second as her back arched and breath after breath exploded from her lips in hastened, sharp bursts.

He began slowly moving back up her body and retracing his steps. He revisited every spot he had touched before and made sure he discovered new ones. He stopped only to reengage her lips. They both ached for approaching moment. Anticipation gripped tighter with every breath. Their hands scurried, frantically clinging to any part of the other they could find. Rhiannon slid her hand down his chest, past his stomach and waistline, and took him in her hand. She slowly pulled him in closer. Beads of sweat began to form on both their bodies as she wrapped her legs around his waist and squeezed. She pulled him the rest of the way in. And as each of them barely drew a single breath, the two became one.

The entire room became a tilted blur around the two of them. As if they were trapped in the fluttering distant view on a steaming summer highway. As their passion progressed neither one was willing nor able to release themselves from the tangles of the other. The slow-starting repetition began to speed up as each of their senses became heightened. Every touch flooded the nervous system like waves crashing onto a beach. Each one stronger than the last. Breathing became replaced by uncontrollable sounds of pleasure and the attempt to utter muffled intimate phrases.

They remained completely one as the two rolled about the bed, stopping with Owen on his back. Rhiannon pressed her hands into his chest as she sat upwards, slightly digging her fingernails into his skin.

Back and forth she swayed, never losing her grip on him. Still in motion, she leaned down and kissed him deeply. Owen brushed her hair back. He wanted to see and memorize the expression on her face. The sight of her biting her bottom lip as she sat up straight again sent a wave of ecstasy through his body and mind. She dropped her head backwards. Her hair fell onto her back and lightly brushed his hands as they moved down to her waist. Further and further backwards she leaned. Owen's hands gripped her waist and followed her momentum until her back hit the bed, and he once again eclipsed her body.

One hand rested on the bed and the other on the back of her neck. Owen pulled her head towards his, meeting her halfway. He watched her face as she looked down to witness the pleasure she was experiencing. "Don't stop," she whispered as she wrapped a hand around the back of his neck. The words were forced out between two panting breaths. She reached up again and wrapped both arms around his neck. Their foreheads pressed against each other. Sweat dripped from his chin and ran from her chest down the length of her body. "I'm almost there," she muttered again, her voice getting slightly louder. She threw her head back and continued to breathe heavily as the sensation grew larger and larger with every breath.

Her body ached for him to never stop as the pleasure filled her so much that she felt she would never have control of her body again. In one final, involuntary gasp, every bit of sound faded from the world. She closed her eyes, and her body was no longer her own as she succumbed to the sweet release.

They each lay sprawled out across the bed. Both with their eyes closed and both teetering between on the edge of lucidity as the dopamine and oxytocin cocktail filled and temporarily paralyzed their bodies. A few moments later, Rhiannon's head was firmly planted on his chest and her leg draped lazily across his. She used her index finger to draw small shapes on his stomach as she visualized them swimming around in her mind. Owen's fingers were intertwined in her hair, gently pulling small amounts out to their full length, and twisting it slowly in his fingers. Each one replaying from their point of view, the strings of intimate moments they had just woven together.

| 10 |

The next morning found them in nearly the same position they had fallen asleep in. The early morning sun poured in through the window casting a warm blanket over the two of them as they lay there sleeping. Soon, Owen began to wake up. Realizing that neither of them had hardly moved. His eyes became fixed on Rhiannon still sleeping on his chest. He began flipping through all the mentally stored visual clips from the night before. Closing his eyes again and smiling a sleepy smile. He wanted so badly to freeze this moment they were sharing. But amidst all the blissful euphoria one thought slowly crept its way back into his mind. In a day's time she would be gone. They shared breakfast that morning, full of smiles and glances and spontaneous laughter, but barely any conversation, before Owen had to leave for campus.

He spent the drive analyzing every detail of what seemed to be their fortuitous reunion. Repeatedly recapping all of their time spent together and secretly wondering, wishing it would be enough to make her stay. *Is that unfair?* he thought. He tossed it back and forth in his mind. Although, he partially felt that it would be unfair to ask her to stay, the thought of her leaving uncontested had become something he felt strongly that he would live to regret.

He had never made a connection like this with anyone. Though his college years had not been filled with random sexual encounters, he had dated a few girls over the years. None of which lasted for any serious lengths of time. Fewer still, resulting in the occasional sexual encounter. But nothing like this. Nothing so gripping, yet so freeing at the same time. He wrestled the entire day with how to approach the evening, scared to say something and force her away, but also scared to say nothing and just let her go.

Without warning, he found that the hour had arrived. It was time to spend his last night with the woman he had fallen so deeply in love with. He arrived at her grandfather's house and took his time getting out of the car. He realized that he had been so preoccupied with what to do about her leaving that he completely neglected to plan anything for their last night together. Feeling like a complete ass, he knocked on the door. As the door opened, Owen quickly began spouting out a partial apology he had conjured up but was silenced by Rhiannon and with her bright smile.

"Come on in, I made us dinner," she said. To which Owen breathed a sigh of relief.

She had cooked a wonderful spread for the two of them. Steak with baked potato, vegetables on the side, salad, and for dessert, an apple pie. Owen was not only impressed, but also thankful that his lack of planning wasn't going to put an unnecessary damper on the evening. They sat in the kitchen, eating, talking, and laughing. It was as though they had spent years in this same routine, blissfully unaware that the outside world even existed. Owen became very aware of the time and waited for a lull in the conversation long enough that he could change topics. When his moment came, he began to feel sick to his stomach. As if he were standing before a judge's bench waiting for his sentence to be handed down.

"Rhi" he said, bringing the conversation to a screeching halt. "We need to talk."

She paused for a moment, staring back at him. He could almost physically see the lump in her throat.

"What about?" she asked as she attempting to smile with little success.

Owen knew at that moment that he hadn't been the only one dreading this conversation. He knew by the look on her face, a mixture of fear and heartbreak, that she too had not been able to fully prepare herself for this point in their time together. The tension in the room increased as if the room were rapidly being filled with water. The silence between them stretched longer and longer, quickly reaching uncomfortable levels and soaring on past uncomfortable, into excruciating.

"About tomorrow," Owen said trying to be vague, but also direct.

"Owen," Rhiannon said looking down at the table.

"Listen," he jumped in quickly, leaning forward onto the table and grabbing one of her hands. "I've tried not to, but this is all I've thought about these last two weeks and I…"

"Owen, I can't stay," she interrupted. She brought her eyes up to meet his. And he could see the truth buried there.

He pressed further, regardless. He knew if he didn't, he would regret it. "But I just wanna…," he started again.

"Owen, please," Rhiannon insisted.

Rhiannon sat there staring back down at the table. Now she couldn't even look at him. Owen couldn't help but sit there and stare at her. Jaw dropped, emotions hastily fleeing in every direction as if the gates to a prison had just opened and everyone was free to go. Nothing. Not a single word from either of them. His thoughts shifted in a flash to clips of the last two weeks he had spent with her. It was as if someone was standing across the room flinging photographs at him. Some he could barely see. Some hitting him and no surprise, it hurt.

He still wanted to try. He wanted to say his piece. He wanted to say *anything* at this point. Instead, he stood up and walked out of the house without another word. He supposed in that moment, that her knowing that he wanted her to stay was as far as he was going to get. He managed to keep himself collected, mostly still in shock at how terribly the conversation had gone before being shot dead. It had been a mercy kill, but a kill just the same. He stood outside the door, and he could hear her breaking down on the other side. He stood listening for only a few seconds then started towards his car.

He got about halfway across the yard and stopped. He stood there like a statue, feeling a pull back towards the house and another toward his car. He wanted to go back in. He couldn't stand the thought of leaving things as they were, dying there at the kitchen table. He took one more step toward his car and thought, *fuck it.* He turned around and marched back toward the house with all the purpose of a soldier determined to accomplish his mission.

His mind scrambled to put back together the pieces of all the things he wanted to say. He wasn't sure how it was going to come out. He didn't care. He knew for his own sanity that he had to get it out one way or another. As he arrived back at the door there was no pause. He turned the knob and walked back in. Rhiannon's head shot up. She was still sitting at the table. Her eyes were wide at his sudden reappearance. He could see the fresh paths the tears had made as they slid down her face. He stood there for a second after making his grand re-entrance, staring at her, and quickly losing himself again. Neither one was jumping at the chance to speak first. Owen took a deep breath and began:

"Why'd you cut me off?" he asked. His breathing became a little heavier. He could feel the uncertainty of the moment settling firmly on his chest. "Why couldn't we at least discuss this?" he continued.

"There's nothing to discuss, Owen," she replied shakily.

She stiffened her posture in the chair trying to maintain her composure. But he could tell by the look on her face that her words betrayed how she truly felt. Still, they cut like a freshly sharpened knife.

"What do you mean there's nothing to discuss?" Owen asked throwing his arms up. "We can discuss whatever we want. I mean––what about the last two weeks?" he asked.

"The last two weeks have to be just that. The last two weeks." She felt rooted to the chair staring up at him. "That's all it can be."

"What do you mean, 'that's all it can be?' It was so much more than that. It could be anything, and we want it to be. And you're telling me you want to just throw it all away. That it meant nothing?"

"That's not what I'm saying, Owen," she said. "And you know it. You know how hard this is. For both of us."

"Then what?" he continued, slightly raising his voice. "What are you saying? Better yet, what are you *not* saying, because you didn't want to let me say anything? You cut me off at the mere mention of a discussion, and…"

"Just say it," Rhiannon interrupted.

"What?"

"Just say what you wanted to say," she repeated in a sharp tone.

Owen stood there confused. He feared now more than ever that he had completely lost any hold he had on himself or the situation.

"Listen," he started, exhaling a giant breath. "All I wanted to say was how much these last two weeks have meant to me. Each moment has been better than the last. I––I can't even really explain it. But I feel like this was supposed to happen. All those years ago, when Tommy and I use to get *so* annoyed that you would want to tag along with us, I never in a million years thought that one day I'd be standing in front of you pouring my heart out."

He sighed again. Only this time it was the sigh of a man making his final appeal.

"Rhi," he said walking toward her. I have never *looked* for anyone. I've never really cared about meeting that special someone and even after running into you at the bar, I still didn't fully realize what was happening, because you were the last person, I expected to see that night. You were the last person I expected to see ever again. But somewhere during these last two weeks I realized that I never was going to meet that special someone…again."

He paused to study the look on her face, hoping it would offer a shred of insight into how she felt about what he was saying.

"It was never going to happen again because it already had. All those years ago. There's no way we could have known it. But it was there, just the same.

Rhiannon sat there, her eyes moving from the floor to Owen, then back to the floor again. *Did she really have nothing to say?* he wondered. He stood there silent and waiting.

"Owen," she said filling the silence with a somber tone. "I need you to know that these last two weeks meant something to me too."

Owen's heart began to race as she sat in her pause for what seemed like an eternity. *This was it,* Owen thought. Whatever she said next, Owen knew he would have to accept. Good or bad. Whether his heart broke or healed, he would have to accept it. He stood there in front of her waiting when she finally raised head. He could see fresh tears forming in her eyes.

"They *really* did, Owen," Rhiannon said as another single tear fell and made its way down her cheek.

With everything he had left, Owen made his final plea. "Then stay," he said.

"I can't," she said softly.

"What's stopping you?" he asked.

"Nothing--Everything--I just can't, Owen. I have a whole life somewhere else."

"Rhi," he pleaded.

"You know," she interrupted. He could see the hurt turning to frustration. "All I wanted to do was spend one more night with you," she said, her words striking like the crack of a whip.

"I just wanted to end this the best possible way we could. That's why I didn't want to talk about it. I know you want me to stay, Owen. I've known the whole time. And if I'm being honest, it's crossed my mind to stay. But I just can't. I came back to do one thing, to bury my grandfather. I wasn't looking for you when I came back."

Owen was sure he could literally feel his heart ripping in two. He had gotten to say his piece and then so did she. He didn't quite understand her frustration. All he knew was that he had opened the door and made way for it. He tried to use the fact that staying had at least crossed her mind to ward off some of the pain he was feeling, but her last statement was too busy running laps in his brain. Too heavy not to feel the weight crushing down on him.

He stood there as long as he could. Not a single word more was spoke between the two of them. In that final moment all Owen wanted to do was wrap his arms around her one more time. Instead, he just stood there. He stared at her and remembered every time she had smiled over the past two weeks. Every time she had rested her head on his shoulder. Every blissful moment they had shared had been sharpened and was now being used to shred his heart into smaller and smaller pieces.

Owen turned to walk away as Rhiannon sat there with her head in her hands. He did not expect her to try and stop him. And she didn't. He made his way out of the house and to his car. He sat for a moment clinging to one last strand of false hope that the door would open, and she would come after him. Or at least have more to say to alleviate some of his pain. But she never did. Owen started his car and pulled out of the driveway, purposely avoiding his rearview mirror as he drove away.

What was done was done. He began to think of a thousand different ways that their conversation could have gone. Even if it still ended with her saying she couldn't stay, it could have gone better than it had. Maybe they would have decided to try some sort of long-distance thing or maybe they would have just agreed that the last two weeks had been great, and it was time to go their separate ways. Maybe either of those could have happened and they still could have spent one last night together. Go out with a bang so to speak. But no. It ended the way it had and even though Owen still didn't fully understand why it had ended that way, all he did know was that it ended in a total disaster.

Owen found himself bypassing campus completely and driving directly to the same bar where Rhiannon had found him alone two weeks earlier. It seemed only fitting that this is where their story would end. It was, after all where it had begun. He ordered up his usual and sat there staring blankly at a TV over the bar. He could have cared less about what was on. His mind was elsewhere. His mind was with her. He wondered if she had gotten up and wiped her face clean and gone about her evening or if she was still sitting there at the kitchen table with her head in her hands. He replayed their dinner from the moment she answered the door with that beautiful smile, right up to the moment that he decided to open his mouth. And of course, the train wreck that followed.

He was broken. He felt as though he had just been run over by a passing car that then refused to stop. Owen made his way to the bottom of three glasses before he realized what he needed to do. The only thing he *could* do. He needed to call Tommy.

11

Tommy showed up at the bar as requested. He had been with Alison that evening and they both had been curious to find out how Owen's night had turned out. Tommy figured the longer he went without a phone call, the better their evening must be going. Then Owen's name popped up on his phone and after a brief thirty second call, Tommy told Alison that he had to go.

About thirty minutes later, Tommy walked through the front door to find a slumped over Owen, sitting at the bar with two empty glasses in front of him, and a third in his hand. Tommy motioned at the bartender as he walked toward the bar. The bartender sat a beer on the bar and Tommy sat down next to Owen and took a drink of his beer.

"So, what do we do now?" Tommy asked staring at the TV.

"I don't fucking know, man," Owen said. "None of that went the way it was supposed to."

"I see," Tommy said. "So, what *did* happen?" he asked.

"She didn't even want to talk. S-she just cut me off." Owen said, his speech a bit slurred.

"Specifics, Owen," Tommy said snapping his fingers.

Owen took a deep breath and sighed. "We were having dinner, and everything was fine. We were laughing and carrying on. And then," he paused. "I opened my mouth, and it all went to shit."

"Okay?" Tommy said.

"I said we needed to talk. She said, 'about what?' and I said, 'about tomorrow.' Then I started to try and say my piece and she cut me off and said she couldn't stay. I tried to continue, but she wouldn't let me. So, I walked out."

"You walked out?" Tommy asked.

"Yeah, but I didn't even make it to the car. I walked back in and said what I had to say." Owen said.

"Which was?" Tommy asked.

"Well at first, she said there was nothing to discuss," he said. "Then when I went back, she told me to say what I had to say. So, I did. I told her what these last two weeks had meant to me and how I felt like this was all supposed to happen."

"And what did she say to that?" Tommy asked.

Owen laid his head back down on the bar. "She said that it meant something to her too," he said. "She said it meant something to her, but that her whole life was somewhere else, and that she wasn't looking for me when she came back."

Tommy sat for a second, thinking about what he wanted to say next.

"Well, to be fair, buddy, you weren't looking for her when you came to the bar that night." Tommy said.

Owen's head shot around looking at Tommy, who sat there with a smile on his face. Owen retreated from his initial reaction.

"Yeah, dipshit, I know," Owen said. "But it happened. It all happened, and I didn't want to just act like it didn't." he finished.

"I know," Tommy said. "Do you think she did?" he asked.

"That's the kicker," Owen said. "I don't think she did. I know she didn't. She said it had crossed her mind too. To stay here, I mean."

"Damn, dude," That's not *nothin'*," Tommy said. "That tells you everything you need to know, if you ask me."

"Whatya mean?" Owen asked."

"Look, she wanted to stay. She told you she thought about it too. In the end, she just couldn't," Tommy said. "Do you think she was just cutting you off and telling you she didn't want to talk about it because it was just that easy for her?" he asked. "No, she was avoiding it, just like you had. Because it was something that she didn't want to do, but when you brought it up, she didn't feel like she had any other choice." Tommy paused, giving the information time to sink into Owen's beer-soaked brain.

"I saw the way she looked at you. The way you two looked at each other. This was the same for her as it was for you. You're just on different paths in life and she just doesn't see a way around that right now. I'm sorry, buddy. I wish it had gone different."

"I know, me too," Owen said. "I wish it had gone different too."

They both drank their beer in silence for a few minutes before talking mindlessly about anything else they could think of. It was clear that Owen was avoiding talking about Rhiannon anymore, and Tommy didn't want to press the matter any further. He knew Owen was hurting, so he engaged him in the mindless topics he would bring up, purposefully steering clear of bringing up Alison and their relationship. Even when Owen asked about it, Tommy answered and quickly changed the subject.

After another hour or so, and a couple more beers, they left the bar and caught a cab back to campus. Tommy walked with Owen back to his dorm, then over to Alison's sorority house. He filled her in on what had happened and what kind of shape he found Owen in at the bar. Alison felt bad for Owen as well, and told Tommy it was a shame, because she really liked him and Rhiannon together.

| 12 |

Owen woke up suddenly the next morning. Almost as if he had awakened from a bad dream. He looked at the clock. It was 7:17 am. He began replaying his conversation with Rhiannon over in his head, hating the outcome even more the next day. He looked at the clock again. *Even if we're not going to end up together, I still don't want it to end like this,* he thought. He flung himself out of bed, got dressed and ran outside, trying to find a cab. He found one quickly and directed the driver to the bar where he and Tommy had left their cars the night before. He tossed some cash at the cab driver once they arrived at the bar, he wasn't even sure how much. Then he jumped out of the cab ran to his car.

He drove through the city as fast as he could and made his way to Long Island. He had to catch her before she left. He had to try. He called Tommy and got no answer, but he returned the call within a couple minutes. Owen told him where he was headed and why, and Tommy cautioned him that he couldn't know for sure what he may be walking into, but all Owen said was, "I have to try."

They got off the phone just as Owen realized that he didn't know any of Rhiannon's flight information. What time she was leaving, which airport, nothing. Not even where she was flying to. *Paris!* He remembered. *She said at the bar, that when she left, she was going back to Paris.*

Excited as he was to have remembered that small piece to the puzzle, it would do him no good without the rest of the pieces. He made it to her grandfather's house in record time, realizing before he even stopped the car that he was already too late. He got out of the car and stared at the house, regretting every second of the night before. Part of him wished he had been a little more tactful. The other part wished he had just kept his mouth shut altogether. Regardless of what he wished had happened, here he stood. She was gone.

He stared at the empty house, then turned to get back in his car when he noticed something stuck to the door. Something he hadn't noticed being there when he walked through the door for dinner with Rhiannon the night before. It was a white piece of paper. *Probably a note for her parents,* he thought. But the curiosity was just too much for him. He walked toward the door. Slow at first, but his curiosity forced him to go faster with each step. He watched as the piece of paper fluttered and flapped in the wind, attached to the door by only a single nail. As he arrived at the door, he grabbed the note in one hand and braced himself against the door with the other to catch his breath. The note wasn't for her parents at all. A fact that caused Owen's stomach to flip. It read:

Owen,
I just wanted you to know that these last two weeks
meant a lot to me too. I'm sorry I couldn't stay.
Love, Rhi

| 13 |

Owen spent the next couple of years clinging to that note. During their senior year of college, on more than one occasion, Tommy had walked into Owen's dorm room to find him lying on his bed or sitting in the chair at his desk just staring at that note. Even after college things seemed to stay the same.

Owen found an apartment in the city and gone to work at his father's shop as planned. Tommy visited frequently and every once in a while, he would see the note sitting out somewhere in the apartment or stuck to Owen's refrigerator. He knew that Owen kept the note in his nightstand, because that's where he kept it while they were still in school. So, when he saw it out, he knew that Owen must be having a particularly rough day.

They talked about Rhiannon and how much Owen missed her. He would think of some detail from their two weeks together that he had previously forgotten to tell Tommy. Those would make him smile. Other times he would go through the many different ways that their last night together could have played out, compared of course, to the way that it actually had play out. Whatever path the conversation took, Tommy sat there and listened. He knew that he was the only one that Owen wanted to talk to about her and it was safe to say that she was all he wanted to talk about.

After a while, quite a while, Tommy started trying to encourage Owen to get out and start dating. He even asked Owen if he wanted Alison to try and set him up with one of her friends. But Owen always declined. He truly had no interest in dating anyone else. He had work. He had Tommy and Alison. And he had his note. He told Tommy, "It reminds me of the good and the bad. What we had, for the time we had it, was good. It was great. As for the bad, even my worst moment with her, was better than never having her at all."

Tommy and Alison found an apartment in the city shortly after college as well. Tommy had just started with the NYPD and was going through the academy. He would be gone throughout the week but was able to be at home with Alison on the weekends.

Alison, of course took over decorating the apartment with very little pushback from Tommy. Not just because he was off at the police academy, but because Tommy could have sat a couple of lawn chairs in front of a TV in the living room and been perfectly content. He didn't seem to mind though. In fact, he seemed a little relieved.

Alison, in addition to her interior decorating, had started her internship at New York-Presbyterian Lower Manhattan Hospital. Right around the same time that Tommy started the academy. The hospital gig came with long hours, an okay salary, and plenty of headaches. Stressful as it was, she became rather fond of the hustle that her job required. During Tommy's weekends home, she would share the new or fascinating things she had learned at the hospital and sometimes details of a tragedy from the night before.

Not to anyone's surprise, Tommy excelled tremendously as a patrol officer after graduating from the academy and racked up a rather impressive arrest record. Sometimes, he and Alison would find that a name that she would mention from the hospital would correlate with someone Tommy had dealt with during the course of his duties.

During his patrol years he was a four-time recipient of the award for most DUI arrests in a single month. He had found it a little difficult in the beginning to determine whether a driver was intoxicated or not, due to the haphazard manner in which most New Yorker's drive. And let's not forget cell phones. They would zig and zag through the flow of traffic, a lot of times without signaling. Speed up to pass, then slow down and honk because they couldn't get around. It was a nightmare. However, it didn't take him long to find his footing and quickly be able to tell the difference between everyday New York driving and intoxicated driving.

Tommy had become more than just a DUI tracking machine. He had gained plenty of experience with domestic violence cases, robberies, shootings, muggings, as well as minor issues like neighbor complaints. He had even been on scene when the New York City Fire Department literally rescued a kitten from a tree. Yes, he had his hand in all manner of things where his police work was concerned. He had proven that he was one of the best. One that they could depend on. One that would go above and beyond.

His stellar performance moved him up the latter at a rather rapid pace compared to other officers that had joined the department around the same time. Again, to no one's surprise, near the end of 2007 he was taken off patrol after passing the detective's exam. Tommy was rightfully proud of himself, as was his mother, and Alison, and Owen.

They celebrated the news with a cookout at Owens parents' house. During which both Tommy and Owen celebrated a little more than everyone else. That left Alison to drive them both back to the city that night. She didn't mind though. There were quite a few laughs to be had. Including Tommy throwing a once-bitten, fully loaded cheeseburger out the window while Alison was driving. He had snagged it on his way out the door and was simply done eating it and didn't want to hold it anymore. "Birds'll get it," he said, followed by a whistling attempt to call whatever birds may be nearby. The three of them laughed hysterically the rest of the way home.

Tommy hit the ground running as a detective. His first case was a drive-by shooting in which a seven-year-old boy had been killed. Terrible as it was, through the course of the investigation, Tommy had discovered that the shooting was caused by a drug deal gone wrong. What made it so sinister, was that the child actually *had* been the target of the shooting, due to his parents' being the ones that had allegedly stiffed their dealer. Through a series of interrogations and statements made by neighbors and family members of the little boy, he learned that this wasn't the first time the parents had tried to get one over on a dealer. In fact, he learned that they owed that particular dealer quite a bit of money, and he decided to teach them a lesson they wouldn't soon forget.

Tommy was finally given a name during an interrogation of the child's aunt. At which time he was able to acquire a warrant and go to the alleged shooter/dealer's home. In the home they found many different types of drugs and more than enough evidence of not only drug use, but distribution as well. He was able to arrest the dealer on site, but the drugs hadn't been what sealed the case. Through a subsequent search of the home, Tommy was also able to recover the gun used in the shooting, and wouldn't you know, rounds from the gun found in the dealer's home matched the round that the coroner has extracted from the seven-year-old-boy.

The jury only deliberated for about an hour before delivering a guilty verdict. The accused was sentenced to fifty-five years in prison, without the possibility of parole. It was a pretty big win for Tommy right out of the gate. The defense attorney tried to argue that the weapon in question did not belong to his client despite the fact that it was found not only in his home, but among the defendant's other possessions. This proved to be a relatively easy hurdle for the prosecution to glide over. They simply provided proof that not only were the dealer's fingerprints found on the weapon, but that his hands also contained a gunshot residue pattern consistent with that specific weapon. At that point, all the defense attorney could do was sit back and watch.

"They won't all be that easy," Bob Stephens told Tommy, when he arrived back at the office after court that day.

Bob was a senior detective. He had all the makings of a great mid-eighties, TV detective. The beat-up, brown leather jacket, the aviator sunglasses, and let's not forget, the classic brown leather shoulder holster that kept his service weapon tucked away neatly under one arm and his magazines under the other.

Bob had been a part of the NYPD since the days of David Berkowitz. The infamous *Son of Sam* killer who stalked New York in the late seventies looking for young women with dark hair. "Ol' Berkowitz caused quite the frenzy," Bob would tell you, if you happened to be the one who got sucked in during one of his story hours. Bob wasn't a bad guy though. God knows he had plenty of wisdom and experience to pass on to fresh-eyed, young detectives. So, Tommy didn't mind trading a little of his spare time every now and then, for some pearls of wisdom or a suggested technique.

2008 was shaping up to be a good one for Tommy. The cases kept coming, but none of them seemed to be out of his league. Some of course, though difficult to solve, required top notch detective skills on Tommy's part. Others proved to be relatively simple. Almost too simple. Like the Wall Street stockbroker found hanging in his office by the night janitor. Obvious suicide. Or so it seemed when they arrived on the scene. That is until reports from colleagues began to show that the victim had plenty to live for. Everything seemed to be going his way. Turned out that one of those colleagues had gotten a little north of pissed off when he missed out on an investment opportunity. And when the profits started rolling in, "Mr. missed out" figured that if his buddy was out of the picture, he may be able to slide in and take his place. In due time, of course. I mean who's never heard of someone on Wall Street committing suicide.

Too bad for him, when he found his buddy working late one night and decided to string him up and set his plan in motion, he didn't know (nor did anyone else, including the victim) that the victims panicky, insecure wife had planted a "nanny cam" in her husband's office one day during a visit. She was able to view the camera from her cell phone and check in on her husband.

She explained to Tommy that back in college her husband, (then boyfriend) had gotten drunk one night and cheated on her. So naturally, when his nights at the office started getting longer and longer, her mind began to wander. She said that she would sit up all night waiting for him to come home. Sometimes until two or three in the morning. She would wait to hear him pull in the driveway then pretend to be fast asleep when he came in. She maintained that she had no other reason to confirm her suspicion other than the late nights, but that that in itself had gotten to be too much for her. So, she paid him a visit him at the office one afternoon, which was not out of the ordinary. He stepped out for a moment to speak with a colleague, and boom, she planted the camera.

"Never in my life did I think I'd capture something like this," she told Tommy through her hysterical sobs. Her tears ran off her cheek and stained her dress. Tommy never forgot that.

Once the discovery of her hidden camera was made and the footage reviewed, it was only a short time before Tommy had the killer in handcuffs.

Tommy was flying high. Leaps and bounds above anyone else in the department. Until the morning of July 8th, 2008.

"Collins!" Captain Spencer yelled from his office.

Captain Dave Spencer was a no nonsense, by the book kind of guy. Very athletic, generally a positive guy. But still, no one you wanted to fuck with. He could be a full-on Drill Instructor, Hartman, if you pissed him off bad enough. He always seemed to be on his game. It was rumored that he once took down two suspects with one bullet. Many had speculated on how it had actually gone down. Theories of ricochets, and various "accounts" of that fateful day's events circulated through the halls of the prescient like the news of someone losing their virginity in high school. But no one had any hard facts, and no one dared ask.

"Tommy," Captain Spencer said, looking up from his morning coffee. "It would seem you may have caught a break in the Johnson case you've been working.

Tommy looked back at him intrigued and immediately began reciting the details of the Johnson case in his head. *Sydney Johnson, female, age nine, alleged that her stepfather had sexually abused her on multiple occasions. Stepfather's out on bond, skips town.*

"Sure, whatya got?" Tommy asks.

"Well," Captain Spencer started. "There was a body found this morning in an alley off East 101st street. The description seems to match your Mr. Jackson Arnold, who decided to leave town once he was out on bond. I want you to go down and check it out."

"Sure thing, sir," Tommy said.

"Let me know what you find out there," The captain said, returning his attention to his coffee.

"Yes, sir," Tommy replied as he turned to leave the captain's office.

"And Tommy," the captain added. "Take Bob with ya, will ya? He needs some sun"

"Will do, sir," Tommy said with a slight chuckle.

Tommy turned and called out across the bullpen, "Bob!" And waited for the seasoned detective to finish whatever clue he was working out in the Times Crossword. "Let's go, it's you and me today."

Bob folded and slapped his paper down on his desk and moseyed out of his chair. Adjusted his holster and threw on his sunglasses. "Ready when you are, champ," he said, with a smile.

The pair walked out of the bullpen and onto the street where Tommy had his car parked and got in. Once they had taken off, Tommy had planned to fill Bob in on where they were headed, but Bob beat him to the punch.

"So, where we headed?" Bob asked in his usual, upbeat manner.

"Well, a body was found this morning, over off 101st. Captain thinks the description matches a fugitive in one of my cases."

"Well, what the hell do you need me for?" Bob said producing a hearty laugh. "I wouldn't know the son-of-a-bitch from Adam."

"Captain said you needed a little sun," Tommy said turning to Bob with a giant grin on his face.

"Oh shit," Bob exclaimed continuing to laugh. "You know, every time I get a good groove goin', layin' low, ridin' that retirement wave right on into the shore, one of you sons-a-bitches comes along, and it all goes to hell."

Bob continued to laugh heartily. Truth is, Bob could have cared less. In fact, he was grateful that someone still found him useful, as much as he would want you to believe the opposite.

They arrived at the crime scene and immediately started perusing the area on their way to identify the body. The body had been left, propped up against a dumpster near one end of the alley. Anyone who didn't know any better could have easily mistaken him for a sleeping homeless person. His clothes were dirty all over, his face and hands covered in dirt as well. There was plenty of garbage and other debris scattered around, some of which even appeared to be concealing the body. All Tommy knew was, he had his work cut out for him.

"So, is it him?" Bob asked.

Tommy bent over in front of the body. He reached with a gloved hand and grabbed the man by the chin, lifting his face up, revealing a sizable neck wound that stretched almost literally ear to ear.

"Yep, that's him," Tommy replied, resting the man's chin back on his chest. "That's Jackson Arnold."

"One case closes, another one opens. That's the way we do it downtown," Bob said with a smirk.

"Well, now we need the 'who', and the 'why'," Tommy said, staring at the body.

Tommy turned around and started scanning the area for possible clues the killer may have left behind. He and Bob spent the biggest part of the morning searching every inch of that alley looking for something, anything to give them a lead. They found nothing. Forensics hadn't reported finding anything on the body or in the alley either. So, now they *really* had nothing to go on.

Tommy and Bob left the crime scene shortly after the coroner left with the body. They reported back to Captain Spencer and confirmed that the body was in fact, Jackson Arnold.

"It's a shame the bonding system in this country works as fast as it does," Captain Spencer said shaking his head. "If we had gotten the DNA results back from the rape kit quick enough, Mr. Arnold here would have never been able to make bond, because they proved that he had molested and raped that little girl. Had to settle for a damn arrest warrant instead."

"Well, somebody got to him before we did. Someone who was obviously paying close attention to the case," Tommy said. "Now we have to find this new asshole, instead of the asshole we already had plenty of shit on."

"That's right, because that's what we do," Captain Spencer said with a grin, as Tommy and Bob stood up to leave the captains office. "Well, that's what you do. All I do is sit here and do fucking paperwork."

"Tommy," the captain said, stopping him at the door. "They'll slip up, they always do."

"Thanks, sir," Tommy said and exited the office.

Bob however, stopped and turned around and looked at Captain Spencer: "Sure was shady in that alley today. Guess I didn't get no sun after all." Followed by one of his hearty laughs.

"Get the fuck outta here, Bob," Captain Spencer said, wadding up a piece of paper and throwing it at Bob. "And pick that up," he yelled, trying to stifle his own laughter.

Tommy left work that evening feeling frustrated. On one hand, he had no qualms about that piece of shit Arnold being dealt with. Now he no longer had to deal with him. The sick son-of-a-bitch was guilty. But on the other hand, the now heavier of the two, a whole new problem had arisen. Many questions raced through his mind. *Was this one of Sydney Johnson's family members? She did have some questionable relatives. Some that had spent some significant time behind bars. Was it someone close to the family who knew where to find him, even when the police didn't? If he fled, why was he back in the city?* All of these questions, Tommy would save for the following day. For now, he just wanted to get home to Alison.

When he walked through the door the smell of Chinese food wafted into his face, pouring from the doorway out into the hallway. Chinese food meant that Dr. Alison (as he so lovingly liked to call her) had a long day as well, and didn't feel like following a recipe, or even making her famous million-dollar spaghetti. He found Alison in the kitchen removing her Chinese takeout from the container onto a plate. She always wanted it to feel like a home cooked meal, even if it wasn't. Tommy on the other hand, preferred the takeout containers. No mess, no dishes, just toss it in the trash. He would always laugh at her about using dishes, then having to clean up afterward, but that never stopped her.

"Hey, honey," Alison said, looking up from behind the kitchen counter. "Let me tell you about *my* day."

She walked into the living room, plated Chinese food in one hand, glass of red in the other, filled to the brim.

"Oh, I ordered you your favorite," she added. "General Tso's. It's on the counter."

"Thanks, babe," Tommy said tossing his keys on the dining room table.

"Let me tell you about my day," Alison started, again.

"Okay, you can go first," Tommy replied, grabbing his food, and joining her in the living room.

Alison leapt into a story about how first thing this morning, a construction worker was struck by a passing car, causing him to fall into a hole at the job site he was working on, where he was impaled through the thigh by a piece of misplaced rebar.

"He was a mess," she said, and went on about how they first had to establish what all injuries the man had from the impact of the vehicle and the subsequent fall. Then without furthering any of those injuries, they had to remove the rebar.

"Luckily for him, it missed his femoral artery," she added. "Just a nick and he could have bled to death before they got him outta that hole."

She dove into his list of injuries from the vehicle and the fall. Broken wrist, fractured leg, and three ribs on his right side seemed to be the worst of it. After the rebar was removed that is.

"Two- or three-days observation, and if all goes well. His wife can wheel him outta there and take him home," she finished.

Alison loved her job. She loved helping people. She loved being the one to meet the ambulance outside as they were removing the patient, listening to the EMT's spout off vital signs and known issues or injuries. It excited her. It motivated her. That's what made her a good doctor.

"So, how was your day?" she asked Tommy.

Tommy had made mention of the Johnson case to Alison back when it first became a part of his caseload. He remembered that it had brought tears to her eyes while he was telling her some, not all, of the details. Someone like Alison, who was so clearly built to help people and save lives just couldn't understand how someone who was supposed to care for and protect a child could do something like that to them. Tommy, however, knew all too well what someone could do to a child. He had lived it.

All that Alison knew about Tommy's father was that he had been killed in an apparent retaliation by someone he had arrested. And that no one had ever been arrested for the murder. At least that's the only answer the police ever gave Tommy's mother. Whatever the motive was, the police had never made an arrest in the case. They never even had a prime suspect. Whoever had killed Tommy's father had gotten in and out as quick as the breeze and left not a single trace. That fact bothered Tommy more than anything. Even more than his father's murder. Finding Arnold's body today reminded him of those facts about his father's murder case. Dead body, throat sliced wide open, no evidence. It was enough to give him goosebumps for most of the day.

"Well, you remember the Johnson case, right?" Tommy asked. "Nine-year-old girl, her stepfath...,"

"Yes, I remember," she said, wielding her fork and cutting him off. "Oh wait, did you find the stepfather?" she asked expecting the next piece of information to lift her spirits.

"Yeah...we did," Tommy said grimly. "But someone else found him before we did. He was found this morning over off 101st with his throat sliced open."

"Oh my God," Alison said, continuing to eat her Chinese food. "But wait, I thought you said he skipped town?" she asked.

"He did. But for whatever reason, and we don't know why yet, he came back. And somebody knew about it. Somebody that wanted him dead."

Tommy continued talking about how they had no leads, no ideas about who it could have been. He talked about how they were going to start with Sydney Johnson's family and work their way out from there. They were, after all, the only ones Tommy knew of who had a clear motive. And in cases like this, sadly, it is most often an act of retaliation.

They finished their meal together over conversation about hospital patients, as well as hospital antics. Then it was off to bed so they could wake up and do it all again tomorrow.

As they lay in bed, Alison slowly falling asleep on his chest. Tommy's mind remained stuck on the freshly opened Arnold case. He couldn't quite put a finger on it, but something felt off. Something felt oddly unsettling. It wasn't that the victim had his throat cut. It wasn't even that it appeared to be some sort of retaliatory killing. He didn't know what it was. He couldn't nail it down. Maybe it was the fact that the culmination of one of his cases had thrusted him right into the middle of a new one. But even that thought didn't seem to satisfy the itch that this case had given him to scratch.

The next morning, before heading to the office, Tommy stopped and grabbed coffee and then stopped by the shop to see Owen. He had previously told Owen about the Johnson case as well because it hit so close to home for him. Owen, being one of only two other people who knew about what his father had done, understood why it was so important for Tommy to close it. Tommy walked through the front door and around the counter and found Owen in his office sitting at his computer.

| 14 |

Christopher's Cleaners was a small, yet respectable business that Owen's father had started after he graduated college and married Owen's mother. It had all the charm of a family owned and operated, New York City business, with none of the corporate chain feel. Owen's father always wanted his customers to feel welcome when they stepped through the door. Like they were part of the family He kept a few chairs along the windows in front of the counter that stretched almost the entire length of the room, with small tables between them filled with magazines for the adults and children's books for the kids. Owen's father did his best to make sure that he paid one on one attention to each customer. And that's what he passed on to Owen.

"Mornin', sunshine," Tommy said stepping into Owen's office. "Thought maybe you could use a hot pick-me-up this morning. I know I sure needed one."

"Damn, bro. You read my mind. Thanks," Owen said. His eyes widening as he stared at the cup of coffee in Tommy's hand.

"So, how are things?" Owen asked. "It's been a couple weeks."

"Oh, you know, things were going just fine, until yesterday," Tommy said.

"What happened yesterday?" Owen asked.

Tommy began refreshing Owen's memory about the Johnson case. Which to no surprise, Owen was able to quickly recall almost immediately. Then on to the discovery of Arnold's body. Owen sat and listened, asking a lot of the same questions Tommy had already asked himself about the case. Unfortunately, a lot of those answers were still unknown.

"It's still pretty early in the game on this one," Tommy said. "I've got to start all over. Just watch your ass. There's some psycho running around out there. And we don't know if Arnold was targeted because of what he did or if it was just random."

"Oh, I almost forgot," Tommy said, changing the subject. "I got something to show ya." Tommy reached into his pocket and pulled out a small, velvety, blue box.

"Oh, you shouldn't have," Owen said fluttering his eyes and laughing at Tommy.

"Smartass," Tommy remarked. Tommy opened the box revealing a beautiful, rather expensive looking diamond ring.

"I'm gonna propose to Alison," Tommy said, as a smile crept up on his face.

"Well shit! Congratulations, buddy! That's Awesome!"

"Owen," Tommy said, closing the box and stuffing it back in his pocket. "I want you to be my best man."

"Well, who the hell else is gonna do it? Of course, brother! Of course," Owen said as he stood up and hugged Tommy.

Tommy looked over Owen's shoulder as he hugged him, at the cork board hanging on the wall behind Owen's desk. It was littered with invoices and receipts. All of which no doubt pertained to the shop. But down in the bottom right corner, Tommy noticed something push-pinned to the board that he recognized all too well. It was Rhiannon's note. He knew that Owen had never fully gotten over her leaving. But he wasn't going to bring it up. Especially after just telling Owen that he was going to propose to Alison.

"It's about time, that's all I can say," Owen said with a chuckle. "So, when you gonna pop the question?"

"I'm not exactly sure yet," Tommy said. "We do have an anniversary coming up. Maybe that'll be a good time,"

"Well, you just let me know if you need anything from me. I'll help however I can." Owen said.

Tommy smiled at Owen and turned to leave. "I gotta head on in," he said. "Plenty to do."

They walked out of the office and back out to the front of the shop. "I'll see ya later, buddy. Let's grab a drink soon," Tommy said as he opened the front door.

"Sure thing," Owen replied and waved goodbye.

Tommy left the shop and hopped into his car and pulled out into traffic. His mind was stuck on the note hanging in Owen's office. He felt like an ass, seeing it hanging there after talking about anniversaries and proposals. He felt for Owen. But the further down the road he got the more his thoughts went back to the crime scene where Arnold's body had been found. He wondered what they had missed. What they could have possibly overlooked. His plan today was to start with Sydnie Johnson's family and ask them if they knew anything or if they heard from Jackson Arnold recently or even knew that he was back in town.

He drove along, lost in preparation for the task ahead, when his phone rang. Tommy sat his coffee in the cup holder and grabbed his phone.

"Detective Collins," he answered.

"Hey, Tommy it's Bob. Listen, since you haven't decided to grace us with your presence yet this mornin', I thought I'd give you a heads up. The forensics report came back. There was some type of metallic dust on Arnold's jacket. They said it was most likely from a grinder or some type of power tool. Not much to go on, I know, but it could mean that he was killed somewhere else, then dumped in the alley."

"You're right, that's not much to go on," Tommy said.

"So, that's all they found?" He asked sounding disappointed.

"Yep," Bob replied. "I was thinkin' we take another look at that alley, see if maybe we missed something the first time. A place like that, you never know what could turn out to be evidence."

"Yeah, that's a good idea," Tommy agreed. "But I'm going to talk with Sydnie Johnson's family first. I wanna see what they know. If anything. She's got a father and a couple of uncles I know wouldn't mind seeing Arnold in a body bag. Wouldn't have minded being the ones to put him there either."

"Alright, just let me know what you kick up," Bob said. "

Will do," Tommy said.

He hung up the phone and drove toward Sydnie Johnson's mother's house. Tommy felt in his gut that this was the best place to start. If for no other reason than rule them out. He hoped that Sydnie Johnson's family didn't have anything to do with Arnold's murder. It certainly would make for a quick, open and shut case. But personally, he would hate to see someone in their family put away for it.

Tommy stopped in front of the Arnold home and exited his car. He stood by his car momentarily, looking both directions, up and down the street, just seeing what there was to see. He walked around the back of his car and just as he stepped up on the sidewalk, the Arnold's front door opened and Sydnie's mother, Sylvia stepped out and closed the door behind her.

It was a nice house, in an upper-middle class neighborhood. A gray two-story with navy blue shutters. Something that Tommy hoped he and Alison would be able to afford someday. It sat on a well-manicured lawn and there was a single oak tree providing a good amount of shade. A single row of boxwoods filled the beds on either side of the front porch.

"Detective Collins," she said, placing a hand on her chest. "I hope you're here to tell me you've arrested that son-of-a-bitch."

She seemed exhausted. She looked as though a good night's sleep was not something she had been privy to recently.

"Well," Tommy started. "Is it okay if we talk inside?" he asked.

"Sure, sure, come on in," she said. "Would you like some coffee?" She asked as they entered the living room.

The inside of the house was just as nice as the outside. Sylvia had a modest taste for cleanliness and some of the nicer things in life. She wasn't rich by anyone's standard, but her home could make guests question just how well off she was. The living room at the front of the house didn't seem to be one that was used often. In fact, it seemed to be a conversation only room. There was no TV, and only two small Victorian style couches, set on either side of a small, ovel shaped, cherrywood coffee table. Tommy could smell the coffee in the kitchen just over the subtle hints of Sylvia's perfume.

"No thanks," Tommy said. "Just polished one off on the way over."

Sylvia continued into the kitchen and poured herself a cup of coffee and then returned to the living room and seated herself across from Tommy.

"So, did you find him?" she asked, looking hopeful. Tommy studied her face for a moment, picking up on the desperation in her voice.

"Yes, Mrs. Arnold, we did," Tommy said.

"Oh, thank God," she exclaimed as her voice cracked and tears started to well up in her eyes. "I can't tell you what this has done to me. What it's done to Sydnie. To know that he was out there somewhere and not rotting in cell like he should be. No one knew where he went. She's been so terrified. We both have."

Tommy watched as Sylvia slumped backwards onto the couch. As if she had only been held up by recently cut marionette strings.

"Mrs. Arnold," Tommy started.

"Please don't call me that," she said, sitting up again, and looking as if she might vomit. "I can't stand being attached to that name anymore. I'm in the process of changing it back to Johnson. You know, so at least Sydnie and I can have the same last name."

Sylvia and Nathan Johnson, Sydnie's biological father, had gotten divorced when Sydnie was about six years old, Tommy recalled from working the first case involving Arnold.

"Sorry, Ms. *Johnson*," Tommy continued. "We did find Jackson, but he's not under arrest."

"What!" Sylvia said, bolting upright onto the edge of the couch. Her posture as stiff as the oak out front. A fearful look washed over her face. "Why the hell not?" she asked angrily.

"We found his body in an alley off of 101st street," Tommy said, watching as the fearful look on Sylvia's face was replaced by a look of confusion. She leaned back on the couch again, much slower this time. Blankly staring out the window behind Tommy. Then her eyes shifted back to him. She did not speak. The shock of what she had just heard had set in almost instantaneously.

"So––he's dead?" she asked. "Jackson is dead?"

"Yes, ma'am," Tommy answered.

"Do you know who did it?" she asked.

"No, we don't. That's actually why I'm here," he said.

"Oh, you don't think…,"

"No, ma'am," Tommy interrupted. "You have not been named as a suspect. No one has as of right now." Tommy said. "I'm just here to see if maybe you had heard from him. Has he tried to contact you recently? Has anyone in the family heard anything that you know of? That sort of thing."

"No, not at all," she said. "In fact, I've been praying that we wouldn't. That's what keeps me up most nights, worried to death that he would come back and try to hurt us. Sydnie too. She hardly sleeps. I certainly would have notified you if I had heard from him."

Tommy expected that to be the answer he got from Sylvia. And based on her reaction, he believed that she was telling the truth. He spoke further with her about the rest of the family. And Sylvia reiterated that she would have contacted authorities if she or anyone else in the family had heard from Jackson Arnold. Sylvia invited Tommy to speak to anyone else in the family he thought he may need to. (Something Tommy had already planned to do) telling him also that Sydnie's father, Nathan had stopped by after work to check on her and Sydnie. Apparently, on the night Tommy said the murder had taken place. Once Tommy felt he had all the information from Sylvia that he needed, he thanked her for her time and started toward the door.

"If you happen to catch wind of anything, please give me a call," Tommy said, handing Sylvia one of his cards. He briefly wondered if Sylvia would be more apt to celebrate with the person that killed the man who raped and molested her daughter, rather than turn them in.

"Absolutely," she said. "But I must tell you, detective. I am more than a little relieved that we don't have to have to look behind us everywhere we go anymore. It's been a living hell. We've barely left the house."

"I know it has," Tommy said. "I'm glad that part is over for you. And for Sydnie. She didn't deserve any of this."

With a parting smile, Tommy left and headed toward 101st street. He called Bob on the way to let him know that he was headed that direction and to see if Bob wanted to join him. Bob agreed and so they met in the same alley where Arnold's body had been discovered. They spent about two hours covering every inch of the alleyway. Flipping over crates, wheeling dumpsters away from the sides of buildings, looking for anything that could point them in any direction. But they found nothing. Forensics had already processed the alley and come up with nothing as well.

"Whoever did this, was very meticulous about the details," Bob said, offering his opinion to Tommy. "Seems to me, like they knew what they was doin'."

"Yeah," Tommy replied, staring intently at the space around the dumpster they had found the body propped up next to. "Well, if they got away with it once, they'll do it again. I hate that, but unfortunately that's what we're dealing with. And if they do, hopefully they'll slip up."

Tommy and Bob left the alley and made their way back to the precinct. Tommy made his way to his desk and sat down and stared at his computer. After a few moments of silence, he decided to give Sydnie's father a call and ask him to come in for questioning. When Nathan Johnson answered the phone, Tommy Identified himself and asked if he minded coming in. Mr. Johnson seemed to be very relieved, telling Tommy that he had already spoke to Sylvia, and how glad he was that this nightmare was over. He told Tommy over the phone that he had been stopping by the Sylvia's house quite regularly to check on her and Sydnie. Then happily agreed to come in for questioning. He said he would leave work immediately and come down to the station.

Once he arrived, Tommy took him into one of the interrogation rooms and grabbed each of them a cup of coffee and sat down to discuss where he was when the murder took place.

"First of all, Nathan," Tommy started. "I just want to say that no one is being considered a suspect at the moment. It's just, with your relationship to Sydnie and the circumstances surrounding her case, this is where we typically start in a situation like this."

"It's not a problem, detective," Nathan replied, sounding anxious to start the conversation. "I'm happy to do it. But let me go on record as saying, after what he did to my baby girl, if I *had* killed that motherfucker, I would be the first one to tell you about it. I would have gladly gone to prison for five minutes alone with that son-of-a-bitch."

"Be that as it may," Tommy said. "We will be recording our conversation. Can you state your name and today's date for me?" Mr. Johnson did as he was asked.

"Okay Nathan, can you tell me where you were the night of July 7th, this past Monday?"

"Sure thing," he said. "I was doing what I do most Monday's. I got off work around 5:00 pm. Drove over to Sylvie's to check on her and Sydnie. I spent about an hour there. Then I went home, had dinner with the wife. Then sat in the garage for a bit and watched the Yankees game."

"Okay," Tommy said. "Is there anyone that can verify all of this?"

"Uh, yeah, actually there is," Nathan said, his eyes shifting up toward the ceiling. "You can check my timecard to see what time I left work. There're cameras there too. Sylvie can verify what time I was over there, and my wife can verify what time I got home. Oh yeah," he added. "And my neighbor, Chuck. Chuck came over and caught the last half of the game with me, in the garage."

"And what time was the game over?" Tommy asked.

"Around 11-11:30," he said.

"Okay, and what about after the game?" Tommy asked.

"Well, Chuck went home, and I went to bed. 5 am comes early," Nathan replied with a chuckle.

"Alright, Mr. Johnson," Tommy said. "If you'll just sit tight for a bit, I'll be right back with you."

Tommy returned to his desk and asked Bob to sit in with Mr. Johnson while he verified his statement. Bob agreed, and Tommy started making phone calls. He had already spoke with Sylvia and remembered her saying that Nathan had stopped by after work on Monday, so that was one less call he would have to make. His employer verified what time he left work that day, and he was able to locate Mr. Johnson's neighbor, Chuck, at his place of employment. He verified that he had been with Nathan Johnson, in the Johnson's garage until approximately 11:30 pm.

Tommy hung up the phone and sat there at his desk for a moment. He didn't want it to be Sydney's father, but the fact that it wasn't meant that he was back at square one. Tommy returned to the interrogation room to find Bob and Nathan Johnson laughing.

"Alright, your alibi checks out," he said as he entered the room and closing the door behind him.

"See," Nathan said. "Like I said, if it was me, I woulda told you."

"Well, I just want to thank you for being so cooperative," Tommy responded. "You're free to go."

"Thanks, detective," Nathan said. "And hey, good luck catching the guy that did this. He don't need to be out there runnin' around either. I'm glad that sick fuck is dead, but we don't need another one takin' his place."

"Thanks," Tommy said. "We'll inform you if we find anything."

Mr. Johnson left the room and Tommy turned to Bob. "If my gut is correct, Sydnie's uncles will have good alibis too," he said. "I don't think Sydnie Johnson's family had anything to do with it."

Tommy was able to get both of Sylvia's brothers, Jake, and Tyler Thomas to come in for questioning. He already knew that both men had prior records. Nothing lengthy, but enough to raise some eyebrows in this particular situation. Even though neither of Sydnie Johnson's uncles had had any run-ins with the law in quite some time, it would be downright foolish of Tommy not to question them. While interviewing Jake, Tommy got about the same reaction he did from Sydnie's father. Jake seemed cool and collected, expressing that he too would have turned himself in if he had been the one to find Arnold. It turned out that Jake was working late the night of the murder, which Tommy was able to verify with his employer.

Then came Tyler Thomas. Once he heard that they had found Arnold's body, Tyler broke down into tears. He folded his arms on the table and buried his face in between them.

"What's wrong?" Tommy asked, wondering if he was about to find out that his gut had been wrong.

"I'm just glad I didn't have to do it myself," Tyler said, looking up at Tommy. His large tears ran down both cheeks. "I didn't plan anything or anything like that. But I knew if I ever saw him again, I would kill him."

To no one's surprise, Tyler also ended up having a rock-solid alibi. He had been at a local sports bar watching the Yankees' game with some friends. The same Yankee's game that sealed Nathan Johnson's alibi. Tyler provided phone numbers for the people he was with, one of which happened to be the bartender who also happened to know Tyler outside of him coming into the bar. Tommy was able to verify that Tyler was there around the time the murder took place, so they were both free to go.

Tommy found himself, again, back at square one. As Jake and Tyler left the precinct, Tommy stayed behind in the interrogation room. He stared at two case files. The thicker one, belonging to Sydnie Johnson, Jackson Arnold's nine-year-old stepdaughter. He had raped and molested her several times before she finally told her mother. It was a casefile that he had spent many hours with already, trying to locate and arrest Arnold for a second time, after he was able to make bond and skipped town.

Tommy had everything in that file that he needed to make sure that Jackson Arnold spent plenty of time behind bars. The other file was much thinner. It now belonged to Arnold himself. The victim of a homicide in which there were no suspects, no clues, not a single shred of evidence to point him in even the faintest direction. It bothered Tommy that he didn't even know if this was a retaliation or just a random murder. But not near as much as the gut wrenching feeling he got when he thought about just how similar these two cases were to what happened with his own father. Down to the way in which they had been killed. For the Johnson family, their nightmare was over. For Tommy, the end of their nightmare, signified the beginning of his.

| 15 |

For months Tommy tried every angle he could think of to get anywhere at all with the Jackson Arnold murder case. And came up short at every turn. If you could even call them turns. November would soon be coming to a close and Tommy found himself just as close to finding Arnold's killer as he was to starting at shortstop for the Yankees next season.

He had primarily worked alone on this case, save his walks through the alley with Bob. He had checked every surveillance camera in the area he could find. Interviewed every all-night business in the area, just trying to get any bit of information. But he always seemed to hit a wall. No one had seen or heard anything. Not one single phone call had come in regarding this case. Not even any false leads or crank calls, which actually did surprise him.

Tommy felt as if he was the only one who knew that it had happened. He had discussed the case with other detectives, as well as Captain Spencer, just trying to maybe find a new tactic, a new angle, or something that would give him a bead on this case. *There has to be something,* he thought to himself constantly.

He walked out of the precinct and got in his car to head home but found himself driving to Owen's shop instead. He couldn't get his mind off the Arnold case and needed to talk to someone about it besides other detectives that had their own shit to worry about. He walked in the shop and straight back to the office as always.

"Hey, brother, what's up?" Owen said, peeking out of his office when he heard the bell ring at the front door.

"Same old shit," Tommy said, plopping down in a chair he had grabbed from behind the counter, on his way to the office.

"Owen looked away from his computer over at Tommy. "Wow, you looked stressed," he said, leaning back in his chair.

"I am," Tommy said. "I can't figure this damn case out."

"Which one?" Owen asked.

"The Jackson Arnold murder case," he said. "There's nothing, I mean *nothing*," he said, waving his arms in that same manner and umpire would if he were calling the runner "safe." "Whoever did this, didn't leave a damn trace of anything. Nothing from the preliminary search of the scene, nothing from the body, forensics, coroner, nothing. I'm at a loss."

"Wow," Owen said. "That's a lot of nothing. What about surveillance footage in that part of town?" he asked.

"Checked that too," Tommy said. "Everywhere I could find."

"You'll figure it out, man," Owen said. "I mean, there has to be *something*. You just need to step back from it. Look at the big picture, ya know?"

"Maybe," Tommy said. "I just don't know how the hell else I could look at it that I haven't already tried." They sat in silence for a long moment. "Anyway," Tommy continued. "What have you been up to? How are things here?" he asked.

"Not too bad. Business has been pretty steady," Owen said. "Had a lady come in the other day, apparently, she had just left a restaurant, where the waiter had tripped and spilled an entire plate of food down the front of her. I guess she got up and walked out and came straight here, because she was still wearing the top."

Tommy started to laugh.

"I told her I could take care of it, especially since it was still relatively fresh, but that I would have to have the garment," he continued. "This woman smiled, said, 'I'll wait,' and started to take her top off, right there at the counter."

Tommy laughed even harder. "Was she at least good looking?" he asked.

"Yeah, she was attractive," Owen said. "Just a couple years older than us, I'd guess. I stopped her, of course, and told her that as much as I could appreciated the urgency of her situation, I wouldn't be able to have it finished until later that day. She looked a little disappointed, but said she understood. She walked out, so I came back here to do some work. And about fifteen minutes later she walked back in wearing a different top, holding the soiled one in her hand."

Tommy was smiling, marveling at the day Owen was describing.

"So, I took the top, she left again and picked it up later that day." Owen said.

"Damn, man," Tommy said. "You shoulda got her number," he joked.

"Nah," Owen said. "Too rich for my blood."

Tommy could see behind Owen, as he turned back to his computer, that Rhiannon's note was still hanging on the cork board behind his desk. He wondered if that was just the new spot Owen liked to keep it or if he was bringing it with him to work every day. He thought about it for a moment, then pointed at the note.

"Are you packing that thing around with you?" he asked.

Owen looked back at the note pinned to the cork board. "Oh that," he chuckled. Tommy sat silent. "I just bring it with me sometimes," Owen said.

Tommy remained silent for a second more. "Dude, I love you, but it's been like four years," he said, staring at Owen. "I know that whole thing meant a lot to you. And I know you were crushed when she left, but don't you think it's time to maybe let go…just a little?"

Owen sat there staring at the computer screen, pretending to be engaged. "I just…," he paused. "Can't." He looked over at Tommy, hoping for some understanding. "I've tried," he continued. "You may not believe that, but I have. But even the thought of 'getting back out there' not only seems exhausting, but I also just feel like if I let go, I'll never find anything like it again."

"Yeah, but you don't know that for sure," Tommy said. The office fell silent again. "Can I ask you a question?" Tommy asked.

"You just did," Owen joked, halfheartedly.

Tommy chuckled. "Seriously. What is it about her? What's kept you hanging on all these years?"

Owen looked at him again, this time as if he had plenty to say. "If you woulda told me when we were kids, that she was the one I was going to fall in love with, I woulda fought you on the spot. I mean, you remember how she used to annoy the hell out of us, right?" A small laughed escaped his lips. Tommy nodded. "When I ran into her at the bar, I was excited to see her, because it had been years. Ya know, we're both adults now. But there was just something about her. The more time I spent with her, the further I fell. I couldn't help it. I didn't even try," he said smiling. "The truth is, every time I was near her, I felt like that was where I was always supposed to be. I hated letting that go. Letting her go."

"I know you did," Tommy said feeling a little sorry that he had forced his best friend to explain everything but wondering if he really minded. "Sorry, I was just curious."

"Don't be," Owen said. "I would probably ask you the same question, if it were reversed."

Tommy waited around with Owen while he finished up things in his office and closed up shop for the evening. He and Owen stood out on the sidewalk in front of the shop, chit chatting just a bit more before they parted ways. Tommy didn't say anything more about Rhiannon, but he did notice that Owen had taken the note off the cork board before he left his office. Tommy wondered again if that was his routine or if it had been something he had said.

| 16 |

Fall was in full swing now that the blistering New York summer heat had given way to cooler, more manageable temperatures. Which, in Tommy's experience, slowed things down just a bit as far as the call rate went. Not a lot, but just enough to notice. Thanksgiving was right around the corner and Tommy was very much looking forward to getting out of the city and back to Long Island to see his mother. He needed to try and take his mind off the Arnold case. Even if it was just for a few hours. Owen and Alison had picked up on it too. They drug Tommy to a Yankees game back in September to try and break the monotony of working this seemingly dead-end case. Tommy enjoyed it for the most part. Particularly when Derek Jeter smacked a three-run homer in the 8th to put the Yankees ahead. It wasn't lost on Owen or Alison that this case weighed on Tommy as much as it did. Alison may not have known exactly why beyond what Tommy had told her, but Owen did. Owen better than anyone knew why this case was affecting Tommy as deeply as it was.

The morning of November 19th, 2008, was a particularly cold, fall morning. The morning runners that frequented Central Park, seemed to be bundled up more than usual for that time of year. Some to hilarious degrees, providing quite the show for their fellow runners and the other park patrons. There seemed to be a dense haze blanketing the city, blocking all possibility of even a single ray of sunlight getting through. Tommy found this morning fitting. Fitting perhaps because it matched the current state of Tommy's mind. He walked into the precinct and followed the hallway back to the area affectionately known to NYPD detectives as the bullpen. The bullpen was a large, mostly noisy room, where the precinct corralled it's detectives like fenced off cattle with only a small field to graze in.

There were various weird smells that would come and go. Usually concocted from the smell of morning coffee and the weird shit some people bring for their lunches. And during the summer months you could add sweat to the list of smells. It also was the last place Tommy wanted to be today. He would have much preferred to have stayed at home with Alison, who happened to have the day off. Or to have talked Owen into taking a day off. Anything besides trying to drown out the noise of that room.

He continued into the bullpen, successfully making his way over to his desk without speaking to anyone or even drawing any attention to himself. He had gotten himself seated all the way down in his chair before remembering that he had intended to grab a cup of coffee before he got to his desk. This of course meant that he was going to have to walk all the way back across the bullpen. He got back up and headed for the coffee pot, trying to be as inconspicuous as he had been when he entered. And he almost made it.

While he was pouring his coffee, Mark Masterson, one of the other detectives, came up to him and shoved a fresh copy of the *New York Times* in his face.

"Can you believe this shit?" Mark asked, waving the paper in front of Tommy.

"What shit?" Tommy asked, not even bothering to glance at the paper.

"They're letting the son-of-a-bitch out," Mark said angrily. He turned to the paper to read the headline again.

"I haven't read the paper yet," Tommy said, barely paying Mark any attention. His main goal at the moment was getting back to his desk.

"Well, you need to," Mark said and once again shoved the paper in front of Tommy.

Tommy took the paper, folded it, and shoved it into his armpit. Without another word to Mark he started back toward his desk. He sat down in his chair and tossed the paper on his desk and sat his coffee next to it. Sifting through that day's edition of the Times didn't top the list of things Tommy had planned on doing to start his day. But he didn't have much else in mind past getting his coffee and planting himself at his desk.

Mark had followed him over to his desk prompting Tommy to grab the paper quicker than he had intended. He stared at the headline and couldn't help but feel a little intrigued himself.

Conviction Overturned, In 2005 Brown Homicide Case

The New York State Supreme Court, in a special session today, ruled that a 2005 murder conviction was to be overturned due to what one of the Justices called, "A miscarriage of procedural integrity by the New York Police Department."

Matthew Hammond was tried and convicted in the 2005 murder of his then girlfriend, twenty-nine-year-old Christina Brown. Police had arrested Hammond just three days after the murder, on a tip from a close friend of the victim, who told police that Brown had planned to end her relationship with Hammond on the night of her death. Hammond claimed multiple times during his trial that the officers that interrogated him, had violated his constitutionally protected rights several times during their questioning.

Once convicted and sentenced, Hammond's attorney immediately began filing appeals, stating: 'The New York Police Department failed to follow their own policies and procedures during Mr. Hammond's interrogation." Hammond claimed, during his trial, and in a written statement to his attorney, that during the interrogation he had not been read his Miranda Rights, and on several occasions, had been denied access to an attorney. Even though, according to his statement, he had repeatedly requested one.

After nearly three years of filing appeals, Hammond's case went before the New York State Supreme Court this morning, where judges were able to view the audio and video recordings of the interrogation, later determining that Mr. Hammond's rights, had in fact been violated. Attorneys for the Brown family brought before the Supreme Court, the evidence that had been used in the 2005/2006 trial, to convict Mr. Hammond of Ms. Brown's murder, claiming, the physical evidence was too overwhelming to overturn the conviction completely.

The District Attorney's Office did say that they plan to review the case, and possibly file new charges, but for now, Matthew Hammond remains a free man.

Tommy remembered the Brown case all too well. Christina Brown had been killed by a single gunshot to the head behind a gas station by her ex-boyfriend, Matthew Hammond. It happened during Tommy's first year with the department. Tommy had provided back-up, securing part of the perimeter for the detectives who served the warrant when Hammond was arrested. It was his first experience as a police officer with a homicide case.

Mark Masterson had pulled a chair up next to Tommy's desk, while he was reading and waited for him to finish.

"Ain't that some bullshit?" Mark asked as Tommy continued staring at the newspaper. "All that fucking evidence pointing straight to that little bastard, and he's gonna walk. They just look for any loophole they can find. It doesn't even matter what they've done. If we mess up one little thing on our end, boom, they can go free. Never mind what they're fucking guilty of."

Tommy wondered why Mark was so up in arms about this case being overturned. Sure, it wasn't justice in any sense of the word. Especially for the victim or victim's family. But Mark seemed overly upset about it being this case in particular.

"Was this your case?" Tommy asked.

"Hell no," Mark replied. "They wouldn't let me anywhere near it."

Tommy looked at Mark confused. It was a very rare circumstance for a detective to be singled out and told to stay away from an investigation.

"That son-of-a-bitch killed my niece," Mark said gritting his teeth. He dropped his head and stared at the floor.

"Wow," Tommy said. "I had no idea."

"Not too many people did," Mark said, looking back up at Tommy. He leaned in closer. "Wasn't exactly something that I wanted spread all over the place. After Christina was killed, the captain sat me down a few days later and told me that they had an arrest warrant for Matt. I couldn't believe it. I begged him to let me go, but he told me 'Absolutely not.' So, I had to sit back and watch during the arrest, during the trial, through the whole damn thing. The captain ordered me not to go anywhere near him. And now he's out."

"That's terrible," Tommy said and paused to let Mark regroup. "Well, they did say they're likely to file new charges."

"Yeah, what good is that going to do if the little cocksucker decides to skip town?" Mark asked, becoming more and more irate with the situation.

"I know, man," Tommy said. "Here's hoping he doesn't, and they can get him back behind bars where he belongs."

Tommy handed the paper back to Mark. The veteran detective stood up without another word and walked back to his desk. Tommy watched, almost able to physically see the weight pressing down on him. He truly felt for his fellow detective. He couldn't imagine being told to stay away from a case that involved someone he was that close to. Especially a homicide case.

Tommy spent the rest of his day trying to avoid looking at the Arnold casefile. He did everything he could to distract himself, but no matter what he found himself thinking about the case. He had already talked to everyone he could think of. He had, for quite some time now, stared tirelessly at everything there was to look at. And still he found nothing.

Quitting time finally came and Tommy disappeared from the precinct just as he had arrived, without saying a word to anyone. He stopped on the way home and picked up a pizza for dinner. When he got home, Alison was in almost the same spot on the couch she had been when he had left for work that morning. Tommy didn't blame her. If he had his way about it, he would have done exactly the same thing. Tommy told Alison about the Brown case, which she said she had heard mentioned on the news earlier that day and had planned to ask him about when he got home. He also told her about Mark Masterson and his background regarding the Brown case. Then, as usual, he filled her in on the lack of anything regarding the Arnold case.

Tommy sat next to her on the couch. He loosened his tie and the top few buttons of his shirt. He leaned forward trying to rub away the stress of the day from his eyes. Alison climbed in behind him on the couch and began rubbing his shoulders.

"Something's going to happen one of these days, and you're going to solve this case," she said.

"I sure hope so," Tommy said. "cause' it's eating me alive."

"Don't let it do that," Alison said with a small laugh. "That's my job."

Tommy couldn't help but smile. He could feel Alison smiling as well. She leaned down, pressing her chest against his back and wrapping her arms around his neck. He leaned his head against her, resting on his shoulder and squeezed her hand.

"I love you; you know that?" Tommy said, continuing to smile.

"I do," she said.

| 17 |

That Friday Tommy was actually looking forward to going into work. Mostly because he wanted to get the day over with so he could start the weekend. He had decided to take Alison's advice and actively try to not let this case drag him down. After all, Alison was probably right. Something *would* break in the case eventually; he just needed to be patient and wait it out. Try and focus on other things. He walked into the bullpen to the usual hustle and bustle that took place there and made his way to his desk. Just as he was about to sit down, Captain Spencer shouted from his office:

"Collins!" Captain Spencer shouted.

"Be right there, sir." Tommy replied.

He picked his coffee back up and made his way back through the maze of desked detectives to the captain's office. Once inside, he sat down wondering what the captain wanted to see him for. It usually wasn't good news.

"Tommy," Captain Spencer said. "You know I knew your father when he was with the department."

Tommy immediately began to wonder where this particular conversation was headed.

"He was a good cop," the captain continued. "Real tragedy, what happened to him."

If you only knew, Tommy thought. But his smile caged the thought behind his lips.

That was not a conversation he ever planned to have with his captain. Nor anyone else at the department. He couldn't imagine what hell he would unleash, not only on himself, but his mother, if he did.

"The reason I bring that up is because I know he would be proud of you," Captain Spencer said crashing through Tommy's thoughts and bringing his attention back to the conversation. "And I don't want you to get discouraged. I know this Arnold case has been tough. There hasn't been shit to go on. I get it."

Tommy didn't see what any of this had to do with his father, but he didn't interrupt the captain.

"Another body was found this morning in a parked car over on Lexington," Captain Spencer said. "And this is where it gets interesting," he paused. "It was Matthew Hammond."

Tommy immediately turned and looked through the glass door of the captain's office, out into the bullpen and directly at Mark Masterson.

"We don't know anything for sure…yet," Captain Spencer said. "This just looks an awful lot like the Arnold case. So, I'm putting you on it."

Tommy turned back towards the captain. "Any witnesses?" he asked, his mind still focused solely on Masterson.

"Nothing as of about forty-five minutes ago, when the call came in," Captain Spencer said. "Except the woman who found the body, she was out on her morning run. She said she thought he was just passed out until she got up to the driver side window and saw the blood. Then she freaked out and called 911. I want you to go down and check it out let me know what you think."

Tommy left the captain's office without another word and went straight back toward his desk. He sat down and immediately began thinking about the possibility of this being the same killer that sliced Jackson Arnold's throat. On the other hand, there was Masterson, who just a couple days ago, seemed ready to kill Hammond himself. In that initial moment, one possibility seemed as likely as the other. Tommy decided that as uncomfortable as it would be to question a fellow detective, he was going to have to talk to Mark. Hopefully, ruling him out as a suspect in the process. Tommy walked out of the precinct, got in his car, and started off toward Lexington Avenue.

When he arrived at the scene he noticed a patrol officer, who appeared to be taking a statement from a woman. Most likely the woman Captain Spencer had already mentioned. Tommy walked up to the officer and the woman and stood there, listening as the woman continued giving her statement to the officer. From what Tommy heard it was just a repeat what the captain had already told him, just in greater detail.

Tommy left the officer to continue taking the statement from the woman and walked over to the car containing the body. The body was slumped over in the driver seat. Blood covered the front of Hammond's shirt and the driver's door was locked from the inside. Tommy walked around to the passenger side of the car to find that the passenger door was unlocked. He opened the door and began peering inside the vehicle. He immediately noticed what appeared to be a muddy footprint on the carpet of the passenger side floorboard. *You're getting sloppy,* he thought as he turned his attention to the body.

He placed a latex glove on his left hand and reached inside the car. He placed his hand on Hammond's forehead and raised his chin to reveal a gaping neck wound. Tommy gently let Hammond's head back down and began looking at the rest of the interior of the vehicle. The inside of the car appeared to be spotless, (minus the footprint in the passenger side floorboard, and the blood from Hammond himself on the driver's side) as did the outside of the car. Tommy began looking at the area around the vehicle when he noticed that the forensics team was arriving at the crime scene. He met them at their vehicle and notified them about the footprint. He told them to make sure that they got photos of it.

Soon after the forensics team arrived, the coroner's van pulled up to the scene. Once they were given the go-ahead from the forensics team, the deputy coroners removed the body from the vehicle.

While the forensics team continued to work, Tommy went to the houses in the immediate vicinity of the crime scene and asked the residents if they had seen or heard anything the night before. Tommy was beginning to have the same run of luck he had had with the

Arnold case. Residents he talked to either weren't home or were home but had nothing to report that would have any bearing on the case.

Just as he finished talking to a woman at one house, Tommy noticed a man two houses down from where Hammond's car had been parked, had decided to come out and sit in his porch swing. Tommy approached the house, and the man maintained his place on the swing.

He was a black man, probably mid to late seventies. He was wearing a hat that said "Vietnam Veteran" across the front. Tommy noticed as he got closer that there was a dog loose in the man's yard. A beefy looking mut, who, if Tommy had to guess, was just as old as the man on the porch swing. The man sat on the swing. Still as a statue, staring unwaveringly at Tommy as he approached his property.

"Don't mind him, he won't bite." The man said as Tommy continued toward his house.

"Good morning, sir," Tommy said as he reached the steps in the man's front yard.

"Is it?" The man replied. "Usually not a good day when it starts with finding a body."

"How do you know there was a body?" Tommy asked.

"Well, first off, my name is Curtis Jenkins, just cause' I know you was gon' ask. And I saw that car pull up and park right there around midnight last night."

"Really?" Tommy asked, his curiosity peaked. "What else did you see, Mr. Jenkins."

"Well, I had to get up and let my dog out. Ol' grumpy ass wouldn't stop whinin' and he never leaves the yard, so I just sat here on my swing and waited for him to do his business." The man passed and appeared to swallow. "Anyway, while I'm sittin' here that car pulls up. There was two people in there when it pulled up. I didn't think anything of it. People come and go all hours of the night 'round here. Now I got a little chilly waiting on ol' Gunner down there, so I got up and stepped inside and grabbed my jacket. When I got back out here, one of them was standin' outside the car. He shut the door and walked off down the street, there."

The man lifted one unsteady arm and pointed a finger in the direction Tommy had come from.

"That was about that time, ol' Gunner finished up, so we went back inside. But that other fella was still sitting in the car. Again, I didn't think anything of it. I mind my own business."

Tommy was jotting down the details of Curtis Jenkins's eyewitness account as fast as Curtis could spit them out. He was after all, very forthcoming with all of his information.

"Mr. Jenkins, where are you from, originally?" Tommy asked as he finished jotting down the last of his notes. "You don't sound like you're from around here."

"You're right," Curtis said with a hearty chuckle. "Tennessee, originally," he said. "Got stationed out at Fort Devens, in Massachusetts, with the 196th Light Infantry Brigade. After we got back from Vietnam, I ended up at Fort Drum. And when my enlistment was up, I got out. I was unsure if I wanted to stick around or not. The city sure was poppin' back then. It was the place to be." Mr. Jenkins smiled at Tommy, and Tommy couldn't help but smile back. "But as luck would have it, I met a girl and decided to stay. We were married soon after we met. Happiest time of my life. She's gone now though. Been gone for about ten years now."

Tommy stood there listening to Curtis, wondering if he was probably the only person Mr. Jenkins had spoken to in a while. Curtis finished his trip down memory lane and sat there quietly on his porch swing.

"Well, Mr. Jenkins, I want to thank you for your time, and for your service to our country," Tommy said. "Please, sir, if you think of anything else, give me a call," he said handing Curtis one of his business cards.

"I will," Curtis said, taking the card from Tommy. "But I'm pretty sure that's all I remember."

Tommy turned around to leave Mr. Jenkins and head back toward the crime scene.

"Hey son," Curtis called out. Tommy stopped and turned around. "Best of luck," Curtis said, tipping his hat at Tommy. "Hope you get the bastard sooner, rather than later."

"I'll do my best, sir," Tommy replied.

He walked back to the crime scene feeling a little bit better about both the Hammond case and the Arnold case, than he had when he arrived. Someone had seen *something*. There was a figure. A shape. He now had to track down this shape, but it sure felt better than chasing smoke. From there

Tommy spoke with the forensics team to see if they had found anything else since the body had been removed.

"Find anything, Simon?" Tommy asked as he walked back up to the vehicle.

Simon Williams was one of the crime scene investigators. He and Tommy had started with the NYPD at around the same time. He was a short, skinny guy. Great at his job. He had an eye for evidence and his size allowed him to get into some places that other C.S.I.'s couldn't. He and Tommy had worked several crime scenes together throughout their careers, so far. Tommy trusted that if Simon was processing the crime scene, that it would be done thoroughly.

"Well, we documented the footprint," Simon said, standing up. "But nothing else, so far."

"Okay," Tommy said. "If you find anything else, let me know the second you do."

"You got it," Simon said.

Tommy then went to speak to the officer who had taken the woman's statement that had found the body.

Officer Joshua Rice was a young uniform, still in his first year with the department. Tommy had taken notice of him when he came from the academy, because he reminded Tommy of himself when he first started out.

"So, Rice," Tommy said, walking in his direction. "What all did she have to say, anything useful?"

"Mostly just a repeat of what she reported when she called it in," Officer Rice said. "Except, she said that after she realized that he was dead and she made the call, while she was on the phone with dispatch, she noticed a homeless man who had been sitting down the block, at the corner. She said he just got up and walked off. Could be something, could be nothing. She said he was white, average height, wearing a dirty green or blue jacket. Pants and a sock cap."

"We need to find this guy and see if he knows anything," Tommy said. "Good work, Rice," Tommy said, patting him on the shoulder and walking back over to where Simon was still processing the vehicle.

"Hey," Tommy called out to Simon. "This lady said she saw a homeless man sitting on the corner, when she discovered the body," Tommy said. "And while she was calling it in, he got up and took off. I'm gonna walk down to the corner and see if there's anything to see."

"Alright, just let me know," Simon said.

Tommy left the crime scene and walked down the block to the corner the women had identified in her statement. As he approached the corner, he didn't see anything that appeared to be unusual. Same old littered street corner that was all too common in the city. However, he did find that at that particular corner, there was an alley between that block and the next. He scanned the ground for anything seeming to be out of place but saw nothing. Tommy then peered around the corner and down the alley way, where he noticed two homeless guys sitting on the ground, leaned up against the side of one of the buildings. He stepped off the curb and started off down the alley towards the men. As he got closer, he noticed that one of them appeared to be wearing a jacket that matched the description the woman gave to Officer rice.

"Kinda cold out, isn't it?" Tommy asked the men as he got closer.

"Yeah, it is," one of the men said.

The other man, the one wearing the jacket in question, just laughed. Both men appeared to have been homeless for a while. Unkempt and dirty, carrying with them the stench of the New York City streets.

"How long have you guys been around this area?" Tommy asked.

"Oh, about a week now," the man in the green jacket said. "We move around every so often, get a change of scenery."

"Oh, it all pretty much looks the same in *this* city, doesn't it?" Tommy asked, jokingly.

"Yeah, I guess it does," the other man said with a chuckle.

"So, let me ask you a question," Tommy started. "If you've been in this area for about a week, what can you tell me about the body we found this morning, right around the corner?"

The two men's laughter stopped. They looked at each other, then back at Tommy. "We got nothing, sir," the man in the green jacket said. Tommy stiffened up.

"Well, I'll tell ya what I got," Tommy said. "I've got a statement from a witness that says they saw a man walking away from *that* corner," Tommy pointed toward where he had entered the alley. "Wearing *that* jacket, when they discovered the body this morning. That's what I got."

Tommy stood there pointing at the green jacket the man was wearing. The two men sat there. Their backs, literally against the wall, staring up at Tommy.

"Here's what's going to happen," Tommy said, in a more authoritative tone. "You two are going to come with me and we are going to go have a little chat.

The two men stood up in front of Tommy. "Gladly," the other man said, sticking both his hands out. His fists balled up, as if he were signaling Tommy to place him in handcuffs.

Tommy grabbed his phone and called Officer Rice and told him to come around the corner to his location. Once Rice showed up, Tommy instructed him to place the man in the green jacket in handcuffs, while Tommy place handcuffs on the other man. Tommy and Officer Rice then escorted the two men back around the corner to Officer Rice's cruiser. Rice places the man in the green jacket in the back seat, and Tommy place the other man in the back seat of his car. Tommy instructs Rice to follow him down to the precinct, and that they will place them in separate interrogation rooms.

"Make sure he stays restrained when you get there," Tommy said.

Just as Officer Rice got in his cruiser, the women that had discovered Hammond's body started over to where Tommy was standing.

"Excuse me, officer," she called out. Tommy looked around and realized that she was headed straight for him. He turned to face her and waited as she approached. "That was the jacket I saw, I'm almost positive. But that wasn't the man I saw wearing it. That, I'm sure of."

"What do you mean?" Tommy asked.

"The man I saw was taller, younger looking," she said.

Tommy turned and looked at the corner the woman had pointed out in her statement. "You could tell that the man you saw wearing the jacket was taller than the man we just took away, from this distance?" Tommy asked.

"Ninety-nine percent sure, yes," she said.

"So, then he must have been significantly taller than the guy we have?"

"Yes, he was definitely taller than him. He had to be around your height, maybe a little taller. I don't know. But that wasn't the guy."

"Okay. Thank you, Ma'am," Tommy said, climbing in his car. "If you think of anything else, please let us know." Tommy handed her one of his cards. The woman stared at it momentarily. nodded, and then walked away.

Tommy informed Simon that he was heading back to the precinct to question the two men he had detained. The whole drive back he thought about what the women had said. He thought about the figure Mr. Jenkins had reported seeing walking away from the car where Matthew Hammond's body was found. The woman's description of the man she saw walking away from the corner matched what Mr. Jenkins had reported. And neither description seemed to match either of the men he had detained. Except for the green jacket. But the woman seemed certain about the jacket. But not the man Tommy had found wearing it.

Once Tommy and Officer Rice arrived back at the precinct, they escorted the two men inside and placed them in separate interrogation rooms. Tommy spoke with Officer Rice before going in to speak with the first of the two men.

"Good job out there today, Rice," Tommy said. "Did he have anything to say on the way back?" Tommy asked.

"Nothing of any interest to the case," Officer Rice said. "He just talked about the weather and where in the city he was likely to end up next. It was funny though; he didn't seem to be the least bit worried about coming down here to be questioned. Even asked if we had hot coffee," Rice said.

"Hmm," Tommy said, gathering his thoughts. "Well, let's see what they have to say."

With that, Tommy grabbed two cups of coffee and went to the first interrogation room where the man in the green jacket was located. He presented himself a little less rigid than he had with the men in the alley way. He sat one of the cups of coffee down in front of the man in the green jacket, then sat down across the table from him and sipped his own cup of coffee.

"It's cold out there," Tommy said in a semi-friendly tone. "Drink up."

The man lifted his shackled hands and retrieved his cup of coffee and took more than the sip Tommy expected.

"First off," Tommy said. "I'm going to read you your rights. You have the right to remain silent. Anything you say can and will be used against you in a court of law. You have the right to an attorney. If you cannot afford an attorney, one will be appointed to you by the court. At any time during this interview, you have the right to exercise these rights and terminate the interview. Do you understand these rights, as I have read them to you?"

"Yes, sir, I do," the man said.

"Okay," Tommy started. "Let's start with your name."

"Cooper. Cooper Stevens," he said.

"Alright, Mr. Stevens," Tommy continued. "So, you said before, that you know nothing about the body that was found this morning."

"That's correct, sir," Cooper replied.

"So, how is it that you came to possess the jacket that my witness claims they saw a man wearing while leaving that area this morning?"

"Well, I woke up, in that alley, just after 7:00 this morning," Cooper explained. "I know that, because I walked to the other end of the alley and looked down the street and saw the clock outside the bank down there. I started thinking about what we were gonna do about some breakfast. So, I woke Allen up and we began digging in the cans in the alley. Didn't find shit until I came to the can near the end of the alley where you came from. That's where I found this jacket. I got nothing to my name, and it's colder than a polar bear's balls out there, so I put it on."

"Allen," Tommy said. "Is that the other man that was in the alley with you this morning?" Tommy asked.

"Yep, Allen Reynolds," Cooper answered.

"Did Allen see you pull the jacket out of the can?" Tommy asked.

Cooper hesitated. His eyes flicked as he searched his recollection of their morning hunt. "I don't know if he did or not," Cooper said. "I believe he was digging in one of the other cans. But I did show it to him right after I found it."

"And you have no idea how that jacket got in that trash can?" Tommy asked.

"Not at all," Cooper replied.

"Well, I know it's cold out there," Tommy said. "But I'm going to have to take that jacket. It's evidence now."

"By all means, take it," Cooper said. "I don't want the damn thing."

Tommy called for Officer Rice to come into the room and instructed him to remove Mr. Stevens's restraints and take the jacket and log it in as evidence. Once the jacket was removed, Officer Rice moved to put the restraints back on Cooper Stevens' wrists, but

Tommy waived him off. Cooper nodded in appreciation and continued drinking his coffee.

"Alright," Tommy said. "You're gonna sit tight for a few and I'm gonna go talk to your buddy Allen."

Cooper nodded again.

Tommy left the room believing that Mr. Stevens was telling the truth. He grabbed another cup of coffee and topped off his own, then walked toward the second interrogation room. When he entered the room he sat the cup of coffee down in front of Allen Reynolds, just as he had with Cooper Stevens. He began the interview the same confirming the man's name and reading Mr. Reynolds his Miranda Rights.

Allen Reynolds' statement confirmed exactly what Cooper Stevens had said during his interview, down to Cooper finding the jacket in a trash can. Allen Reynolds also claimed that he had no knowledge of how the jacket ended up in the trash can at the end of the alley, and before long, Tommy concluded that interview as well.

He had guessed when the woman at the scene told him that Cooper Stevens wasn't the man, she saw wearing the green jacket earlier that morning, that the two men wouldn't have much more information to offer than what they did in the alley way. Tommy thanked them for their cooperation, and then he personally escorted them out of the precinct.

"Gentleman," Tommy said as the three of them exited the building. "I want to apologize for disrupting your morning and thank you again for your cooperation. I hope that you can understand my position under the circumstances."

"We can," Cooper said.

"Yeah, this ain't the first time we've been questioned by the cops," Allen added. "We just try to stay out of the way."

"Listen guys," Tommy said reaching into his back pocket and pulling out his wallet. He pulled out a one-hundred-dollar bill. "Here's for the jacket," he said handing the bill to Cooper Stevens. "And I want you guys to get some food."

Cooper took the bill from Tommy's hand, staring at it as if he had just won the New York State Lottery. The men both thanked Tommy and then were on their way.

Tommy walked back inside the precinct to the bullpen and sat back down at his desk. *Two murders,* he though. *Possibly the same killer.* He sat there for only a moment longer, then got up and walked toward Captain Spencer's office and knocked on the door.

"Come in," Captain Spencer said still flipping through some papers on his desk.

"Sir," Tommy said. He walked in and took a seat. "I think you were right. This looks a lot like the Arnold case. Only this time, we have a shred of evidence, and a witness."

"Which is?" Captain Spencer asked.

"Well, there was a muddy footprint in the passenger floorboard of the car. And our eyewitness, Curtis Jenkins, who lives about four doors down from where the car was parked, said that he had been out on his porch letting his dog out when the car pulled up. He said that here were two men in the car when it arrived. He stepped inside to grab a jacket and when he came back outside, the passenger was outside of the car and took off walking in the opposite direction. He said that the driver was still sitting inside the car, but he didn't think anything of it. He just went back inside when his dog was finished."

Captain Spencer sat at his desk for a moment. His hands folded together. "What about the two men you brought in this morning, for questioning?" he asked.

"Well, I think our killer stuck around," Tommy said.

"How so?" the captain asked.

"So, the woman that initially called in the body said in her statement to Officer Rice, that after she discovered the body and called 911, she noticed a man sitting down the block at the corner. She said that the man got up and walked away while she was on the phone and described to Rice, the jacket he was wearing. I walked down the street and found a couple of homeless guys in the alley, one of which was wearing a jacket that matched the description the woman gave in her statement. I brought them in for questioning and took the jacket as evidence. They didn't have much to offer as far as information goes. They both claimed that the jacket was found in a trash can in the alley. Plus, as we were putting them in the car, the woman approached me and claimed that Cooper Stevens, the guy who had the jacket on in the alley, was not the same guy she saw wearing the jacket earlier. She said the man she saw was taller and younger looking."

"So, what's your next move?" Captain Spencer asked.

"Well, that's the tough part," Tommy said. Captain Spencer looked at him, confused. Tommy dropped his head. He knew the gravity of what he was about to say. "I think we need to question Mark Masterson."

| 18 |

"What?!" Captain Spencer said, raising his voice.

Tommy waited for the reverb of the captain's voice to fade out before speaking again.

"Sir, I understand, but the day that Hammond's conviction was overturned, Masterson brought me the article and seemed pretty upset about it," Tommy said, explaining his reasoning to the captain." "

"Mark told me that during Hammond's arrest and trial, you had ordered him to stay away from Hammond as well as the investigation. Why was that?" Tommy asked.

"Are you interrogating me now, son?" the captain asked.

"No sir, just asking a question," Tommy said quickly realizing his mouth may have worked a little faster than his brain.

"Of course, I did," Captain Spencer replied. "You should have seen how distraught he was. He was barely fit to return to work, let alone have anything to do with that case. Plus, it was a conflict of interest. A big one. I just wanted him to keep his head straight and not do anything stupid."

"Exactly," Tommy said. "And Hammond's release obviously jump-started all of those old emotions and feelings." Tommy prayed that the captain would see and understand his point. "Only this time, he wasn't ordered to stay away," Tommy continued

Tommy paused for a second, giving the captain time to consider what he was saying.

"Now, I'm not saying he's guilty, but knowing his feelings about the case being overturned, his connection to the victim, I think we at least need to rule him out."

The room fell silent. Captain Spencer sat at his desk thinking about everything Tommy had just laid out for him. "Okay," Captain Spencer said. "But I want this done tactfully. And I don't want any serious accusations made. All we need to do is find out where he was when the murder took place."

"Agreed," Tommy said.

"I want it done in here," Captain Spencer said. "If we find anything solid, if he has no alibi, then we can move it to a room, but what I don't want, is the media getting wind of us questioning one of our own in this case. They'll have a fucking field day with that."

"Works for me," Tommy said.

Captain Spencer got up from his chair and walked to the door of his office. "Masterson!" he shouted, signaling for him to step into his office.

Mark walked in and took a seat next to Tommy. "What's up, Cap?" Mark asked.

"Mark," the captain started. "We need to ask you some questions."

"Okay," Mark said, sitting there puzzled. "We need to know where you were when Matthew Hammond was killed." Captain Spencer said.

"What the fuck, guys, come on!" Mark replied, throwing his hands in the air. "What, you think I killed the little bastard?" Mark asked.

"That's not what we're saying," Tommy interjected, turning in his chair toward Mark. "Listen, we just need to rule you out. Your niece was the victim in his case. Understandably, you're feeling pretty pissed off about that conviction getting overturned. You're honestly the perfect suspect," Tommy said.

Mark scowled at Tommy. "You little prick, who the fuck do you…,"

"Mark, listen," Tommy started. But the room only filled with the jumble of their two voices, each trying to be heard over the other.

Captain Spencer sat shaking his head for a moment then slammed his fist down on his desk. "Enough!" he shouted. And the room fell silent. He stared at both of them. "Tommy," he started. "I said 'tactfully.' I didn't say beat him with it and see what he has to say."

"Sir, I just...,"

"Shut up," the captain said calmly. "And Mark," he continued. "Tommy's right."

Mark's face paled with disbelief.

"You *are* the perfect suspect, and for the reasons Tommy just described. That's why we are having this conversation. Not because we think you did it, but because we want to take care of it before the media catches wind of it. If they even do. Either way, we want to be ready. And you should too."

Mark sat there looking at the floor. Both Tommy and Captain Spencer felt like assholes for even bringing any of this up to him. But they also knew that it had to be done. Mark raised his head and looked at the captain, then at Tommy. They could see the tears welling up in his eyes.

"I get it, man." Mark said, looking at Tommy. "I would do the same thing if I was in your position. It's just a hard thing to hear, ya know?" Mark paused. The air in the room felt a little less heavy. "The truth is," Mark continued. "I was at home all night last night. And the only one that can verify that is Diane." Tommy sat, giving Mark a second to gain his composure.

"Are you alright with me calling Diane to verify?" Tommy asked, trying to ease the question at Mark.

"I don't give damn," Mark said. "Hell, call her right now."

Captain Spencer stared at Tommy and Tommy nodded back at him. The captain reached forward, picking up the phone sitting on his desk. "You're sure about this, you wanna call her now?" the captain asked.

"Yeah, let's get it over with," Mark replied.

"Just one thing though, can I explain to her what's going on?" Mark asked. "I don't want her thinking that something is wrong, or something happened to me, because one of you are calling. She'll freak out as soon as she hears one of your voices."

"Sure thing," Captain Spencer said. Tommy nodded in agreement.

Mark took the phone and dialed his home number, then pushed the speakerphone button so all three of them could hear. The phone rang once, twice, three times before Mark's wife, Diane answered the phone.

"Hello," Diane answered, sounding worried.

"Hey baby, it's me," Mark said.

"Oh, hey," Diane said.

"I got a little worried, this isn't your desk phone, but I knew it was from the department.

"No baby, I'm in with Captain Spencer, and Detective Collins," Mark said. "Listen baby, I need you to verify where I was last night."

"Why, what's going on, Mark?" Diane asked in a concerned voice.

"I'm going to explain, honey, but right now I just need you to verify where I was last night," Mark continued.

"You were at home," Diane said.

"Okay," Mark said. "And what time did I get home?" he asked Diane. Her breathing was staring to get heavier as the confusion grew bigger and bigger.

"Around 5:30," Diane said. "What is going on, Mark?"

"Okay baby, last question," Mark said. "Did I leave the house at all last night after I got home?"

"No," Diane replied, realizing now, that she needed to give all the information she could. "We had dinner shortly after you got home, then sat down and watched a movie, then went to bed around 10:00."

Mark looked at the captain, then at Tommy. Tommy nodded his head in approval.

"What is going on, Mark?" Diane asked, again, starting to sound inpatient.

"Honey, Matt Hammond was found dead this morning." Mark said.

"What?" Diane replied. The phone fell silent for a moment before she spoke again. "Wait, what? And they thought you…"

"No, no, no, baby," Mark interrupted. "No one is accusing me of anything. It's just with Christina being my niece, and him getting released and now turning up dead, they had to rule me out as a suspect before someone *did* try to accuse me." The phone fell silent again, then the sound of Diane crying crept across the phone line.

"What's the matter, baby?" Mark asked.

"I know this is so wrong of me to say," Diane said. "But I'm just glad it's over and we don't have to worry about him anymore."

"I know, baby," Mark said.

"May I?" Captain Spencer whispered to Mark. Mark nodded his head at the captain and turned the phone toward him on his desk.

"Diane," Captain Spencer said. "It's Dave Spencer."

"Hi Dave," Diane said, composing herself. "It's been a while."

"Yes, it has," Dave replied. "Listen, I just want you to hear it from me that this was all just a formality. Neither I, nor Detective Collins thought for one second that Mark had anything to do with this."

"I know," Diane replied. "I know you're just doing your job. It's just a tough phone call to get, ya know. A lot of questions and information all at once."

"I completely understand," Captain Spencer said.

"Well, I'm gonna turn you back over to Mark."

"Hey babe," Mark said. "Listen, I'm gonna go ahead and go, but I'll call you in a little bit, okay?" Mark said.

"Okay," Diane replied. "I'll talk to you in a bit."

"Okay, I love you," Mark said.

"Love you too," Diane said.

Mark hung up the phone and slid it back across Captain Spencer's desk. "So, are we good here?" he asked, looking at both Tommy and the captain.

"Yeah, I think we are," Tommy replied.

"Mark," Tommy said. "On a personal note, I hope you really believe what you said. That we weren't accusing you of killing Matthew Hammond."

"I know," Mark said. "You did what you had to do. It wasn't an easy thing to do, but you did it anyway. You got some balls, kid."

"Thanks," Tommy said.

Mark looked at them both, then got up and left the office. The sound of the door closing behind him filled the office like the firing of a cannon.

"Shew," Tommy said to Captain Spencer. "That was rough."

"Yeah," Captain Spencer said. "But Mark was right. It *was* a tough thing to do. And even after my initial reaction, you went through with it anyway. Bold move, Tommy."

"Thank you, sir." Tommy stood up gathering his things and moved toward the door of the captain's office.

"Where ya headed?" Captain Spencer asked.

"I'm gonna see what surveillance footage I can find for that area," Tommy said. "See if I can get a visual on our mystery passenger and see if I can get any idea where the vehicle was coming from."

"That's as good a start as any." Captain Spencer said.

Tommy left the precinct and drove back toward the crime scene. He checked with some businesses around the area and asked to see their surveillance footage. He was able to find footage of the vehicle approaching the spot where it was found parked, but not a clear shot of the passenger, even as he walked away from the scene. He was also able to trace the route of the vehicle back, but not far enough to see where the passenger had entered the vehicle. When Tommy returned to the scene, Simon Williams was finishing up with the vehicle.

"Tell me you found something, Simon," Tommy said, approaching the car.

"Not a damn thing," Simon said.

"Shit!" Tommy exclaimed. "What about the footprint?" Tommy asked.

"Not sure yet, but I don't think we're gonna get much off of it," Simon replied. "I mean, unless we have a shoe and an owner to go with it, it's really not much help."

Tommy stood there for a minute, knowing that Simon was right. Still, he could feel the weight of not knowing which way to go next. *Just like the Arnold case,* he thought. Tommy left the crime scene, feeling as if he was being tossed around in the wind, blowing aimlessly from place to place with no particular purpose. He had nothing to go on but a jacket and a figure. Some would say, that was still more than he had before. But for Tommy, he felt as if he were trying to catch a shadow. A shadow that only came out at night.

| 19 |

Tommy, Alison, and Owen carpooled back to Long Island for a Thanksgiving dinner with both, Owen's parents, and Tommy's mother. They all gathered in the Christopher's dining room to share the dinner their mother's had prepared. According to their mothers, Owen's father was of no help, planting himself firmly on the couch, keeping up the tradition of watching football until they arrived. Everything seemed perfect. The spread was amazing. There was Turkey, of course. Surrounded by most of your traditional Thanksgiving side dishes. Mashed potatoes, green beans, gravy, and of course, Owen's mother's broccoli casserole. Everyone ate their fill, then the parents took turns telling stories on Tommy and Owen from their younger days, trying to embarrass them. Anything they thought would get a laugh out of Alison. And though she did laugh heartily, as did everyone else, she later revealed that Tommy and Owen had already shared most of their youthful shenanigans with her.

Around 10:00 pm that night the three of them decided to head back to the city. Alison, who shared a little too much wine with Tommy and Owen's mothers, talked most of the way back to the city about how much she loved both their parents. She always felt welcome anytime they visited.

They arrived back in the city, stopping first at Owen's apartment to drop him off. They pulled up in front of his building, where both he and Tommy exited the car.

"Hey," Tommy said jumping out of the car and running up to the door. "I'm off work tomorrow. I'm gonna swing by and we can discuss the engagement party."

"Sounds good to me," Owen said, turning the knob, and opening the door to his building.

"I'll see ya then." Tommy waved and turned back toward the car.

He got inside and started driving toward his and Alison's apartment building. Alison sat there in the passenger seat glancing over at Tommy and smiling every so often. Tommy caught this in his peripheral vision but tried not to let on that he saw her. When they arrived at their apartment building, Tommy parked and rushed around to open Alison's door.

"My handsome man," she said as she exited the car. "Aren't you just the sweetest."

She leaned forward and kissed Tommy. The chilled winter wind wrapped around them causing Alison to shiver as they kiss ended.

"Ooh, it's chilly," she said, smiling at Tommy. "Let's get upstairs."

They walked into the building and got on the elevator and exited once they got to their floor. Once they entered their apartment, Tommy walked into the kitchen to grab something to drink and Alison took off toward the bedroom, flinging her purse and jacket onto the dining room table as she passed.

Tommy stood there at the counter and poured himself a small glass of Woodford Reserve. He swished it around in the glass, admiring the shades of brown and amber as the bourbon flowed in a circular motion around the bottom of the glass like a tilt-a-whirl. The deep bourbon smell tickled his sense of smell. He brought the glass to his lips, threw his head back with the glass following closely, and took the drink in one quick swallow. He could feel the warmth of the bourbon coursing throughout his body like a cold chill, only warmer, and with the same goose pimple effect on his body. A warm chill.

Just as he sat the glass back on the counter, he caught Alison, again in his peripheral, entering the room. He turned to look at her and there she stood, leaning up against the doorway of the kitchen, wearing a black, see-through bra, with matching panties that left absolutely nothing to the imagination. Tommy stared at her, marveling at her beauty and her body. She smiled and started walking toward him. She grabbed him by the shirt and pulled him in closer to her and whispered in his ear.

"Do you like what you see?" she asked.

"Absolutely," Tommy whispered back.

"Well then," Alison continued. "It's all yours. You better come take what's yours."

Alison kissed him softly on the cheek and smiled. She let go of his shirt and turned around and walked toward the bedroom. Tommy stood there stunned, frozen in place, watching Alison walk out of the kitchen. He started toward the bedroom and entered, finding Alison leaned back on the bed waiting for him. Shadows bounced off the walls as the soft orange glow of candles flickered throughout the room. Alison got up off the bed and walked toward him. She lifted his shirt and began kissing his chest while undoing his belt. Tommy's pants fell to the floor as Alison's lips made their way up to his. She gasped in the split second her lips left his body to find his own and then pressed firmly against them. He ran his hands down to her waist and squeezed, prompting her to pull him in even closer. She moved backward toward the bed, slowly, not releasing him from the kiss for even a second.

When she reached the bed, she sat down and laid back and pulled him down with her. Tommy left her lips and began kissing her neck as her body began to rise and fall like a wave in the ocean. Up then down, and then back up again. Tommy's hand grazed her body. Every caress calculated. He knew exactly where she liked to be touched, and how.

Alison's breathing began to speed up as his hands roamed free. Her hands were slowly sliding down his back. Her nails pressed against his skin digging in with only the tiniest sliver of restraint. She could feel him touching her, teasing her as the two moved tangled up in their passion.

Tommy reached down and grabbed her panties and pulled them to the side, revealing all of her. Again, he teased her and watched as her body rose and fell. He could feel her moving around his fingers.

Reacting to them. He leaned forward and kissed her stomach, and then came back upright again. He moved forward, ever so slightly, and put himself inside her. Alison let out a gasp as Tommy entered her and kept going. Back and forth, Tommy moved. Slowly increasing his pace second by second. Alison began breathing heavier and heavier each time he thrusted himself into her.

"Harder," Alison begged. "Don't stop."

Tommy watched her body. He memorized everything about it. The way it moved. The way the shadows moved across it in the candlelight. She moaned involuntarily as pleasure radiated throughout her body. Each sound coming at exactly the right moment. They moved in almost perfect unison as their bodies clashed against one another in the fit of sexual mania they were creating. Faster and faster Tommy moved. In and out.

"I'm almost there," Alison said, between breaths.

Her screams were getting louder. She could feel the sensation rising. Her body was reaching for it. Fully extended. She wanted to grab it. Squeeze and release. It was right there, grazing her physiological fingertips. She could feel it building, swelling, ready to explode.

"Now--n-now," Alison shouted, but Tommy didn't stop.

He pressed on and maintained his pace. He watched and felt her body begin to quiver as she came. She grabbed him and gripped him as tight as she could. When her eyes opened again, she stared first at his face, then at his body, lustily watching what he was doing to her.

She could feel it building again. She looked up at him and their eyes met. She took notice of the sweat beading on his chest and rolling down his body. It was coming faster now. And before she even had time to reach for it, she closed her eyes and threw her head back

"I'm gonna come again," she said, the words barely escaping her lips in the instant before her body tensed up and began to quiver once more. Tommy wrapped his arms around her and pulled her close to him as he found his release as well.

Still bound together, both physically, and in their passion, they collapsed on to the bed. Neither one was able to catch their breath.

Tommy rolled over onto his back and stared at the ceiling which seemed to be moving in waves. His legs hung off the side of the bed. After a moment, Alison crawled over to him, her arms, and legs only partially useful, and lay beside him in the same position.

"That––was amazing," she said, in two separate breaths.

A smile fell across Tommy's face. "Yes, it was," he said, working to catch his own breath.

They lay there for just a moment before Alison rolled over and laid her head on his chest. She ran her fingers down the center of his stomach.

"I love you, so much," she said, looking up at him.

Tommy looked back at her, smiling again. "I love you too," he said.

They stayed in that position until both of them almost fell asleep. Alison rolled back over to her back and stretched. She reached her arms above her head and curled her legs upward. Tommy lay there with his hands on his chest, watching her, laughing.

"You're too damn cute, you know that?" he said.

She smiled, squinting her eyes as she finished her stretch.

Alison got up and walked over to her dresser. She opened the drawer and stared inside, trying to decide what pajama pants she wanted to wear. Tommy got up and grabbed a pair of shorts from his dresser, put them on and climbed back in their bed. He sat there watching Alison change from her seductive, see-through lingerie, into her pajama pants and an oversized t-shirt. He admired her. He cherished her. He loved everything about her.

She climbed in the bed next to him and placed her head on his chest as always. He turned the TV on and found something mindless that they could fall asleep to. His focus was still on her. He held her close, and they both drifted off to sleep.

The next morning Tommy woke up around 7:00 am. He had the day off, but Alison had to work, so he decided to make her a pancake breakfast before she had to go in. He made too many, as he always did. He finished up just as Alison came shuffling out of the bedroom, and into the kitchen.

"Mmm," she said, in a sleepy tone. "Smells good in here."

She made her way to the barstool at the counter, sitting down and leaning on her elbows. Tommy grabbed a plate and put three pancakes on it, knifing a bit of butter on each one and smothering them in syrup. He sat the plate in front of Alison, whose eyes widened at the sight of her breakfast, and a child-like smile crept across her face.

All Tommy could do was laugh at her. He grabbed a cup and poured her some orange juice, which didn't last long. She finished it in no more than a couple gulps.

Tommy sat his own plate of pancakes on the counter, across from Alison's. "I'm going to go hang out with Owen at the shop, see what he's up to."

"I wish I had the day off," she replied. "I'll be at work."

"That sounds fun," Tommy said, sarcastically. Alison merely looked up from her plate, giving a half smile.

"Just be careful," he said.

She knew that Tommy worried about her being out in the city alone. He had seen firsthand what type people were roaming the streets. She didn't show any hesitation when he brought home a bottle of pepper spray for her to carry in her purse.

They sat and finished their breakfast together, passively commenting on the previous night's events. Each passively complimenting the other on their performance in the bedroom through smiles and glances.

Alison finished her pancakes and went to the bedroom to get herself ready for work, while Tommy cleaned up the breakfast mess he had made in the kitchen. Once he was finished, he threw on some clothes, said goodbye to Alison, who was begrudgingly ready to walk out the door herself, and left the apartment.

The instant he sat down in his car, he began thinking about the Arnold and Hammond cases. These two cases had plagued his every free moment since the idea popped into his head that it could be the same killer. Forensics had processed the green jacket from the Hammond crime scene and found nothing but traces of the garbage from inside the can where it was found. As far as the fleeting shadow he was chasing after, no traces there either. Tommy felt relieved that someone had seen this person leaving the crime scene and that the killer had possibly stuck had around, but the relief never lasted long. Having so little to go on, coupled with the only increasing probability of more victims wouldn't sit well with anyone. It sure didn't with Tommy.

He arrived at Christopher's Cleaners and hurried inside to get out of the cold New York air funneling its way down the street and between the buildings. He walked in to see Owen at the front counter discussing a wine stain with a customer who was concerned that their clothing was now permanently ruined. Tommy walked directly behind the counter and back to Owen's office where he sat down and got on the computer. He pulled up Solitaire to play until Owen was finished with his customer. After a few moments Owen made his way back to the office.

"What's up, bro?" Owen asked.

"Almost done," Tommy replied, staring intently at the screen.

"So, I was thinking about this proposal," Owen continued. "I definitely think you should do it at the engagement party."

Tommy sat silent for a moment, still focused on the screen. "There, I beat it!" Tommy exclaimed, sliding the mouse forward and sitting back in Owen's chair. "What were you saying?" Tommy asked, smiling at Owen.

"The party, dipshit," Owen said. "You should propose at the party."

"You think so?" Tommy asked.

"Yeah, it's perfect," Owen said. "She's already not expecting the party, she *definitely* won't be expecting a proposal on top of that."

Tommy thought for a minute, spinning side to side in Owen's chair. "That's a good point," Tommy said. "Everyone *will* already be there. Good idea, buddy."

"So, you stayin' busy?" Tommy asked.

"It's been steady," Owen replied. "A lot of repeat business. How about you?" he asked.

"Oh, ya know, still runnin' in circles," Tommy said.

"Still nothin', huh?" Owen asked.

"Not a damn thing," Tommy said. "So, listen, I'm gonna need your help setting up the party. I'm taking her out for an early dinner at Puglia's, and I need someone to get everyone to the apartment and have everything ready before we get back."

"I can do that," Owen said.

"Awesome," Tommy said.

The bell hanging over the front door of Christopher's Cleaners chimed. Owen glanced back over his shoulder to see the silhouette of a customer entering his store.

"I'll be right back," Owen said, turning and walking out of the office.

Tommy sat back up in the chair, re-focusing on the computer and starting a new game of Solitaire. After he finished, and not so successfully this time, Owen was still at the front counter helping other customers that had come in. Tommy made his way out of the office and toward the front door. He opened the door, grabbing Owen's attention and waving goodbye to him as he stepped out.

The air seemed colder, sharper than when he went in. Cutting almost to the bone. Tommy walked toward his car and began thinking about Cooper Stephens and Allen Reynolds, having nowhere to go, being stuck out in this weather. *That must be terrible,* he thought. He felt bad for people in their position, those two specifically. They seemed like nice enough guys to him.

Tommy stopped and grabbed some lunch from Subway. Spicy Italian foot long, on wheat, toasted, with a large Coke and a bag of Barbeque Baked Lays. He always ordered the same thing. After getting his food, Tommy went back home and planned to spend the rest of his day on the couch watching mindless television. So that's what he did. He walked in and sat his food on the kitchen counter and walked into the bedroom to change. He threw on some basketball shorts, kept on the t-shirt he had thrown on that morning, and returned to his food. He grabbed it off the counter and planted himself on the couch.

The TV didn't have a lot to offer, so he settled for a re-run of *Friends*. A show which Tommy had seen every episode of, several times, and got a laugh every single time. In some cases, he would even be able to tell you what was going to happen in the entire episode just by watching the opening scene or hearing someone talk about a scene from an episode.

Tommy waited a while after lunch and found himself hungry again. He grazed in the kitchen and then back to the living room once he had amassed a couple handfuls of snacks. Alison came home around 5:30 that evening. She walked in and couldn't help but laugh at the sight of Tommy on the couch, surrounded by single serving sized chip bags and snack cake wrappers.

"Had yourself a real productive day, did ya?" she asked still laughing.

She sat her purse and car keys down on the table. Took off her white lab coat with her hospital ID clipped to front and draped it of a chair next to the door. She walked over toward the couch and sat down next to Tommy.

"I did exactly what I wanted to do today." He replied, chomping on a chip, and smiling.

"Well good for you, babe," Alison said, rubbing his head, and mimicking the way you would talk to a puppy or a small child. "I, on the other hand, had a hell of a day."

"Yeah?" Tommy said, shoving another few chips in his mouth.

"Yeah," Alison said. "Anything that could happen, did happen. We had six broken bones, four head traumas, three car wrecks, and two gunshot wounds."

"And a partridge in a pear tree," Tommy sang, smiling proudly and laughing at the joke he had just made at Alison's expense.

She lifted her head and gazed at him, wondering if some screw had come loose during his "productive day." It only took her a second, but she began to laugh as well.

| 20 |

December 11th, Tommy, and Alison's fifth anniversary (and oh, what a wonderful five years it has been) began with the two of them lying awake in bed. Alison, as she could usually be found, had her head on Tommy's chest with her arm draped across his stomach. It was around 9:00 am. A time at which the both of them would usually be out of the house having gone their separate ways to work. Tommy off to the bullpen surrounded by chatter and case files. Or off at a crime scene somewhere in some cordoned off section of the concrete jungle. Alison making rounds at the hospital, seeing patient after patient, doing her best ease their pains and cure their ales. But not this morning.

This morning was theirs, and they were taking it. They lay there silent, watching the morning sunlight fill up the room as it pierced its way through their bedroom window and onto the walls. Alison repositioned herself, climbing on top of Tommy and straddling his waist. She leaned forward and placed her hands around his shoulders. Her un-brushed hair still showing the signs of just waking up, flowed down toward his face, shrouding their faces in an unkempt veil of her hair. He looked up at her wondering to himself, how he got so lucky. *She really is the whole package,* he thought.

She stared deep into his eyes for a few seconds and with a soft, sincere whisper said: "I am so in love with you." Tommy sat upward, kissing her as deeply as he possibly could. He pulled her body closer to his. They made love on their morning. Slow, passionate, unbridled love. The kind of love making that shakes you to your very core and leaves your once independent souls tangled and intertwined and floating about the stratosphere.

They didn't escape euphoric clutches of their bed until around 10:00 am that morning. They lazily made their way into the kitchen where they sat and enjoyed only their morning coffee and each other's company. Glances and infatuated smiles made up most of the conversation. Their understood silence surrounded by the distant buzz and hum of the busy New York City streets

Tommy had spoken with Owen once more about the anniversary/engagement party over the phone since visiting him at the shop. Owen assured him that he had everything under control and that all he had to do was get Alison to dinner and back to the apartment. Tommy was eternally grateful for Owen's willingness to oversee the party. Not that he would expect anything less from his best friend, but he found himself overwhelmed with all the natural nervousness a man goes through when preparing to propose to the woman he loves. Even though he was sure she would say, "yes."

"I have something for you," Tommy said, reaching to. The top of the refrigerator and pulling down an envelope and handing it to Alison.

Her already permanent smile widened even further as she took the envelope from Tommy and began to open it. Inside the envelope were three gift certificates. One for a morning massage at a parlor Alison had talked about going to for months but had never made the time for herself to go. A second for a manicure and pedicure at the same nail salon where she would treat herself every so often, when, as she would say, wanted to make herself feel pretty. And a third for an afternoon appointment at her favorite hair salon, so she could doll up however she wanted.

Alison's lit up with a new excitement for the day that Tommy had laid out for her.

"Thank you!" she said, walking around the kitchen counter and hugging him.

"You better get going," he said. "I need you back here by five."

Alison looked at him with a happy suspicion but didn't say a word. She left their apartment about fifteen minutes later to set out on her day of pampering. Tommy had nothing to do but wait around for her to get back, so that's what he did. He tidied up around the apartment and prepped it as much as he could for Owen. After that he just sat and watched TV. Sure enough, Alison came walking through the door at 5:00 on the dot.

She walked into a freshly groomed Tommy, standing in the middle of their living room. He wore a black suit, complete with white dress shirt, black tie, and black dress shoes. His left arm behind his back in parade rest fashion, and a single red rose in his right hand. The room was dimly lit by a few strategically placed candles flickering in the darkness causing the shadows to dance around on the walls behind him.

Alison stood there, slightly shocked at first. Tommy walked toward her. He presented her with the rose, then leaned in and whispered in her ear, "You should get dressed," he said.

Alison took the rose from his hand and placed it under her nose. She closed her eyes and deeply inhaled its fragrance. She smiled and softly kissed him on the lips and walked away toward the bedroom. Tommy waited in the flickering candlelight pacing around the room, the way a father-to-be would wait just outside the door of the room where his wife was giving birth to their child.

It only took about fifteen minutes seeing as how her hair and nails had already been checked off the ever-increasing list of things women need to do to get ready. Tommy heard the small, familiar click of their bedroom door opening behind him and turned toward the hallway. He stopped dead in his tracks. His eyes widened as he gazed at the door. It seemed to open at the same eerie pace doors open in horror movies, but his eyes awaited what would come next. Out she came. Looking as stunning as Tommy had ever seen her.

She wore a black floor-length dress with a slit climbing all the way up her left side, stopping only a few inches south of her waistline. The straps covered very little of her shoulders and descended into a cut low enough that it would surely steal Tommy's glances more than a few times during dinner. Alison had done a little planning of her own it seemed. He involuntarily held his breath as she took her first few steps out of the bedroom, then let out a gasp in the same manner.

"Wow," he uttered at the end of his gasp.

She smiled. "I take it you like the dress."

"You look…amazing," he said.

Tommy grabbed her coat and placed it on her then grabbed his own. He held out his arm for her and she smiled and the two were off.

Once they were down on the street, they hailed a taxi. He opened the door for her, and she climbed in. He climbed in after her and closed the door. *"Puglia's,"* Tommy said, and Alison snapped a look and a smile in his direction. It was Alison's all-time favorite restaurant in the city. She loved the authentic Italian food and the way your senses were already enjoying everything before you even got through the door. The atmosphere always made her feel as if she were in some quaint foreign eatery, where just a glance out a window would reveal the beautiful Italian architecture. Something she had always wanted to see.

The cab pulled out front of the restaurant. Tommy paid the driver and stepped out. Alison followed and he closed the door to the taxi. She took his arm again and they walked inside. Once they were seated, Tommy ordered up the fried calamari, a dish he got whenever available, (knowing what it was, Alison couldn't bear the thought) as well as a bottle of merlot. Robert Mondavi Private Selection, to be exact. Alison however, enjoyed only the wine saving herself for the homemade Manicotti. Reading "homemade" on the menu entrenched her in the experience even more. Not to mention that the portions were always more than she could enjoy in one sitting.

Dinner couldn't have been tastier. They polished off the bottle of wine, but both ended up leaving with leftovers. They took a taxi back to their apartment and as they entered the elevator on the first floor, Tommy offered to carry Alison's leftovers for her. She of course thought it was just another small part of her pampering for the day.

But really, he wanted to ensure that she didn't drop her food once she opened the door and realized that their evening wasn't over. So, he simply made sure her hands were free.

They exited the elevator and walked toward their door. Tommy handed Alison his keys, which could have seemed a little odd, but she either dismissed such a thought or didn't pick up on it at all. Could've been the wine. She unlocked the door and pushed it open and reached for the light switch and flipped it on. As the light brought life to their apartment, a thunderous "Surprise!" erupted from their guests hidden in the shadows of their once dark living room. Alison jumped and dropped Tommy's keys.

A small scream flew from her mouth just as she covered it with both hands. She bent at the waist and knees from the shock, then stood upright again and turned to Tommy. He was laughing hysterically at her reaction. She punched him in the arm for laughing at her, then grabbed his face and kissed him for the lengths he had gone to make their evening such a special one.

They walked inside and greeted the now laughing group of family and friends that had been secretly stationed in their apartment. They looked around at all the faces staring back at them. Their expressions and laughter continuing.

Alison's parents were there, Tommy's mother, Owen and his parents, and a few friends of Alison's from the hospital. They continued through the door, coats and leftovers making it to the dining room table and no further and began greeting their guests.

Alison continued to laugh at herself while clearing her eyes of the tears that had begun form. Either from the shock of the surprise or simply just the thought of it all. She wasn't even sure. But either way, it didn't matter. It had been, to that point, the perfect evening.

Alison greeted her parents while Tommy hugged his mother, then walked over and shook hands with Alison's father. Her mother hugged him and gave him an appreciative smile before he excused himself and walked over to Owen who was standing off to the side watching everything unfold.

"This was perfect, buddy," Tommy said, shaking Owen's hand. "Thanks again."

Owen smiled at Tommy, "It was no problem, my friend. I'm happy to help."

Tommy looked around the room, spotting Alison who was speaking with her work friends. No doubt thanking them for coming and trying to pry out of them how long they had known about the surprise and been able to keep it a secret from her. He couldn't help but fall in love with her all over again. With every move, every gesture, she exuded everything he could ever desired. He couldn't help but stare. She turned and caught his gaze and excused herself from her colleagues and walked over where he and Owen were standing.

"You've out done yourself, Mr. Collins," she said, tiptoeing and kissing him on the lips. She smiled and then turned to Owen. "You, no doubt had your part in all of this," she said and hugged him.

"I made a few calls," Owen said, cracking a smile and hugging her back.

"Well, I want you both to know that I really appreciate it," she said, smiling back and hugging him again. "It's perfect."

Alison walked back over to their guests, leaving Tommy and Owen standing off from the rest of the party.

"You ready for phase three?" Owen asked.

"Ugh," Tommy grunted back quietly. "You know, I thought the wine would help with my nerves. But as luck would have it, I seem to be immune this evening."

"It's probably best," Owen said. "You don't want to stumble through that anyway. So, when you gonna pull the trigger?" he asked, smiling at Tommy's nervousness.

"I want to let her settle in first," Tommy said. "Let the surprise of the party wear off a little."

"Good choice," Owen said, as they both rejoined the party.

Owen had already made use of the alcohol Tommy and Alison had available at their apartment. He poured and mixed drinks for anyone that wanted one before the happy couple had arrived. Tommy walked into the kitchen and grabbed his bottle of Woodford. He poured himself a small drink and surveyed the party. He noticed that one of Alison's work friends had taken the liberty of pouring her a glass of wine, which she appeared to be nursing. Her portion of the bottle of merlot at Puglia's had taken a stronger hold on her than it had on him.

He finished his drink in one swallow, almost immediately feeling it kickstart the effects of the wine he drank earlier. He breathed a sigh of relief and poured another for himself and one for Owen. He walked back in the living room past Alison, momentarily stealing her attention from the conversation she was having. She reached out and touched his arm as he walked by, and he smiled back at her.

He walked over and handed the drink to Owen. They each downed their drinks and continued talking. After about thirty minutes, Tommy told Owen he thought he was ready. Owen got the attention of the group and asked everyone to raise their glasses to Tommy and Alison in celebration of their five years together. Everyone held their glasses high while Tommy and Alison stared at each other. Once the toast was finished, Owen turned the floor over to Tommy.

"I believe Tommy has something he'd like to say," he said.

"Thanks, Owen," Tommy said, stepping to the middle of the room and addressing the group. "Couldn't have pulled this off without this guy," he said pointing at Owen.

"I would first just like to thank everyone for being here. This means the world to Alison and me. To have all of you here tonight, celebrating with us."

Tommy then turned and faced Alison.

"Alison, the night we met, we had both intended to study our butts off in the library. Instead, we ended up completely abandoning our books and going out for coffee. I can say with the most certainty I've ever spoke with, that was one test I'm glad I didn't study for. I want you to know that now, five years later, I still feel as certain about you as I did that night. I love you. There is no one else in the world like you and I'm glad you're all mine."

Tommy reached in the inner pocket of his suit jacket and pulled out the small, velvety blue box. He looked at Alison and knelt down on one knee. Alison watched in disbelief. Her eyes widened and immediately filled with tears. Her mouth dropped and hung open. One of her work friends took the wine glass out of her hand without even asking. Alison didn't even seem to notice. She covered her mouth with her hands and stood there staring at Tommy kneeling in front of her.

"Alison, Will you marry me?" Tommy asked.

A resounding "YES" flew out of Alison's mouth, faster than the tears could roll down her cheeks. Their guests clapped and cheered as Tommy stood in front of her. He took her left hand and placed the ring on her finger. Alison looked down at the ring, astonished at its beauty, then back up at Tommy. More tears filled and fell from her eyes. She flung her arms around his neck and pressed her lips against his in a tear-soaked kiss that lasted more than a few seconds. Alison turned back around to their guests; her face still soaked. She saw the tears in her mother's eyes and walked over to her. Tommy followed and walked up to her father.

"Congratulations, son," her father said and extended his hand. "You make her happier than I've ever seen her."

"Thank you, sir," Tommy said. "That's all I've wanted to do since we met."

Their remaining guests congratulated them both several times over. Alison's friends from work marveled at her engagement ring, offering their praise to both her and Tommy on what a good job he did picking it out. His mother was elated for the both of them. She hugged them both and told them how proud she was that they had found each other. When she caught Tommy by himself a little later. She laughed and cried at the same time and told him that she believed he was well on his way to the life she always hoped he would have. He knew his mom tended to get a little over emotional. He was sure too, that the wine had played its part as well.

Alison's mother had about the same reaction with her. She shed plenty of tears and talked about how bright the path was that Alison was headed down. Tommy walked over to Owen, who was talking to his father. No doubt business related. Tommy tapped him on the arm, gave him a directional nod and the pair walked into the kitchen. Owen excused himself from his parents and followed Tommy. They stood at the counter where Tommy poured each of them a drink. They stood silent for a moment, both watching Alison surrounded by the party guests.

"You did good," Owen said, raising his glass to Tommy.

Tommy tapped his glass against Owen's and they both drank.

"Yeah, she really is great, isn't she?" Tommy said.

"Yeah, she is," Owen said.

The party lasted another couple of hours. Everyone mingled around the apartment, involved in their different conversations. Then they started to filter out as the hour got late. Owen was the last one to leave. He congratulated his friends one last time and left them to spend the remainder of their evening alone. Once everyone was gone, Alison walked over to Tommy and wrapped her arms around his stomach and placing her head on his chest and closing her eyes.

"Tonight, was perfect," she said.

Tommy held her, loving everything about her. "It sure was," he said. "I'm just glad you said yes," Tommy said, laughing.

"Oh, shut up," Alison said, playfully hitting him in the chest with her fist. "You knew I would."

Tommy continued laughing at her. He *did* know that she was going to say yes, but that didn't change the fact that he had been nervous about asking. And now that it was over, he could breathe a sigh of relief.

They went off to the bedroom where they changed clothes and then climbed in the bed. Alison found her usual spot, nestled in close to Tommy with her head on his chest and her arm half draped over his stomach. Only half draped this time because she had her hand propped up, fidgeting with her new engagement ring. She moved it back and forth around her finger so that it glimmered in little bit of light sneaking its way through their bedroom window. Tommy lay there staring at the ceiling, re-playing the evening in his mind. He was overjoyed that everything went off without a hitch.

Alison fell asleep first, leaving Tommy awake in the silent darkness. He soon drifted off to sleep himself almost immediately falling into dream.

| 21 |

It seemed to be a pleasant dream. He found himself standing in the middle of a neighborhood street facing a house, probably back on Long Island somewhere. It reminded him of his and Owen's old neighborhood where they grew up. Although, he didn't seem to recognize any of it. It was beautiful though. White house, with dark green shutters and a large green door with a gold door knocker. The green on the door was so dak, it almost looked black. But for whatever reason, Tommy knew it was green.

In the yard were two small kids, a little boy, and a little girl. Neither of them could've been older than six or seven years old. Toys were scattered across the yard and a German Shepheard zig zagging through the toys and around the kids. Tommy watched in his mind's eye, trying to understand exactly what he was looking at. When suddenly, the big green door opened, and a woman stepped out. *Their mother,* he though.

Tommy walked a little closer to the white picket fence that surrounded the front yard to get a better look. The woman brushed the hair out of her face as she knelt down to speak to the little boy. It was Alison, he was sure of it. As sure as you can be of anything in a dream, but he could feel her there somehow.

He watched even closer now and tried to memorize every detail. As he focused in on her and the children, he became distracted by the sound of an approaching vehicle. He turned and looked to his right and sure enough, there was car headed his direction. He didn't recognize the car, but it began to slow down as it got closer to where he was standing. Even slower still, then it turned into the driveway of the house, he was standing in front of. Tommy watched as the children abandoned their toys and ran toward the car as fast as they could. He waited as the door to the car opened. He found himself wondering in that moment who was going to step out, surely it had to be him.

Tommy watched himself step out of the car and breathed a sigh of relief. He leaned down and came back up with both children in his arms. Alison had walked behind the rushing children, over to the car. Her smile matching that of the children. She leaned between the little boy and little girl in Tommy's arms and kissed him. He sat the kids back down and hugged Alison, then the four of them walked inside the house.

Tommy stood there watching as the big green door closed. Then he was alone. He wanted to go inside. He wanted to see more of what their life was like together. He wanted to see more of himself as a father, but he couldn't. Tommy wasn't allowed past the fence surrounding the front yard. He stood there on the sidewalk realizing he had seen all he was going to see for now. He backed out, into the middle of the street. He was still trying to commit every detail he could to memory when suddenly, distraction befell him again.

This time there was no sound of an approaching vehicle. No sound at all, in fact. Only a piercing, high pitch ring that seemed to swell and fill the entire scene. Louder and louder, it grew until Tommy had to cover his ears. He tried to scream and thought that he was. But there was nothing but the ringing.

It only grew louder and seemed to now buzz as the sound had yet to reach its peak. Tommy could feel the sound vibrating throughout his entire body. He tried again to scream. He tried block it out. He tried to be louder than the sound, but it wasn't working. He couldn't even hear his own scream in his own head.

He fell to his knees, feeling as though the sound could possibly cause him to explode. He bent forward and hit his head on the pavement. Then suddenly, the sound stopped. It was as if it were never really there.

Tommy looked up. He felt exhausted now. His eyes squinted as if someone were shining a very bright light in his eyes. He climbed to his feet looking around. He hoped to see the source of the sound, but there was nothing. He looked down the street, or rather where the street had been. It wasn't really a street anymore. The house was still there, but the street he had looked down earlier, the one his car had drove down, was no longer there. There was nothing but beyond. Nothing but an enormous white light blanking out the rest of the space in his dream.

In the center of the light a small black dot appeared. He stood there on the street focused on the black dot in the middle. It was blocking out more and more of the light as it grew. Bigger and bigger it swelled, never taking an actual shape. Almost all the light was gone now. The black spot had grown and grown. Suddenly the light flashed a brilliant brightness, blocking out the black spot then going out completely.

Tommy opened his eyes. The black spot was still there. But it was no longer just a spot. It was a man. The dark, faceless figure of a man. It walked toward Tommy. A shadow moving all on its own with nothing there to cast it. It was coming toward him, but he couldn't move. He looked at the house and panic began to fill his entire body. He looked back at the figure. It was getting closer. Tommy stood frozen to the spot as the figure got closer when suddenly it stopped.

Tommy stood facing the figure. The figure stood facing the house. The house where Tommy, Alison, and their kids were. The figure appeared to turn its head and look at Tommy. There was no face. Only the vast, deep of the dark, almost liquid shape of a man. The figure turned his attention back toward the house and began to walk toward the fence. Tommy began to yell. He screamed at the figure, pleaded with it not to go in the house. But the figure paid him no mind.

It walked up the driveway and to the front door. Tommy screamed louder and louder, but the figure did not acknowledge him. Tommy stopped and watched as the figure knocked on the door. The figure stood there waiting and Alison opened the door.

"Don't, Ali! Close the door!" he screamed. But she stepped aside and let the figure walk into the house and closed the door.

Tommy continued screaming, desperately trying to get someone in the house to hear him, but somehow, he knew they wouldn't.

He could hear his screams again. And he was free again. No longer frozen in place in the middle of the street. He took off running toward the fence. He knew he hadn't been able to cross over last time he had been so close, but he had to try. He ran hard and fast. Just a couple feet from the fence he leapt into the air and to his surprise, over the fence he went. *It worked!* he thought in mid-air.

He hit the ground on the other side of the fence and continued running to the front door. He beat on the door and screamed for Alison to open the door, but there was nothing. He stepped back and looked at the front of the house. He ran to one of the windows and tried to see inside, but the curtains were drawn, and he couldn't see a thing. Panic was filling him fast. He ran to the back of the house. He grabbed the knob on the back door and turned it and the door opened. Tommy stood there staring at the open door, realizing that he hadn't really expected that it would open. He instinctively reached for his weapon, quickly realizing that he didn't have it. He stared at his empty hand, then looked through the open door and waited to hear any sound at all from inside the house. It was eerily silent. He took one step inside the house. Then another. And then another. There was no sound at all. In fact, there was nothing at all. The house appeared to be empty. No Alison, no kids, no Tommy, and no figure.

Tommy walked through the kitchen into the living room. The house was a blank canvas. Not one stick of furniture. It didn't appear that anyone had ever been in the house, but he knew what he saw. He noticed stairs leading to the second floor and started toward them. He ascends the stairs slowly, not even hearing the sound of his own footfalls as he took each step. He searched every room upstairs. Each one just as empty as the last. He's cleared the entire house and there was no one, no *thing* to be found. He walked back through the kitchen toward the back door. It was still open.

He started to walk back out into the back yard when he heard the unmistakable sound of hurried footsteps behind him. They were moving fast. Running at full speed now. He turned around and saw the figure running toward him. His body filled with fear as he reached again for his nonexistent sidearm. The figure drew closer. He could see the immeasurable depth of the blackness as it closed in. It was on him now. The figure pulled back its shadowy arms and shoved him out the back door. Tommy went flying through the door and landed in the yard. And just as he landed, he heard the back door slam shut. He got back up and ran back to the door. He was almost there. He reached for the doorknob. Grabbed it and started to turn. He pushed in on the door as he turned...

As he pushed the door open for the second time in his dream, Tommy sat straight up in his own bed. He stared at the wall beyond the foot of his bed, replaying everything he could remember about the dream in his head. He was covered in sweat and starting to feel cold now. He looked over at Alison who was sound asleep in the bed next to him. He thought about waking her to make sure everything was okay, maybe tell her about the dream, but he didn't. He let her sleep. *No since in both of us being interrupted,* he thought. He sat there in the bed for another moment still thinking about the dream. He looked over at Alison again and climbed out of the bed. He walked into the bathroom and leaned over the sink to splash some water over his face. He looked in the mirror and watched as the water ran down his own face. *The killers in the house,* he thought.

Tommy's eyes shot open as wide as they could. He rushed out of the bathroom and grabbed his service weapon off his nightstand. He walked to the bedroom door and listened for any sound throughout the apartment, but he didn't hear anything. He opened the bedroom door, listening again, but still nothing. Step by careful step, he crept out of the bedroom and down the hallway, eventually clearing the entire apartment. He found nothing, and no sign that there had even been anything. He looked at the clock on the microwave. *It's only 12:30 am,* he thought, and felt as though the dream he had just awakened from had lasted for hours.

He sat his gun down on the kitchen counter and poured himself a drink. He threw the drink back swallowing it all at once. He was thinking about the dream again. If it hadn't meant that the killer was in their apartment, what did it mean? Who or what was the figure?

| 22 |

Tommy sat at his desk in the bullpen with his morning coffee and his latest casefile. A New Year's Eve liquor store robbery in which the clerk had been shot. The shot wasn't fatal. The shooter had become inpatient and panicked when the clerk took too long to retrieve the money from the register. The shooter ran toward the entrance of the liquor store throwing his arm back and firing his weapon, blindly at the clerk. The clerk was wounded in the shoulder. There was video of the incident, but the perpetrator had done a pretty good job of concealing his identity, so no arrests had been made…yet.

The Arnold and Hammond casefiles however, had found their way inside one of the lower drawers of Tommy's desk. A wishful stop no doubt, on the road to becoming cold cases. Tommy hadn't been able to stomach the idea of ridding himself of those two files just yet. He wanted to badly, just not before he solved them. No matter how much they haunted him. He still hung on the hope that someone would come forward with something leading him in the direction of the killer.

He got up from his desk and walked across the bullpen to refill his coffee. He stopped and chatted with Bob for a minute then returned to his desk. As he sat down, his phone lit up showing a text message from Alison. *Call me when you get a chance.* The message read.

She's at work, Tommy thought. *And she never texts or called during the workday.*

He quickly picked up his phone and called her back. Her message immediately made him anxious, but he hoped he was wrong. The phone barely rang for the second time when she picked up.

"Hello," Alison said.

"Hey babe, everything ok?" Tommy asked.

"Um," she started. "Well, I was doing fine this morning. I was in with a patient when something hit me, and I had to run to the bathroom, and I got sick."

"Holy shit, babe, are you okay?" Tommy interrupted.

"Yeah, yeah, I'm fine." Alison said. "It's just not that common for something to onset that quick, except for maybe food poisoning and I had only had coffee this morning. So, I spoke with Dr. Davis and there was only really one thing left that I didn't think to check. And, well…I'm pregnant."

Tommy shot up out of his chair without saying a word. He started walking in a small circle next to his desk. He noticed that his fellow detectives were beginning to look at him as if he had just had some sort of sudden mental lapse.

"So––I'm gonna––I mean––we're gonna be––parents?" Tommy stammered.

"Yes, baby, we are," she said, her voice cracking.

Tommy could feel the butterflies forming in his stomach. They quickly grew larger and larger. He felt nervous at first, then went into full blown excitement. Tommy pulled the phone away from his ear, shot his arms into the air and let out an exclamatory "YES," causing the rest of the bullpen (the ones who hadn't noticed him yet) to jerk around from their desks and stare at him. He turned and looked at everyone in the room with a large goofy smile on his face. He locked eye with Captain Spencer who was now standing in the doorway of his office, surveying the room to see what the commotion was all about.

"I'm gonna be a dad!" Tommy shouted, his arms still in the air. The room erupted in applause and cheers. Tommy stood there, celebrating, overcome with the joyful news, and completely forgetting that Alison was still on the phone.

"Yo, Tommy," Another detective yelled, pointing to the phone still in Tommy's hand.

"Oh shit," Tommy said. "Sorry, babe," he said quickly putting the phone back up to his ear.

"I take it you're excited," Alison said. She was beginning to cry.

"Of course, I'm excited," Tommy said. "Listen, I'm leaving the office now. I'm taking you to an early lunch."

"Okay, I think I can swing that. I'll get someone to cover me for a bit." Alison said. "I'll see you when you get here."

Tommy hung up the phone and sat back down at his desk letting the news sink in. He stood back up and grabbed his keys, phone, and jacket and walked over toward the captain's office. He opened the door without knocking and before he could get a word out, Captain Spencer looked up from his desk.

"See ya tomorrow," he said.

Tommy smiled and shut the door then turned and walked out of the bullpen. His pace hurried as he reached the front door of the precinct and burst through. He rushed over to his car and climbed in and pulled out into traffic. His mind continued racing, going over the phone call again and again. He had forgotten all about the dream from the night before. He had forgotten about the black, liquid shadow figure.

He drove down the streets so full of excitement. He had the urge to roll down his window and proclaim to everyone he passed that he was going to be a father. He got caught at a red light, so he reached into the inside pocket of his jacket and grabbed his phone. He scrolled quickly through his contacts finding Owen's number and pressing the "call" button. The phone rang over and over, so many times in fact, that Tommy assumed Owen had probably left it in his office. Just as Tommy was about to hang up, Owen answered the phone.

"What's up, bro?" Owen said.

"Man, have I got some news for you," Tommy said.

"Alright?" Owen said. "What's up? You sound excited."

"Well, I just got off the phone with Ali," Tommy started. "And, um…she's pregnant."

"Oh my God, that's awesome!" Owen said. "Congratulations, to you both!"

"Thank you, I'm pretty damn stoked about it," Tommy replied. "I'm on my way right now to take her out to an early lunch."

"Buddy, that's great," Owen said.

Tommy and Owen continued talking. Tommy told him about his initial reaction to Alison's baby news, and how he had acted in the middle of his office. Owen laughed hysterically. He told him that he wished he could've been there to see it firsthand. Their conversation ended just as Tommy pulled into the parking lot of the hospital. Once he was parked, he jumped out of his car and quickly made his way to the door. He hurried across the parking lot looking like one of the goofy speed walkers he and Alison would see in the park.

Once inside the hospital doors, Tommy momentarily lost all sense of direction. He had completely forgotten which way he needed to go to get to Alison in the ER. He quickly got himself oriented and sped off in the right direction. About halfway to the ER, he spotted her heading toward him. Good thing too, because he thought all his excitement could possibly cause him to implode if he had to wait much longer.

Once they locked eyes, Tommy's pace increased until he came to an almost screeching halt in the hallway. He stood there in front of Alison. He stared at her and smiled a large goofy grin. His mouth and mind void of anything useful or even appropriate to say. She only smiled back at him. Her face was still wet from the tears.

"Are we sure?" Tommy asked, finally breaking the silence.

"I had them run the test twice," Alison replied.

"I love you," Tommy said, stepping toward her and wrapping his arms around her. He started to pick her up off the floor then thought better of it.

"I love you too," she said, resting her head against his chest.

Tommy held out his arm. She took it and they walked back out to Tommy's car. Each with a giant smile on their face.

They drove to a small café where they sat eating lunch and talking and sharing in their excitement about the future of their now expanding household.

They were both thrilled about the pregnancy. It had only been about eight short weeks ago that Tommy had proposed, and the elation of that night couldn't touch how they were feeling now. Especially seeing that the other not only shared in their excitement but magnified it as well.

They decided to call and inform their families of the news. Both Alison's parent's and Tommy's mother shared in their celebration. Their parents couldn't have been happier. Tommy's mother revealed to them that she didn't figure it would be too long after the engagement before they would be blessing everyone with a new addition.

Once the phone calls were over, they just sat there at the table staring at each other. They held each other's hand atop the table until their food came, lost in the happiness of their moment.

They finished their lunch, and Tommy drove Alison back to the hospital. He pulled right in front of the doors, kissed her, and she got out and walked inside. He watched her walk until he couldn't see her anymore then he pulled off.

He took his time getting home, not bothering to be upset about sluggish New York traffic conditions. Once he arrived, he walked inside and changed his clothes and sat down on the couch. He didn't immediately turn on the TV. Instead, he sat there in the silence letting the day's information sink in even further. There were countless questions bouncing around in his mind. How would he feel when the child arrived? When should they start buying things for the baby? He assumed it would be soon. In the midst of reveling in his happiness about the pregnancy his dream from the night before popped back into his head. He felt a chill all over, remembering first the sight of him and Alison with children, then the figure. What had it been? Who had it been? Was it a person at all or just shaped like one?

Tommy remembered standing beside the figure on the street, in his dream. He remembered that it appeared to turn and look at him, but there was nothing there. Only a fluid darkness.

Tommy fought his way back to reality. He turned on the TV and kicked back on the couch, trying to shake the chill his dream had given him. However, he didn't pay much attention to what was on the TV. He lay there staring at the ceiling, *I'm going to be a dad, I'm going to be a dad,* circling through his mind over and over again like a banner attached to the back of a plane. The thought filled him with excitement. But it also frightened him. He found his thoughts drifting again to his father. He wondered how his father reacted to the news that *he* was on the way. *Was he excited? Was he upset? Did he even care either way?* Tommy wondered. *Did he wonder what kind of dad he would be?* These were questions that Tommy didn't have the answers to. He didn't know if he even wanted the answers. All he did know was that there was no way in hell he was going to turn out like his father.

| 23 |

The bitter New York winter gave way to spring, and then the spring to summer. It had proved to be a mild spring, semi-warm temperatures, a fair amount of rain, but when the sun was out, it was almost perfect. Summer, however, was projected by every local new outlet to be one of the hottest in recent years. Something Alison was not looking forward to during the last couple months of her pregnancy. As her belly grew bigger so did her aches and pains. Tommy did his best to accommodate when and where he could, but between the ever-growing hormonal imbalance Alison was suffering and with the increasing temperatures all his efforts seemed to be an exercise in futility.

Despite all the hardships Alison had so far suffered throughout her pregnancy she actively tried to show her appreciation for Tommy's efforts to make her more comfortable. He would rub her feet or back, whichever needed the most attention. Often both.

During the middle of the pregnancy, he made a habit of running a bath for her at least once or twice a week, just so she could relax. But the bigger she got the harder it was for her to get out of the bathtub without assistance. For obvious reasons, this began to upset her, and the baths were quickly phased out of Tommy's assistive routine.

Alison suggested replacing the baths with heating pads and foot baths.

Around the end of June Tommy's mother threw a baby shower for them at her house. The weather wasn't too hot that day, which made things a little more enjoyable for everyone, especially Alison. Owen and his parents attended. As well as some of Alison's co-workers, friends from her sorority and her parents. They brought gift after gift for the mommy and daddy-to-be. And along with almost every gift came a pack or two of newborn diapers, or a large box of baby wipes. The shower guests also enjoyed traditional baby shower games such as Guess the Baby Food, A diaper derby, (a team game, which consisted of diapering a team member in toilet paper in the most creative way possible.) Followed by the all too popular Baby Shower Bingo. It was the same concept as traditional Bingo. Only instead of corresponding number and letters, the players simply filled in the space on their card labeled with baby items that matched the one drawn out of the hat.

It was everything Tommy and Alison hoped it would be. Alison did her best to show her appreciation to Tommy's mother, thanking her several times throughout the day. The heat of the day eventually caused Alison to sweat in places she didn't realize you could sweat from.

As the daylight faded and the night drew closer, the guests began to filter out. Alison found her place in Tommy's mother's living room. Owen was the last to leave, saying his goodbyes, and heading across the street to his parent's house. Alison sat on the couch in the living room with her head back and her eyes closed. Her bare feet propped up on the coffee table and an oscillating fan his mother had planted across from the couch in front of the TV, roaring at full speed. The cool air struck her directly in the face.

"So, Alison," Tommy's mother said, walking into the living room and sitting down next to Alison on the couch. "What do you think it is?"

Alison smiled. "In my heart, I feel like it's a boy." she said. "I keep trying to think of what it would be like to have a little girl. All the flowers and princess stuff. All the pretty colors. But my brain always kicks me out of my little daydream and says, 'don't worry about that, you're having a boy.'"

"Oh, honey," Tommy's mother said, laughing. "You had better just listen to your gut. I went through the same thing with Tommy. I wanted a little girl ever since I could remember. I tried so hard to convince myself that I was having a girl, even on the day of my ultrasound, I made them check twice." She laughed.

"What about Tommy?" his mother asked. "Has he said what he thinks it's going to be?"

"He always says he doesn't care," Alison said. "And I don't think he really does, but I know he'd love to have a son. Plus," Alison continued. "Whenever I'm thinking about him with the baby, it's always a boy.

Tommy's mother smiled at Alison. "Well, I think it's safe to say that it's going to be a boy. I'd put my money on it if your gut is that strong."

"At this point I just want it out," Alison said, looking over at his mother and laughing.

"Oh, I remember that feeling," Laurie said, laughing along. She got up and walked back into the kitchen. "Can I get you anything?" she shouted from the kitchen.

"Some ice water would be great," Alison shouted back.

"Okay, just a sec," his mother said.

Alison laid her head back on the couch. The cool air from the fan still whipping against her face. She was so relaxed that she didn't even move when she heard the door start to open.

Tommy stepped inside the house and took one look at Alison sitting on the couch and stopped dead in his tracks.

It was the way she was sitting. Motionless. Her head flung back. A memory flashed in his mind of being frantically carried down the hallway back to his room, and the brief glimpse he had caught of his father dead on the couch.

His mother had long since replaced the couch. In fact, she had replaced it several times over the years. Tommy always thought it was just one of the weird ways she delt with everything that had happened. But the room was the same.

Tommy stood there in his daze. "Babe," he heard Alison say. Her voice sounded far off to him at first. Then a little louder. "Babe." Even louder still. "BABE!" she called one final time, snapping him back to reality. Tommy just smiled at her and shrugged it off. It was that exact moment that Tommy was reminded of the fact that he had never told Alison the full story about his father.

They left his mother's house that evening and drove back to the city. Alison was exhausted from the heat and the events of the day and fell asleep almost immediately after Tommy pulled out of his mother's driveway. Tommy drove toward the city with only the hum of the tires gliding across the asphalt and the whoosh of passing cars to break the silence. He thought about his daydream. He thought about telling Alison about everything. But he also worried about her reaction.

Will that make her question me *as a father?* he though. Tommy had kept this secret from everyone for so long. He really didn't know what to expect. In spite of the unknowns and the uncertainties, he knew that he was going to have to tell her the truth.

24

The baby shower had been an exciting day for both Tommy and Alison, but Alison had another reason to celebrate. That day also marked the beginning of her maternity leave from the hospital. With many miles and hours already logged during her pregnancy, up and down the hospital halls, standing bedside with patients. Her feet were really going to thank her for the much-needed break in the action. Her first day home she slept until around 11:00 am after being pummeled from the inside all night long by their unborn child. Once she woke up and had the apartment all to herself, she had breakfast and retired to the couch where she planned to spend most of her day with her feet up, watching TV. As much as she loved not *having* to be on her feet all day every day for the remainder of her pregnancy, she knew that there was a high probability that she and boredom were going to become great friends. She knew she could find things to do to pass some of the time if she needed to, but for now, laziness was her ally, and she intended to take full advantage.

Back at the precinct, Tommy sat at his desk in the bullpen staring at his computer screen. It had been stuck on the screensaver for approximately thirty minutes. He was thinking about seeing Alison sitting on his mother's couch and the subsequent memory that froze him in place. He thought about the car ride home afterward and the questions that had plagued his mind ever since. He knew that he needed to talk to her, but that was a conversation that he didn't even know how to start. But he knew she deserved to know. Tommy looked at the drawer on his desk that contained the Arnold and Hammond case files. He caught himself briefly reciting snippets of the reports in his mind. Almost as if he were looking at them with a fresh set of eyes. He knew that he was no closer to solving either of those cases than he was the day he set foot on the crime scenes. Still, they haunted him. Tommy got up from his desk and without saying a word to anyone, he walked out of the bullpen, down the hall and out the front doors of the precinct. He stood on the sidewalk outside watching the city move as it always did, at a thunderous pace. He didn't know where he was going, only that he had to get out of that office. He walked to his car and got inside. He sat in the silence. The noise of a city in full swing, now just a distant hum. *Owen,* he thought. *I need to talk to Owen.* He started his car and pulled into traffic and made a beeline for Owens shop.

He pulled up out front of the shop and without a second's hesitation he jumped out and walked inside. He found Owen as he usually did. At the front counter tending to a customer who was desperate to restore some article of clothing they were sure they had destroyed. He walked past the counter and straight back to the office where he sat in Owen's chair waiting for him to be finished. He sat swiveling in the chair in little half circles until he heard the chime of the bells above the front door, and Owen's footsteps moving toward the office. He stared up at Owen who had stopped in the doorway and stared at him, wondering how he must look right now

"I need your help," Tommy said.

Tommy explained to Owen what had happened at his mother's house. Walking in and seeing Alison sitting in that certain way on the couch. Then the flashback of his murdered father as he was being carried down the hallway. Then the car ride home where he finally realized that he was going to have to tell Alison the truth about his father and the fears that accompanied sharing that part of his life with her. Owen stood there in the doorway listening and watching the fear grow on his best friend's face.

"How do you think she's gonna take it?" Tommy asked. "Fuck, I should have told her before now."

"Listen, man," Owen said. "It's not like your confessing something to her that *you* did. None of that was your fault. Not what he did to you. Not his death. None of it. It's not something you tell just anyone. She's going to understand why you haven't said anything."

"I sure hope so," Tommy said. "I just don't want to lose her."

"Bro, if she left you over something like that, then that says more about her than it does you," Owen said. "But that's not going to happen. Alison loves you."

Just as Owen finished talking the bells over the front door to the shop chimed and they heard a customer walked in.

"You're right, you're right," Tommy said. "I'm just scared, ya know"

"I know, brother," Owen replied. "But you don't have anything to worry about. Hang on just a sec."

Owen backed out of the office and turned toward the front counter. Tommy sat in the chair with his head in his hands.

Owen turned around looking at the floor and started to greet his customer. "Hello, how can I..." He didn't take another step. He didn't say another word. He just stood there staring. His gut immediately twisted tighter and tighter until he was sure his body would begin to twist with it. He could feel the beads of sweat beginning to form on his forehead. He just stared into those eyes staring back at him from across the counter. Rhiannon's eyes.

There she stood just inside the front door of the shop staring back at him with her hands clasped together. Owen heard the squeak of his office chair behind him, followed by Tommy's footsteps coming out of the office. Then they stopped. Owen immediately remembered the last time he saw her

"Hi," Rhiannon said, nervously. But Owen just stood there. Still and silent. Tommy walked up next to Owen.

"I'm going to get out of here," Tommy whispered, patting him on the shoulder.

"K...bye," Owen whispered back, not even bothering to look at him. It was all he could muster.

Tommy walked around the counter and gave Rhiannon nod and a small wave. She waved back and he walked out the front door.

Rhiannon watched him walk out then turned back to Owen. The two stood there gripped in the silence that had filled the room like rushing water through a broken dam. Rhiannon nervously fidgeted with her fingers.

"Sorry to just show up like…," she started nervously.

"What are you doing here?" Owen blurted out, interrupting her.

He didn't really mean it as harshly as it sounded. But it was literally the first thought that came to his mind once he had locked eyes with her. He could tell by the confused look on her face exactly how she had taken it.

"Sorry," he said, trying to recover. "That's not what I––I mean––I was just––never mind." Owen stood there staring at her. Again, there was silence. "How are you?" he asked.

"I'm good," Rhiannon said, nodding her head. How have you been?"

"I've been good," Owen said.

This was true, except where she was concerned. Since the day he read the note she left on her grandfather's door for him, he had missed her terribly. He had spent days and nights wondering what it could have been like, what *they* could have been if she had stayed. He had tried on several occasions throughout the years to put the thoughts and daydreams of her having stayed out of his mind, but he always seemed to fail miserably. He had simply given up on the idea of erasing her from his memory and settled for having her note and letting her linger in his mind. Often times she would take over his thoughts and pull him into a full-on daydream where she had stayed, and they had their happily ever after.

"That's good, Owen," she said. "I'm really glad to hear that you've been doing well."

"Well, I've just been keeping busy, running the shop and all," Owen said, looking down at the counter. He saw her shadow move as she stepped toward the counter.

Owen raised his head and looked at her. The smile on her face was gone.

"Would you like to have a drink with me tonight?" she asked.

Owen looked into her eyes, then back down at the counter. Here she was standing in front of him. Asking to spend time with him, something he had literally dreamed about. Now only one thought crossed his mind, he didn't know if he could stand to lose her again.

Before he could think any further the words simply popped out of his mouth.

"I'd love to," he said betraying his thoughts.

"Great," she said, smiling. Her eyes lit up just as they had before. Just as he remembered. And with that, he sunk even further into the reverie.

"Same place?" she asked.

"Sure," he said as a smile worked itself out on his face. "I'll meet you there at eight."

Rhiannon's smile got a little bigger, then a little smaller. "I'll see you then," she said. Then she turned and walking out of the shop.

Owen stood there at the counter and watched her walk out and then up the street until she was totally out of sight. He stood there for a few seconds more before going back to his office and sitting down in his chair. He was still trying to convince himself that it had actually happened. She had really been there, and this wasn't the work of some subconscious fantasy he had conjured up. He could still smell her in the store, even from where he sat in his office. Her scent still triggered the same feeling it had when they were last together. He looked at the clock on his desk. 12:32 pm. The numbers sat, mocking him at how much time he now had to fill before seeing her again. He knew that only meant that he had more time to over analyze the whole situation.

He picked up his phone and stared at it. He flipped through his contacts stopping at Tommy's number. On one hand he knew that Tommy already had enough on his mind, worrying about telling Alison the truth about his father. But on the other hand, Tommy was there when Rhiannon showed up and he was probably very curious about how things had turned out. He hit the call button, and the phone didn't finish the first ring before Tommy answered.

"Hello," Tommy said, sounding like he had been waiting on Owen's call.

"Hey, it's me," Owen said. "Rhiannon just left a few minutes ago."

There was a brief silence before Tommy spoke again. "So…what'd she say?" Tommy asked.

Owen sighed. "She wants to get together for a drink tonight."

"And you're *not* excited about this?" Tommy asked

"I don't know, man," Owen started. "I was so excited to see her. I mean really excited. But the more I think about it, the more nervous I get that this is just another visit and she's just going to leave again. I lost her once a–and I don't really want to do that again.

"Listen buddy," Tommy said. "This is a *good* thing. I know you've been through some shit over her leaving before. I've seen it. But this is a good opportunity.

"For what?" Owen asked.

"For some closure," Tommy said. "Look, I know you hated the way things ended last time. Then she left you that note. And even though I know it made you feel a little better, I also know that you still wished that there hadn't been a need for it. This is your chance to change that. I mean…you *know* it's going to come up at some point. At least now you'll get to say what you wish you had said before.

Owen sat silent, absorbing what Tommy had said. "I know you're right. Everything just came flooding back so quick, ya know?"

"Oh, I could tell. It was very clearly written all over your face," Tommy said with a chuckle. "Look," Tommy continued. "This is a big city. It would have been all too easy for her to come back here and completely avoid seeing you. But that's not what she did. She came to you, and she wants to see you. That tells me that there is probably more that she wants to say as well.

"True," Owen said. "I didn't think about all that."

"Listen, buddy I gotta go," Tommy said. "Let me know how it goes."

"You know I will," he said.

Owen hung up the phone and leaned back in his office chair. He ran through everything Tommy had said. But every time he started to feel a little confident about the situation, he remembered how he felt when he realized that it was Rhiannon that had walked into his shop and his confidence slipped away. He began to drift off in thought, plotting out the different ways the evening could go, but was interrupted by the chime of the bells above the door once again. He could see a customer walk up to the counter from where he was sitting. A couple of garments in hand. "Be right with you," he shouted. He leaned forward and placed his elbows on his desk. The clock read 1:01pm. *Six hours, fifty-nine minutes,* he thought to himself. *If I don't go crazy before then.*

| 25 |

Tommy looked up from his desk realizing that the workday had flown by. He collected his things and walked out of the precinct and to his car. He sat there ready to go home, but not ready for the conversation he and Alison were going to have. He started the ignition and pulled into traffic. Traffic was typical rush hour congestion which he usually hated. But today it provided him with the extra time he needed to calm his nerves and collect his thoughts. He pulled into his apartment building, parked, and shut off the car. *Here we go*, he thought.

He got out and walked inside the building. He took the elevator to their floor and walked down the hall to their door. He opened the door to find Alison laid back on the couch, feet propped up, watching TV.

"Hey baby," Alison said, starting to work herself upward. "How was your day?"

"Oh, it was fine," he said, hanging his jacket on the chair next to the door. He walked over and sat next to her on the couch.

"What about your day?" he asked.

"Ugh," Alison grunted. "This child of ours is as backward as could be. Not a single movement all day long. But I just know as soon as I try to go to sleep tonight, it's going to start doing cartwheels in there."

"That sounds amazing," Tommy said, sarcastically.

"Yeah, it's the best," she said catching her breath.

She looked at Tommy fully expecting a smile at her last comment but didn't see one. His face was stressed. There was worry in his eyes.

"What's wrong," she asked.

Tommy paused momentarily. He looked at the TV but wasn't paying any attention to what was on. "I need to talk to you about something," he said, pausing again.

"Okay," Alison replied hesitantly. "Is everything okay?"

"Yeah, everything is fine," he said, placing his hand on her leg. "I just need to tell you something. Something that I've never told you before. But it's something that you deserve to know."

He could see the fear on her face. Like she didn't quite know what to expect.

"You can tell me anything," she said. "You know that."

"Well," Tommy started. "It's about my father."

"Your father?" Alison said, with a confused look on her face.

Tommy never talked about his father, and she hadn't expected that he would be the topic of discussion now either.

Tommy took a deep breath and began. "You know the weird circumstances surrounding his death, about how the killer was never caught and how they suspected that it was possibly someone he had arrested. You know all that."

"Yeah," Alison said, waiting for him to continue.

"Well, there's something about him that you don't know." Tommy continued. Alison sat there looking at him. Frozen in her seat. Worried and fearful of what she was about to hear.

"I used to have these dreams… Or at least that's what I thought they were at the time. But they were terrible. My father had me convinced that they *were* dreams and told me that if I ever told my mom or anyone else about them, that they would basically think I was crazy and I could be taken away from them. And of course, I didn't want that to happen. I was just a kid. So, I kept my mouth shut."

Tommy paused and took another deep breath.

"I thought I was dreaming that my father was molesting me."

One hand flew up and covered Alison's horrified face.

"Then one night, I decided I was going to see for myself, once and for all, if I was really dreaming or not and I purposely stayed awake.

And sure enough, later that night he came into my room. I pretended to be asleep, and…well…he started trying to touch me."

He felt Alison tense up as she grabbed his hand.

"I jumped out of my bed and lost my shit and started screaming at him. He just started beating me. Then my mom came running in and stopped him and I told her everything. He tried to deny it of course, but there was no more denying it. I had caught him red handed."

"Oh my God!" Alison said, choking on her words and beginning to tear up. All she could do was stare at Tommy as he continued talking.

"After that," Tommy continued. "He kept me, and my mom trapped in the house for a few days. I guess until he thought it was safe to let us out or until he figured people would start to question it. But either way, it was hell. He was killed shortly after that, and they never found out who did it.

Alison tried not to, but she was bawling now. She sat there facing the floor. He could see where tears had fallen from her eyes and landed on the hardwood beside her feet. She looked over at Tommy, her eyes still full of tears and her face red from sobbing.

"I am so sorry, baby," she said, leaning over and wrapping her arms around one of his. The tighter she squeezed him, the harder she cried. The sleeve of Tommy's shirt soaked up her tears.

"I just needed to be honest with you about that," Tommy said. "Because honestly, him being as shitty of a father as he was, has had me questioning what kind of father I'm going to be.

Alison's posture stiffened as she sat upright and wiped her face clean.

"You listen to me," she said, turning his face toward her own. "You are nothing like him. You hear me. You are kind and gentle and I know you would never do anything to hurt our child. You are going to be a wonderful father. I know it. Just the fact that you're worried about being a good father tells me that you're going to be great. I am so sorry that happened to you, baby. But that doesn't define you or what kind of father you're going to be."

Tommy breathed a sigh of relief and laid back against the back of the couch. "You feel better now?" she asked.

"Yeah," he replied.

"You should, honey," she said. "You shouldn't keep something like that locked up inside. It's not healthy."

"Well, I've kinda had to," he said. No one else knows about it except my mom and Owen. After he was killed, my mom sat me down and talked to me about it all and told me that since he was dead, she didn't want to say anything because there would be nothing that could be done about it. And she didn't want to go public about what he had done and then me to have to tell the story a bunch of times, to a bunch of different people. I mean, it made sense."

"She was just trying to protect you," Alison said. "You had clearly been through enough already."

"Yeah, I know she was," Tommy replied.

He looked at Alison, feeling more in love with her than he had ever been. He wrapped his arms around her, and they sat there on the couch holding each other. The weight that Tommy had experienced all day was gone. He felt as if he could float away and that holding on to Alison was the only thing keeping him grounded.

"On a completely different topic," Tommy said, cracking a small smile. "I stopped by the shop today, to see Owen, and something very interesting happened."

"I'm interested?" Alison said, looking up at him.

"Well, like I said, the only people that know everything that I just told you are my mom and Owen. I was nervous about having this conversation with you, so I stopped in and talked to Owen. We were sitting in his office talking when someone walked in…"

Alison stared at him, patiently waiting for him to finish his sentence, which based on the smile on his face, he was not doing on purpose.

"Well…who was it?" she asked impatiently.

Tommy's smile grew a little larger. "Rhiannon," he said.

Alison's jaw dropped open. "No F'n way!" she exclaimed.

"Yep," Tommy said, continuing to smile.

"What fo––what did she––I mean––," She paused to collect herself. "What happened?" she finally asked.

"Well, I left almost as soon as she got there. The interaction was tense enough without me standing in the background just staring them, waiting for one of them to say something. But Owen did call me after she left and said that she wanted to go have drinks tonight."

"How did he sound?" she asked. "I bet he was excited to see her."

"Yeah, he was," Tommy said. "But he was also very nervous about the whole 'having drinks' portion. I told him not to be nervous and that he needed to look at this as a good thing. Maybe they would be able to clear some things up, ya know?"

"Yeah, I just remember how hard it was on him last time. How hard it's been this whole time," Alison said.

"That's what he was worried about too. I told him to just go into it not expecting anything. Just drinks with an old friend."

"That's probably for the best," Alison said.

But Tommy knew that more than anything, Owen already wanted her to stay.

| 26 |

Owen turned the sign on the front door of the shop so that the side that read "closed" was facing the outside. He walked to the back into his office and sat in his chair. *Tommy's right,* he thought. *It's just drinks.* He sat there for another minute before he locked up and drove home. He got home around six, showered and got himself ready to go. He went outside and stood on the curb and waited for a cab to pop up.

On the way to the bar, he tried hard to focus on what Tommy said to him on the phone, but the closer he got the more his focus shifted to all the thoughts and feelings of doubt that ran through his mind when he saw her standing in the shop. He had the driver drop him off about a block away from the bar. He figured he needed the extra walk time to prepare.

He stood there on the sidewalk and watched the taxi drive away, then turned and started walking toward the bar. He arrived at the bar but stayed outside, staring through the front window at the inside of the bar.

There she sat at the bar. He stared at her, remembering the night they reconnected in this very bar. He walked over to the door, worked up his nerve and walked in. The door squeaked as he pulled it open, the same way it had every time he had opened it since the very first. It was just loud enough to disrupt the buzz of the chatter in the bar causing Rhiannon to turn her head and look toward the door. She smiled at him and waved. He smiled back and walked over to her. She got out of her seat at the bar and wrapped her arms around him. He wrapped his arms around her and slowly breathed in deep, inhaling her familiar, enchanting scent. Something he had been sure that he would never be able to do again after the last time they had seen each other.

That was all it took. Every single one of his defenses were down. Disabled, inoperable, however you wanted to phrase it. It only amounted to one thing. Before they had even spoke a single word to one another, he already didn't want to let her go. He had forgotten everything he had tried so hard to remember before arriving at the bar. He found himself, once again, scared to let go of her. Everything in him wanted her to stay.

Rhiannon unwrapped her arms and stood there before him smiling. They each ordered a drink, then found a table and sat down as a warm, powerful, female voice poured out of the jukebox singing the words, "Well, maybe I'm just thinking that the rooms are all on fire, every time that you walk in the room," Owen happened to catch the words as they were seating themselves and almost laughed at irony between the lyrics and how he was feeling at the moment.

"So, how's the shop doing?" Rhiannon asked.

"It's doing well," Owen said after taking a sizable gulp of his beer. "Stays pretty steady."

"That's good," she said, looking down at her drink.

Owen could tell that she was just trying to make small talk. What he didn't quite know was why. She looked as though there was something she wanted to say but she was avoiding saying it for some reason. *Why would she ask me out for drinks, just to make small talk? She could have done that at the store,* he thought. *Why would she come find me at all if that's all she wanted? There's plenty that we could be talking about. Maybe that's it, maybe she just wants to clear the air between us.*

Owen felt a sense of having a little more control over the conversation. Just as Tommy had suggested, this was a good opportunity to do just that. To clear the air. Owen took another drink of his beer and decided to keep the conversation going.

"So," he said, with a smile. "Where all have you been? Anywhere exciting?"

Rhiannon's face lit up a little. She began talking about how when she left the last time, she went back to Paris where she spent about a year. Then it was back to Germany where she found a job working at a small pub. "It wasn't a lot," she said. "But I was able to get an apartment and take as much time as I wanted to visit all the 'touristy' spots. Then it was off to England for a while with some friends.

"That all sounds amazing," Owen said, watching her face. "You've definitely led an interesting life, that's for sure."

Rhiannon smiled and looked back down at her drink. She brought it to her lips and to Owens surprise, she finished it. Owen was a little surprised at this and thought maybe she had suddenly changed her mind about their conversation. She sat her glass back down on the table and looked at Owen with an almost urgent look on her face.

"You wanna get out here?" she asked. "Take a walk or something?"

Owen sat there a little shocked at the sudden detour the evening had taken but found that he was willing to follow.

"Sure," he said. He grabbed his beer and finished it, left a tip on the table and they walked out of the bar.

"Where'd ya wanna go?" Owen asked once they were outside.

"I don't know," she said, shrugging her shoulders. "I just thought it would be a nice night for a walk."

"Alright," Owen said, and they took off down the sidewalk. "I think it's supposed to rain though."

They walked for a few blocks, not talking about anything relevant. Mostly catching up on how each other's families were doing and whatever else they could come up with to avoid any silent gaps in the conversation. Anything it seemed, to avoid the one subject that Owen was sure was hanging in the balance of each of their minds just waiting to be plucked for discussion.

It was obvious to Owen that she was not acting like her usually free-spirited self. A walk through the city on a summer evening would normally prompt her to do something spontaneous or even a little risky, but not tonight. Tonight, she seemed closed off, guarded, almost nervous.

They walked for more than a few blocks making their pointless conversation before they arrived at Central Park.

"Wanna walk through the park?" she asked.

"Sure," he said, even though he knew the park was not the safest place to be at night, especially in the summertime. "It's the best of what's around," he said.

"Good song," she said, looking back at him and smiling.

They took off into the park and followed one of the usually crowded concrete walking paths. They followed the path and continued the mindless chit-chat about nothing at all. It seemed to fill the empty space between them, and they both seemed to be okay with that. For now, at least.

They soon found themselves in an area along the path shrouded by trees on either side. It was nearly pitch-black with only drops of silver moonlight leaking through the branches. Rhiannon stopped walking and turned to face Owen. The slivers of the penetrating moonlight falling across her face as she stood there. She stared at him, then at the dark concrete path. She looked even more as though she had something she desperately wanted to say, and maybe the darkness was giving her the courage to do so. But not a single word escaped her lips.

Owen stood there waiting, affording her every opportunity to say whatever it was that was weighing so heavily on her mind. Whatever it was that was so difficult for her to talk about in the light, but she stood silent. Her eyes moved between him and the path. He opened his mouth to speak. His internal curiosity had nearly reached its boiling point. What did she want to say? Why wasn't she saying it? He started to speak, but he was interrupted when Rhiannon stepped toward him, maintaining her silence. She stood there in front of him, even closer now, staring directly into his eyes. Owen could feel that same all too familiar knot beginning to form and twist in his stomach. He attempted to speak again when Rhiannon grabbed him and pulled him towards her hurriedly and pressed her lips against his. Owen could feel what little control he had maintained throughout the evening slipping through his grasp and floating away like smoke on the breeze.

He had spent years since their last night together longing for this very moment. *Soak this in,* he thought. *It may be the last.* Then suddenly, unbeknownst to even him, he pulled away. It was as if lightening had struck the concrete surface of the path between where the two of them stood. He took a step back away from her, staring at the still nervous look on her face.

"What are you doing, Rhi?" he asked, quietly. He could hear the evenings forecasted rain begin to fall all around them, splashing into the trees above their heads and on the grass behind them. She stood silent.

"You know what?" he continued, throwing his hands in the air. The frustration in his voice was very clear. "I don't wanna know."

He turned and walked out from under the cover of the trees and into an open area of the park. The rain began to pick up, turning from a light drizzle into a full-on down pour.

"Wait," Rhiannon called out to him, but he didn't stop.

He didn't look back. He continued walking in the opposite direction. She took off after him, also abandoning the cover of the trees and into the now torrential rainfall. She continued calling his name, but he stayed his course.

"Owen, wait," she cried out once more. This time sounding slightly angry and annoyed. She caught up to him grabbing him by the sleave of his rain-soaked jacket.

"No, you wait," Owen said, sharply, as he spun around to face her. The rain like TV static between their faces. "Since I walked out of your grandfather's house that night, I have spent every second of every day trying to get over the fact that I couldn't make you stay. That *I* wasn't enough of a reason for you to stay. I hated the way we left things. I hated myself for even bringing it up. Because I knew if I had just left it alone, we could have at least had that one last night together. And yeah, I probably would have still been miserable when you left. I would have still missed you just as much as I already did, but at least I would have had that to hold on to instead of what I was left with."

"But…," Rhiannon started, but was quickly interrupted.

"I'm going to tell you something that you have no way of knowing. But it's too important for me not to tell you now that I have the chance. You don't know what it feels like to be the other person in this equation," he said gesturing at each of them. "You don't know what it feels like to stand beside you, to hold you, to taste you. Just to sit across a table from you. To watch you smile or make you laugh. Just to look at you and *maybe* catch your eye. You don't have any clue how amazingly wonderful each of those things truly are and it's because of those reasons, and many others that I almost didn't come tonight. I didn't want to come because I was scared."

Owen watched as the anger in her face melted away.

"Scared to death that just sitting there having a drink with you would undo everything and I would crumble. I was scared I would just fall apart. I just––I can't do it. I can't have you like this. I can't have you whenever it suites you, just to turn around and watch you leave again. I'm sorry, Rhi, I *really* am. I just can't do it. I don't think I'm strong enough to do it twice. I wish you nothing but the best, I really do. But I gotta go.

He turned to walk away again, leaving her standing there in the downpour. Every inch of both of them now completely soaked.

"Owen," she cried out as he walked away. But he didn't stop.

"Owen Christopher!" she shouted over the pounding rain in a demanding tone as she followed in his direction.

Owen stopped and turned around facing her once again. She walked quickly over to where he stood, water splashing up at her from the ground with each powerful step.

"You didn't let me speak," she said harshly. "Yes––okay––yes, I left.

She was breathing heavily now. Owen supposed he was about to hear what she had avoided saying all evening.

"But I had a plan for my life, Owen. I came home for one reason and one reason only. None of this was supposed to happen…"

"But it *did* happen, Rhi!" Owen interrupted, shouting over the rain.

"Yes, it happened," Rhiannon said. "And *because* it happened, every single thing I had planned fell apart."

Owen stood there confused, staring back at her.

"I had a plan, Owen," Rhiannon continued, calming the tone of her voice. "My plan was to come home, bury my grandfather, and get on with my life. Because that's what he would've wanted me to do. I came home prepared for loss. I had already made peace with that. What I wasn't prepared for was you."

Owen stared back at her. Anger and confusion creeping into his already tangled emotions.

"I wasn't even prepared to see you. And even after I did, I wasn't prepared to get as involved as I did. But I couldn't help it. And most of all, oh my *God*, most of all, I was nowhere near prepared to fall in love with you."

She paused. And in her silence, Owen could feel the knot twisting and tightening in his stomach once again.

"That last night at dinner," she continued. "I *prayed* that me staying wouldn't even come up. That we just both understood what was going to happen. What *had* to happen. I knew it was on your mind. I saw it all over your face the moment you walked through the door. It was all you were thinking about the whole time. And I don't blame you for that. It was on my mind too. But when it did come up, I––I panicked. On one hand I had this wonderful, exciting life elsewhere. That at the time, I didn't want to just abandon. And on the other hand, there was you. And I'm sorry, Owen, but I just didn't know what to do. I was scared too. But let me tell you," she said pointing her finger at him harshly. "The second I sat down on that plane I wanted to get right back off and come find you. I had to tell myself, over and over again, *it'll be better once you're in the air.* Then, *it'll be better once you land. It'll be better once you get settled back in,* but it never––got––better. It never got any easier being away from you. No matter what I did. It didn't matter what my friends said or where they took me or what fun and exciting thing, they drug me off to do. All I wanted to do was come back. I spent the next few *years* forcing myself to live a life, that at one time, I wanted more than anything else in the world. Desperately hoping that one day it would be what it once was. That it would feel the way it did before. But I couldn't stand it anymore. So, I left it all behind. I came back.

She paused and stared at him, trying to gauge what he was thinking.

I *do* understand what it's like to be the other half of this equation. Because I have hated being away from you every single day, just as much as you've hated being away from me. I don't have a plan anymore, Owen. I came back for one reason, and one reason only."

She paused again. Owen hung in the balance, waiting for what she would say next. The sound of the rain falling all around them seemed to fill his head. He couldn't think about anything except the one thing he knew for sure. This was either the beginning or the end. It wasn't at all how he imagined it, but he knew it rarely was.

Rhiannon sighed. Her eyes fell to the sopping grass beneath their shoes. It seemed to Owen that she understood and accepted that everything hinged on what she said next.

"I came back to find you," she said meeting his eyes with her own. "And now that I have, I'm hoping that you still love me and want me in your life me as much as *I know* you did before."

Owen threw his head back and stared into the starless, night sky. The rain splashed against his face. He closed his eyes and felt the drops pelting him all over. He looked back at Rhiannon. She was standing there staring at him, nervously waiting for him to say anything. The pounding storm continued all around them.

"Listen, Owen," she said. "If you're still scared, I unders...,"

"Stop," Owen said, cutting her off. Everything she said was now bouncing back and forth in his mind. "Just stop." He looked back at her, and she back at him.

He stepped toward her and grabbed her. He lifted her off the ground and pulled her to him. Her legs wrapped around his waist. Her hands cupped his face as he pressed his lips against hers and felt her fall into his kiss. She felt like dead weight in his arms. She wrapped her arms around his neck and continued kissing him as if it were going to be the last time. They stood there inseparable, clinging to each other and utterly drenched from the storm.

Owen briefly pulled his lips away from hers. "I *do* still love you," he said, staring into her eyes.

"I love you too," she said, staring back at him, breathing heavily. Her heart was nearly pounding out of her chest. "And I'll never leave you again."

They continued holding on to each other as tightly as they could. The roaring rainfall echoing throughout the park all around them and the city beyond. They had found each other once again and no amount of bad weather was going to take this moment away from them.

Owen sat her back down on her feet. He took her by the hand and without saying another word they walked out of the park together.

They made their way back to the street outside the park and caught the first taxi they could find. They both climbed in the back seat, waterlogged, and on the verge of laughing at the extent of their circumstantial dampness. Owen started to give the cab driver his address when Rhiannon interrupted and gave the driver the address to her grandfather's house. The driver took off toward Long Island with the two of them still silent in the back seat exchanging glances and smiles. During one such glance, Rhiannon reached over and took Owen's hand. She interlocked her fingers with his and rested their two hands on the seat between them.

They reached Rhiannon's grandfather's house in what seemed to be a record time. The storm seemed to have forced more New Yorkers to stay inside than usual. It was almost as if it had paved their way for the evening. Owen paid the driver who took off back toward the city and left them once again standing in the downpour. He grabbed her by the hand and started toward the house. Rhiannon followed for a few steps then stopped. He stopped as well and turned to find her found her smiling.

"Come on," she said and pulled him in the opposite direction.

Through the gate they ran not stopping or slowing down until they reached the pond. When they reached the dock, she let go of his hand and stood there staring at the wall of rain slamming into the surface of a water. The sound reminded her of a waterfall crashing into the body of water below. She turned and faced him. She held out her hands to each side and let the rain splash off her palms.

"It'd be a shame to waste this weather," she said.

She pulled the straps of her dress off each shoulder and let it fall to the dock. She stepped out of the dress toward Owen and kissed him once again. She ran her hands under the front of his shirt and lifted it upward until he took it the rest of the way off. The two continued shedding their clothing until the rain was falling on nothing but their bare skin. Owen grabbed her by the waist and pulled her in as close to him as he could get her. The warmth of their naked bodies their only shield against the cool summer rain.

They knelt down on to the sodden wood surface of the dock, managing to continue their kiss all the way down. Rhiannon laid back onto the dock. Large drops of rain pelted every inch of her body and splashed off every surface that surrounded the two of them. Owen followed her down, positioning himself on top of her. He removed his lips from hers and stared at her for a long moment. He was memorizing her face as she stared back at him. With a look of want, of *need*, in her eyes, she placed a hand on his cheek and caressed his face. Then she pulled his head down and raised her own and rested her cheek against his.

"Make love to me," she whispered.

| 27 |

He stared down at her, taking all of her in. The moonlight on her skin. The trails of rainwater, first forming, and then quickly rushing off her body. He could feel her moving against him, aching for him. Her hands desperately seeking purchase, and her legs tightening around him as he slipped into her and an audible gasp escaped her lips.

The rain pelted them from all sides, splashing onto every surface and surrounding them in white noise. The staticky hum serenaded them as their pleasure rose and rose, threatening to expose their deepest vulnerability.

They would reach the end together It was only a matter of letting go. Of allowing their tangled bodies, a moment of weakness. A moment of release.

Owen ran one hand through Rhiannon's hair and pulled her mouth up to his own. The storm responded with a roll of thunder the instant their lips met. A long, deep, roll of thunder, and every touch a bolt of lightning. He bit down gently on her lip as her fingers clinched and her nails dug into his back. They were sprinting toward the end now. They could see it. They could *feel* it in every cell in their bodies as thunder rolled once more all around them.

The rain seemed to fall harder, cooling their bodies against the warmth they were creating. He felt her legs tighten around him. Her ankles locked and she squeezed as her back arched up, off the wooden surface of the deck, simultaneously pressing into him and pulling him closer. The rainwater that had pooled in her naval spilled over and ran down the side of her body. And then she let go. Thunder rolled once more as the release came for them. Found them. Enveloped them. And then, as if someone had flipped a switch, the rain stopped, and he heard her pleasure echo into the stillness of the night.

Owen slowly lowered himself down against her rain-soaked, naked body. He could hear her breath slowing against the backdrop of the storm. Her heart was thudding in her chest. Her hands roamed his back for one long moment, unsure where they wanted to settle, and then her fingers were in his hair. He pushed up and looked down at her, wanting to take all of her in again. The moonlight glistening off every drop on her body, making her sparkle like the treasure she was to him.

A relaxed, satisfied smile rose from the corners of her mouth. And she pulled him down and kissed him again.

The walk back to the house was a quiet one. The night sounds slowly resuming since the passing of the storm. Once inside, Rhiannon took their dripping clothes and threw them in the dryer. She found Owen some sweatpants and a t-shirt that had belonged to her grandfather and gave them to Owen. Mr. Thurman was much bigger than Owen in the mid-section, but he was able to make do.

Rhiannon changed into pajama pants and a t-shirt as well and the two of them climbed in the bed and wrapped themselves in one another.

"I have something to tell you," Rhiannon said, her head laying on Owen's chest

"What's that?" Owen asked, intertwining his finger in the length of her damp hair.

"I found out right before I left, last time that my grandfather left his house to me." She craned her neck and looked up at him. "That means we never have to leave this place. It's ours. Forever."

Owen couldn't help but smile. She laid her head back down and didn't wait for him to say anything. He didn't need to say anything. She knew that meant just as much to him as it did to her. This place had been a large part of both their lives since they were kids. And now it was theirs. It was where they had met. And now, it was where they had fallen in love a lifetime later. But tonight, it was where they had outlasted the storm by creating one of their own.

It didn't take long for the two of them to fall asleep. Neither one let go of the other. They slept through the night and well into Saturday morning. When Owen did wake up, he checked his phone. The screen showed a couple of missed calls from Tommy. He sat his phone back down on the nightstand and lay there staring at the ceiling, replaying their night together in his head from beginning to end. He thought about the chain of events. How it started, the rain, how it unfolded, *the rain*. He would never look at the rain the same again. *I almost walked away,* he thought. He didn't like how that thought made him feel. How close he actually came. *But she wouldn't let me*, he thought. He stewed on that thought for no more than a minute or two then quickly moved on.

He thought about how she described her life abroad after she had left. All these years he never once suspected that she was just as broken about leaving him as he was about her leaving. Part of him still had trouble believing that she was really laying here with him or that last night had really gone the way that it did. Yet it had. And here she was.

Rhiannon started to stir. Moving just a little, then working herself onto her back and into a full-on stretch.

"Good morning," she said, looking over at him and smiling.

"Good morning," he said, smiling back at her.

"How'd you sleep?" she asked.

"Like a rock," he said.

Rhiannon closed her eyes and raised her arms above her head and stretched once more. "You want some breakfast?" she asked. "I'm making pancakes."

"Mmm," Owen grunted. "That…sounds…incredible."

Rhiannon sat up in the bed and smiled. She leaned over and gave him a kiss then got out of bed and made her way to the kitchen. Owen could hear the sound of the pancake prep work being done in the kitchen, so he grabbed his phone and sent a text message to Tommy.

Sorry I missed your calls…we were sleeping…call you later.

He sat his phone back down and got out of the bed. As soon as he stood up his phone chimed showing a reply from Tommy. *We?* the message read. Owen chuckled at Tommy's reply having said "*we* were sleeping" on purpose, just to leave Tommy hanging. *Call you later,* Owen replied. He stared at his phone for a few more seconds to see of another reply would come through. Tommy did not disappoint. Owen's phone chimed again. *Asshole,* the message read to which Owen laughed even harder.

He walked into the kitchen where Rhiannon stood at the stove working on the pancakes. He walked up behind her and wrapped his arms around her waist. She rubbed his hand and leaned her head back on to his chest, looking up at him. They sat down and enjoyed breakfast together, catching up on everything they had neglected to talk about at the bar the night before. Owen gave her all the details about Tommy and Alison's anniversary/engagement party that he had a hand in planning. As well as Alison's pregnancy. How the shop had been doing and their families. Trying to make sure he covered all the bases. There was a lightness in the air between them now. Complete opposite of the thick, staggering tension that occupied the space between them at the bar.

They talked well into the afternoon before Owen left for his apartment. He spent the drive thinking about how the evening started. Everything that happened at the park. And of course, how the evening ended. Even after waking up next to Rhiannon this morning, it was still hard for him to wrap his mind around the two of them finally being together.

Together, he thought, analyzing the word. His mind stuck there for a bit. It just didn't seem real. Yet, it most certainly was. And he couldn't be happier.

After getting back home, showering, and sitting down to relax for the evening, Owen finally got back in touch with Tommy, who had clearly been impatiently awaiting his call. Owen told him the entire story. From the bar to the park and the rain, and then of course the dock. Tommy was thrilled for both of them. Alison was as well. Tommy had been relaying information to her while on the phone, before just turning on the speakerphone so they could both get the story firsthand.

After finishing his conversation with Tommy and Alison, Owen sat on his couch and stared at the TV. The light flickered in the dark living room, jerking the shadows back and forth into different positions. His mind was with Rhiannon. He thought again, about how close he came to actually walking away from her and what she said that caused him to stay. He had lived it. He had told Tommy the entire story from beginning to end. But part of him still thought that he would wake up any moment to the heartbreaking reality that it had all been a dream. But that moment never came. Only sleep where he dreamed of her in his arms.

| 28 |

"What are you doing up?" Alison asked walking into the living room and finding Tommy on the couch, painfully staring down into two open casefiles on the coffee table in front of him.

She had woken up in the middle of the night due to the tiny acrobat growing inside her and realized that Tommy wasn't in the bed. She thought at first that he had gone to the bathroom, but the light wasn't on, and she couldn't hear anything.

"I just couldn't sleep," he said, still staring at the files.

"What's this?" Alison asked as she sat down on the couch next to him. But inside she felt she already knew.

"It's just a couple of files from work," he said, not wanting to say the names out loud. He knew she would be concerned that he was bringing his work home with him.

He had told her previously about placing the files in his desk drawer rather than filing them as cold cases. She had looked at him then as if she was concerned about him not letting go of cases he couldn't solve, but she hadn't said anything. But she never forgot the look on his face.

"Hmm," Alison said. "Okay."

Tommy sensed that she was aware of exactly what files they were without him saying a word. He waited for the questions. For the worried look on her face.

"Don't stay up too long, honey," she said. She stood up and kissed him on the top of the head and walked back toward the bedroom.

"Hey, babe," Tommy said, looking up at her as she walked away. She turned around and looked at him. "I love you," he said like a man losing his grip on something.

"I love you too," she said.

Tommy watched her walk the rest of the way into the bedroom and when he heard the door close, he went back to his files. *She has to know,* he thought, immediately feeling guilty for not being completely honest with her about the files.

This wasn't the first time he had brought them home. It was just the first time she had found out about it. Tommy closed the files and left them sitting on the coffee table. He sat back on the couch and stared at the wall behind the TV. The apartment was silent. He thought about Alison and their child that would be here very soon. He started to wonder himself, why he was unable to let these cases go. Why couldn't he take them to that place where, sadly, a lot of cases went to die? Was it the elusiveness of the killer? It hadn't *really* bothered him that stepping out of Sydnie Johnson's case, he had stepped directly into a new one that seemed to be directly related. He would have been assigned a new case either way. *But then there was a second murder,* he thought.

Tommy rubbed his hands across his face. He was tired. He looked at the clock on the microwave. He had to leave for work in just a few short hours, but the files wouldn't let him sleep. Sure, he could go back there and lay down. He may even drift off. But he had dreamed about doing exactly what he was doing right now. Sitting at his desk, trying desperately to work this puzzle, and coming up short every time.

Work the next day was more of the same. He had placed the files back in their drawer in his desk with no intention of looking at them for the rest of the day. He did have other things he could be working on, but that didn't last long. Before lunch, he found himself pushing everything else aside and sitting at his desk with the files opened, reading over the same reports he had been reading almost every day since the second body was found. It was like a novel he just couldn't put down. He read the notes, the statements, all the reports. He stared at the pictures. He had already seared this stuff into his brain. He didn't know what else he could learn from these files that he didn't already know. But that was exactly what he was looking for. Something he didn't already know.

His head was pulled out of the files by the sound of his phone ringing. I was Alison. Tommy picked up his phone and stared at her name on the screen. The phone had rung three times now. Was she calling to talk to him about last night? About the files he brought home. Was she *that* concerned? He knew he couldn't blame her if she was. The phone rang again. He knew in his heart that she knew what files they were when she walked into the living room last night, even though neither of them had actually said it out loud. *How could she not?* he thought. The phone rang again. He snapped out of his thought process and answered the phone to a frantic Alison on the other end.

There was a mixture of crying and laughter pouring out from the other end of the line. He tried hard to understand what it was she was trying to say through this borage of mixed emotions but had no such luck at first. He spoke over her ramblings, finally convincing her to calm down and tell him what she was trying to say.

"I'm in labor!" she said, the tears and laughter immediately picking back up.

Tommy paused for a long moment as her words burrowed into his brain. "I'm on my way," he said and grabbed the files and flung them back into the drawer. The same drawer he had intended on keeping them in earlier.

He notified the captain that their ticking clock had made a significant leap forward and ran out of the precinct. He drove straight to their apartment and ran inside, leaving the car running outside. Alison met him at the door, go-bag in hand and ready to go. In the car on the way to the hospital, Alison's vacillating emotions continued causing Tommy to wonder how he should be responding at the moment. Although, he was content with his surprisingly calm demeanor.

They arrived at the hospital, quickly parked the car, and got inside as fast as they could. Tommy, still calm and reserved, approached the information desk just inside the hospital doors and informed the nurse that his wife was in labor. Alison stood behind him red-faced and trying to catch her breath. The nurse sat Alison down in a wheelchair and informed the maternity floor that she would be up momentarily.

The three of them climbed on the elevator. The nurse pushed Alison in the wheelchair and Tommy carried the bag. They got off on the fourth floor and the nurse wheeled her down to another information-type desk where another nurse sat waiting. Alison did her best to answer the second nurse's questions in her emotional state, with some help from Tommy. The nurse finished her line of initial questions and had them take a seat in the small waiting area next to the desk. Across from the desk there was a single, large door with a small black plastic plate mounted to the front, the plate read, "Triage" in white capital letters.

Alison's face had started to return to its normal shade. Although the shades of pink and red would return every few minutes when the contractions came. After about fifteen minutes a nurse walked out of the "Triage" door, addressing Alison, and asking her what her pain level was and about how long there was between the pains. Alison gave the nurse all the information she had requested, and the nurse wheeled her through the triage door and into another exam-type room.

Tommy followed Alison and the nurse, and when the nurse closed the door to the exam room, she handed Alison a hospital gown and asked her to change out of her clothes and have a seat on the exam table. The nurse left the room and Alison began to undress. Tommy sat down in a chair tucked away in the corner of the room smiling, and ogling at her, and jokingly making comments about the two of them seizing the opportunity and being "adventurous" in a hospital room. Alison shot a half-annoyed glare back across the room at him. He quickly quieted himself, retreating further into his corner and playing with latex glove he had taken from one of the boxes mounted on the wall.

Alison got changed into the hospital gown and slowly climbed on the exam table. It was another twenty minutes before the doctor, along with the nurse from before, joined them in the exam room. He spoke with Alison, asking her a lot of the same questions that the nurse had asked her in the waiting area, as well as others pertaining to the current state of her pregnancy. Once the doctor was finished with his questions, he instructed Alison to place her feet in the stirrups and to lie back and try and relax. When she was positioned, the doctor placed a glove on his hand and checked to see how far she was dilated.

Tommy sat there in his corner, feeling a little uncomfortable with what was happening. Not that he thought the doctor was doing anything wrong, he just wasn't sure if he was supposed to be in the room for it. To Tommy's relief, the doctor finished the exam rather quickly. He removed his gloves and told Alison that she was only dilated two centimeters at the moment. He informed them that what she was likely experiencing were Braxton Hicks contractions. In other words, false labor. Alison began to tear up when she heard the doctor's prognosis. The doctor asked if she had already been scheduled for an induction and she told him she had, and that the appointment was for the following Monday. He excused himself from the exam room and informed her that she could change back into her clothes and a nurse would be in momentarily with her discharge papers.

Tommy sat silent in the corner watching a disgruntled Alison change from the hospital gown back into her clothes. The nurse came in a few moments later and handed him some papers. She told Alison that if the pain got to be more than she felt she could handle, she should feel free to come back and they would check her again. Alison smiled half-heartedly at the nurse, looking at the words "false labor" on the first page under the heading "Doctors Notes."

After the nurse left the room, she turned to Tommy and nodded towards the door. Alison didn't utter a single word for a good part of the drive back to their apartment. She sat there in the passenger seat leaned up against the window with the saddest look on her face Tommy had ever seen. They were about halfway home when she said, "I really thought that was it." All Tommy could do was sympathize with her.

When they got back to their apartment, Alison went to the bedroom to take a nap and Tommy retired to the couch for the remainder of the day. He sat there flipping through the channels, content with getting an early start on the weekend. After the morning he'd had at the office with his face once again buried in the Arnold and Hammond files, and then Alison's false labor, it seemed they both needed to relax as much as they could before her scheduled induction on Monday.

He hoped that they didn't have any more false alarms before then. She was sad enough over this one, he didn't know how she would handle another trip to the hospital that didn't end with them having the baby.

He thought about the files in his desk drawer. He was glad he had rushed out of the precinct the way he had, leaving the files behind. He didn't have to suffer that end of the day pull to bring the files home with him again.

They spent the weekend doing nothing but lounging around the apartment. They were both anxiously waiting for Monday when they would be able to see their new baby for the first time. Tommy had spoken to Owen on the phone Friday evening and told him about Alison's false labor. So, he showed up at their apartment late Saturday afternoon to hang out with Tommy and see how Alison was feeling. He walked through the door with two large pizzas. One with all of Alison's favorite toppings and the other for him and Tommy. Alison was thrilled about the pizza, ready to feed herself and the baby, but in her emotional state, she almost cried when Owen sat the pizza down in front of her.

The three of them sat around for the rest of the afternoon and into the evening, eating and talking. Alison told Owen how pissed she was that it was only false labor and that if it happened again before the induction, she didn't know what she would do. "If it happens again, we're not leaving until my water breaks," she said, as if a light bulb had lit inside her head.

Alison went to bed around 8:30 pm. The pizza had put her in a sort of food coma, and she was barely able to stay awake sitting on the couch. Tommy and Owen got a couple good laughs watching her nod off while trying to participate in the conversation, sputtering random things that had nothing to do what they were talking about. Tommy suggested that she go on to bed, which didn't bother her at all. She was content with sleeping the weekend away if it meant Monday would get here quicker. Then her pregnancy would be over, and she wouldn't be so uncomfortable. She hoped at least. She hugged Owen and thanked him again for the pizza. Then she kissed Tommy and went off to bed.

"So, how's things with Rhiannon?" Tommy asked.

"It's going great, Man" Owen said. "I'm so glad she's back.

"I know you are," Tommy said. "I can see it all over your face." Owen couldn't help but smile again, just thinking about her.

"So, you excited, nervous, or what?" Owen asked.

"Man, I'm all over the place," Tommy said.

"What do you mean?" Owen asked.

"I'm excited about the baby, of course," Tommy said. "And nervous. But man, just shit with the job, ya know."

"Such as?" Owen asked. He knew exactly what Tommy was talking about.

"Man I––I keep finding myself buried in these case files." Tommy said. "I've been over them a thousand times and I never find anything new."

"Maybe there just isn't anything else to find," Owen said.

"I've thought about that," Tommy said. "I've tried to let it go. But every time I get myself motivated to do that; I always think that there *has* to be something else."

"Listen, bro," Owen said. "Now more than ever you need to let that shit go. In two days, you guys are going to be parents. Then you'll have a whole new batch of shit to worry about." Tommy laughed. "My point is you need to be here. Your mind and your focus need to be here, with Alison and the baby. Work will be there. Those cases aren't going anywhere and if something comes up, you can do something about it then."

Tommy knew he was right. He needed to get his head in the game, because the game was going to be here very soon, and he had been very much looking forward to filling that position. He also knew that Alison was going to need him more in the beginning because of her recovery time and the fact that neither one of them had any real experience with newborns.

"You're right, man. I gotta get my shit together," Tommy said.

"You will," Owen said. "I have all the faith in the world in you, brother."

| 29 |

The Sunday before her induction seemed to move by so slow that Alison wondered if time might actually go backwards. And though she had begrudgingly accepted what the doctor had said, she was still none too happy about it.

Monday morning finally arrived, and Tommy and Alison couldn't have been happier. "Induction day!" she cheered, still in the warmth of their bed at five in the morning. Her doctor had told her to be at the hospital at eight-o-clock that morning and they would get her set up for the induction. They ended up arriving at the hospital around 7:30 am because once Alison was ready to go, her nerves wouldn't allow her to sit and wait any longer. She was literally standing by the door, so Tommy agreed that they could go ahead and go to the hospital.

They arrived at the hospital and took the elevator to the fourth floor for the second time. They stopped at the nurse's desk again, where Alison, very excitedly, informed the nurse that she had an eight-o-clock appointment. The nurse looked at the computer, confirmed their appointment, and asked them to have a seat in the waiting area. And once again they were told that the nurse would be with them in a moment. Fifteen, twenty, thirty minutes passed, before the Triage opened and a nurse walked out. She wore a blue surgical gown with a matching face mask and a surgical cap with her hair tucked up inside. She walked over to Tommy and Alison, sitting in the waiting area, and removed her mask.

"Ms. Taylor," she asked.

"That's me," Alison said, smiling at the nurse, and standing up.

"I'm sorry, Ms. Taylor, but it doesn't appear that we have a room available at the moment to put you in," she said.

"I––I'm––I'm sorry," Alison said, slowly sitting back down next to Tommy, her smile completely wiped from her face. "I––I don't understand,"

"It would seem," the nurse said empathetically. "That every woman in the city, near the end of her pregnancy has gone into active labor within the last thirty-six hours. When those patients come in, they unfortunately take priority over scheduled inductions."

Alison sat there defeated and feeling as though she were shrinking further and further into the waiting room chair.

"So, what are we supposed to do?" Alison asked, visibly frustrated but trying to remain civil. She was a doctor, after all, and had been the one to deliver unfortunate news to patients on many occasions, so she could understand the nurse's position. But that didn't make it any less heartbreaking.

"Well," the nurse said doing her best to reassure them. "There is a possibility that a L&D room will open up today. I'm almost sure of it. We have some that are on the verge of giving birth right now and we have others that have already given birth, they're just waiting on a room in the Mother/Baby wing." The nurse paused and gave the information time to sink in. "So, you're welcome to stay and wait. Although, I can't tell you how long that wait will be. Or you could find something to do close to the hospital and we can call you when a room opens up,"

Alison looked at Tommy, who had been silent the entire time. He recognized the fragile state Alison was in and knew that even a single word from him while the nurse was still there would expedite the impending burst into tears.

"What do you suggest?" she asked, looking back at the nurse.

"If I were you, honey," she said. "I would find something to do. Something that's going to hopefully take your mind off the waiting. I know that will be near impossible, but it beats sitting in this tiny waiting area, for God knows how long."

Alison looked back at Tommy; he looked at the nurse. "Thank you, ma'am," he said.

The nurse apologized again. She took down Alison's number and reassured her that they would call her the second a room opened up. She walked back through the Triage door and as the door closed behind her, Alison sat in the waiting area and broke down. Tommy sat beside her and rubbed her back, trying to comfort her.

"You wanna get out of here, find something to do?" he asked her. She wiped her face and looked at him.

"I am *not* leaving this hospital until I have this baby," she said.

Tommy didn't say another word. He could see that she was in no mood to compromise on anything. They sat there for about thirty more minutes before he was able to convince her to at least go down to the cafeteria and get something to eat. She had been in such a hurry to get to the hospital this morning that neither of them had eaten anything. Even as angry as she was, she *was* hungry, and so they went down to see what they could find to eat.

They arrived in the cafeteria and stood there looking at the menu board and deciding what they wanted before getting in line. They got their food and sat down in the dining area. They mostly ate in silence. Tommy was desperately trying to think of something to talk about that may lighten the mood or at the very least, steer her mind away from the unknown amount of time they were going to spend waiting on a room. Nothing that good came to mind.

They finished their food and slowly made the long walk back to the elevators and up to the fourth floor. They walked past the nurse's desk and sat themselves back in the tiny waiting area. Alison pulled out her phone and called her mother to let her know that there had been a slight delay and that they didn't need to rush to get to the hospital. Tommy thought this was a good idea, as his mother was planning on coming as well. So, he stepped away from the waiting area and called his mother to let her know what was going on as well.

They each finished their phone calls and once again sat silent in the waiting area. Two-–hours had passed since the nurse told them about the room shortage and no one's mood seemed to be getting any better. Tommy worried with every passing minute that Alison was going to break down again. His worry got worse every time the Triage door opened, and it wasn't someone with good news. Well into hour three, Alison was still very much toeing the line between impatiently waiting and losing her shit on the next person that came through the Triage door. When the door opened again and a nurse stepped through, again, wearing all the surgical get up. It was the same nurse they had spoken to when they arrived that morning. The same bearer of bad news that told them there wasn't a room available. She walked over to the waiting area and looked at Alison, who was staring up at her. Eyes wide and expectant, ready to burst into tears depending on what she said.

"Let's go, sweetie," she said to Alison. "We got you a room."

Alison burst into tears anyway, which Tommy fully expected regardless of what the nurse had to say. They both stood up. Alison tearfully thanked the nurse several times as she led them into the exam room. The same room they had been in when Alison had her false labor. She once again changed into a hospital gown and sat down on the exam table. A few minutes later the nurse returned and told them that the room was finished being cleaned and was ready for them.

The look on Alison's face morphed from a look of excitement to a look of complete and total awareness. Almost scared. This was really going to happen. It was time. The nurse escorted them to their labor and delivery room and helped Alison into the bed, while Tommy got their bags situated in the corner.

"How are you doing?" the nurse asked, Alison.

"Uh…a little nervous at this point," Alison said, trying to work up a smile.

"Well," the nurse said. "We will be in and out, checking on you and getting you ready for the procedure. First, we will break your water then you will get an IV of Pitocin to help the labor along. Hopefully, not too long after that we will have us a baby."

The nurse gave a large, genuine but clearly practiced smile.

Minutes seemed to move in breaths for the both of them. Nurses were in and out checking on Alison and monitoring the baby's heartbeat. Tommy knew that she was scared. He was scared too. Neither of them had been through this before. Everything from here on out was going to be new territory. About thirty minutes later the nurse appeared again, this time with Alison's doctor. "It's time to break your water," he said, producing an instrument that looked to Tommy like a large crocheting hook.

Tommy looked at the instrument, then at Alison. Her eyes were as wide as he had ever seen them. He imagined that she saw the same thing when she looked back at him. The doctor prepared Alison, telling her that she was going to feel a bit of pressure. It was over in just a few seconds, but after the doctor and nurses left the room, Alison told Tommy that she felt like she had peed herself. It was the first time they had laughed all day.

The nurses returned periodically to check on Alison and monitor the baby. The doctorless frequently to check how dilated she was. Her doctor said that her labor seemed to be moving along slowly and after a while the nurse returned with a bag of medicine that they hooked to the IV in Alison's arm.

"This is Pitocin," the nurse said. "The doctor wants us to get this started and hopefully it will speed up the labor. If it does your contractions are going to get more intense, and more frequent. Just wanted to give you a heads up so you didn't think something was wrong."

Alison looked at Tommy as if she wanted to call the whole thing off and go home. But they both knew that wasn't an option.

"Dad," the nurse said, addressing Tommy this time. "Your job is going to be keeping track of the time between her contractions. The shorter the time between, the closer we are to push time. When they get about five minutes apart, we'll be really close. So, if one of us isn't in here when that happens just hit the button and let us know."

"Five--button--contractions--got it," Tommy stammered, as the nurse smiled and left the room.

He looked back at Alison, who's face had shifted from nervous, to full on frightened. Once the door closed Alison laid her head back and took some more deep breaths. No doubt preparing for the inevitable. Tommy stood up from his chair in the corner, near where he had stowed their bags, and walked over to Alison's bed.

"You doin' okay, baby?" he asked.

"Yeah," she said, in a large exhale. "I'm just ready for it to be over with. I'm ready to see our baby."

"I know you are," he said. "I am too."

Alison laid her head back down and closed her eyes. Tommy began brushing her hair back with his fingers. He kissed her forehead, and after a few minutes, walked back over and sat back down in his chair. He wanted to let her rest. If he knew nothing else about this process, he knew she was going to need all her energy very soon enough.

Sitting there silent, watching Alison in the hospital bed, Tommy's mind began to wonder. It wondered away from Alison and their baby and back work. Specifically, the two case files not so neatly tuck away in one of his desk drawers. He started to feel a slight panic that something may develop in either of the cases and he wouldn't be there to handle it. *Would they even call?* he wondered. *The captain knows why I took today off. He knows Alison's induction was scheduled for today.* Fear churned in his stomach at the thought of something breaking in either one of the cases and him not knowing about it. His brain instinctively began reciting the notes and reports contained in the files as if it were trying to compensate for being unavailable to their beckon call. Sending out some kind of signal that it hadn't forgotten about them. He stood at the window of their labor and delivery room. Orienting himself from where he was in the city and staring out in the direction of the precinct.

He wondered who would handle it if something *did* happen? The thought of not being at his desk, not at least being within reach of those damn files began to make his stomach flip even more. His concentration was broken suddenly, by the sound of the door opening to their room. Tommy turned and looked at the door, then at Alison.

She was sitting up and looking toward the door as well. *I hope she hadn't been staring at me this whole time,* he thought, immediately feeling ashamed. He felt that if she had been, she would have been able to hear what he was thinking. And what kind of husband, what kind of *father* would turn his thoughts and attention away from his wife and unborn child at time like this. When they both needed him more than anyone else.

The doctor walked in followed by the nurse. Tommy looked at his watch. It had been just under an hour since the nurse had started the Pitocin. Tommy imagined, one day after an appointment where her and her doctor discussed her being induced, that after they broke her water that it would only take about an hour to have the baby.

"We just need to check and see how dilated you are," the doctor said, in his cheerful, matter-of-fact tone.

Tommy looked back at Alison who was nodding at the doctor. She got herself in position and he checked. "You're at about a five," the doctor said. "You're moving along nicely." He took off his gloves and tossed them in the trash and opened the door. "We'll be back to check again in a little while," he said. And then he and the nurse followed him out of the room.

Tommy walked over to Alison, who he could tell was thankful for the progress, but wished it had been more.

Within the next hour the intensity of Alison's contractions had started to increase significantly. So much so that Tommy began to worry that their baby was going to come with only him there to assist her. Tommy grabbed his chair and sat next to the bed holding Alison's hand, his focus finally where it needed to be. They talked about anything they could to keep Alison's mind, (and secretly, Tommy's as well) from wondering to places it didn't need to at that moment. Soon the doctor/nurse duo came back into the room asking about the contractions. Intensity, length, frequency. The doctor checked Alison's dilation once more. Only this time, when he was finished, he looked at Alison and said, "It's just about time to push." He and the nurse left the room again. Tommy looked at Alison and she back at him. They were going to meet their baby soon.

Within minutes, the doctor returned with not only the one nurse, but what seemed to be a team of nurses, all of whom were wearing full surgical attire. One of the nurses walked over to Tommy and handed him a set of the same surgical scrubs for himself. Once he was dressed and ready the nurse said, "You're going to help mom." And she directed him back to Alison's bedside where she told him that he was going to have to help hold her leg. Everyone seemed to be getting in position, poised and ready, exactly where they knew they needed to be. The doctor placed himself at the foot of the bed and looked up at Alison. "Get ready to push," he said. Alison sat up a little farther in the bed, and hen the doctor told her to do so, she took in a deep breath and pushed. Once the push was over, Alison laid back down on the bed breathing heavily.

There was a not much chatter in the room. Mostly the doctor instructing the nurses if he needed something. And soon, it was time to push again. The doctor asked if she was ready. She got herself in position and pushed again. Tommy wondered if there was more that he was supposed to be doing besides holding her leg back while she pushed. But no one was directing him otherwise or telling him he was doing it wrong, so he just focused on Alison.

The doctor once again prompted her, she got herself into position and pushed. Push after push, he watched Alison. Amazed at her strength. She pushed again. He held her leg with one hand and wiped the hair from out of her eyes with the other. She pushed again and flopped back onto the bed trying to catch her breath. "One more push," The doctor called out from the foot of the bed. "Get ready." Alison sat back up, getting herself in position, for what Tommy hoped was the last time.

"And...push," the doctor called out. Alison leaned forward with a nurse pushing one leg back, and Tommy pushing the other. She closed her eyes, bared her teeth, and screamed through the push with every ounce of energy she could find. Tommy stared at her through the entirety of the push and watched her collapse back onto the bed when she was finished. One of the nurses who had been standing away from Alison's bed walked over to the doctor and took the baby. Tommy leaned down and kissed Alison on the side of her head.

"I'm so proud of you, baby," he said. "You were wonderful. That––that was amazing."

Alison reached up, her hand shaking of exhaustion, and felt around for Tommy's hand. He grabbed hers and held it while she lay there still trying to catch her breath.

"Is it…a boy…or…a girl," she asked between breaths. Tommy looked back at her, instantly realizing that he didn't know either. He had been so preoccupied with Alison that he hadn't looked.

"I don't know," he said, smiling at her. "I forgot to look," he laughed.

"Are you okay?" he asked her, watching her breathing start to slow.

"Much better now," she said.

Tommy kissed her again, just as one of the nurses walked toward them carrying a small bundle of blankets. The nurse told Tommy to help her sit up and pull down the shoulders of Alison's gown. Tommy assisted Alison as instructed, then the nurse laid the naked baby on her bare chest and covered them both with the warm blankets.

"It's a boy," the nurse said, smiling at them both.

Alison looked up at Tommy. Tears filled her eyes and her lip beginning to quiver. "We have a baby boy," she said as the tears started to roll down her cheek and onto the bed.

Tommy stared back at her, then at their son. He found himself, again, not believing what he had witnessed. What he was seeing that very moment. He was finally here. *He.* Their son. Their baby boy. They both stared at the baby watching his tiny face, memorizing every feature and watching every movement.

The nurses took the baby to run some routine tests in the nursery. Tommy stayed by Alison's bed just watching her rest. Occasionally, she would open her eyes and look at him and smile, but she didn't have much say. Tommy didn't need her too. One of the nurses brought the baby back and handed him to Alison swaddled in a white baby blanket with a tiny blue sock cap on his head. She quickly recognized the faces of two brand new parents completely enamored with their first-born child, and quietly slipped out of the room. Alison looked at Tommy,

"We never settled on a boy name, you know," she said.

"You're right," he said. "We didn't."

They looked at each other then back at the baby. Both now wondering what they should call him. Tommy's phone began to ring over on the windowsill, but he ignored it. The phone chimed on several times but still he made no move to answer it.

"Go on, answer it," she said. "It's okay. It's probably just someone asking about the baby," she said. Tommy kissed her forehead again and walked over to the window and grabbed his phone. He looked at the screen, which read, "Owen, incoming call." Tommy stared at the phone a second longer then looked over at Alison, who was looking back at him.

"Who is it?" she asked.

Tommy looked down at his still ringing phone, then back at Alison with an inspired look on his face. "How about, Owen?" he asked.

Alison smiled, looked down at the baby resting on her chest. "I love it," she said.

She stared at him with tears in her eyes and a smile on her face. With all the love she could muster she softly whispered, "Hello, Owen."

| 30 |

Owen and Rhiannon dove headfirst into their relationship after fighting it out in Central Park. Rhiannon did elect to stay at her grandfather's house, while Owen maintained his apartment in the city. They liked the idea of having both places at their disposal. It worked well if they were out late in the city and didn't feel like driving or taking a cab back to Long Island. Despite having separate places, they were still together nearly every night.

Rhiannon and Alison had no trouble reconnecting and building on the friendship they had started before. Being close to Owen, Alison saw what her leaving did to him. She never told anyone, but she saw how confusing it was for Rhiannon just as well as she saw how hard it had been for Owen. She felt for them both really. But Rhiannon had left, and Owen was the one she witnessed being so heartbroken. However, she was more than thrilled for them both after hearing the all the details of their waterlogged walk through the park. Rhiannon was always happy to fill her in on how Tommy and Owen were when they were younger. Like how she *knew*, even back then, that they didn't care for the times when she would tag along with them to the pond, but she didn't care.

"You know," she told Alison at dinner one night. "Sometimes I would go, just to annoy them. Even if I didn't really want to. Annoying them was just something to do."

They would double-date sometimes. And on occasion, Owen and Rhiannon would babysit, Owen 2.0 when Tommy and Alison needed a night out. They celebrated birthdays and holidays together. Owen and Rhiannon even had a set up at both his apartment and her house so they could keep little Owen overnight if need be. They had become their own little family and Tommy and Owen couldn't have been happier about it.

Owen and Rhiannon were engaged in the spring of 2010. Right around the same time that Tommy and Alison started planning for their wedding. Owen thought and planned meticulously, trying to make it as special and memorable as he could, but always seemed to be unsatisfied. He never found himself finalizing any of his proposal plans because in the end, he realized that it had been so simple all along. The answer had been right in front of him the entire time. All he had to do was wait on the weather. When it was just right, or at least supposed to be just right according to the weather forecast. He took Rhiannon out to dinner and afterward, a walk in none other than Central Park. They took the same concrete path they had walked the night Rhiannon had come back to town and at one point veered off into the open lawn, just as they had before. Owen hoped that he wasn't giving it away and judging by her demeanor at that point she hadn't put it together.

Once they were out in the open, Owen stopped. He turned to Rhiannon and shared with her how happy his life had been since she became a part of it and how he never wanted to lose that. It was at that very moment, just as if Owen had queued it up himself that it began to rain. Owen dropped to one knee, looked up at Rhiannon and asked her to spend the rest of her life with him. She cried and sounded off with a tearful "YES!" then cried a little more. That was the que for Tommy and Alison, who had been discretely following them through the park, to come out onto the lawn and join them in their celebration. They left the park soon after and went out for drinks. It had all been a part of Owen's plan. The only uncontrolled variable was the rain, but even the rain was right on time.

| 31 |

The Arnold and Hammond casefiles sat in Tommy's desk drawer for nearly a year collecting dust and nearly forgotten. Tommy had made a conscious decision after Little Owen was born that he was going to set them aside and focus on his family. However, when it did cross his mind to file them as cold cases, he found that he still didn't have the stomach to do it. *Not yet,* he'd tell himself. *Just not yet.* He had long since hit the proverbial wall in both cases. Until the fall of 2010.

The chilly morning air blew steadily through every corridor of the city, whipping trash and debris down the sidewalks, across streets and into alleyways. The previous evening's rain glistened off the surface roads creating a dull, reflective glare. On one of these rain-soaked streets, Tommy found himself staring down at another body. Another throat flayed open. Another homicide victim that just so happened to have a list of victims all his own.

His name was Chance Hall. Chance Hall was a husband and a father, and not a very good one on either account. He had on several occasions during the 10-year span of his marriage to his wife, Heather, been arrested and convicted of different sorts of abusive behavior toward her and their children. If being beaten wasn't enough, he would threaten to do more harm, or on one of his worst days, threaten to kill all of them if Heather ever tried to take the kids and leave or is she ever told anyone what he had done. It became a common occurrence with the two of them. So, often times the police ended up being called by a neighbor who happened to hear the screams of Heather or the kids.

Whenever he was incarcerated, he would always call or write home, apologizing to Heather and the kids. Promising that it would never happen again, begging Heather to stay. "Don't take the kids away from me," he would plead from a jail somewhere in the city. "I love them, I love you." But it never stuck.

After returning home there was always a small period of overcompensation where he tried to win her and the kids over with gifts and promises. But he always managed hit that slippery slope and pick right back up where he left off before. As a result of the most recent incident, Heather ended up having to go to the hospital where doctors discovered that she not only had a concussion, but a broken arm as well. Dr. Alison Taylor tried to convince her that it was in her best interest to stay overnight for observation, but Heather insisted that she needed to get back to her children. And once she was treated, she left the hospital against medical advice that same evening.

When she arrived back at home, she packed the kid's bags and headed for her mother's house. She dropped the kids off and told her mother that she was going to go back home, just to have some time to herself. Chance was released from custody three days later. When he walked through the front door of their house after taking the bus home, he found Heather slumped over in a chair in the living room. His gun in her hand and a bullet in her head. Next to her on the coffee table was a note that read, *I can't protect them, I can't protect myself, I'm sorry.*

Three days later Heather's mother received a letter in the mail, from Heather. She had apparently stuck it in the mailbox and raised the flag before putting the gun to her head and pulling the trigger. The letter apologized to her parents and asked them to apologize to the kids, and to make sure that her mother told her kids that she *did* love them. She just couldn't protect them. This broke her mother's heart. Especially because she had been begging Heather to get away from him since the first year of their marriage. In the end she did.

32

Tommy and Alison agreed early on in her pregnancy that all wedding planning would be postponed until a few months after the baby was born. After the baby arrived and they had the whole new world of parenting to try and navigate, they quickly realized they had made the right decision. It wasn't until seven months after Baby Owen arrived that they even sat down to discuss planning their wedding. And twelve months later, on March 21st, 2011, they were married.

Big Owen stood at the altar with Tommy, as his best man, of course. Watching and laughing as his namesake waddled down the aisle. Tied to Little Owen's tiny wrist was a small piece of white ribbon looped through two rings. Big Owen stepped out of the line of groomsmen and grabbed 2.O, as he called him. He untied the ribbon and placed one ring in the inside pocket of his tuxedo jacket and handed the other off to Alison's maid of honor, Hannah.

Hannah was a sorority sister of Alison's and happened to be the one who Alison had been abandoned in the campus library the night that she and Tommy met. Hannah had, of course, ultimately decided after waiting too long for Alison to return to their cram session, to take her studies elsewhere and leave the two of them entangled in their conversation.

Hannah and Owen had met on a few occasions before the wedding. At least once or twice during college that he could remember. Tommy and Alison's engagement party, and again at the baby shower. Alison had made it a subtle point to re-introduce them at both the party and the shower, and They had hit it off pretty well each time. Just not the way she, or Hannah for that matter, had hoped.

All members of the wedding party returned to their assigned places just in time to watch Alison walk down the aisle to an instrumental version of *Wonderful Tonight,* by Eric Clapton. That song had played in the diner Alison and Tommy visited after leaving the library all those years ago. Alison smiled when it came on and couldn't help but sway back and forth a little in the booth. She told Tommy that it was one of her favorite songs. "It's not just the lyrics, it's the whole flow of the song. Everything about it. You could slow dance to it anywhere, at any time and it would be perfect," she said, with what Tommy thought was the cutest smile he had ever seen. And she did look wonderful. Then and especially today. It was a good thing Owen had control of their son, because Tommy couldn't take his eyes off her.

Tommy was back to work soon after the wedding and found himself running into the same issues with the Hall case, that he had with the Arnold and Hammond cases. No evidence, no witnesses, no suspects. He began to feel the cloud hovering over his head again. Following him around the city, shadowing him in doubt and frustration. He read and re-read the report. He re-visited the crime scene, looked at surveillance footage, spoke with business owners, all the while feeling in his gut now more than ever, that three were somehow related. *Two cases could have been a coincidence,* he thought. *Three cases, there's no way in hell.*

He spoke with Heather's family but got exactly what he expected to get. Nothing. "He didn't even try to get the kids from us after Heather––passed," her mother told him. Tommy tried to narrow his focus comparing the three cases, looking for any similarities aside from the gaping throat wounds. The only thing he could come up with was the most obvious detail of all. All three were men who victimized others, and because of that there were likely more than a few people that wouldn't mind running across their obituary while skimming through their copy of the morning paper. He continued analyzing the files every day only taking on new cases if they were assigned to him. He would close those cases as quickly as he could, then back to the drawing board he went.

A particularly wet morning in April 2011, Tommy was at his desk staring at the aging casefiles when he was called into the captain's office. Tommy shoved the three files back into the desk drawer and walked over to the door. Captain Spencer barely got the first few words out of his mouth before Tommy knew. He could feel it in his gut. There had been another murder. He was right. The captain gave him the details and Tommy rushed to the scene hoping that this one would yield something that could link them all together. He took notice of every detail, even the smallest. But as usual there was nothing to there to find and he was lead nowhere. This gruesome morning scene repeated itself again one morning in June of the same year, and again in January 2012. Tommy was now staring at six unsolved murder cases. All the same manner of killing. All yielding no evidence except for a single footprint in one of the earlier cases, which may as well have not been there at all. He now knew to be certain, what he had only speculated when he arrived at the second of the six crime scenes all those years ago. They were in fact dealing with a serial killer.

Tommy began taking his work home with him again. It worried Alison. She would watch him stare at the files each night, as if he hadn't already been staring at them for most of the day. He tried to assure her that he only brought the files home because he knew that he and the rest of the department had missed something. But that was a lie. He hadn't missed anything, and he knew it. There was nothing there to miss. He had investigated these murders as thoroughly as anyone possibly could have. Of course, he didn't see it that way because the cases were still unsolved. He had followed every instinct, every gut feeling, and every procedure he could think of and still come up with nothing. However, now, he was beyond policy and procedure and following his gut. He was becoming obsessed. And Alison knew it.

She had seen him work tough cases before. But she had never seen him like this. The department kept any news about there being a serial killer loose in the city, out of the media for a little while as to not insight a city-wide panic. But eventually, with six bodies and no answers, they had to feed the beast and hope that someone knew something. The first media release was simply to inform the public that there had been a string of homicides, spanning the last few years, that could possibly be related and that everyone should keep a more watchful eye when out and about in the city. Especially at night.

They encouraged New Yorkers to report any suspicious activity to the police and not attempt to apprehend anyone themselves. It didn't cause a panic, but there was an almost overnight increase in the sale of guns and ammo. Calls began coming in non-stop. At first people claiming that they knew who the killer was or even that they themselves were the killer. Such claims and allegations were investigated but were all quickly proved to be false.

It had been about nineteen months since the last body was found. The concern of the citizens as well as a lot of the department about free-running serial killer had started to diminish. But not for Tommy. He couldn't help himself. He thought about and analyzed these cases even when they weren't in front of him. Even when he wasn't at the office. It was a mental part of everything he did. At work and at home. Working completely unrelated cases failed to distract him as well. He had become prone to feeling beckoned by those six files tucked away in his desk drawer, even when he was standing in the middle of another unrelated crime scene. He would make attempts to not to be so distracted by the daunting weight buried in that drawer, especially when it came to his home life. But he was failing. He could see it on Alison's face almost daily when he would get home from work.

Alison woke up in the middle of the night to find that Tommy was not in the bed...again. She rolled over facing away from his side of the bed and stared at the distant glow of the city lights outside their bedroom window. *A detective that never sleeps, in a city that never sleep,* she thought. She didn't like that that was the first thought that crossed her mind, but it was. She wanted to feel for Tommy. She wanted to support him, but her support meant that he had the freedom to go as far as he needed to. And he was already far enough away. She knew he was in the living room, and she knew that those damn case files were spread open all over the place with Tommy pacing back and forth, from one file to the next. She had witnessed this scene many times. Just as those files were to Tommy, this was the problem that *she* couldn't solve. The only difference being she knew exactly who to talk to. She grabbed her phone and looked at the time. It was 2:34 am. She got out of bed and walked over toward the bedroom door. She stood there for a second before opening it, mentally preparing for what she was about to do. She opened the door and walked down the dark hallway toward the soft glow of light in the living room. She stopped in the kitchen and watched him from the doorway. Sadly, it was just as she had feared. Case files open on the coffee table, on the couch, and one on the chair. Tommy standing off to the side with one in his hand flipping through the pages. He hadn't noticed her yet. She wondered if he would have noticed if the building was burning down around him.

Tommy closed the file in his hand and walked over and sat down on the couch. He still hadn't noticed that she was watching. He tossed the file on the coffee table with a couple of the others and rested his head in his hands. Alison knew this was her opportunity. She knew she had to say something now before he jumped up and grabbed another file. She walked into the living room and stood across from him on the other side of the coffee table.

"Tommy," she said. His head popped up out of his hands. He stared at her, then looked around at the mess he had created in their living room. "We need to talk."

Tommy dropped his head back into his hands. He knew in the back of his mind that this time would come eventually, but these cases had pushed that thought so far back that he wondered if he had ever really thought it all. Or was he was just trying to pretend he had at least *thought* about his family. He didn't know anymore.

"Tommy, look at me," Alison said, sharpening and softening her tone at the same time.

Tommy raised his head and looked at her.

"Tommy I'm scared," she said. "You stare at these files at work all day. Then you bring them home and stare at them all night. You never get any sleep. I wake up every night and you're gone. It's like *we* don't exist. Even if you're not staring at them, I know that's what you're thinking about. It's written all over your face all the time. Everyone can see it except you."

Tommy jumped up off the couch, startling her. "What am I supposed to do, Ali, act like this isn't going on?" he asked. "Act like there isn't some fucking psycho out there that keeps leaving bodies for me to find, huh?" His voice rebounded of the walls of their quiet apartment. The sound lingered in her head as the shock began to fade.

"Your *family* is what's going on," Alison said sharply. "And it's going on without you. You may as well just sleep at your damn desk. You bring those Godforsaken things home with you and walk around pretending that that you're here, but you're not. You're just waiting for us to be out of the way, so you can get back to your precious fucking files."

"Don't you see what I'm doing here, Ali?" he asked. I'm not doing this just for me. I'm doing this for us. This is my job; to get people like this off the streets so this city can be just a little bit safer. For all of us."

"No!" she said, barely leaving the space of a breath between his words and her own. "This *used* to be about us. It used to matter. *We* used to matter. But we don't anymore.

"What the hell is that supposed to mean?" he asked.

She couldn't stand the look on his face. Like she was somehow out of line for bringing this to his attention.

"It means that you have allowed this to take over your life," she said. The words poured out of her as if they had been trapped inside and now had the chance to flee. "I am all for you doing your job. I'm all for you going above and beyond, but this is insane, Tommy. You're trading your family for something that you have no control over, and you don't even realize it. But you know who's going to eventually? Our son," she said pointing down the hallway toward Owens bedroom. "He's going to realize one day that you were more worried about solving a damn case than anything else. And it's not going to matter to him what you were *trying* to do. All that's going to matter to him is that his daddy was always too busy or too caught up to pay any attention to him. I know that seems unfair, Tommy, but you can't expect a child to understand what the hell you're doing, when you don't even fully understand it yourself. Hell, I don't understand it either."

"Don't do that, Ali," Tommy said lowering his voice. His face carrying the weight of her words.

"No, Tommy!" she said. "You need to hear this. This could go on forever and you know that. Are you seriously willing to hand over your life and your family, so that you can put this thing together?" she asked. "Do you really not see what is happening to yourself, to us? We are falling apart, Tommy. I know deep down, that's not what you want. I don't want it either. But you aren't doing anything to stop it. You're pushing us away."

Tommy stood silent for a long moment, then sat down on the couch. He looked around at the open files littered around their living room. The lingering mess he had brought into their home.

"*Please* come back to us," Alison begged.

Tommy looked up and saw that her anger was gone. There was nothing but longing and pleading in her eyes. He knew she was right. He had reached a point where he would have sold his soul to for the missing piece to this puzzle. And he would have done so with a smile on his face. He stared up at her. He could see the trails of tears running down her cheeks that he had yet to notice because he had only been focused on proving his point. He could feel them welling up in his own. His stomach wrenched at the thought of how far he had run away from his family without realizing that one day, it may all be gone. He stood up again and walked over to Alison. He wrapped his arms around her and pulled her to him. He held her as tight as he could. Alison laid her head against his chest and closed her eyes. A fresh pool of tears that had been building in her eyes streamed down her cheeks and she began to weep.

"Please come back," she whispered again.

Tommy could feel the tears running down his own cheek. He could see now, what he couldn't before. He had gone too far. "I'm right here," he said. "I'm staying right here."

That marked the last time Tommy would bring his work home with him.

33

Owen Grant Collins had weighed in at just over eight pounds when he was born. A healthy weight for a newborn. He took his first glimpse at the world through his father's blue eyes and that turned out to be the only feature he would get from Tommy. The rest was derived from his mother. He was as much a copy of a little Alison as was the finished product of an artist painting still life. He *did* act like his father according to Tommy's mother, Laurie. Who not once in four years had missed a chance to have the pitter patter of his little feet scurrying through her house. Tommy's old bedroom had since been repurposed as a playroom, complete with a toddler bed just in case Little Owen was spending the night.

Tommy, Alison, and Rhiannon sat on the outside of the fence just behind home plate, while Coach Owen was busy on the field wrangling a herd of twelve, four and five-year-old's. Shuffling them to their assigned positions. Little Owen among them, standing in the dirt between first and second base in his yellow jersey. His glove resting on his head, flinging handfuls of dirt into the air, and watching the floating trail that follows being taken away by the breeze.

When Little Owen's t-ball league was having trouble finding sponsors, Owen stepped up to not only sponsor, but he also volunteered to coach his team. With Owen's team finally taking the field, the other team, the *blue* team, sent their first batter to the plate.

The league didn't keep score during the games. Though a few of the more competitive parents did. Even if the fielding team managed to get three outs, which almost never happened, the team at bat still got to run through their entire line up before taking the field.

The blue team batter stepped into the batter's box. The boy eyed the ball on the tee sitting just in front of home plate. A couple of wobbly practice swings at the demand of his father sitting in the bleachers, and with the third swing the dull knock of the small aluminum bat hitting the ball sent the batter running crazily toward first base.

Once the ball hit the ground every kid on the field, outfield, and infield alike, ran from their positions darting toward the ball that had stopped rolling just to the left of the pitcher's mound. The first few kids arriving at the ball caused a pile, with one boy emerging victoriously with the ball in hand. He threw it as hard as he could toward first base watching it hit the ground short of its intended target and roll the rest of the way. But the parents cheered as if they were watching their child in their first Major League game.

Soon, the blue team took the field and Owens team was up to bat. After three yellow team batters, 2.0 stepped up to the plate. He stopped just short of the batter's box and waved at his parents, and his *Aunt* Rhi, sitting behind home plate, and then stepped up to the tee.

He took a couple of practice swings of his own and raised the bat up to the ball just as his uncle had taught him. Then wound the bat back and swung forward with everything he had. The ball flew off the tee, hitting the pitcher's mound, and rolling to the backside into the grass in front of second base. "Run, Owen, run!" Big Owen yelled from across the field. Little Owen took off toward first base, bat in hand, dragging the ground behind him. His little legs moved as fast as they could. "Go, buddy, go, go, go!" Tommy cheered from behind the plate, raising up out of his chair. Little Owen ran and ran. Cheers erupted from behind home plate and the yellow team bleachers as he reached first base. Only he didn't stop running. Little Owen dropped his bat ran clear past the base. Past the blue team dugout and through the gate and clear off the field. People in the bleachers started to laugh as Big Owen called out, "Owen, where ya going?" from across the field. Parents on both sides laughed as little Owen continued running around the backside of the bleachers, all the way around behind home plate and straight up to his father. Tommy picked him up and Owen wrapped his arms around Tommy's neck. "I just needed to give you a hug," Owen said. Tommy kissed him on the cheek and sat him back down and watched as he hustled back the way he had come. Onto the field and back to first base. The rest of the game, Tommy sat beaming with pride. The smile on his face said it all.

After the game, they all went to Pizza Hut for dinner. Big Owen reached over, ruffling the hair on Little Owen's head, "You did good out there today, buddy," he said. "Fanks Spunkle," Little Owen said, shoving his half-sized piece of cheese pizza into his mouth. "Spunkle" was the result of trying to teach 2.0 to call him, *Uncle* Owen. It stuck, and Big Owen loved it. Three large pizzas, one personal pan pizza, and a couple pitchers of beer later, they said their goodbyes and headed home.

After his bath Little Owen lay there in his bed ready to be tucked in. Tommy sat on the floor next to his bed and read him a story. When the story was finished, they said their prayers and Tommy kissed him goodnight. Tommy checked the front door one last time to make sure it was locked, then headed off to bed himself. Alison was laying in the bed looking at her phone, waiting on him to get done putting Owen to bed. She sat her phone down and stared at him silently, a smirk stretched across her face while he changed into his bed clothes and climbed in the bed. She continued to stare at him as his head hit the pillow.

"How proud are you?" she asked, still smirking.

Tommy smiled a huge smile, and looked over at her, "Couldn't be prouder," he said.

"You're a good dad," she said, staring back at him. "That boy loves you."

Tommy looked up at the ceiling, still smiling, "I love him too.

It had been nearly five years since the first murder. Four of which, Tommy had spent riding a dangerously obsessive wave unable to let the cases or his mind rest. Ultimately, he crashed. Soon after the last conversation he and Alison had about the cases he decided that enough was enough. He had to face the fact that he was no closer to solving any one of the cases than he was the day he had been assigned the first one. So, he finally took the step he had dreaded all along and filed all six as cold cases. It took Alison a little while to be sure that Tommy was serious about letting go of the cases. But he had stuck to his word. He had quit cold turkey.

The space in Tommy's desk drawer where he had once hidden the files was now home to an array of different snacks for him to munch on while conducting the desk riding portion of his job. His most recent case was a string of burglaries which he had received several tips on. Most of which implicated the same man. This guy must have been in a bad way with a lot of people, because they seemed to be lining up to turn him in. Tommy already had the warrant, he just had to find him. And on May 5th, 2014, Tommy got his shot.

He received an anonymous tip that morning that his suspect would be attending a Cinco De Mayo party that evening, along with an address to the party. Tommy called Alison and told her he would be working late and set up surveillance down the block from where the party was supposedly taking place. A little while into the party a vehicle matching the description of the one belonging to the suspect pulled up and a man got out and joined the party. Tommy gave him a minute to get settled in and knocked on the door. He stationed a couple patrol officers near the back of the house just in case their man decided to run, and one at the front door with him. Surprisingly, the guy went quietly and without incident. He did, however, seem to find it humorous that it had taken so long for the police to find him. Tommy reported back to Captain Spencer that evening and was complimented on a job well done.

Tommy sat at his desk working to finish the paperwork for his burglary suspect. He had finally started to feel that all important sense of accomplishment again. When he finally got to file the case as closed, he couldn't help but smile. The following week, Tommy sat at his desk looking over his newest casefile. A hit and run, *vehicle versus pedestrian*, when he was called into the captain's office.

"Hey, Tommy," Captain Spencer said, motioning to a chair at the front of his desk.

"Morning, sir," Tommy said.

"Tommy," he started, leaning back in his chair. "I hate to have to tell you this, but I think it's starting again."

"What's that, sir?" Tommy asked even though he immediately assumed the worst.

"We just got a call about a body in an alley off Central Park West. Officer Nichols is the responding officer. He reported a male, mid to late thirties, throat slashed wide open."

Tommy tried not to react. But his body betrayed him and fell almost limp into the back of the chair. He didn't want to believe what he was hearing. He didn't want to re-open that door. He leaned forward in the chair and tried to clear his head.

"Any witnesses?" he asked, barely getting the words out.

"No one has come forward yet," the captain said. "Except the guy who found the body. But I want you to get down there and see if this is what we think it is."

"Sir, with all due respect, I don't know if I'm...," Tommy started.

"Listen," the captain interrupted. "I know how you must feel about this. I hate even asking you to do it. I saw how you were with this before and I know Alison is going to hate me for this, but no one knows those cases better than you do and we need to know if this is starting again." He paused. "I'll tell you what, if it gets to be too much, we'll stick somebody else on it."

Tommy nodded and stood up and walked toward the door. "Hey, Tommy," Captain Spencer said. "Make sure you let me know if this is too much."

Tommy nodded again and left the office. He went back to his desk and sat down. He leaned back in his chair and stared at the ceiling dreading what he was about to do. He knew he didn't have long, so he got up and walked out to his car. The closer he got to the crime scene the more nauseous he felt. He thought about his family. What it could possibly mean for them that he was having to re-visit what he had worked so hard to bury. He arrived at the scene and walked over to the where Officer Nichols was taking the statement of the man who had found the body. He stood there for a moment listening to the man's statement then walked past the officer over to where the body was. He didn't recognize him, but it would have been difficult to identify anyone with that amount of blood covering their face. So, he spoke to the officer after he was finished taking the man's statement.

"What are we looking?" Tommy asked.

"Well," Nichols said. "The vic's name is Jason Warner. I looked him up, he just got out a few months ago. Did a nickel for some pretty nasty shit."

"What about this guy?" Tommy asked nodding toward the man who found the body.

"Oh, he said he was out walking his dog. Said he was looking at his phone and didn't even realize what happened until his dog was already sniffing the body. Kinda fucked up if you ask me."

Tommy looked around the scene to see if there was anything too obvious to ignore, but nothing stuck out. He could feel the wheels in his brain beginning to turn. He started to think about the six cold cases and immediately began comparing this one to the rest. He had seen enough. He informed Officer Nichols that he was going to report back to Captain Spencer and that he needed him to continue to secure the scene for the C.S. I's and the Coroner. Tommy walked back to his car and sat down inside. He didn't drive off right away. Something Nichols said had stuck with him. That Warner had served time for some "nasty shit." Tommy needed to know what he was locked up for. He hurried back to the precinct and to his desk. He searched the name "Jason Warner" in the system and found exactly what he was looking for. He was sickened by what he read. Not just because of what Warner had done to get locked up, but because it also confirmed what the captain thought. It was happening again.

"Come in," Captain Spencer said, after Tommy knocked on the door.

"Sir," Tommy said, walking in and taking a seat in the same chair he had occupied earlier that morning. "I hate to say it. I hate to even think it. But I think you're right. It's happening again."

34

Captain Spencer leaned back in his chair and sighed. "Shit," he said.

"Victims name is Jason Warner," Tommy said, laying paperwork on the captain's desk.

"Warner––Warner," the captain said quietly, his eyes darting around the room. "Why do I know that name?"

"Jason Warner," Tommy continued. "Was a convicted child molester who served five years for raping his own daughter. Age ten at the time. As well as one of her friends (same age) during a sleepover. Not only that, but the sick son-of-a-bitch videoed the whole damn thing. Trial moved pretty quick with all the evidence. The courts terminated his parental rights and basically, he was never allowed to see his daughter again. Not to mention be around any other minors."

"Sick fuck," the captain said, his face openly displaying his disgust.

"Now, he was released about three months ago. I did a little digging and since he's been out there have been several reports from his ex-wife that he's been calling, asking to talk to his daughter. He's stopped by their house unannounced or been seen following her places. I mean, she walks out of the store and this guy's there watching. He's even been reported to have shown up at the girl's school to try and see her. But he always manages to be nowhere around when we show up. Looks to me like someone knew what he was up to after he got out."

Captain Spencer sat there staring at the papers Tommy had given him. "Certainly, fits our guy's M.O.," the captain said.

"My thoughts exactly." Tommy agreed.

"Okay," Captain Spencer said. "Keep this under wraps for now, until we know a little more."

"Will do, sir," Tommy said.

Tommy collected his paperwork and left the office. He didn't waste any time. He left the precinct and went to speak to Warner's ex-wife, Carrie. Her reaction to the news that Jason was dead reminded him of Sydnie Johnson's mother, Sylvia. She seemed relieved. Tommy could see the fear draining away from her face as he gave her the news. They sat talking for a few minutes before her now fifteen-year-old daughter, Jamie happened into the room. She looked frightened at first to see a police officer sitting in her house. She asked her mother what was going on and broke down in tears after hearing the news. Tommy asked her if she was okay. "Oh, I'm much better now," she replied and then walked out of the room.

He finished up with Carrie Warner and then went to speak to Jamie's friend, Emma Cole. She was Jason Warner's second victim. He needed to know if Warner had contacted them as well or if they had seen him around anywhere since his release. Emma said she had or at least she thought she had. She said that Jamie had told her one day at school about the phone calls and the surprise visits.

"She just wanted to warn me," Emma said. "I ran to the bathroom and threw up after she told me. Then called my mom to come and get me. I didn't go back to school for a week after that."

Emma and her parents seemed relieved as well. Her parents said that Emma pretty much refused to leave the house except to go to school and even then, they had to drop her off and pick her up. "She wouldn't come out of the building until she saw one of our cars pull in front of the doors," Emma's mother said.

Tommy thanked them for their time and got up to leave. Emma's father stopped him as he walked out their front door. "Detective," he said. "I just want to thank you for this."

"What do you mean, sir?" Tommy asked.

"If that son-of-a-bitch hadn't been arrested as quick as he was, I would have killed him myself," he said. "When Jamie told Emma that her father was out and had tried to contact her, and even showed up at the school, I started sleeping with my gun on my nightstand again. If he had shown his face around here this is where you would have found the body."

"I understand, sir. Believe me," Tommy said.

"Well, somebody did us all a favor," her father said.

"That's certainly one way to look at it," Tommy said.

Emma's father smiled and nodded at Tommy. "Thanks again, Detective," he said and turned to walk back inside.

Tommy returned to the precinct feeling no need to question anyone else regarding Jason Warner's death. Even after Emma's father's comments about killing Warner himself he had no real suspicion that he had anything to do with his death. He knew he was dealing with the same killer. He was sure of it. As sure as he knew water was wet. He briefed Captain Spencer about speaking to Carrie and Jamie Warner, and Emma Cole and her parents and that he had no reason to suspect any of them were involved. He returned to his desk and sat there with his head in his hands trying to prepare himself for what he was about to do. It may have seemed so simple to anyone else. The logical next step even. But pulling those six files out of the cold cases and breathing new life into them meant diving back into a pool he had no desire to swim in. This pool was infested with creatures that seemed to have no other purpose in life except to pull him far down beneath the surface. And for some reason, despite the many hours and days logged treading water as a kid, when Tommy was in *this* pool, he always forgot how to swim.

He stayed at his desk trying to muster up whatever emotion he had to, to physically go and pull the files out. He thought of Alison and their son. Her concern for him before when he had buried his life in these cases. He picked up his phone and walked out of the bullpen and out the front door to the sidewalk. Her phone rang three times before she picked up.

"Hello?" she answered.

Tommy sat silent for a second or two before he responded. Her voice already made him regret what he was about to tell her. "He…hey, baby," he said. "Listen, we need to talk." He paused. "Ali, it's starting again," he said, exhaling sharply.

Alison knew in an instant exactly what "it" he was talking about. She didn't know she knew, but it was the first thing that popped into her mind. She could have asked what he was talking about. She could have spat out any one of a thousand questions, but she didn't need to. She knew.

"Are you sure?" she asked, hoping there would at least be some doubt in his voice. No matter how small, she would take it. But she also knew he wouldn't have called if he had any.

"Yeah, I'm sure," he said, regretfully. He could hear her voice begin to crack.

"Tommy, I don't know what to say," she said. "I don't like this. Not one bit."

"I knew you weren't going to be happy about it," he said. "But listen, I'm going to do my investigation and if I don't find anything, fine. That's it. It can go in the cold cases with the rest of them. I'm not bringing this shit home with me again.

"I'm scared, Tommy," she said.

"I know, baby," he said. "I just needed to call and let you know what was going on. I didn't want to keep you in the dark about it."

"Okay," she said. "I do appreciate that."

"I love you; baby and I'll see you tonight," he said.

"I love you too," she said, her voice still cracking.

"Bye," he said.

"Hey, Tommy," she said, catching him just before he hung up. "Just promise me this isn't going to be like it was before."

The sadness in her voice seemed overwhelming. "I promise, baby," he said.

"Okay. I'll see you when you get home," she said.

"Okay," he said.

Tommy hung up the phone and stood there on the sidewalk, watching the city pass. He knew her concerns were valid, and he knew that it was his fault that she had them in the first place. He had gone too far before. He knew even though she stayed as calm as she did on the phone with him, that she was probably in tears right now. Again, his fault. He walked back in and grabbed a cup of coffee and sat down at his desk. Alison's words ran through his head. *Promise me this isn't going to be like it was before.* He knew he had to keep that promise above everything else. No matter what, he could not let her down again. Not over this. *Work stays at work,* he thought. *And right now, I'm at work.*

He sat the hot coffee down on his desk thinking to himself that it needed to cool off a bit anyway. Then he got up and left the bullpen. He walked down the hall to retrieve the files belonging to the six cold homicide cases that he had been unable to solve. He sat back down at his desk with the stack of files. He stared at them for a second knowing nearly every word contained within each of them. He cracked the first one, The Arnold case, skimmed through its pages. Then on to the second, the Hammond case. So on, and so forth, until he had reached the end. Once he was finished with the cold cases, he opened the Warner casefile. The Warner and the Arnold cases shared a common thread. Both victim's bodies were found in an alley which seemed to be the only new piece of information he had. There was still no witness, no evidence, nothing useful. Just like before. Then he remembered, there had been one witness. *Old man, Jenkins,* he thought.

Tommy looked back over his report of what Curtis Jenkins told him when he had interviewed him before. He decided to go and speak with him again. Tommy studied over the files for a good portion of the rest of the day before leaving and driving to Curtis Jenkins's house.

He walked up the steps at the front of the house and knocked on the door. The door opened and to Tommy's surprise, it appeared to be Curtis Jenkins, only about thirty years younger.

"Hello," Tommy said, pulling out his badge and showing it to the young man. "I'm Detective Collins with the NYPD. I'm looking for Curtis Jenkins. Is he home?"

"I'm Curtis Jenkins," the young man said, looking confused. "What's this about?"

"Oh, I'm sorry, I'm looking for the older gentleman that lives here,"

"You mean my dad," young Curtis said.

"Yeah, I guess so," Tommy said, offering a smile

"I'm sorry sir, but he passed away last night," Curtis said. "Died in his sleep."

"Oh," Tommy said, now feeling slightly intrusive. "I'm really sorry to hear that."

"He told me about you though," Curtis said, smiling. "Even showed me your card. Said you were one of the good ones."

Tommy smiled. *One of the good ones* was all he had ever set out to be. "I really appreciate that," Tommy said. "Listen, I'm *really* sorry to intrude, but your father was a witness in a case I was working a while back and we've had some new developments. I was just going to stop by and speak to him again. My apologies for your loss."

"Yeah, he told me about that," Curtis said, with a laugh. "Showed me the paper clippings and everything. He was proud that he got to help. Even if it was just a little."

"He sure did," Tommy said. "I wish he could've helped more." Tommy extended his hand. Curtis shook it and Tommy walked back down the front steps to his car.

| 35 |

Tommy spent nearly a month going through all seven files again, and again. Hitting the same wall every time. He knew there was going to have to be a break in at least one of these cases before would be able to move further with any of them. So, he did the one thing that he had been so difficult for him to do before, he gave up. He skipped the purgatorial desk drawer where the first six had existed in limbo for quite a while and dropped all seven files into cold case status. He told Captain Spencer where he was at with the Warner case and what he was doing with the files, not leaving much room for him to suggest otherwise. Tommy had been down this road too many times before and knew where it led. Captain Spencer didn't argue or suggest anything else. He nodded and acknowledged Tommy's decision and that was that.

Tommy went home that night and peeked in on Owen, who was already fast asleep in his bed. He told Alison about the case (something he had made a habit of doing to keep her mind at ease) and what he had done. She couldn't have been happier. Alison smiled and hugged him. "I'm proud of you," she said. She knew it was a tough thing to do, to set aside such a serious case so soon. But he had kept his word and for that she adored about him. Tommy did lay awake that night thinking about the cases after Alison had fallen asleep, but it didn't last long. Soon he drifted off into a dreamless sleep.

Tommy and Alison lay there asleep as the morning sunlight pierced through their bedroom window. Tommy was pulled from his sleep by the creaking sound of their bedroom door opening. He laid there as still as he could, his eyes remained closed as the sound of footsteps got closer and closer to the bed.

"Daddy," a tiny voice whispered.

Tommy slowly opened his eyes and found himself staring directly into his son's. Only they were about a half inch from his face. "Hey buddy," Tommy whispered back.

"Daddy, I'm hungry." Owen whispered again.

"Okay, give me a sec," Tommy said.

Tommy sat up in the bed and looked at Owen standing at the door, waiting to make sure that he was going to get out of bed like he said he would. He looked over at Alison who was still very much asleep. He flipped the blankets back and climbed out of bed and followed Owen in the kitchen. Tommy poured each of them a bowl of cereal and they sat and talked. Owen mostly, about a dream he had in which he had a full-grown Tyrannosaurus Rex named Bumpy as a pet. And how his mommy let him take Bumpy to daycare for show and tell. All his friends loved Bumpy and took turns riding him around the playground. When Tommy asked why his name was Bumpy, Owen replied, "Because his skin is bumpy, daddy" All Tommy could do was laugh at his son's overactive imagination.

Later that day, Tommy and Alison packed the three of them up and drove out to Long Island to Rhiannon's house where they were having a cookout. As soon as they pulled up, they saw Big Owen outside firing up the grill. Steaks for the adults and hotdogs for 2.O. Owen stood at the grill with cold beer in hand and walked back inside to get Tommy one as they parked the car. Tommy and Alison walked over to the grill while Owen ran ahead making a beeline for his uncle.

"Spunkle!" Little Owen shouted, running toward the grill.

"2.O!" Big Owen shouted back, bending as the boy raced into his arms.

As Tommy and Alison got closer, Owen reached around to the grill and grabbed the beer he had taken out for Tommy and handed it to him. "What's up, brother?" Owen said, greeting Tommy.

He held Owen in one arm and wrapped the other around Alison. "How you doin', Ali?"

"Good…hungry," she said, wrapping an arm around Owen. "Where's Rhi?" she asked.

"She's in the house," Owen said.

He sat Owen down and he ran towards the house screaming, "Auntie Rhi, we're here!"

Alison followed behind walking toward the house, leaving Tommy and Owen at the grill. Alison walked inside, into the kitchen where Rhiannon had scooped up little Owen and was tickling his stomach. His laughs echoed through the house. Alison helped Rhiannon finish up the sides while Tommy watched Owen grill and shot their usual shit.

They sat around a picnic table Owen had purchased for the house for just such occasions. They ate and laughed. Big Owen and Little Owen even had their ceremonial food fight which usually ended up involving everyone. After dinner they cleaned up, then they all took a walk down to the pond where the boys went for a swim and the girls sat on the dock with their glasses of wine and dangling their legs into the water.

Tommy found himself treading water and soaking in the scene. His best friend splashing around with his son, who love him so much. His wife and his best friend's fiancé sitting on the dock talking and laughing like they had been friends their whole lives. He couldn't have been happier in that moment and work was farther from his mind than it had ever been. As the sunlight began to fade away and the pastels began to cover the sky in thick swipes, they left the pond and walked back to the house. All except, Little Owen that is. Tommy carried him. his head rested on his father's shoulder nearly falling asleep. They changed Owen into the pajamas they had brought and laid him on the couch in the living room. Then the four of them sat around the kitchen table playing spades while Alison and Rhiannon enjoyed their second bottle of wine. Just before midnight, Tommy and Alison loaded a sleeping Owen back into the car and headed back home.

"Today, was a good day," Alison said.

Tommy smiled, looking out the windshield. "Yeah, it was," he said.

"I saw you tonight. Hanging back, watching everyone," she said, smiling at him. "I noticed it too."

Tommy's smile grew even bigger. "Just looking at what a lucky man I am," he said.

Alison leaned over and put her head on his shoulder. She stayed there until they arrived back home.

| 36 |

The next couple weeks seemed to be unusually busy. Not just for Tommy, but Alison as well. Each night seemed like it had been when they were both starting out in their careers. They each had so much to share with each other about their day. So many stories. Some with overlapping names, some without. But the best thing, they both thought silently, was that Tommy had not had to remove any of the seven files from their resting place amongst the other cold cases. No news was good news. And nothing had changed. There were no tips, no physical evidence. Therefore, no need to bother with them.

Tommy spent that Friday working late wrapping up a case involving an overdose with a single witness. A twenty-three-year-old man named Joey Sams had called 911 and reported that his friend, twenty-two-year-old, Seth White had overdosed on heroin. Police and paramedics responded and attempted to revive White, but they were unsuccessful.

In the statement Joey Sams gave to police at the scene he stated that the two of them had purchased the heroin then returned to his house intending to "shoot up." They were both getting their shots ready. His was ready first, so he shot up. Then White shot up a few seconds later and according to Sams, almost immediately hit the floor and was unresponsive.

He told officers that that was when he called 911, to try and save his friends life. Joey Sams was arrested at the scene and charged with possession of heroin and Seth White was taken to the coroner's office. Joey Sams sat in jail on a simple possession charge awaiting his day in court. On Wednesday of that week, Tommy received a call from the coroner's office and was informed that White's time of death had actually been approximately six hours before the 911 call had been made. This contradicted Joey Sams's statement. So, Tommy went to the jail to question him again. Sams insisted that his story was the truth until Tommy told him what the coroner had reported. Joey Sams heard this and immediately became emotional. He began blubbering and crying about how Seth had gotten high with his ex-girlfriend, and they ended up sleeping together. "So," Joey said. "After he shot up, he sort of knocked out. So, I loaded his syringe again and shot him up again." Tommy was able to get a signed confession, effectively closing the case.

Tommy was on his way home that night, feeling pretty good about wrapping up the Seth White case so quickly. He still had to go to court and testify, but it was pretty much a slam dunk at this point. He was about halfway home when a call came out over the police band that a woman had called in stating that she believed she had just witnessed a kidnapping. Tommy instantly got that same old gut twisting feeling. The same one he would get every time he found himself staring down at a different body with their throat slashed open. He couldn't shake it. This wasn't going to wait until morning. He didn't want to wait until morning only to find himself staring down at another body.

Tommy whipped his car around in the middle of traffic and sped toward the location where the woman who called in stated that she would be waiting. He sped through the New York streets, weaving in and out of traffic to get there as quickly as he could. He could feel himself starting to sweat. *This has to be something,* he thought. He arrived, screeching to a halt, and was soon out speaking with the caller.

"I'm Detective Collins with the NYPD. Are you the one who called in the possible kidnapping?" Tommy asked.

"Yes," she said, still panicking. "It was a silver car. I'm not sure what kind. But it looked like the one guy didn't want to get in the car, but the other guy was kinda forcing him to.

"Okay, which way did they go?" Tommy asked.

"They went down the street, there," she said, pointing. "And they took a right a couple streets down. That's the last I saw them."

"Okay," Tommy said. "Just wait here. Another officer will be here shortly to take your full statement." Tommy said, running back to his car.

Tommy Jumped back in his car and sped off in the direction the woman had showed him. He did as she said the suspect vehicle did and took a right a couple streets down. He looked for any silver car he could find, but quickly found himself in a rundown area of the city. It was filled with festering warehouses most of which had been abandoned by the former occupants, as well as the rest of the city. He reached an area where there seemed to be no signs of life anywhere. It seemed that even the homeless had abandoned this part of the city. He slowed down creeping through dark, lifeless streets. Carefully examining every building, every alley way, looking for the vehicle the woman had described. It wouldn't have been hard to spot. There was no one else around. Nothing but darkness peered back at him through the mostly glassless windows of the forgotten buildings. Tommy was starting to kick himself for acting so impulsively when the call had come across the radio. Everything had come flooding back so fast he just knew that it had to be related to his unsolved cases. He drove a little further down the street. He just about cut his losses when he saw a single light in the distance.

| 37 |

A literal light had flicked on in the distant darkness in front of him. The faint glow peeking through the partially blackened windows of one of the warehouses up ahead. It caused him to jerk his car to a stop in the middle of the street. He squinted, peering through the windshield to make sure he wasn't seeing things. He let off the brake pedal allowing the car to roll on its own steadily in the direction of the light. Sweat began roll from his brow, down his face the closer he got to the light. The rock-solid knot in his gut felt as though it would tighten to the point of rupturing as he slowly approached the building.

Tommy stopped the car in front of the building where he had seen the light. He got out of the car and quietly pushed the door closed. He looked around. There was still no vehicle in sight. Tommy could still see the faint, yellowish glow of the light through the window. Just barely, but it was definitely there.

He drew his weapon and moved stealthily on foot toward the side of the building. He moved along the side of the building unable to get a good look at the inside through any of the windows. He slowed his move as he approached the back corner of the building. He paused at the corner and peeked around slowly. It was pitch black. It amazed Tommy for a second just how dark it was. It would seem the city lights, even the moon had forgotten about this place. Then, as his eyes adjusted to the thick darkness, he saw it. A vehicle tucked deep in the shadows behind the building. He left the corner and moved closer to the vehicle sinking into the blanket of shadows himself. He quickly realized that he had found the silver car the woman described.

Tommy peered inside the care and saw nothing, then moved back to the opposite corner of the budling from where had been. He slinked around the corner of the building, still looking for a way in. He could feel it in his bones. He was so close. He continued around to the far side of the building. He was about halfway back toward the front of the building when he came upon a door. He stared at the door and listening for any noise he might hear on the other side. There were soft muffled sounds, but nothing that Tommy could make out. He could see traces of the light from inside sneaking under the door to the outside. Tommy stepped toward the door gently grabbing the knob and giving it a slight turn to see if it was locked. It wasn't. He was in.

38

"Show me your hands!" Tommy shouted, as he flung the door open and entered the warehouse.

He stood there with his weapon drawn, staring at the ghost that had eluded him for years. Evaded him like the whisper that wakes you from a dream in the middle of the night.

The smell of water damage and garbage and rust filled the room, creating a stench that rivaled that of a rotting corpse. It seemed that there was a fresh one of those as well. Tommy did his best to ignore the reflexive gag building in the back of his throat as the rancid smell of the room mixed with the sight of the victim's blood as it poured off the table onto the floor in small splashes. Tommy thought back to when this case began. This being. This shapeless, faceless shadow had plagued his mind and his family for so long. Now, here he stood. Mere feet away, drawn down on the killer, hovering over the body of its latest victim.

"Show me your hands!" Tommy yelled again; his weapon aimed center mass of the killers back. He tried like hell to maintain a steady, authoritative voice. Despite the sweat racing down every inch of him, a chill set in that rippled throughout his entire body.

The killer hadn't moved. They didn't even seem startled when Tommy belted out his initial command. They only stood there, still as a statue. Just as Tommy prepared to belt his directive for a third time the killer began slowly raising their hands.

"Slowly." Tommy said, feeling a slight hint of relief in his stomach.

Tommy tightened his grip on his pistol, now wrestling between fear and pride, but he knew the pride would have to wait. This wasn't over yet.

He could see the knife in the killer's hand, the blood still fresh and glistening in the light on the blade, falling victim to gravity as the killer turned the knife skyward. He knew this night wasn't going to end until the killer was in handcuffs or one of them was dead. Suddenly, the killer threw his hands the rest of the way up quickly. He struck the light bulb dangling above the body with the knife, causing the room to go pitch black.

"Stop!" Tommy screamed, simultaneously firing a pair of gunshots at the fleeting silhouette now disappearing into the darkness.

Tommy rushed into the blackened room chasing after the killer. He rushed down a hallway, whipping in and out of doorways frantically trying to gain even an inch of ground on his target. His breathing was heavy and loud. Tommy stopped just outside one of the doorways. He had followed the killer into the darkness of the abandoned building and now, as his eyes adjusted, he realized that he had no idea where he was. Or where he was going for that matter. He knew he had to intentionally slow his heart rate so he could focus. This could very well mean that he may be searching for someone who was already long gone. It could also mean that he was going be the killer's next victim.

Tommy started moving again. This time at a crawl. He soon realized that the only sound he was hearing were his own muted footsteps. As quiet as possible, Tommy took a step every few seconds, taking time in between to listen. The deafening silence surrounded him, and his mind began to race as feelings of paranoia sat in. *Make a noise,* he thought. *Something, anything.* Tommy knew he couldn't just stand there waiting for a sound that may never come. He tried to stare through the darkness of the hallway using only the scant amounts of intruding moonlight scattered throughout the building. He realized that he had been in such a rush to get here that he had neglected to radio anything in. No one knew where he was. No one would know where to start looking if he didn't come home and Alison reported him missing. He stood there in the dark not knowing which way to go. He didn't know if he could even find his way out at this point. He darted glances and his weapon all around hoping to catch a glimpse anything that could lead him in the killer's direction. Panic began creeping up his spine. *Am I alone?* he wondered. *Well, minus the body in the other room, of course.*

The doorway in front of him seemed to lead to a deeper darkness. Following his gut, Tommy turned around and went back the other way and tried to retrace his steps. As he exited the room, he noticed that the hallway he stepped into went further down than he had originally thought. He turned and made his way down the hallway approaching a door to his right. He pied the door, quickly realizing that the room was empty. It also mirrored the room he was just in. He stepped into the room to clear it completely, noticing again, a doorway on the far side of the room. Reluctant and unsure of either direction he moved towards the second doorway. Frustration began to cloud his mind. He stood at the doorway having to face the real fact that he may be searching an empty building. As he got closer to the doorway, he began to feel a slight breeze that sent a cold chill screaming throughout his entire body. Fear and anticipation rose again as he prepared to make his way through the door.

He positioned himself against the doorframe. He peeked to see as far as he could in both directions, but the darkness shrouded his view no matter where he looked. He listened and still there was nothing. He was kicking himself even harder now for missing his two initial shots when the killer took off running. *If only I'd landed just one,* he thought. They would possibly be loading up the body about now and this would all be down to the paperwork and court proceedings. Or at least they may have had a blood trail to follow. *Blood trail means DNA,* he thought. *Fuck.*

He had all but given up when he heard the unmistakable sound of a creaking floorboard coming from the hallway just outside the door. Tommy's eyes widened. He waited only a split second before realizing he was going to have to act fast. He peaked his head through the doorway and there he was. To his surprise, he had somehow found himself with the offensive advantage. He was standing approximately thirty feet behind the man he had seen when he entered the building. And this man seemed to be completely unaware that Tommy was anywhere near him. Tommy's stomach twisted and tightened as he watched the killer slink down the blackened hallway towards the door Tommy had been at earlier. He realized that if he had gone through that door instead, he would have stepped out right in front of the killer and be in a very different position right now.

He knew what he had to do. With every step the killer took the distance between them became greater. He holstered his weapon, took a deep breath. He took a couple of quiet steps out into the hallway, then launched himself down the hallway. He closed the distance between them as quickly as he could and plowed into the killer with everything he had.

| 39 |

Both Tommy and the killer fell, crashing to the floor. Tommy's weapon flew out of its holster on impact and slid across the floor and out of Tommy's reach. The two rolled around on the dusty, grimy floor, punching, and kneeing each other. Tommy fighting to gain control of a serial killer, the killer trying to escape, kill Tommy, or both. Tommy knew he was fighting for his life as the killer tried to inch his way toward his sidearm. They found themselves back on their feet, striking one another and grappling to gain control of the other. Tommy took a punch to the left jaw which knocked him down to one knee. The killer quickly made a move for his gun. Tommy looked around in a panic and grabbed the first thing he could find. He found a misplaced chair, and as the killer bent over to pick up the gun, Tommy broke the chair across his back. The man crashed onto the floor face first.

"Don't… fucking… move." Tommy said, in three separate breaths. The killer lay there groaning and desperate to catch even a single breath. Tommy stumbled over to him and dropped to one knee, nearly collapsing on the floor beside him. Barely breathing himself, he reached over and grabbed his sidearm. Suddenly, the killer flipped himself over with an unexpected burst of energy catching Tommy in the jaw for a second time with his elbow. Tommy crumbled to the floor nearly passing out while the killer scrambled to his feet. The shadowed man limped over and picked up Tommy's gun from the floor.

Tommy now lay there on the floor staring down the barrel of his own gun. He was certain this was how it was all going to end. He thought of Alison, his son, his mother. All of whom he was now sure he would never see again. They were all sleeping by now. They had no way of knowing that Tommy was about to be killed with his own weapon. It brought tears to his eyes, the thought of never seeing them again. His son growing up without him. But he choked them back. The killer stood there silent and shrouded by the darkness. He stared at down the sights at Tommy now kneeling on the floor. Tommy had always heard that you never hear the shot that kills you. In that moment, Tommy decided that if he was going to die, he was going to die on his feet. Tommy slowly began to stand up keeping his hands in plain sight, as he would be telling the killer to do if the gun were in the other hand. Still silent, still drawn down on Tommy, the killer began to back away slowly.

All Tommy could do was stand there. Bloody and breathless. Aches and pains in places he had never experienced before. The killer suddenly turned and tried to make a run for the exit when he tripped over the splintered remains of the chair that had been shattered across his back. Before he even hit the ground, Tommy made his move. As the killer crash landed an oddly shaped piece of the broken chair delivered a breath-taking blow to his stomach and sent Tommy's gun sliding across the floor once again. Before he could move an inch, Tommy dove on top of him, re-emphasizing the blow to his stomach from the piece of chair beneath him. The killer tried to fight back but was unable to conjure up even a single full breath. Tommy wrestled to maintain control of the struggling killer and delivered a deciding blow, connecting with a right hook to the killer's jaw, causing him to go limp and fall back to the floor.

Tommy reached down and grabbed him by the collars of his shirt. He pulled him in closer. He needed to see the face. He wanted to look into the killer's eyes and see what evil truly looked like. Tommy could hear the distant sound of a lone car from outside the building. The headlights of a passing vehicle burst through one of the nearby windows and sliced through the darkness and rolled slowly across the killer's face as the vehicle made its turn. Tommy froze. All the air had been sucked out of his lungs. "Owen?" Tommy said, hesitantly.

| 40 |

The name tasted like vomit coming out of his mouth. As if saying it would breathe life into some horror story that Tommy had been living. But it was true. It was real. And they both knew it now. Owen, still gasping for a breath, couldn't get a word out. Tommy stared at him in utter shock for a few seconds then let go of his collar and dropped his limp body to the floor.

Owen tried to stop his head from smacking the floor but just simply didn't have the strength. Tommy stood up and limped over to where his gun was. He picked it up and holstered it. Owen was attempting to stand up and just as he got to his feet, Tommy came barreling back toward him. Before Owen could blink, Tommy grabbed him by the shirt again and slammed him against the wall.

"What the fuck are you doing here, Owen?" Tommy asked, still full of disbelief. "What is this? Huh?"

Owen could hear the mixture of anger and sadness in his voice. This was not where Tommy had expected this road to lead him. Tommy had rightfully envisioned this moment being victorious. Catching the killer and closing the case. Even a sort of "saving the city" childish feeling. Now here he was in the middle of his big moment, angry and confused. Staring at his best friend.

"Answer me!" Tommy screamed, pulling Owen toward him, and slamming him into the wall again.

Owen stood there unwillingly soaking in the grief he had caused his best friend. A thousand things to say were running through his head, but not one seemed that it would be of any use.

"I was...only doing what...had to be done." Owen said, still gasping for each breath.

"Oh, bullshit!" Tommy exclaimed, pulling Owen so close their noses almost touched, then slamming him against the wall for a third time.

He let go of Owen's shirt and took a couple steps in the other direction. He stood there scratching his head. His brain feeling as though it had been tampered with, rewired somehow. "I can't fucking *believe* this!" Tommy yelled into the emptiness of the building.

Confusion clouded his mind as he tried to make sense of any one part of what had just happened. Then he suddenly realized that he had just turned his back on a killer. *But it's Owen,* he thought, automatically. He wrestled with what that actually meant at this point.

Owen couldn't imagine the extent of Tommy's confusion and frustration in that moment. The weight had to be enormous and overwhelming. He just stood there staring at Tommy wondering from second to second, how this was going to play out. For the first time in a long time Owen was scared. It was the uncertainty.

"Listen, I...," Owen started.

"Shut up, shut the fuck up!" Tommy yelled, turning back toward Owen. "We've been friends our entire lives and you just failed to mention that you're a fucking psychopath?"

Owen opened his mouth to speak, but Tommy interrupted.

"I'm a cop, Owen!" he said throwing his hands in the air. "That kind of puts us on opposite sides of the fence here." Tommy paced in circles around the room, still hoping to wake up from what a small part of him hoped was just some twisted, fucked up creation of his subconscious. "How could you do this?" he asked, bringing his tone down just a bit.

"These are awful people, Tommy," Owen said, slightly raising his voice. "They do nothing but spend their days feeding off of other people and destroying lives. They're parasites."

"That's not for *you* to decide!" Tommy said, raising his voice again.

"Well, someone had to." Owen said, becoming a little frustrated that Tommy wasn't seeing any part of where he was coming from. "These people do whatever the hell they want, to whoever they want, and they don't even worry about the consequences. Because they end up right back out on the streets. It's a minor inconvenience for them and then there right back to…"

"That's not how this works!" Tommy yelled, cutting him off.

"So, you just let them go on living?" Owen asked, angrily. "Brutalizing and victimizing everyone and everything around them?"

"You can't throw everyone in jail for life, for everything they do." Tommy said with a sudden burst of energy that moved him back in Owens direction. "We have a system. There are rules," Tommy continued. "Rules that we all have to follow. And this is so fucking far outside those rules… wh--what am I supposed to do with this, Owen? What about Rhiannon? What about our family? What about Owen?"

"We're not talking about petty crimes here, Tommy!" Owen snapped back. "These people are animals."

"Yeah, and what makes you any different?" Tommy asked.

"I did this to protect the people I love. So, they didn't end up like…like…"

"Like what, Owen?" Tommy said, sharply.

"So, they didn't end up becoming just another victim," Owen said.

Owen's anger increased. He had only ever put himself in the role of "monster" to frighten those who he had decided needed to get what they were due. Owen saw himself as having to momentarily become more than they were, something they would fear. He believed that what he was doing as more of a public service. Saving everyone, especially their victims, the trouble of having to worry about being affected by these people any longer.

Silence filled the room like a thick morning fog on the highway. They both stood there, exhausted and beat down. Both of them at the end of a rope, both hanging on for dear life.

"All I've ever tried to do was stop people from having their lives destroyed by people like that," Owen said, pointing towards the body in the other room. "This wasn't some sick game I liked to play; I wasn't victimizing these people. I was stopping them from making victims out of more innocent people."

"It doesn't matter!" Tommy screamed at the top of his lungs.

"You can't tell me that even a small part of you doesn't think the world is better off without these people," Owen fired back.

"It doesn't matter what I think, Owen!" Tommy said, grabbing his hair as if he were going to rip out two handfuls. "This is wrong. This is not the way." Tommy said. "Who do you think you're helping? I mean… do you think you're out here saving people?"

Owen *did* feel like he was helping people. He knew it wasn't the preferred method, but it sure got the job done. He felt himself beginning to boil at Tommy's misunderstanding or outright disregard for his intent. Whichever it was. He did his best to contain it, but the words crossed his mind and shoved their way to the front of the line. They came flying out of his mouth before he could even think of stopping them.

"I saved you, didn't I?" Owen said. He immediately wished he had choked to death on those words rather than breathe an ounce of life into them.

Tommy's face morphed from angry and frustrated to pure confusion. Owen tried to guess what he was thinking. Hoping he was headed down a different path. *Maybe he didn't hear it,* he thought. *Maybe he's so lost in everything else that he missed it completely.* But he hadn't. Tommy had soaked those words in just as quickly as Owen had spit them out. Now he stood there, Owens words bouncing around inside his brain like a pinball. Trying to trigger some sort understanding as to what Owen had meant.

"What do you mean you saved me?" Tommy asked, still very much confused.

"Nothing, Tommy. I was just…," Owen said, desperately trying to move the conversation in a different direction. It was all Owen could come up with. The only attempt He had at making a U-turn in this fuck-up of his, and he knew immediately that it didn't work. Tommy stood fully upright, lost in the translation, but refusing to let it go.

"No, Owen," Tommy interrupted. "What do you mean you saved me?"

Owen had backed himself into a corner. He stood there silent and staring back at Tommy with an almost lifeless look in his eyes. He scrambled his brain to come up with anything that might divert the conversation, but there was nothing. Why didn't Tommy want to know more about the body in the other room? Why was Tommy stuck on those three words that he didn't even mean to say? Owen knew he no longer had a choice. This was it. The one moment that he dreaded. It was never supposed to be, but here it was. The only thing he could do was accept it. Owen took a breath and said the one thing about himself that he never wanted Tommy to know.

"I killed your father," Owen said. It was the first time he'd ever said it out loud.

Tommy stood there frozen in place with Owen's words still echoing off the walls of the abandoned warehouse. The color completely drained from his face as he stared at Owen so hard that he began to look past him. Tommy tried to make any sense of what Owen had just said. He heard the words, and he knew he had heard them correctly, but he still couldn't believe it.

"How could––why––Owen, why?" Tommy said, in a failed attempt to piece a sentence together. "We were twelve, Owen!" he shouted.

"Look at what he was doing to you, Tommy; his own son," Owen screamed back.

Owen didn't really know what tone he should've taken. He couldn't tell if Tommy was a breath away from expending every round of ammunition, he had on him or was he a little closer to understanding why Owen had done such terrible things? He could only stand there waiting. Tommy stood there not saying a word, so Owen compulsively continued talking.

"I'd never had a friend until I met you," Owen said. "I didn't even know I wanted one. The day you told me what he had done to you, that was the first time I had ever truly felt bad for someone. And it was so much worse than I ever imagined it ever could be. You were my best friend, Tommy. You still are. I just couldn't leave you to rot like that and I knew that's what would happen. Yeah, he might have gone to jail eventually, but when? How much worse would it have gotten before something was actually done about it? And then how bad would the damage have been? On top of all that, he wouldn't have been in forever, and you know tha…"

Tommy raised his hand, silencing him mid-syllable. Owen stood silent, waiting for Tommy.

"How did I not see this?" Tommy said, sounding frustrated with himself. "All this time." He finally looked back at Owen. The anger poured from his face "I've talked to you about these cases. I've complained to you about how hard this shit was to solve, and it was *you* the whole fucking time." Tommy started pacing around the room. "You watch me spiral out of control over this. Alison came to you, to talk to me. You know what these cases did to my family, and you just sat back and watched. You must have got a real kick out of watching me run around trying to find *you*!"

"No, I didn't," Owen replied. "Quite the opposite, in fact. I hated what this was doing to you, and it broke my heart when Ali came to me. Something told me when you got assigned to the first case that this would be where we would end up."

Silence once again filled the room. Under the weight of everything spilled, Tommy felt as if he was drowning.

"I'm sorry you got drug into this." Owen said. "I never wanted you to be involved in any way."

Tommy still hadn't said a word. He looked at Owen, then back at the floor.

"You said it yourself; we've been friends our whole lives. I would've been drug into this somehow, at some point, even if I wasn't a cop."

Tommy pushed himself up off the table he'd been leaning on and stood with his back to Owen. Suddenly, Owen found himself feeling like that twelve-year-old kid, standing there at the pond, looking at his best friend. Even though he couldn't see Tommy's face, he knew he was fighting back tears. There were no words that were going to make this any easier for either of them. Tommy took a step towards the door and stopped.

"Get the hell outta here, Owen." Tommy said, gritting his teeth.

Owen couldn't believe what he had just heard. *He's gonna let me go.* he thought to himself. As much as he wanted to walk out of there a free man, Owen found himself torn between his freedom, and his best friend.

"What are you doing, Tommy?" Owen asked.

"Just leave, Owen!" Tommy said, slightly raising his voice. "Go. Now!"

Owen simply didn't understand. As much as he wanted to run, he was too thrown off by what Tommy was saying. Suddenly, Tommy turned and hurried toward him.

"Why are you still here?" Tommy said, his anger and sadness now fully displayed on his face. "Leave town. Leave the country and don't come back. Don't send for Rhiannon. Don't try to contact any of us. Just go."

Owen would have guessed that given this opportunity he would've already been halfway out of the country by now, but he couldn't do it.

"No," Owen said. The anger melted away in Tommy's face and there he stood again, confused.

"What do you mean, no?" Tommy asked.

"I mean, no," Owen said loudly.

"You wanted to get caught, didn't you?" Tommy asked, starting to get angry again.

"Not at all," Owen said. "I just can't let you do this."

Owen could tell that, that was not what Tommy expected to hear. Tommy was back to waiting for the ball to drop and there would be some sick and twisted reasoning behind all of this.

"If you do this now, you'll be headed down the same slippery slope your father did, and I can't let you do that." Owen said. "You're my best friend, Tommy. My only friend. I can't let you make the same mistakes he did. If you do this, then all of this was all for nothing."

Tommy was still angry. Angry that Owen was the one he had been chasing all this time. Angry at the position he had found himself in. Angry because a part of him wanted to let Owen go, but he knew he was right. Tommy stood there just staring at Owen for a moment then reached to the back of his belt and pulled out a pair of handcuffs.

| 41 |

"Turn around" Tommy said, still partially expecting to wake up from a dream at any moment. "You have the right to remain silent…"

As Owen stood there being handcuffed, listening to Tommy read him his rights. He could hear the sad relief in his voice. Relief because all the cold cases would soon be solved and closed. Sad, because what was supposed to be a triumphant moment had turned into something dark and terrible. Something that would surely weigh Tommy down for his remaining years. He was losing his best friend. The one person he had always been able to count on. Tommy walked Owen out of the building in handcuffs and placed him in the back of his car. Even in the dead of winter, the night air had never felt colder. Owen sat there knowing that both of their lives had changed forever starting in that warehouse.

Tommy walked around to the back of his car and popped the trunk. He threw his jacket in the trunk and stood there staring into the darkness. His mind struggled to make sense of everything that had just taken place. He thought of Alison and Rhiannon. He thought of his son. He thought of Owen's parents. All of them were losing someone they loved, and he didn't know how he was going to tell them about it.

He closed the trunk and walked around to the driver side of the car and got in. He picked up the radio and called dispatch and gave them the address of where he was and what he needed to secure the scene. Once he was finished, he got back out of the car and waited outside for the other officers to arrive. It wasn't long before the once pitch-black section of the city was blazing with red and blue and white strobes.

Tommy explained to one of the other officers on the scene exactly how he wanted the scene secured, then he got back into his car and drove off with Owen handcuffed in the back. Not a single word was said between the crime scene and the jail, where Tommy took Owen. When they arrived at the jail. Tommy pulled in and got Owen out of the back seat and walked him inside. He handed Owen over to the jail staff and informed them that he would be back with the paperwork once they had finished processing the scene. Tommy left the jail without so much as looking at Owen again.

| 42 |

He walked back out to his car and stood there, knowing, and dreading what he had to do next. And it had nothing to do with processing the crime scene. He got in his car and started towards his and Alison's apartment. He called Rhiannon on the way and asked her to meet him there, then called Alison and told her that he was on his way and that Rhiannon would be coming too. By the time he got home, Rhiannon had already arrived.

Tommy walked through the door of their apartment looking as though he had just been jumped on the street. He was dirty and bleeding. His shirt was torn. Alison and Rhiannon both jumped up in a panic to help him but sat back down on the couch when he instructed them to and insured them that he was fine. They both stared up at him, unsure of what they should expect to hear.

"What's going on, Tommy," Alison asked, scared, and confused at the state he was in. "What's wrong? What happened to you?"

Tommy grabbed a chair from the dining room table and sat it down in the living room, facing the two of them. He sat down and covered his face with his hands.

"Tommy," Rhiannon said. "Is this about Owen?" she asked. Tommy looked at her as the tears began to well up in his eyes. "Oh my God, is he…,"

"He's fine," Tommy interrupted. "He looks about like I do, but he's fine."

"What do you mean?" Alison asked. "What the hell happened, Tommy? Where's Owen?"

Tommy stared at them dreading what he was about to tell them. He still hadn't processed it himself. The lingering thought that he would wake up at any moment had held on this long, but he could feel it fading until it was completely gone. But the pain he was feeling was real and present. Physically and emotionally. He knew it was real. It was all too real.

"Owen," Tommy started, unsure whether to look at them or the floor. "Is in jail."

"I––I don't understand," Rhiannon said, her voice cracking. She looked from Tommy to Alison, then back to Tommy. "Why is he in jail? What did he do, Tommy?"

Tommy took a deep breath. "God, I don't even know how to say this."

He looked up at the ceiling, then back at the two of them. Alison's eyes hadn't left him since the moment he sat down in front of them. A realization had started forming in her mind that even she herself wasn't fully aware of. Her eyes pierced into him trying to piece it together between the bits of information he was giving them. She thought later that somehow, she had known before he even said the words.

"It's him," he said. Alison stared at him. She didn't want to accept it, but she knew exactly what he had meant.

Rhiannon looked at Tommy then at Alison. "What do you mean, 'it's hi…" she paused.

"He's the one I've been chasing all these years," Tommy said. Alison and Rhiannon stared at him in complete disbelief.

Tommy told them the whole story. Every detail. Every detail except one. He did not tell them that Owen had been the one who killed his father when they were only twelve. That single piece of information stayed between him and Owen. Besides, everything he *did* tell them was more than enough to make them question everything they thought they knew as it was.

Alison and Rhiannon sat there stunned, barely able to cry or comprehend, listening to Tommy explain how everything had happened.

Neither of them wanted to believe it. Tommy didn't want to believe it. But there was no way to ignore it. Both girls tried to ask questions. But neither one did so successfully. Each question fell incomplete as they would break down halfway through, unable to force the words out. Tommy shared their heartache. He shared their questions. Lord knows, he had plenty of his own that he wanted answers to, but he had already decided that he wasn't going down that road. Besides, he still had the gut-wrenching task of informing Owen's parents to look forward to.

Tommy returned to the jail that night to officially question Owen. He wasn't sure if he had the stomach for it, but as it turned out, he did. Just barely though. He sat in the small room the jail provided waiting for them to bring him in. When they sat Owen down across from him, Tommy stared across the table at him for a long moment before dropping his eyes to the table at the pen and paper he had in front of him. He started to ask his first question when Owen interrupted.

"Can I just write everything down?" he asked. "I think that would simplify things, wouldn't it?"

Tommy nodded and slid the pen and paper across the table. "Everything from June 2008, until tonight," he said flatly.

Owen stared back across the table at him. His eyes had questions that he didn't want to ask out loud. Questions about what happened when they were younger. He had told Tommy everything. Yet, Tommy had given him specific dates to write about. *There's no way he's forgotten,* Owen thought. He stared a few seconds longer.

Tommy stared back and waited for him to begin writing his confession. He knew what question was on Owen's mind. He could see him working up the nerve to ask it. And just as Owen started to, Tommy stopped him.

"June 2008, until tonight," he repeated.

Owen nodded and did as Tommy had instructed him to.

The day after Owen's arrest, after the scene had been processed and everything was finalized, Tommy faced what he had to do next and spoke with Owen's parents. Part of him wished he were going to tell them Owen had died somehow. He thought even that would be easier to swallow then what he actually had to tell them. He drove out to Long Island and sat with them in their kitchen and told them what had happened at the warehouse.

They were aware that Tommy had been chasing *someone* for quite a while and were understandably devastated to learn that it was their son who had been responsible for those deaths. But he knew it was better for them to hear from him, rather than read about it in the paper or hear it on the news.

Owen's mother sat there in the kitchen and cried. She repeatedly apologized to Tommy, and he tried his best to comfort her, but it was no use. She just covered her face with her hands and sobbed uncontrollably.

His father didn't say a word. His life just seemed to stop in place when he heard what Owen had done. He looked from Tommy to his wife, then back to Tommy. Then he simply stood up and left the room.

Christopher's Cleaners stayed open for exactly one week after Tommy visited Owen's parents in Long Island. Just long enough for Owen's father to call everyone that still had items that were waiting to be picked up, and then he locked the doors for the final time. He died of a heart attack six months later. Tommy, Alison, and Rhiannon attended the funeral with Owen's mother as well as his own. Tommy stood at the gravesite stone-faced and furious that this had happened because of everything Owen had done. Owen's father had been the only good example of a father, Tommy had ever known.

Over the next year the court dates came and went. Tommy found it increasingly harder and harder to look at Owen during the proceedings. With every question he was asked, and every gruesome detail he had to convey to the court, he was forced to publicly face that his best friends name was somehow carved into every single word.

Owen had signed the confession and pled guilty, despite the fact that his attorney advised him to plead not guilty and let him try to have the initial confession thrown out. But Owen refused and the trial moved rather quickly. During sentencing the jury only deliberated for about forty-five minutes before returning with their verdict. "Guilty on all charges." The judge imposed a sentence of life, without the possibility of parole. And as soon as Tommy heard the sentence. He stood up and left the courtroom and went straight back to the office.

He grabbed the eight case files connected to Owen's trial and filed them as "closed." He sat down at his desk and stared off into space, wishing he could have done something else with them. Burned them perhaps. But sadly, that wasn't an option. Tommy could still hear the verdict being read as he laid in bed that night, wide awake and staring through the ceiling, rather than at it. He tried to imagine how life was going to be now that everyone he loved had the weight of this to carry with them forever.

| 43 |

Owen spent his time learning to adapt to prison life. During that first year he saw Tommy on the news quite a bit. At first it was during a press conference where he shared with the public the names of people whose cases had been solved by Owens arrest and subsequent confession. Tommy mentioned every name except one. His fathers. Tommy hadn't told anyone about Owen being responsible for his father's murder when they were just kids. Not Alison and Rhiannon, not Owen's parents, not even his own mother.

Owen looked at that as a silent gesture on Tommy's part. As the microscopic bit of understanding he had been looking for the night it all ended. As it turned out, it was enough for Owen. Then there were news segments showing Tommy had received an award from the NYPD for his diligence and dedication to the unsolved cases and his success in ridding the city of New York, and the world of such a person. Owen was proud of him. Tommy had done what he set out to do. He had become a better cop than his father. But Owen could always see a sadness in his eyes. No matter what the situation, Owen could always tell that there was something else behind the bleak smile he would see on the news or in the papers.

It made Owen smile to see his friend doing so well, but he knew it had all come at a price. Owen knew that Tommy wasn't happy about the way things had ended. He wasn't either. He knew that no matter what Tommy a police officer from this point on did as, this would always be the case that took a piece of him with it when it closed. And Owen knew he was to blame. Owen missed his best friend. He missed their friendship. At night he would think about Rhiannon, wondering if she had stayed or if it had all been too much for her and she left to try and resume the life she had given up, to be with him. He thought about their little family and how for a little while, everything had been perfect. The worst part of all was knowing that no matter what happened from here on out, he had spent his last summer with Tommy.

www.ingramcontent.com/pod-product-compliance
Lightning Source LLC
LaVergne TN
LVHW010310070526
838199LV00065B/5513